STAND YOUR GROUND

Look for these exciting Western series from bestselling authors William W. Johnstone and J.A. Johnstone

The Mountain Man

Luke Jensen: Bounty Hunter

Brannigan's Land

The Jensen Brand

Preacher and MacCallister

Fort Misery

The Fighting O'Neils

Perley Gates

MacCoole and Boone

Guns of the Vigilantes

Shotgun Johnny

The Chuckwagon Trail

The Jackals

The Slash and Pecos Westerns

The Texas Moonshiners

Stoneface Finnegan Westerns

Ben Savage: Saloon Ranger

The Buck Trammel Westerns

The Death and Texas Westerns

The Hunter Buchanon Westerns

Will Tanner: U.S. Deputy Marshal

STAND YOUR GROUND

WILLIAM W. JOHNSTONE
and *J.A. Johnstone*

PINNACLE BOOKS
Kensington Publishing Corp.

www.kensingtonbooks.com

PINNACLE BOOKS are published by

Kensington Publishing Corp.
119 West 40th Street
New York, NY 10018

PUBLISHER'S NOTE: Following the death of William W. Johnstone, the Johnstone family is working with a carefully selected writer to organize and complete Mr. Johnstone's outlines and many unfinished manuscripts to create additional novels in all of his series like The Last Gunfighter, Mountain Man, and Eagles, among others. This novel was inspired by Mr. Johnstone's superb storytelling.

Special book excerpts or customized printings can also be created to fit specific needs. For details, write or phone the office of the Kensington Sales Manager: Kensington Publishing Corp., 119 West 40th Street, New York, NY 10018. Attn. Sales Department. Phone: 1-800-221-2647.

PINNACLE BOOKS, the Pinnacle logo, and the WWJ steer head logo Reg. U.S. Pat. & TM Off.

First Printing: August 2014
ISBN-13: 978-0-7860-5039-0
ISBN-13: 978-0-7860-3357-7 (eBook)

10 9 8 7 6 5 4 3

Printed in the United States of America

God grants liberty only to those who love it,
and are always ready to guard and defend it.
——DANIEL WEBSTER

"Our top story tonight . . . the Supreme Court, in a closely divided five-to-four opinion, has ruled that the 150 alleged Islamic terrorists still in the custody of the United States military must be turned over to civilian authorities and transferred out of the military prisons, where they have been held, into a civilian facility. They will no longer be subject to military tribunals but rather will be tried in civilian courts. The deciding vote in the case was cast by newly appointed Chief Justice Sofia Hernandez Mkwame, who wrote in the majority opinion: 'The rights enjoyed by citizens of this country must be extended to those who have come to our shore as guests, or else this isn't America anymore.'

"In response to this opinion, the Senate Minority Leader, Senator Carl Alvarez, R-Texas, had this to say:

"'I hate to say it, but Chief Justice Mkwame is right about one thing—this sure as hell isn't America anymore.'"

BOOK ONE
The Battle of Fuego

CHAPTER 1

Fuego, Texas

The bright lights on the tall metal standards around the stadium lit up the night for hundreds of yards around. The cheers of the people in the stands filled the air. An autumn Friday night in Texas meant only one thing.

Fuego had gone to war.

And the enemy was the McElhaney Panthers.

The undefeated Panthers were ranked number six in the state in the 3-A classification and had come in here tonight expecting to crush the lowly Fuego Mules, who currently owned an unimpressive record of two wins and four losses.

Yet here it was, middle of the third quarter, and Fuego held a slender 14–10 lead on the visiting Panthers.

The people in the home grandstands were going nuts. They were on their feet with almost every play as they cheered for the local high school team. The band played the fight song at high volume.

Across the field in the smaller stands where visitors sat, Panther fans who had made the ninety-mile drive from McElhaney were fit to be tied. Their shouts were edged with disbelief as they implored their boys to hold the line. Their dreams of an undefeated season were fading. The Mules had the ball and were driving for a score that would pad their lead.

At the big concession stand on the home side, operated by the Fuego Booster Club, Lucas Kincaid leaned forward and said over the racket, "I'll have two chili dogs and a Coke, please."

The booster club mom who was tired and harried from the press of hungry and thirsty customers blew a strand of blond hair out of her eyes and said, "Sure, hon. You want onions and jalapeños on those dogs?"

Kincaid shook his head and said, "No thanks. Just chili and cheese."

"You got it."

He saw her casting glances at him as she fixed the chili dogs. Probably wondering if he had a kid playing in the game or maybe in the band. He was fairly youthful in appearance but had touches of gray in his close-cropped dark hair, which made him old enough to have a child in high school. She didn't know him, though, and even in this day and age, everybody knew 'most everybody else in a small town like Fuego.

But not Kincaid. He didn't have any relatives around here, didn't have a kid who was a football player or a cheerleader or a trombonist or anything else.

That didn't stop him from attending the games. He wanted to fit in, because the more he fit in, the lower a profile he could keep. Everybody in Fuego went to the games, so he did, too. He didn't want to get a reputation as a reclusive loner. People remembered reclusive loners.

Kincaid didn't want to be remembered. He didn't want to be noticed.

That way if his enemies came looking for him, they'd be less likely to find him.

Make that *when* his enemies came looking for him, not *if*, he thought. It was only a matter of time.

The blond woman set the chili dogs in their paper boats and the canned Coke dripping from the ice chest on the counter in front of him and said, "That'll be five dollars."

"Thanks," Kincaid said as he laid a bill on the counter beside the food.

"Can you handle that okay?" she asked as he started to pick up the food.

Kincaid smiled and said, "Yeah, I think so." His hands were pretty big. He had no trouble holding the two hot dogs in one hand and the Coke in the other. He opened the can before he picked it up and took a long swallow of the cold, sweet liquid.

"Thanks," the woman said. Kincaid could tell that she wouldn't mind if he stayed and talked to her some more, even though more customers waited in line behind him. He had seen the appreciation in her eyes when she cast those hooded glances at him. He was a good-looking stranger, and she probably didn't have much excitement in her life.

Lucky woman, he thought as he turned away.

In his experience, he'd found that excitement was *way* overrated.

Andy Frazier's nerves were jumping around all over the place. He struggled to bring them under control as he leaned forward to address the other players in the huddle. He had to make them think he was calm so they would stay calm. He was their quarterback, after all. Their leader.

"Red fire right on two," he said, relaying the play that one of the offensive tackles had brought in from the sideline. "Break!"

The team broke and went up to the line. As they took their stances, Andy looked over at the sidelines. He saw Jill Hamilton leading cheers, her long, dark brown pony-tail bouncing as she jumped around and waved blue-and-white pompoms.

She must have felt his eyes on her, because she paused and turned, and the connection between them over the green turf was electric. They'd been dating for six weeks and Andy knew she'd be riding him in the front seat of his pickup before the night was over, but it would be even better if they could beat those asshats from McElhaney first.

Andy bent over center and barked, "Hut, hut!" and Charlie Lollar snapped the ball to him. Andy turned, faked to Brent Sanger charging past him from the run-ning back spot, and slid along the line with the ball on his right hip as he waited for Spence Parker to make his cut and come open on his pass route.

But then one of the linemen—Ernie Gibbs, big but slow and stupid—lost his block and suddenly a McElhaney linebacker was right in Andy's face. *Gibby, you son of a bitch!* Andy screamed mentally as he twisted away from the rush.

There was no pocket—the play was designed to look like a rush, so the linemen had fired out rather than dropping back—and as Andy curled back across the field he saw a sea of McElhaney red and silver coming at him. He dodged this way and that and looked downfield to see if anybody was open, or at least close enough to open that he could heave the ball ten yards over his head and get away with it. They were almost in field goal range for Pete Garcia, but an intentional grounding penalty, with its loss of both yardage and down, would push them back too far.

Then Andy caught a glimpse of a seam in all that red and silver and cut into it without stopping to think. Hands grabbed at him, but he shook loose. Bodies banged into him, but he bounced off and kept his feet. He pulled the ball close to his body to keep it from getting swatted loose in all the traffic.

He was just trying to reach the first-down marker, but suddenly he came free and saw nothing but open field in front of him. The line of scrimmage had been the McElhaney 35, and he was past that now so there was no point anymore in looking for a receiver. Andy put his head down and ran as frenzied shouts went up from the stands on both sides of the field.

He passed the 30, the 25, and cut to his right as he sensed more than saw one of the McElhaney safeties coming in from his left. The diving tackle fell short, but the safety had forced Andy back toward the pursuit. He angled left at the 20 and saw the flag at the front corner of the end zone.

Now it was a race, and a hope that nobody behind him held him or threw an illegal block.

By the time Andy reached the 10, he didn't hear anything except his own pulse pounding in his ears. No, that wasn't his pulse, he realized, it was a couple of McElhaney players closing in on him from behind. He crossed the 5, left his feet at the 3-yard line just as they hit him. Momentum carried all three of them forward, and when Andy came crashing to the ground with nearly 400 pounds of McElhaney on top of him, the ball tucked under his arm was a good eight inches beyond the goal line.

Andy saw that, realized he had scored, and felt a moment of pure elation before he started screaming from the pain of his newly broken leg.

Up in the stands, George Baldwin turned to his friend John Howard Stark and said, "That's a sign of true greatness, being able to make something out of nothing. You know good and well that was a busted play, John Howard, and it wound up being a touchdown."

"Yeah, but it looks like the kid paid a price for it," Stark drawled. "He's still down."

Baldwin, a burly, bear-like, middle-aged man with close-cropped grizzled hair, frowned worriedly toward the group of players, coaches, and trainers clustered around the fallen player.

"Damn it, I hope he's all right. That's Andy Frazier. His dad Bert works for me out at the prison."

"I hope he's all right, too," Stark said. He was taller than his old friend but weighed about the same. Stark had lost a little weight over the past couple of years, but to all appearances he was still a vital, healthy man despite being on the upward slope of sixty.

An apprehensive quiet settled over the stands during this break in the action. The crowd became even more hushed when a gurney was brought out from the ambulance that had pulled up on the cinder track surrounding the field. Everybody on both sides stood up and applauded when Andy Frazier was loaded onto the gurney and taken to the ambulance. His right leg was immobilized and probably broken, but he was awake and talking and holding the hand of a pretty brunette cheerleader.

The kid would be all right, Stark thought. Even with the way things were today, he had everything in the world to live for.

As the teams lined up to kick the extra point, Baldwin said, "You never have told me why you showed up out of the blue to pay me a visit, John Howard."

"Can't a guy stop by to see an old army buddy?" Stark asked with a smile.

"Sure, but you've never been what I'd call the sentimental type. Anything you ever did, you had a good reason for it." Baldwin frowned again. "I heard about your health problems. Hell, everybody heard about them. There was the trial, and all that crap with that drug gang—"

Stark winced and said, "I could do without all the notoriety. I'm just glad things have settled down and I can go places again without being recognized. I've been traveling around, seeing some of the old outfit I haven't seen in years."

"You're not going around and, well, saying good-bye, are you, John Howard?"

Stark laughed and shook his head.

"No, this isn't a farewell tour, George. Fact is, I'm in remission and feel better than I have in a year or more. But none of us are getting any younger."

"Boy, that's the truth," Baldwin said. He clapped as the Fuego kicker drilled the extra point and made the score 21–10. "I've got a hunch I'm about to get a lot older, too."

"The terrorists," Stark said.

"Yeah." Baldwin sighed. "All the places they could have put them, and instead of spreading them out they've sent all hundred and fifty of the bastards to Hell's Gate."

Stark knew exactly what his friend was talking about. The official name of the place was the Baldwin Correctional Facility—a privately run penitentiary with a contract with the United States government to house federal prisoners—but nearly everyone knew it as Hell's Gate because of a geographical feature just west of the prison.

A long line of cliffs ran north and south there, and the red sandstone of which they were formed made them as crimson as blood when the morning sun hit them. Then, in the afternoon, the setting sun lined up perfectly with a gap in the cliff, and anyone looking through that opening at the blazing orb would think that Hell itself lay just on the other side . . . hence the name "Hell's Gate."

The prison had been an economic boon to this isolated county in West Texas, which was larger than many northeastern states but had more jackrabbits and rattlesnakes than people, making it a good location for a maximum security facility. Hell's Gate was actually the largest employer in the county these days.

Because of the seemingly permanent economic downturn that had gripped the country for the past ten years, ever since the Democrats had learned how to buy national election victories by passing out benefits to low-information voters and how to steal the elections they couldn't buy, for a time it had seemed that Fuego was going to dry up and blow away.

Hell's Gate had changed all that, providing jobs for many of the town's citizens. Guards, administrators, service personnel, all benefited from the prison's being there. If the trade-off was having hundreds of violent offenders housed just a few miles west of town . . . well, so be it. Prices had to be paid.

But now, with the recent closure of Guantanamo and other off-the-books military prisons, finally fulfilling the promise of the president who had started the nation's precipitous slide into mediocrity, the population of Hell's Gate had swelled dramatically, and nobody wanted the newest prisoners: hard-core Islamic fundamentalists who had nothing in their hearts but hate for America and a burning desire to harm the country. Stark had run up against their kind before and knew how dangerous they were.

The Supreme Court had ruled that they had to be held in a civilian prison, though, and tried in civilian courts. It was a farce, an invitation to catastrophe, but age had picked off enough of the Justices so that the gate was wide open for anything the so-called progressives wanted to do, without any way to rein them in.

And *that*, John Howard Stark thought as he watched a football game on a Friday night in Texas, was the true gate to Hell for a once-great nation.

"Well . . . maybe it'll work out all right," he said to Baldwin, although he didn't believe that for a second.

"Maybe," Baldwin said, not sounding convinced, either. "Hey, you want to come out to the prison, have a look around?" He grinned. "I'll buy you lunch in the cafeteria. The food is actually pretty good."

Stark nodded and said, "I'll just take you up on that, George."

CHAPTER 2

Despite losing their quarterback to an injury, Fuego hung on to eke out a 21–17 victory over the previously undefeated McElhaney Panthers. It took a great effort by Brent Sanger, who played defensive back as well as running back, to slap away a Hail Mary pass in the Fuego end zone as time ran out on the clock.

Jubilation filled the town as people in the stands used their phones to post the final score on social networks. Car horns began to honk, not only at the stadium but all along Main Street to the Dairy Queen and McDonald's at the other end of town. Soon there was such a cacophony it seemed more like the team had just won a state championship, instead of improving its record to one game under .500.

So yeah, maybe folks were overreacting to the win, Lucas Kincaid thought as he made his way through the parking lot toward his Jeep, but he was happy for them anyway. With the world the way it was, people needed a little something to celebrate every now and then.

A long line of red taillights stretched from the parking lot along the road in front of the high school to the state highway that ran past the school and the football stadium. Kincaid figured he would sit in his Jeep for a while and let the traffic thin out before he left. He hated inching along in traffic.

Loud voices from his left drew his attention as he walked across the asphalt with his hands in the pockets of his denim jacket. He looked in that direction and saw three men confronting a man and woman who had a couple of small children with them.

The three men were angry, and their comments were pretty profane. One of them said, "You people don't even realize what you've done. We were undefeated! You've ruined the whole season!"

The other two shouted obscene agreement.

So, disappointed McElhaney boosters, thought Kincaid. And from the sound of them, drunken ones at that.

The man and woman tried to lead their kids around the angry visitors. The trio cut them off.

"Whassamatter? You too good to talk to us? You think one lucky win makes you better than us?"

"Mister, my wife and I just want to take our kids home," the man said. He was in his thirties, a little heavyset, wore glasses. Kincaid thought he looked like a teacher.

As if three-against-one odds weren't bad enough already, the three men from McElhaney were all bigger and rougher-looking, the sort of men who worked outdoors in construction or oil and gas. Kincaid's eyes narrowed as he studied them. He had never liked drunks, especially mean drunks . . . like his old man.

One of the men shoved the guy in glasses and sent him stumbling back a step. The guy's wife made a sound that was angry and frightened at the same time. She maneuvered the kids, a boy and a girl, behind her.

Kincaid had slowed, but he hadn't stopped walking. He could just go on to his Jeep and forget about what was happening in this corner of the parking lot. He knew that was exactly what he should do.

No, he thought. He couldn't. Who was he trying to fool by pretending that he could?

"Stop that!" the guy in glasses said. "Leave us alone!"

"You gonna make us?

"No," Kincaid said as he came up behind the three men. "I am."

They turned toward him, startled, and he hit the one in the middle in the belly hard enough to double him over. Then in a continuation of the same movement he slashed right and left and caught the two flankers on the sides of their necks with the hard edges of his hands.

The one on the left went down like a puppet with his strings cut, but the one on the right stayed on his feet. He was a little tougher than the other two, Kincaid supposed, and probably not as drunk, either, because he reacted fairly quickly. He bulled forward and caught Kincaid around the waist, slammed him back into the passenger door of a parked pickup.

If he could have just gone ahead and killed them, it would have been easier, but Kincaid knew he couldn't do that. Even getting in a fight was more notoriety than he ought to risk. Since he had to hold back, it threw him off a little, slowed him down, allowed the guy to ram him into the pickup. Kincaid's head bounced off the glass in the window.

Yeah, and maybe he was a little rusty, to boot, he thought. He had been lying low for a while. Skills deteriorated with disuse.

But muscle memory never went away completely. Kincaid jerked his head out of the way as the man tried to punch him in the face. Another second and he would have the man on the ground, puking his guts out like the one Kincaid had hit in the belly.

Kincaid didn't get the chance. The guy in the glasses tackled the third man from the side. Both of them spilled onto the pavement. Glasses swung a punch into the man's face. The blow was slow and awkward and probably didn't have a lot of power behind it, but it landed squarely on the man's nose and broke it.

That ended the fight. The third man rolled onto his side, cupped his hands over his nose, and squealed in pain. Glasses climbed to his feet, where his wife grabbed his arm and asked, "Honey, are you all right?"

He pushed the glasses up on his nose and said, "Yeah, I think so. Thanks to—"

He stopped as he looked around for Kincaid.

It was too late. Kincaid was gone. He'd faded into the shadows because a crowd was gathering and somebody was bound to call the cops and Kincaid didn't need that.

As it was, nobody involved in the incident knew his name. Nobody would be able to describe him except in vague terms: medium height, medium build, dark hair, blue jeans and denim jacket. That description would fit dozens of guys who'd been at the game tonight.

"Stupid," Kincaid muttered to himself as he circled through the parking lot. Getting mixed up in a brawl in a high school parking lot wasn't keeping a low profile. Not low enough.

Not when a lot of dangerous people would have liked nothing better than to kill him.

Andy Frazier floated on a cloud of painkillers. He didn't even feel his broken leg anymore. He was just co-herent enough to realize he had a silly grin on his face as he looked up at Jill, who stood beside the hospital bed holding his hand.

"Did we win the game?" he asked her.

"We did," she told him. "Twenty-one to seventeen. Ashleigh texted me and let me know."

From the other side of the bed, Lois Frazier, Andy's mother, said, "He's asked you that four times already, Jill. I think there's something wrong with his brain. Did they check him for a concussion?"

"For God's sake, Lois, he's just doped up," Bert Frazier said. Andy's dad stood at the foot of the bed. "He doesn't know what he's saying."

He was tall and had the same shade of brown hair as Andy, but his was straight and thinning, instead of thick and rumpled. His face was broad and beefy, and his shoulders were heavy. He was a supervisor out at the prison, in charge of the correctional officers when he was on duty, which he wasn't tonight because he always arranged to have Friday nights off during football season.

Andy was glad his dad and mom were here. That made him feel better. So did having Jill hold his hand. But as he looked up at her, he felt a pang of disappointment.

"My leg's broke," he said.

She smiled and nodded and said, "Yes, I know."

"That means we can't—"

Her hand tightened on his and made him stop.

"I know," she said. "That means we can't hang out at the Dairy Queen with everybody else and celebrate the victory. But it wouldn't have been possible without you, Andy, and everybody knows that. We'll just have to celebrate later, when you're feeling better."

"Okay," he said. That wasn't what he'd meant at all— he had been thinking about what they would have done out at the dry lake bed, just the two of them, alone—but if she wanted to act like that's what he was talking about, that was fine, because . . .

Oh, yeah, his folks were right here. So it was probably better not to say anything about the lake bed. Jill was smart that way, really smart. Probably gonna be valedictorian. Vale . . . dic . . . torian.

Andy started to giggle.

"Ah, he's stoned out of his mind," Bert said. "Come on, Lois. Let's go home and let him sleep it off."

"I'm not going anywhere," Andy's mom said. "I'm going to stay right here at the hospital. I can sleep in one of those chairs out in the waiting room."

Bert rolled his eyes. That just made Andy giggle more.

Then he stopped and asked Jill, "Did we win the game?"

There was only one motel in Fuego, down on the same end of town as the fast-food joints. It had been built in the fifties, with a one-story office building that also held the owner's living quarters in front of a two-story L-shaped cinderblock building with thirty rooms, fifteen on each floor. A swimming pool sat inside the L. Guest parking was on the outside of it. It was a fairly nice place, well kept up despite its age.

Stark had checked in earlier that day and told the clerk, who was also the owner, that he would probably be staying for a few days but didn't know exactly how long. That wasn't a problem, the man assured him. The motel did a steady business, since it was on an east–west U.S. highway, but it was seldom full.

When Stark got out of his pickup after the football game and started through the open breezeway leading to the stairs, he saw the motel's owner doing something to the ice machine that sat in the breezeway next to a soft drink machine. The man looked up and nodded to him.

"Hello, Mr. Stark."

"Mr. Patel," Stark said.

"Did you enjoy the game?" Patel grinned. "I could tell from the racket that we won."

"Yes, it was very exciting." Stark gestured at the ice machine. Patel had taken a panel off the side of it, exposing some of its works. "Problem with the machine?"

Patel shook his head and said, "Not really. Just doing a little fine-tuning on it." He chuckled. "You know, when things get older, they don't work as well. You always have to be messing with them."

"That's the truth," Stark said with a smile of his own. "Well, good night, Mr. Patel."

"Good night, Mr. Stark."

Stark didn't think any more about the encounter as he climbed the stairs to the second floor and went to his room.

What he had told his old friend George Baldwin about being in remission was true. The last time he'd seen his doctor, he had gotten an excellent report, which came as a surprise to both of them. A couple of years earlier, the doctor had told Stark he had maybe a year left.

So every extra day was a blessing, Stark told himself, but at the same time the days carried with them a curse. The longer he hung around this world, the longer it would be before he was reunited with his late wife, taken from him by violence several years earlier.

But Elaine would have wanted him to live as long as he could and enjoy every day of it, Stark knew. His friend Hallie Duncan, waiting for him back home, was the same way. She had encouraged him to go see his old friends, so that was what Stark was doing.

Despite what he'd told George, in a very real way this *was* a farewell tour, because Stark didn't know from one day to the next what was going to happen. It was all too possible that he would never see any of them again.

But then, every day on this earth was a farewell tour of sorts, because the past was gone and nothing else was promised to anybody but the present.

Tomorrow might not ever come . . . and the day after that was even more iffy.

* * *

As Patel was tightening the screws on the service panel after putting it back in place, a figure drifted out of the shadows to the side of the breezeway.

"That was him," the newcomer said in the foreign tongue that he and Patel shared. "The big American who has caused so much trouble for our friends in the cartel."

Patel nodded. His mouth was dry with fear—this man caused that reaction in him—so he had to swallow a couple of times before he could speak.

"Yes, that was John Howard Stark. I . . . I have no idea what he is doing here. He said he came to Fuego to visit an old friend, and it must be true. He could not have any idea what we plan to do."

"Well, it doesn't really matter," the other man said with a shrug. "If he chooses to stay here, in a few more days he will be dead, too, along with thousands of these other decadent Americans."

Patel looked down at the ice machine and tried not to shudder.

CHAPTER 3

He had been born in Alaska, of all places.

Unlike the American president a decade earlier who finally had been proven, beyond a shadow of a doubt, to have been born overseas, Phillip Hamil really was a native-born American. To add to his credibility, his parents were both naturalized Americans who had immigrated from Pakistan and gotten their citizenship before Phillip was even born.

His father worked for an oil company—that was what the family was doing in Alaska—and his mother was a housewife. Nothing in that background to make anybody suspicious.

But from the time he was old enough to understand the teachings of the Prophet, Phillip Hamil had been raised to hate America.

To destroy America.

As good looks did in every aspect of life, it helped that he was movie-star handsome. With his dark hair and skin, he could pass for Hispanic if he needed to. He spoke Spanish as if he had been born and raised in Guadalajara. But he was also as fluent in Russian as if he had grown up in Minsk. He spoke every dialect of every Middle Eastern language. And his English was perfect.

Why wouldn't it be? He was an American, after all.

His facility for languages was just one area in which he shone. He was a brilliant mathematician and scientist, and his grasp of world history was enough to have earned him several doctorates. He was one of those rare individuals who mastered everything he turned his hand to. Degrees from Harvard *and* Yale, president of a smaller but still major university, best-selling author of several volumes about political relations between the U.S. and the Arab world, advisor to presidents . . .

And at the moment, lover to a United States senator.

She gasped and clutched at him and then her head fell back on the pillow as she tried to catch her breath. Hamil rolled off her, left her splayed on the hotel bed, and padded over to the window to part the curtains slightly and look out at the night. They were in suburban Virginia, and he could see the lights of Washington, D.C., glowing in the distance.

For a moment he allowed himself the fantasy of seeing a mushroom cloud rising over that cesspool of American evil. Such a sight would be so satisfying.

But even better was the knowledge that ninety-nine percent of what came out of Washington these days harmed and weakened the Americans without an electoral majority even knowing it. The place was a necessary evil that in the long run did the work of Islam.

The Americans, in their damnable arrogance, should have listened to that old man when he said, "Government is not the solution. Government is the problem."

If only they had known then that it would be all downhill from there for them, to use one of their own sayings.

"Phillip, that . . . that was incredible," the woman said in a throaty voice, still slightly breathless from their exertions.

Hamil let the curtain fall closed and put a smile on his face before he turned back to her. She was a powerful woman, rumored to be a strong contender for a vice-presidential slot on the next Democratic ticket, that is, if she didn't make a run for the top spot herself.

It was a shame she was ugly as a camel. With rare exceptions, the hated Republicans had much better-looking women, from the politicians and the pundits down to the ones who attended rallies and waved signs demanding that no more rights be taken away from them.

Those rallies were futile, of course. The Democrats and their lapdog media just called anyone who opposed their stranglehold on power racists . . . or misogynists . . . or homophobic . . . or anti-immigrant . . . or religious bigots . . . or gun nuts . . . or if all else failed, Nazis . . . and their followers swallowed the lies whole.

For a short time, after an American president had gone too far, ordering the use of nerve gas on American citizens who opposed his policies, then been impeached and removed from office for his crimes—literally removed, since he had barricaded himself in the White House and refused to leave—the pendulum had swung back in the other direction. Hamil, already a power in academia but not yet in politics, had feared that the Americans had finally woken up and come to their senses.

But then a movie star had died of a drug overdose, and a young pop star had lost most of her clothing during a scandalous performance on live television, and a rap singer and his longtime girlfriend had gotten married, and another rap singer had beaten up his longtime girlfriend, and a new cheating scandal had broken out in professional football, and by that time enough people had forgotten what had happened that it was safe for the media to go back to telling everyone on a daily basis how wonderful the Democrats were and how terrible the Republicans were, and the Republican leaders, who really just wanted to be liked and patted on the head by their Democratic masters, quashed any real dissent in their ranks, and everything went back to the way it was before, with the United States on a long, slow slide into oblivion and irrelevance.

But then the politicians, thinking they were doing a good thing, had made the mistake of moving those prisoners—those holy men and martyrs—to a place called Hell's Gate. It was an insult to Allah that could not be borne.

Anyway, letting the Americans destroy themselves was taking too long. It was time to act.

And so the order had gone out. Phillip Hamil's order. He had picked up a phone, called a certain number, and said one word in Arabic: "Judgment."

The man on the other end of the line had called two more men, each of whom had called two more men, and by the time the Americans finished with their unholy prisoner transfer, the word had gone out across the country to thousands.

Some were members of small cells; others were individuals. Many had been born in this country, like Phillip Hamil. They had jobs, small businesses, families. They lived like Americans because they *were* Americans.

But they answered to a higher calling, and now they had been summoned. By ones and twos and small groups, they would travel to Texas to liberate their brothers and strike a blow to the heart of the Great Satan. They would travel to a place called Fuego . . . Spanish for "fire."

The Americans would know fire, Phillip Hamil thought. Fire and death.

"Phillip . . . you look so . . . intense."

The woman's words shook him out of his reverie. He smiled and slid into bed with her.

"Intensely in love with you, my dear," he said as his hands began to move on her body.

She responded, of course. Her fool of a husband—an academic like Hamil—had no idea how to satisfy her, but she had been faithful to him anyway, unwilling to risk the damage an adulterous affair might do to her political career, even in this liberal day and age.

Until she had met Phillip Hamil at a Washington cocktail party. She had been an easy target, and a worthwhile one since she served on a Senate committee that made her privy to a great deal of inside foreign policy knowledge.

It had taken only a few weeks for her to agree to a series of clandestine meetings in anonymous hotels like this one. No one knew she was here tonight.

No one.

She looked up at him and stroked a hand across his cheek.

"I don't know what I would have done if I hadn't met you," she whispered. "You made me realize that my life was just an empty shell. I've never been more truly alive than when I'm with you, Phillip."

"I'm glad I've been able to give you that, Mercedes," he murmured. "I'm glad you've been able to know true pleasure at least a few times in your life."

A slight frown creased her forehead. She said, "That sounds sort of . . . I don't know . . . final. You're not . . . ending this, are you?"

"I have to leave Washington for a time. My presence is required elsewhere."

"Oh." She sounded relieved. "I understand about having to travel. I mean, I have to travel quite a bit because of my Senate duties, too." She smiled. "A politician's work is never done, you know."

"I know," Hamil said as he stroked her face and slid his hands down to her neck. She seemed not to think anything of it as they began to tighten. "But yours is, my dear."

He would hang the Do Not Disturb sign on the door when he left. He had paid for the room for four days. It might not be that long before her body was found, but he would still have plenty of time to get to Texas.

Under normal circumstances the murder of a United States senator would be big news. With what was coming, it would just be a footnote.

But her usefulness to him was at an end, and her continued existence was an affront to him.

When she finally realized something was wrong, her eyes barely had time to widen in terror before he broke her neck with a quick, clean snap.

CHAPTER 4

"Remember," Bert Frazier said to the members of the guard detail assembled in front of him, "everything is by the book. All of you know the drill, or at least you'd damned well better. If we do anything to get the press on the old man's back, he won't be happy about it. And he can make life hard for all of us."

"You mean we're gonna have to hold the hands of those camel-humpers and tell 'em everything's gonna be fine, Bert?" Ed Remington chuckled in amusement at his own comment.

Bert's face flushed. He felt his hands clenching into fists. He didn't like the balding, hatchet-faced Remington, and never had. But he controlled his temper and said, "You see, that's just what I'm talking about, Ed. You say something like that, and somebody records it on their phone and leaks it to the media, and before you know it there's a big stink."

"Nobody in here has got a phone," Remington pointed out. "They're not allowed."

"Yeah, plenty of people have thought before that there was no way they could be recorded, and they wound up neck deep in crap because of it. Just don't take any chances, okay? Keep your words, your actions, and your attitude professional at all times. Got it?"

"Got it, Mr. Frazier," Mitch Cambridge said.

Of course he'd be the one to speak up, Bert thought. Cambridge was a brown-noser, an ambitious kid. But even though he sometimes rubbed Bert the wrong way, he was smart, he followed orders, and he had done a good enough job that he had been picked to help guard the new prisoners.

Bert stifled a yawn and said, "All right. Shift change in five minutes. You got any business to take care of, do it now."

They split up to hit the can or grab a last-minute snack. Bert went over to the table in the corner of the assembly room and poured himself a cup of coffee.

He was tired because he hadn't gotten much sleep the night before. It had been after midnight before he was able to convince Lois that it would be okay to go home. Andy was fine. The fracture was clean, the doctors hadn't had any trouble setting it, and other than having to wear a cast and use crutches for the next couple of months, once Andy got out of the hospital he could go on about his everyday life.

Well, he couldn't play quarterback anymore, Bert amended, and screwing that cute little cheerleader he'd been dating probably would be more difficult, but Bert had confidence in the ingenuity of horny youth. They'd find a way.

Bert swallowed the last of the bitter coffee from the foam cup and belched. He already felt the heartburn it was giving him. But that was all right. The heartburn would help keep him awake and alert.

A short time later, the ten uniformed guards moved into the wing of the prison where the terrorists were housed. Six at a time, the prisoners were taken from their cells and escorted to a small exercise yard separate from the much larger one used by the general population.

The orders from the Attorney General's office were quite clear: the alleged terrorists, foreign nationals for the most part, would never mix with Gen Pop. They were to be kept totally segregated.

That was just fine with Bert. It was easier to keep up with them that way. There were some really hard-nosed cons in here—it was a maximum security facility, after all—and many of them would have liked nothing better than to get their hands on a bunch of Arabs who'd been plotting to destroy the country.

They might be criminals . . . but that didn't mean they weren't patriots.

The new prisoners were cooperative. Not polite, really. There always seemed to be sneers lurking on their faces and hate gleaming in their eyes.

But they went along and did what they were told and hadn't caused any trouble in the time they had been here. Admittedly, that had only been a few days. If they kept that up, Bert supposed he could tolerate them.

But there was something about them . . . something about the way they looked at their captors . . . that worried Bert.

They looked like they knew their victory was inevitable.

Like it was only a matter of time until all their enemies were destroyed.

"What do you think, Albert?"

"What do I think?" Albert Carbona said. "I think these orange jumpsuits look like hell. They got no style at all. You know, I once paid ten grand for a suit, Billy. Ten grand just to look snazzy. And then they stick us in these pieces of crap." Carbona sighed. "It's cruel and inhumane, I tell you. Cruel and inhumane."

"You're right, boss," Billy Gardner said. "If they're gonna make us stay in here for life, at least they could let us dress nice. But that's, uh, not what I was talkin' about."

"Well, then, what *were* you talkin' about?"

"The new prisoners." Billy lowered his voice. "The Arabs."

Carbona said, "Phhhtt! All they wanna do is kill, kill, kill. They got no style at all."

"That's what you just said about these jumpsuits."

Carbona glared at the big guy who had once been one of his right-hand men, and demanded, "It's still true, ain't it?"

"Yeah, sure," Billy said quickly. Carbona was half his size but that didn't matter. He was still the boss.

Carbona hunched forward on the bench bolted to the floor next to the table, which was also bolted to the floor, and frowned at the cards in his hand. He and Billy were playing hearts, as they did most days to pass the time, but right now Carbona wasn't really seeing the cards.

"We never wanted to destroy the country," he went on. "We just wanted our piece of the action. Those guys, they're crazy. Can you imagine what it'd be like if they took over, with all the rules they got? And if you break one of those rules, they don't just send you to jail. No, they stone you, or chop your hand off, or even your freakin' head, just like it was still the Middle Ages instead of the twenty-first century." He revolved his index finger next to his temple. "Crazy."

"Yeah, guys like us would be in real trouble, wouldn't we?" Billy asked.

Carbona narrowed his eyes and said, "We're sitting in a damn max security prison for the rest of our lives, you big dumb ox. Ain't we already in trouble?"

"Well, yeah. That's not what I meant."

Carbona snorted. He had a lot of affection for the big ox, who had taken a bullet for him more than once, but sometimes the guy just didn't have any sense.

Of course, the same was true of him, Carbona told himself. They were both throwbacks, men out of their time. And that had been true even before the Feds convicted them on a few dozen counts of murder, racketeering, and income tax evasion and threw them into Hell's Gate for the rest of their lives.

The fifties and sixties, that had been the golden time for guys like him and Billy, Carbona mused. He had been just a kid then, but he remembered those days well, remembered his father Giovanni and his uncles Sal and Bruno and Petey. Snappy dressers. Men who got things done. Nobody in the outfit crossed them. Nobody. Albert had wanted nothing more than to grow up and be just like them.

Even when his father and Bruno had been killed in a hit and Sal and Petey were crippled for the rest of their lives by the same hail of bullets, they were still role models to Albert.

Except he would be tougher, more ruthless. Nobody would ever take him out like that. He would crush his enemies before they ever got the chance.

Unfortunately, by the time Albert grew up and started rising in the ranks of the family business, most of the old bosses were gone. And the guys who took their place were freakin' accountants. Guys with MBAs. It was an era when greed was good—hell, greed had always been good, as far as Albert was concerned, but now everybody believed that—but the way of going about it was changing. There was more money to be made on Wall Street and in corporate boardrooms than in back alleys.

So there wasn't much room for somebody like Albert Carbona who wanted to do things the old way. Oh, he'd been able to claw out some territory of his own. He had attracted guys like him who had grown up in the waning days of the previous era and still thought that was the way to run this thing of theirs. It had been a lot of work and trouble, but he was on his way to putting together an old-fashioned empire.

So what had the damn suits done? Betrayed him. Set him up. And the Feds had swooped in and gathered up him and his inner circle, of whom Billy was the only one left. They had been split up, and all the others had been shanked, victims of payoffs from the new bosses who wanted anybody who represented the old days gone for good.

He and Billy had stayed alive, though, because Billy was a monster. Not even those Aryan Brotherhood nutjobs would mess with him.

So here they sat, two guys who weren't young anymore, playing hearts and living out their days behind the walls. It was pretty crappy, Carbona thought.

But at least it couldn't get any worse.

Kincaid tapped at the keyboard and looked at the results that came up on the monitor in front of him. The high school football team's upset win over McElhaney was plastered all over the front page of the Fuego *Star*'s online edition, but there was nothing he could find about a fight in the parking lot after the game.

If it wasn't important enough to rate a mention in

the local paper, that was good. That meant giving in to impulse and getting involved in something that was none of his business hadn't done any harm.

This time.

Next time he would have to be more careful, whether he liked it or not.

A man wearing an orange jumpsuit and sitting at a desk in the corner muttered a curse. Kincaid shut down his monitor and swiveled his chair behind the counter in the prison library.

"What's wrong, Simon?" he asked.

Simon Winslow, whose carrot-colored hair didn't go well with the jumpsuit at all, waved a hand at the typewriter in front of him and said, "How did anybody ever write anything on these? Those keys just wear out your fingers and when you make a mistake it just sits there mocking you. Even after you x it out." A wheedling tone came into Simon's voice as he went on, "It would be so much easier if I could work on a computer, Mr. Kincaid."

"You know you can't get anywhere near a computer, Simon," Kincaid said. "You hack into people's bank accounts and steal millions of dollars, then leak a bunch of government secrets, you can't expect to be allowed online ever again."

"Ever?" Simon looked aghast as he said it.

Kincaid shrugged and said, "As long as you're here, I guess. What is it? Forty years?"

"I'll be an old, old man," Simon said with a sigh.

"Sorry," Kincaid said, and he really was. He wouldn't want to be locked up for most of the rest of his life, either.

That was one reason he had gone on the run after what happened at Warraz al-Sidar.

So in order to avoid prison, what had he done after making it back to the States with a lot of back-channel help from spooks he'd done some favors for?

He had gone to work in a prison, running the library. It made sense in a perverse way. Who would think to look for a deserter and fugitive in a place like this?

"So I take it the novel's not going well?" Kincaid asked as he leaned back in his chair.

"I keep getting sidetracked by the characters. I know the readers don't really care about all that backstory. They just want the survivors in the moon colony to blow away the zombies that were infected by the alien virus. I've got to get that out of the way so the girl can go ahead and fall in love with the guy who's a vampire."

"You're making all this up," Kincaid said. "That's not what the story is really about."

"Authors shouldn't talk about their work in progress. It ruins the spontaneity."

Kincaid chuckled and shook his head.

"Sorry, but you're gonna have to get back to it later. There are books that need to be shelved."

Simon sighed and said, "All right. I guess my muse will just have to wait." He stood up and came over to the counter to pick up a stack of books that had been turned back in. "I'll bet your backstory is pretty interesting, Mr. Kincaid."

"You'd lose," Kincaid said. "My life is boring as hell."

CHAPTER 5

Stark had made arrangements with George Baldwin to visit Hell's Gate on Sunday afternoon, so that meant he had Saturday to himself. He'd never been that fond of fast-food breakfasts, but there was a café within walking distance of the motel, so he strolled over there to get an actual breakfast of scrambled eggs, bacon, and pancakes that wasn't mass-produced, washed down with plenty of coffee. His appetite had come back as his health improved, and he was glad of that. He had always liked good food.

When he got back to the motel, he went into the office and found the owner's wife behind the counter.

"Hello, Mrs. Patel," Stark said. "I was wondering what there is to do around here."

The woman gave him a weak smile and said, "Nothing, I'm afraid, Mr. Stark. There is nothing in Fuego to interest a tourist."

"Looks like I'm going to be here until Monday. Any suggestions how to pass the time?"

"We have satellite TV."

"Thanks. Maybe I'll just walk around town for a while."

"All right. Do you need anything for your room? Some . . . some ice, maybe?"

"No, thanks. I'm good."

As a matter of fact, Stark had filled up a bucket with ice as soon as he checked in, but he hadn't used any of it. It was probably melted by now. But he could always get some more later.

Stark left the motel and started walking up Main Street. In boots, jeans, a long-sleeved khaki shirt, and straw Stetson, he looked right at home here in Fuego. Other than being tall, with an impressive spread of shoulders, there wasn't much to make anybody look twice at him.

That was the way he liked it. He'd had his share of being famous. More than his share. First that war with the cartel that had taken Elaine's life, then that crazy business at the Alamo, and finally, when he'd tried to retire and actually live a quiet life, more trouble had cropped up at Shady Hills, the mobile home community where he had moved after selling his ranch.

He'd had his face plastered all over the TV news and the Internet, and he didn't like it. Luckily, enough time had passed so that he didn't get recognized all that much anymore. Maybe there would come a day when nobody except his friends knew who he was, and that would be just fine with John Howard Stark.

But it wasn't going to be today. He was standing in front of a hardware store looking at some riding lawn mowers parked there on the sidewalk when a police car pulled up at the curb.

The man who got out wore brown uniform trousers about the same shade as his skin and a lighter brown shirt. He didn't have much hair left, and what there was of it was gray.

"Mr. Stark," he said as he crossed the sidewalk and

extended his hand. "Charles Cobb. I'm the chief of police here in Fuego."

"Chief," Stark said as he shook hands. "Glad to meet you." He paused, then asked, "Am I in some sort of trouble?"

"Should you be?" Cobb asked with a smile.

"Sometimes it seems like it finds me, whether I'm looking for it or not."

Cobb looked more solemn as he nodded and said, "I can see how you'd feel that way, given your history. But no, you're not in any trouble, Mr. Stark, not as far as I'm concerned. I just wanted to welcome you to Fuego. We don't get many celebrities here."

Stark winced slightly.

"I never have been very fond of the idea of being a celebrity," he said.

"Well, you'll have to get used to it. Not many people have done the things you have."

"Only did what I had to," Stark said.

"I understand. What brings you to Fuego?"

Cobb asked the question like he was just casually curious, but Stark knew better. A question like that from a cop was always serious.

"I came to visit an old friend of mine. George Baldwin."

"The warden out at the prison?"

"That's right. We served together in Vietnam. A lifetime ago."

"No, Desert Storm was a lifetime ago. Vietnam was two lifetimes."

"That was your war?"

Cobb nodded and said, "Yeah. A lot quicker and cleaner than yours. Neither of them really got the job done, though, did they?"

"Ancient history," Stark said.

"It certainly is. Well, you enjoy your stay in our town, Mr. Stark." Cobb started to turn back to the police car, then paused. Stark thought the move was genuine, not some sort of take-the-suspect-off-guard trick. "You were at the game last night, weren't you? I heard that you were."

"Yep. It was a pretty exciting game."

"Sure was. You didn't happen to notice anything going on in the parking lot afterward, did you?"

Stark frowned and shook his head.

"No, I'm afraid not, Chief. Did something happen?"

"Just a fight," Cobb said with a dismissive wave of his hand. "Three sore losers from McElhaney jumped some folks from here in town. Somebody pitched in to give them a hand."

"The sore losers?"

"No, the hometown folks. They didn't know the guy, but they said he made short work of a couple of the guys from McElhaney. Sounded like something you might do."

Stark shook his head again and said, "I don't know a thing about it, Chief. George and I were together right after the game. Went to the café and got a little something to eat. You can ask him about it if you want."

"No need for that," Cobb assured him. "I didn't really think you were mixed up in it, but since I saw you here—"

"You thought you might as well ask."

"That's right."

"What will you do if you find the guy?" Stark asked. "You said those sore losers started it. Wouldn't seem like they'd have any real grounds for filing a complaint."

"Maybe not, but I'd still have to question whoever was involved." Cobb grinned. "Then thank him for a job well done . . . off the record, of course."

Stark returned the chief's smile. Cobb lifted a hand in farewell, got into the police car, and drove off.

Stark resumed his walk. He didn't know if the chief had believed him or not, and he didn't really care.

Whatever had happened in the parking lot after the football game, it didn't have anything to do with him.

The two men arrived at mid-morning. They didn't give Jerry Patel their names, just came into the motel office and said in English, "Judgment."

Patel's hands were resting on the counter, palms down. Although outwardly calm, he involuntarily pressed down hard with them for a second as he tried to bring his rampaging emotions under control. He believed in the glorious cause, he truly did, but he had never really thought he would be called on to do the things he had done.

The things he still had to do.

He called to his wife, who was back in the office, and said, "Lara, keep an eye on the desk, please. I'll be right back."

"All right, Jerry."

Patel came around the counter, nodded to the two men, and said, "Come with me."

He led them along the sidewalk in front of the ground-floor units until he reached the one on the end. A few years earlier, the motel had been renovated and all the old door locks had been replaced with the electronic card key type. Patel had a card that would open any of them and he used it now, sliding it into the slot and pulling it out. He twisted the handle and opened the door.

A middle-aged couple had rented the room the previous afternoon. They were driving from Dallas to see their son and his family in Arizona and seeing some sights along the way, the man had told Patel as they were checking in.

Patel had said that he was sure the trip would be a good one.

Ten minutes later, another man had walked through the office door, and everything had changed.

Now Patel saw the woman lying on the floor next to the bed, curled in a ball around the pain that had filled her in her dying moments. The man was half in the bathroom. Maybe he'd been trying to reach the toilet and make himself throw up before he collapsed.

Even if he had made it, it wouldn't have done any good. The poison was too fast-acting.

Patel hadn't been able to bring himself to go into any of the rooms until now. Some of the guests had survived; he knew that because he had seen them pack up their cars and leave. That meant they hadn't used any of the ice.

That was true of Mr. Stark, as well, but he hadn't checked out. That might cause a bit of a problem before this was all over, but that didn't really matter. When the time came to act, Stark would be greatly outnumbered. One man couldn't make a difference.

"Put them in the bathtub," Patel told the two men who had just arrived. "They'll be out of the way there."

The man's trousers were lying on a chair. Patel dug in the pockets and found a set of car keys. He had all the license numbers on the registration computer, so he could tell which car belonged to whom. In a little while one of the men would drive the couple's car out into the badlands south of town. The other man would follow in their vehicle and bring him back.

This was just the beginning, Patel thought. The day would be spent piling bodies in bathtubs and disposing of vehicles. By the next morning, several hundred men would have arrived here. The motel would be very crowded, but it wouldn't be for long.

There were a number of other rendezvous points in Fuego, but the largest group of fighters would be gathered here at the motel. In the morning—Sunday morning—

while the Americans were either sleeping in or attending their churches, all the men would converge . . .

And Judgment Day would arrive for one town full of infidels, anyway. The Americans would pay for all their affronts to the one true religion. Patel knew he was doing the right thing. He was just carrying out the will of Allah.

But many of the people who would die . . . they had been his friends and neighbors. He had talked with them, laughed with them. They had done no real harm.

"You are all right, brother?" one of the newcomers asked after he and his companion had dropped the woman's body on top of her husband's in the bathtub. "You look ill."

"I'm fine," Patel said. He tried to put a fierce look on his face, but he thought he probably failed.

By the time he got back to the office, two more men were waiting. Patel sighed and took them to the next room in line to clean up *that* mess.

CHAPTER 6

"Just be sure the camera crew is there tomorrow," Alexis Devereaux said as she wheeled the powerful sedan through a long, gentle curve in the highway. The speedometer needle hovered right around 90.

"The producer promised me they would be."

The reply came from the car's speaker, through the built-in phone.

"Well, stay on him," Alexis told her assistant back in Washington. "This place is way out in the middle of nowhere. I don't want them getting lost."

"Yes, ma'am. By the way, Colin Evans from the State Department called."

Alexis took her right hand off the wheel, clenched it into a fist, and hammered it down on the seat beside her.

"By the way?" she repeated. "By the way? You didn't think that was important enough to lead with, Crystal?"

"I—I'm sorry, Ms. Devereaux. There's an awful lot to keep up with—"

"That's why you make the big bucks," Alexis said coldly, although she knew perfectly well that Crystal *didn't* make big bucks. She did. But Crystal ought to be happy earning what she did, because a lot of people didn't have jobs these days, and many of the ones who did worked part-time for minimum wage and no benefits. "What did Evans want?"

"He didn't really say, but I got the impression he'd found out somehow about that court order you got—"

"Well, that's no surprise. The administration can promise all it wants to that they've stopped reading everybody's emails and listening in on everybody's phone calls, but nobody believes that for a second. And with good reason. Is State going to try to quash the order?"

"He didn't say. He just told me to have you call him."

"Fine."

"Do you want me to give you the number?"

"No, I've got it," Alexis said, without explaining how she happened to have the cell phone number of an undersecretary at the State Department. It was none of Crystal's business that she banged Colin Evans twice a week when they were both in town.

Alexis added, "Just stay on that news producer," and then broke the connection.

She would call Colin later. She wasn't in the mood to do it now. If she did, she might say things she would regret later. He was a good source. Better as a source than he was in the sack, when you got right down to it, although Alexis couldn't really complain about that part of their relationship, either.

She had come up behind a truck. Without slowing down, she swung out into the other lane and zoomed past it.

That was one good thing about this godawful state, maybe the only good thing, she thought. You could see a long way on these flat, straight, mostly empty highways. You didn't even have to take your foot off the gas.

Alexis didn't like taking her foot off the gas, on the road or in life.

She had gone to Washington as a very junior White House counsel, a member of the legal staff working for the first female president. By the time that chief executive's two scandal-marred terms were over, Alexis had risen to the position of senior White House counsel. Her rise in power had been fueled by intelligence, hard work, and a great deal of subtle, discreet back-stabbing.

Once that administration had drawn to an ignominious close, Alexis had gone to work for a K Street lobbying firm and done good work for it for several years before becoming an associate at one of the city's most prestigious law firms. She had assisted in several cases at the Supreme Court. She took advantage of her blond, slightly square-jawed, girl-next-door good looks to get plenty of airtime on the cable TV news networks as they began seeking her out to appear as a consultant on their broadcasts. Eventually she had left the firm and established her own practice, smaller but more visible, and it wasn't long before most of the country knew her as a beautiful, tireless crusader for liberal causes.

Those prisoners who had just been transferred to Hell's Gate were tailor-made for her.

Alexis had been campaigning for years to have Guantanamo and the other military prisons closed down and the so-called terrorists moved to civilian facilities where they belonged. The military had too much power and couldn't be trusted.

Of course, a previous president had promised to do that very thing, but that was just one more broken promise in the tsunami of broken promises that had swamped his administration. Healthcare reform disaster? What healthcare reform disaster? Nothing to see here, move along, move along. This wasn't the healthcare reform you were looking for.

And so Gitmo and the political prisoners being held

there illegally—as far as Alexis was concerned—had been all but forgotten as just one more scandal among many.

Or they would have been if not for Alexis and a few others continuing to beat the drums. Writing magazine articles, appearing on TV, organizing fund-raisers complete with Hollywood stars. Until finally somebody got around to doing something about the things Alexis and the others had been demanding.

It hadn't taken her long to realize what a terrible development that was for her.

She had lost the main thing that kept getting her on TV.

But it also hadn't taken her long to figure out a way to salvage the situation. Now she could use her standing as one of the nation's top celebrity lawyers to make sure that the prisoners were being treated properly and that their rights weren't being violated. That ought to be worth some airtime, and a producer at one of the news networks agreed. He had promised Alexis that a field reporter and a camera crew would be in Fuego to document her unannounced and unexpected visit to Hell's Gate.

Now, she thought as she sped across the flat West Texas landscape, if only she could discover that the guards were mistreating the prisoners. Mistreating them physically and disrespecting their religion.

That would be a wonderful example of just how bigoted and intolerant those awful Christians were.

'

A lot of what was on TV these days bored Stark, unless he happened across a channel that showed old movies, so he always traveled with several books stuck in his suitcase. His favorites were Western novels.

He read one of them Saturday afternoon. The motel seemed to be busy, with lots of people coming and going, although he didn't really pay much attention to it. When he left to go to dinner, he frowned slightly as he saw that the parking lot was full.

More than full, really. A number of vehicles were parked on the vacant lot next to the motel, and the No Vacancy sign was lit up. It appeared the Patels were doing a booming business. Nobody was moving around the complex, though. Stark couldn't help but wonder where they had put all those people.

It was none of his affair, he decided, so he walked on to the café and enjoyed a good chicken-fried steak for dinner.

He was lingering over a cup of coffee and a piece of apple pie when a good-looking woman came into the café and asked the cashier behind the counter, "Is there another motel in town besides the one right over there?"

"No, ma'am, I'm afraid not," the cashier replied.

The stranger blew out an exasperated breath, shook her head, and said, "Great. Where am I supposed to stay? Who would've dreamed that every room would be booked in a place like this?"

"I'm sorry, ma'am," the cashier said with the sort of genuine sympathy one found in small towns. "You might find something in McElhaney. It's ninety miles farther west—"

"My business is here," the blonde interrupted. She reached into the pocket of her tight, stylish jeans for a phone.

Stark was about as far from being a member of the fashion police as anybody could be, but he thought the jeans went well with the dark blue silk blouse the woman wore. The outfit suited her. She wasn't young anymore, but she was still extremely attractive.

And he wasn't so old that he failed to notice that.

Something about the woman interested him besides her looks. She seemed familiar somehow, as if he had seen her before. He was trying to figure out if they had ever met when he suddenly realized who she was.

He left a twenty and a five on the table with his ticket to pay for the meal and a generous tip. Then he stood up, carried his Stetson, and walked over to the counter.

"Hello, Ms. Devereaux," he said.

"Hi," she said, nodding distractedly in his general direction without really looking at him. Clearly, she was used to people recognizing her and coming up to her to say hello. Why wouldn't she be? She had been on TV quite a bit, after all. Everybody knew people who had been on TV.

"I couldn't help but overhear about your problem," Stark went on.

She had her phone out now and was scrolling through something on its screen.

"Unless you've got a motel room in your pocket—" she began.

"I might," Stark said.

That prompted her to look at him, finally. Interest sparked in her eyes at the sight of his tall, broad-shouldered form.

"What did you have in mind?" she asked.

Not the same thing she obviously believed he did, he thought, but he was flattered that she hadn't rejected the idea out of hand. He said, "I have one of the rooms over at the motel—"

"You do, do you?"

"And I thought maybe if I could find somewhere else to stay, I could give it up and let you have it," Stark went on.

"Oh."

He wasn't sure if she sounded disappointed or relieved—or both.

Then a look of recognition appeared on her face, and she went on, "Wait a minute. I know you. Don't I?"

"We've never met in person," Stark said, "but you've talked about me on television, when you were being interviewed as a legal expert, and before that as a spokesman for the White House."

"Oh, my God," she breathed. "You're—"

"If I recall correctly," Stark said, "you called me a murdering, right-wing, vigilante lunatic."

"You're him. John Howard Stark."

"Yes, ma'am. And you're Alexis Devereaux. And this—" Stark waved the hand holding the Stetson to indicate their surroundings. "I think this is what they call in the movies a meet-cute."

CHAPTER 7

Phillip Hamil arrived in Fuego that evening, as well. He had caught the red-eye from Washington to Dallas, where one of the members of his organization had a car waiting for him. Then he had spent the day driving across Texas, one of the places he hated most.

This was one of the last bastions of Republican strength in the country, and even it threatened to turn purple because of the growing liberal enclaves of Dallas, Houston, San Antonio, and Austin.

Over the past decade, the Democrats had become as adept at getting the illegal alien vote as they always had been at turning out the dead vote, so it was only a matter of time until a tipping point was reached.

Hamil didn't really care about American politics except for putting the system to use in furthering his own cause, the cause of Islam. The Democrats were the most useful because they were the most easily manipulated. Appeal to their emotions and they would fall into lockstep behind any idea, no matter how stupid and obviously unworkable it might be, especially if it involved raising taxes and soaking the evil rich.

The Republicans came in handy, too, because they

gave the Democrats an enemy and kept them united. The pundits kept saying that the Republican Party would eventually wither away and disappear because of demographics.

Hamil hoped that wouldn't actually happen. If the Democrats ever attained complete control, with nothing to hold them back from implementing their ideas, the United States would collapse into complete and utter chaos, probably within twenty years.

That was obvious to anyone who looked at the situation with clear, unbiased eyes. Hamil and those like him needed the country to stay at least somewhat functional.

Who wanted to take over a madhouse? That would be more trouble than it was worth.

None of which kept Hamil from despising Texas and everything that it stood for. Thanks to the relentless politically correct drumbeat of the American media on both coasts, "cowboy" was an insult these days, but that didn't stop many of the people in Texas from continuing to embrace what it had originally stood for.

In fact, there was one of them now, Hamil thought as he turned the car into the motel driveway. The man, tall and broad-shouldered and wearing one of those ridiculous-looking cowboy hats, was going into the office with a stunning blond woman in jeans and a dark blue blouse.

Hamil brought his car to a stop. His hands tightened on the wheel. *Wait a minute*, he thought. He recognized that woman.

She was Alexis Devereaux.

A smile slowly appeared on Hamil's lean face. He hadn't known that the Devereaux woman was going to be in Fuego this weekend. This was an unexpected but welcome development.

The whole world needed to know about what happened here, and Alexis Devereaux could help get the story out.

He would have to be sure that she wasn't killed right away, Hamil decided.

The blond American bitch could die *after* she had served her purpose.

Jerry Patel leaned on the counter in the office lobby, feeling dizzy and trying not to collapse. If he didn't know better, he might have worried that he had been exposed accidentally to the same poison he had used in the ice machine.

He knew that wasn't the case, though. He was all too aware of why he felt so weak. He had spent the day running to the toilet and throwing up, and he hadn't been able to eat a thing.

So much death. So much.

And most of it seemed completely pointless to him. The motel could have served as a rendezvous point without it. Nearly all of the guests would have checked out and moved on, and if anyone else stopped during the day looking for a room, Patel could have told them that the motel was booked up. Mr. Stark was the only one staying for several days, and somehow he was still alive. Patel had seen him walking to the café a while earlier.

But Fareed's orders had been explicit. He had shown up the night before with the cylinder of poison and instructions to hook it up to the ice machine's water supply line so that the odorless, tasteless, deadly stuff would go into the ice and kill anyone who used it.

Dozens of Americans would die for no good reason except . . . dozens of Americans would die.

Patel supposed that was reason enough for Fareed and the other leaders of the clandestine network that ran across the entire country. All he knew was that he was too afraid of Fareed not to follow the man's orders.

The office door opened. Patel looked up and saw a woman coming into the office. Mr. Stark had opened the door and held it for her.

Patel caught his breath and straightened as he recognized the blonde. He couldn't put a name with the attractive face at first, but he was sure he knew her from television or the movies. She was that beautiful.

Stark followed the woman into the office, nodded, and said, "Mr. Patel, this is—"

"Alexis Devereaux," Patel interrupted as he realized who the woman was. "Ms. Devereaux, I've seen you on the news so many times. It . . . it's an honor to have you here in my motel."

She smiled and said, "Thank you."

She was so gracious, Patel thought. But then, she would have to be, the way she must be surrounded by admirers all the time. She would have learned how to deal with them.

"Ms. Devereaux saw your No Vacancy sign," Stark said. "She's looking for a place to stay, and I hoped you might be able to help her out."

An image suddenly flashed into Patel's mind. A horrible, dreadful image of the beautiful Alexis Devereaux lying on the floor with her lovely face contorted in agonized lines of death.

"No," Patel said instantly. "I'm sorry. The motel is completely full. There is no room."

Stark said, "Well, actually, I was thinking that maybe you could give her my room. I can find somewhere else to stay."

Patel shook his head.

"No," he said again. "There is nowhere else. I . . . I am very sorry, Ms. Devereaux. It would be such an honor for you to stay here with us, but it is impossible."

She let out an exasperated sigh and said, "This is ridiculous."

"It certainly is," a new voice said. "Hello, Alexis."

Patel had been so busy staring at Alexis Devereaux and trying to banish the awful mental image of her dying that he hadn't noticed the office door opening again. Now he looked toward the door and saw a handsome, well-dressed, dark-haired man coming in. He wore a smile on his face, and as Alexis turned toward him, he held out his arms to her.

"Phillip!" she exclaimed. "Phillip Hamil, is that you?"

"Of course it is," he said.

She threw herself into his arms and said, "I never expected to see a friendly face in this godforsaken place!"

Stark thought the well-dressed stranger—Phillip Hamil, Alexis had called him—looked familiar, and that name rang a bell, too. After hugging him, she stepped back slightly and said, "What are the odds that two old friends from Washington would find themselves in Fuego, Texas at the same time?"

"Well, I don't know about you," Hamil said, "but I'm here to pay a visit to my old friend Jerry Patel." Hamil extended his hand over the counter. "Hello, Jerry. It's good to see you again."

"And you as well," Patel said as he smiled and gripped Hamil's hand.

The funny thing was, it seemed to Stark like the motel owner had never seen this visitor before. That was just an impression, a hunch, really, but it puzzled Stark anyway.

Alexis kept her right arm linked with Hamil's left as she turned and said, "Phillip, this is John Howard Stark."

Hamil's carefully plucked eyebrows rose as he said, "Really? Yours is a famous name, Mr. Stark."

"Infamous is probably more like it in certain circles," Stark said, "such as the ones the two of you travel in."

Stark had remembered why he recognized Hamil's name and face. Like Alexis Devereaux, Hamil had appeared on TV often enough that he would seem familiar to anybody who watched the news very often. Whenever he was interviewed, the graphic at the bottom of the screen always identified him as "Dr. Phillip Hamil." He was some sort of professor, Stark recalled, not a medical doctor, and he was an expert on U.S.–Arab relations.

Hamil laughed and said, "I'll admit, you've gotten under the skin of a number of my political acquaintances, Mr. Stark. Several presidents have gotten some gray hairs over the activities of you and your friends."

"Just trying to do the right thing," Stark said.

"Of course." Hamil put out his hand. "It's all politics. There's nothing personal in it."

Maybe that had been true at one time, Stark thought as he shook hands with Phillip Hamil, but not anymore. Politics had become the religion of the left, since they had no real religion of their own, and as true believers everything became intensely personal to them, including politics. No one could disagree with them simply on the basis of logic and reason. No, anyone who opposed even the smallest part of the "progressive" agenda was not only wrong but also evil, to be demonized, spat upon, and destroyed.

It was a damned shame people had to get like that, Stark had thought more than once, instead of being able to sit down and work out their differences like reasonable human beings.

But elections had consequences, even stolen ones, and one such consequence over the past decade had been a hardening of the Democrats' belief that "compromise" meant that they should get everything they wanted all the time, every time, in every way, and anybody who didn't go along with that was just a crazy Republican obstructionist.

Stark tried not to let any of that show on his face as he shook hands with Phillip Hamil, who asked, "What brings you to this part of Texas, Mr. Stark?"

"Like you, I'm just visiting an old friend," Stark said.

"Who might that be?"

Being a lifelong Texan, Stark was too naturally polite to tell the man it was none of his business. Instead he said, "George Baldwin."

Hamil cocked his head to the side.

"From the prison?"

"That's right. George and I served in the military together, a long time ago."

"I see. Well, I hope you enjoy your visit." Hamil turned toward the counter again. "Now, Jerry, what's this about you not having a room for Ms. Devereaux?"

"We're . . . we're full up," Patel said. Stark heard an undercurrent of nervousness in his voice. "I'm sorry, but—"

"But you're holding one of those rooms for me, right?" Hamil broke in.

"I am? I mean, yes, of course I am."

"Well, there you go. Give her my room."

Alexis said, "Oh, no, Phillip, I couldn't put you out of your room. That just wouldn't be right."

"Nonsense. I insist."

"But where will you stay?"

Hamil gestured at Patel and said, "I'll bet Jerry here can put me up. Hate to put you on the spot like this, Jer, but hey, what are old college buddies for? You've got a sofa you can make up for me, don't you?"

"Of course," Patel said. "Of course you can stay with Lara and me. We'd be glad to have you."

Despite his effusive words, Patel looked like he was welcoming a scorpion or a diamondback rattler into his home, Stark thought.

"So it's all settled," Hamil said.

"And nobody gets put out of a room," Alexis said. "Mr. Stark was trying to give up his for me when you came in, Phillip."

"You know how chivalrous Texans are," Hamil said with a chuckle. "Maybe we'll see you again before you leave, Mr. Stark."

"Could be," Stark said. He tugged on the brim of his Stetson and nodded to Alexis. "Good night, Ms. Devereaux."

"Good night, Mr. Stark," she said. "It's been a pleasure to meet you."

Stark gave everybody a smile all around and left the office. He wasn't smiling inside. Something really odd was going on here, and he thought he knew what it was.

It couldn't be a coincidence that just a few days after those Islamic terrorists had been brought to Hell's Gate and locked up there, a couple of liberal icons like Alexis Devereaux and Phillip Hamil showed up in Fuego.

There was only one explanation that made any sense.

One of the networks was going to do a live broadcast from here. They might even try to get into the prison. A little ambush journalism at its finest.

Tomorrow when he went out there, Stark thought as he let himself into his room, he would have to warn George Baldwin that trouble was likely on its way.

Once both of the Americans were gone, Fareed came out of the office into the motel lobby, where he and Hamil embraced and slapped each other on the back. Hamil was glad to see his second-in-command.

Fareed Nassir was tall and lean, with wiry muscles, a shock of black hair, and a face pockmarked from a childhood illness. Hamil knew that he had personally executed at least three men, traitors to their cause who had tried to sell them out to the infidels. It was quite likely that Fareed had killed more than that, but the details didn't matter.

Patel was staring at them. Obviously, he was unaware of Hamil's place in the organization. Hamil smiled thinly and said, "Judgment."

Patel swallowed and nodded.

"Judgment," he replied. "I had no idea—"

"That's all right. You weren't supposed to know about me. But you did a good job of playing along. For now there are only two things you need to know."

Patel nodded again, indicating that he was ready to hear them.

"One, I'm in charge here, and two, you need to go shut off that ice machine and put a sign on it saying that it's out of order. Lock it up if you can. Do it quickly, before Ms. Devereaux has a chance to get any ice out of it."

"You don't want her to—"

"Absolutely not," Hamil said. "The more media coverage we can get tomorrow, the better." He smiled. "We want the whole world to know that the triumph of Islam is inevitable. We want everyone to watch as we plunge a dagger into the heart of America."

CHAPTER 8

Sunday morning promised a beautiful autumn day when the sun rose in a deep blue sky dotted with puffy white clouds. The temperature was around fifty degrees, just low enough to be pleasantly cool. A light wind blew out of the south, indicating that the day would warm up nicely later.

The café near the motel was the only place open for breakfast, and it was doing a fairly good business when Stark came in. Empty stools were plentiful at the counter, though, so he took one of them. The café wasn't really that busy because most people didn't go out for breakfast before heading to church, and Fuego was a churchgoing town, at least compared to most places these days. Christians had been so belittled for so long that many of them elsewhere had drifted away from attending services.

"Coffee, hon?" the redheaded waitress asked Stark as she came along the counter toward him. She already had the carafe from the coffeemaker in one hand and a cup and saucer in the other.

"Yes, ma'am," Stark said with a smile.

She filled the cup, pushed a bowl with little plastic containers of half-and-half and packets of various sweeteners within his reach, and asked, "What'll you have?"

"Stack of pancakes with bacon and hash browns," Stark replied.

She grinned at him, nodded, and said, "Can't beat the classics, can you?"

"No, ma'am, you sure can't."

An elderly man in overalls, a flannel shirt, and a gimme cap sat two stools over. He gave Stark a friendly nod and asked, "You go to the game the other night?"

"I happened to be there," Stark said. He knew how important high school football was to the folks in towns like Fuego. They'd be talking about the McElhaney game all week . . . until the next game.

"Mighty excitin'," the old man said. "Ain't had much of a team so far this year, but that game might've been enough to turn it around." He sighed. "If our startin' quarterback hadn't broke his leg, that is. Gonna have to go with a underclassman now."

"Have you heard how the boy's doing?" Stark asked, mildly curious.

"He's still in the hospital. Ought to be able to go home in another day or two, his daddy said. Bert Frazier—that's Andy's daddy—stopped by here for coffee a while ago on his way to work. He's a guard out at the prison, you know. Good fella. Used to be a cop. He'd been by the hospital to see his boy."

"Well, I'm glad to hear the youngster's doing as well as can be expected."

"Yeah, he'll be all right. Done for the year, though, as far as playin' football. That'll hurt his chances of gettin' a good scholarship. Tough break." The old man grunted. "No pun intended."

Stark smiled and drank some of his coffee.

The waitress brought his food a minute later, and he dug in with enjoyment. The talkative old-timer let him eat a while, then asked, "You ain't from around here, are you, mister?"

"No, just visiting," Stark said.

"Thought so. I know just about everybody in town. Ain't hard for me to pick out a stranger . . . and the town's full of 'em this mornin', let me tell you."

"It is?" Stark said with a slight frown.

"Yep. Seen some of 'em down at the grocery store parkin' lot and here and there around town. Funny-lookin' fellas, too. Thought at first they was Mexicans, comin' in for some sort o' construction project, but I ain't so sure about that. Looked to me like they might be some other kind o' foreigner."

That was odd, Stark mused. His first thought at hearing the old man's words had been a worry that cartel soldiers might be moving into the town for some reason. The whole area had had so much trouble with drug smugglers, with the problem continuing to grow worse over the past decade because of budget cuts and what passed for immigration reform to Democratic politicians, and Stark's personal history included so many violent clashes with the cartel that it was natural his thoughts would turn in that direction.

But then the old-timer had said that he thought the men he'd seen weren't Hispanic. What did that leave?

Middle Eastern, Stark thought as his frown deepened.

Alarm bells went off in the back of his head.

He finished his food, then asked the waitress, "Where's the police department?"

She looked surprised as she asked, "Something wrong with the food?"

"What? Oh, no." Stark laughed and shook his head. "The food was great. Perfect. Wonderful bacon. No, I need to talk to somebody about something that doesn't have anything to do with the food."

She blew out a mock sigh of relief and said, "That's good to hear. The police department's a couple of blocks up Main, on the other side of the street."

Stark nodded and said, "Yeah, I think remember seeing it when I was walking around town yesterday."

"You probably won't find anybody there but the dispatcher, though," the waitress told him. "And there'll only be one officer on patrol on a Sunday morning like this."

"Well, it probably doesn't amount to anything," Stark said. "I just want to check on something."

"All right, hon. Hope it works out for you."

Stark paid his check, nodded, said so long to the old-timer he'd been talking to, and left the café. He walked back over to the motel, and as he did, he saw a couple of men striding quickly from one of the units to another.

With their dark hair and skin, they could have been taken for Hispanic, all right, he thought. But like the old man in the café, he didn't think they were.

Instead of going to his room, Stark got into his pickup and started it. He backed out of the space and pulled from the parking lot onto Main Street. It took him less than a minute to reach the Fuego Police Department, which was housed in a tan brick building with some shrubs growing along the front. The entrance was down at the end of the building, facing a parking lot to the side.

When Stark went inside, he found a burly young man sitting behind a counter at a console that included a radio and a computer. He wore the same sort of uniform that Stark had seen on Chief Charles Cobb the day before. The dispatcher swiveled his chair around to face Stark and asked, "Help you, mister?"

Now that Stark had a better look at the young man, he realized the dispatcher had Down syndrome. He said, "The chief doesn't happen to be here, does he?"

"Nope. Just me. Officer Raymond Brady. Who're you? I don't know you, do I?"

Stark smiled and said, "No, I don't live here in Fuego. I'm just visiting. My name's Stark."

"Pleased to meet you, Mr. Stark. What can I do for you?"

"You're the dispatcher?"

"That's right. Do you have a crime to report, or an accident, something like that?"

Stark shook his head. "No, what I'd really like to do is talk to the chief."

"Give me your cell phone number. I'll see if I can get in touch with him and tell him to give you a call."

That seemed reasonable to Stark. He couldn't very well claim this was an emergency and insist that Officer Brady call the chief on the radio right this minute. For all Stark knew, there was absolutely nothing threatening going on in Fuego this morning. It was just a hunch on his part that something might be wrong.

But given the fact that 150 Islamic terrorists had been locked up in Hell's Gate a few days earlier, and now there was a sudden influx into town of men who might be Middle Eastern . . .

Well, it didn't take a genius to see that *something* might be up.

Stark took a business card from a plastic holder on the counter, turned it over, wrote down his name and cell phone number on the back, and handed it to Raymond Brady.

"The chief can get hold of me at this number anytime."

"Maybe you should tell me what this is about, so I can pass it along to the chief," Raymond suggested.

Stark hesitated, but only for a second. Raymond seemed competent and sharp as a tack.

"I'm a little worried because there seems to be a lot of strangers in town."

"*You're* a stranger in town," Raymond pointed out. "You said so yourself."

"That's true, but I think the ones I'm talking about might be looking to cause some trouble." Stark thought about the fact that Alexis Devereaux and Phillip Hamil were both in town, too, and went on, "I think there's going to be some sort of protest demonstration about those new prisoners out at Hell's Gate."

"The terrorists, you mean."

"Yeah. I wouldn't be surprised if there were TV crews here later."

"Fuego's gonna be on TV?" Raymond asked.

"I don't know. Maybe."

"That would be something."

"But maybe not something good," Stark said. "Anyway, that's what I want to talk to the chief about. I was going to suggest that he be on the alert for some sort of disturbance."

"Chief Cobb's always on the alert for trouble," Raymond said with a note of pride and admiration in his voice. "And I'm his number one lookout."

"I'm sure you are. If you'll give him my number . . ."

"I will," the young man promised.

Stark smiled again, nodded, and said, "Thanks." He went back out to his pickup, hoping that it wouldn't be long before the chief got in touch with him.

As he started to pull out of the parking lot, he hesitated

again, then turned left instead of right, back toward the motel. There was nothing he needed from there right now, and even though he wasn't supposed to show up at the prison until 11:30, he decided to drive out there now. He suspected that the demonstration, if there was one, would take place here in town, but it might move out to the prison later.

Stark had already planned to warn his old friend that trouble might be on the way. Now he was more sure than ever that George needed to know something was up.

CHAPTER 9

Fuego was small enough that it had just one of numerous things. The town's lone apartment complex sat on the western edge of town. Kincaid had rented an efficiency there when he arrived some eight months earlier, paid for with money some of his friends had gotten to him.

Men who lived and worked in the shadows knew that there might come a day when they would need to disappear with little or no warning. Untraceable funds were stashed all over the world for just such emergencies. They had access to all sorts of well-documented false identities as well.

Officially, Lucas Kincaid was not one of those shadow warriors, but he had worked with many of them—Special Forces operators, SEALS, Company men. When the incident at Warraz al-Sidar occurred, Kincaid had known that his military career was over. He had gone too far off-book. If he turned himself in, he would be court-martialed, and he knew that getting off with just a dishonorable discharge would be an incredible stroke of luck.

It was more likely he would have wound up in some deep, dark hole nobody even knew about, spending the rest of his life in the most secret of top-secret, black-site prisons.

So he had reached out—into the shadows—and wound up with a new name, a new life, a new job.

"Lucas Kincaid" had the background to get him hired at the Baldwin Correctional Facility. It hadn't occurred to him that he might wind up in charge of the prison library, but Kincaid had surprised himself by finding that he liked it. He had always been a big reader, and he had organizational skills.

The best part about it was that nobody ever got killed over an overdue book. At least they hadn't so far.

And nobody at the prison or in Fuego had a clue who he really was. Things might stay that way indefinitely if he was just smart enough not to call attention to himself.

On Sunday morning he slept late. When he got up he worked out for an hour. The fight a couple of nights earlier had told him that he needed to get back into better shape. Then he fixed himself an egg-white omelet, washed it down with a couple cups of coffee, and felt pretty darned good. He didn't feel like sitting around all day and watching TV, that was for sure.

There was always work to do at the prison. The library was closed on Sunday, but he could go in and update the circulation statistics. Of course, he could get one of his assistants to do that—but not Simon Winslow, who wasn't allowed on computers even if they weren't connected to the Internet. One of the other guys could handle the job, though.

But in that case, what would he do today, Kincaid asked himself, and with that thought in his head he got dressed, piled into his Jeep, and headed for Hell's Gate.

Not for the first time—not hardly for the first time— he felt uneasy because he wasn't armed. He could have gotten a CHL using his new identity, but that was one more digital trail. He could have carried illegally, or at least had a knife in his pocket.

But he would have had to leave any weapons in the Jeep when he got to the prison, in order to get through the metal detectors, and it didn't seem worth the trouble. He had a tire iron that was easy to grab if he needed to, and it wasn't illegal anywhere.

The Jeep had satellite radio. That was necessary out here in far West Texas, where regular radio signals could be few and far between. It was tuned to a news station, and as Kincaid drove toward the prison he heard a breaking story about how the body of a United States senator had been discovered in a motel in Virginia, not far from Washington, D.C. The police were being stingy with the details, of course, but a source close to the case had leaked the fact that the woman had died of a broken neck and her death was considered a homicide.

That was a damned shame, thought Kincaid. He didn't know the senator, didn't agree with her politics at all—she'd made a habit of saying inflammatory things about the military, about the Second Amendment, about economic redistribution—but still Kincaid hated to hear about anybody being murdered. Life was a precious thing and shouldn't be squandered.

Well, most of the time that was true, anyway, he told himself. Anybody who had killed as many people as he had ought to qualify such statements.

The only things the cops were admitting at the moment were that they had no suspects and no clue as to the motive behind the senator's death. When the report was over, Kincaid pushed the tuning button on the Jeep's steering wheel, found a metal station playing a Hammerfall song, and cranked up the volume as he drove toward the cliffs, shining red in the morning light.

* * *

Charles Cobb's hand hovered over the butt of the revolver holstered on his hip. As he waited for the other man to make his move, Cobb kept his breathing steady. A man needed calm nerves at a time like this.

The other man—visible only to Cobb since he was imaginary—slapped leather. Smoothly, Cobb pulled the double-action Colt .45 and squeezed off all five rounds in its cylinder in less than three seconds. The shots came so close together they sounded like one long roar instead of individual blasts.

As the echoes rolled away across the flats, Cobb studied the target he had set up. The shots had a nice grouping, all within the chest of the man-shaped silhouette. Cobb didn't think his draw had been quite as fast as the others he had made earlier that morning, but it was still pretty fast.

He reloaded the Colt and returned it to the gunfighter's leather he wore. Other than the holster and gun belt, he wore his regulation uniform because he was taking the afternoon shift. Most of his officers were football fans, so they could see the NFL games that way. Cobb enjoyed watching football, but he didn't really keep up with it. Baseball was his game, yet another way in which he was sort of a throwback.

Nobody expected a black man to be interested in Old West gunfighters, but ever since seeing Western movies starring Fred Williamson and Jim Brown when he was a kid, deep down Charlie Cobb had wanted to be fast on the draw. Police work gave him a familiarity with handguns, so eventually he had taken the step of getting a Colt .45 replica and starting to practice with it. He wasn't married, so he had his work and his hobby, and he devoted long hours to both of them.

He was pretty good with the Colt by now, he thought. Probably nowhere near as fast as the true pistoleers like

Wild Bill Hickok, Smoke Jensen, Ben Thompson, John Wesley Hardin, and Frank Morgan, but still pretty slick on the draw. Of course in this modern era, five rounds in a revolver didn't amount to much—he kept the sixth chamber empty, just like the old-timers—but Cobb still took pride in his ability.

He had driven out to his favorite spot to practice, several miles north of town, the same way he did most Sunday mornings. There were no houses anywhere around, so the shots wouldn't disturb anybody. And nobody could see what he was doing and make fun of him, either.

He packed up his targets and headed back toward Fuego. He had driven about a mile when his cell phone rang. There was no service in the area where he practiced, but Raymond could reach him there on the radio if something important came up.

It was the station calling now, Cobb saw as he picked up the phone from the seat beside him. He thumbed the button to answer it and asked, "What is it, Raymond?"

"A man came in looking for you a while ago, Chief," Raymond Brady replied. "He wanted you to call him."

"You get his name and number?"

"Yes, sir. He said his name was Stark."

Cobb frowned slightly and asked, "John Howard Stark?"

"He didn't say the rest of his name, just Stark. Let me look at the card where he wrote down his number . . . Yes, sir, he wrote John Howard Stark. You were right."

Cobb had felt a little tingle of . . . something . . . when he realized John Howard Stark was in Fuego. Not fear, certainly, and not even apprehension. More of an awareness that trouble had a habit of following John Howard Stark around.

"Did he say what he wanted to talk to me about?"

"He said that there were strangers in town and Fuego was gonna be on TV."

That didn't really make sense to Cobb, but he supposed Stark could explain. He said, "Go ahead and give me the number, Raymond."

The dispatcher did so. Cobb had a remarkable memory and knew he wouldn't have any trouble recalling it. Then Raymond asked, "Should I have called you on the radio about this, Chief? I didn't want to disturb you while you weren't on duty."

"No, it's all right," Cobb told the young man. "I'm sure that whatever this is about, it won't amount to anything."

He said good-bye and broke the connection, then dialed the number Raymond had given him.

A single two-lane blacktop road ran from Fuego to the Baldwin Correctional Facility. That isolation and difficulty of access made it even more secure.

Some modern prisons looked like industrial and manufacturing facilities—although with a lot more barbed wire—but Hell's Gate was everything grim and gray that a prison should be. The main building was an imposing three-story heap of concrete, steel, and bulletproof glass. A narrower two-story wing jutted out from its north side. Windowless, it was a secure, bunker-like structure where the worst of the worst were housed.

Those prisoners had been shifted around, however, some confined in solitary, others deemed lesser risks mixed in with the general population. The ultramax wing was now home to the hundred and fifty Islamic terrorists who had been brought here.

George Baldwin explained that to Stark as they stood

in the warden's office and Baldwin pointed to a map of the prison mounted on the wall.

"There's an old-fashioned sally port between the rest of the prison and the ultramax wing," Baldwin said. "That wing has its own backup generator for lights, water, and ventilation if something happens to the power in the rest of the prison. There's also a supply of food in case of emergency. Just MREs, but enough to keep the prisoners from starving for a while. We can isolate that whole wing if necessary."

"I can see why the Justice Department picked Hell's Gate to house those terrorists, if they were bound and determined to transfer them from military prisons," Stark said.

Baldwin grunted and said, "If you ask me, the best thing to do with those bastards would be to stick 'em in front of firing squads. It wouldn't take long to solve the problem."

"I don't know if that would solve anything. It would just make the fanatics in the Middle East regard them as martyrs even more than they already do."

"Yeah, well, that's the problem, John Howard," Baldwin said. "The fanatics aren't in the Middle East anymore. They're here, right in our own backyards."

Stark couldn't argue with that, not after what he had seen in Fuego this morning. Two men didn't make a mob of protesters, but that's what the signs pointed to. Baldwin agreed with him, too.

"How about the National Guard, or even the regular Army?" Stark asked. "Can you call them in to help keep order if you need to?"

Baldwin grimaced and shook his head.

"I'm only allowed to request assistance from civilian authorities. No military. The Federal Protective Service was disbanded after that nerve gas fiasco, or at least it was supposed to be, but from what I hear it was just absorbed back into the Department of Homeland Security. It's still the same bunch of jackbooted thugs."

Stark nodded. Like everybody else in the country, he had heard about how the former president had tried to bypass the Second Amendment and use his own personal Gestapo to seize all the guns in the little town of Home, Texas, about 150 miles from here. As if that weren't bad enough, the president had then ordered his men to use a new chemical weapon developed at a secret government lab on American citizens. It had cost the president his job, and he was now living in exile overseas, where he had come from to start with, rather than do time in prison where he belonged.

A lot of people had hoped that near-disaster would permanently alter the direction of the country, but after a short time when it appeared that might happen, the media had gone back to propping up their sacred "progressive" cause and smearing anyone who dared to oppose it, and things had returned pretty much to the sorry state that resembled "normal" in the United States these days.

"Sounds like it could be a mess, all right," Stark agreed with his old friend. "I suppose we'll have to wait and see what happens, though."

Baldwin sighed and said, "Yeah. In the meantime, you want to have a look around?"

"Sounds good to me," Stark said.

CHAPTER 10

The police chief was supposed to set a good example, so Cobb tried not to use his cell phone while he was driving unless it was an emergency. For that reason, he radioed John Howard Stark while he was still at the site where he practiced his fast draw and did his target practice.

"Hello?"

"Mr. Stark, this is Charles Cobb. We met yesterday in Fuego."

"Of course, Chief. How are you?"

"I'm fine," Cobb said. "My dispatcher said you wanted to talk to me. Something about strangers in town?"

Stark didn't answer the question directly. Instead he said, "Do you know who Alexis Devereaux is, Chief?"

"The name's familiar," Cobb said, frowning slightly. "I can't quite place it, though."

"She's a lawyer, used to work at the White House. Now she shows up on TV a lot. The cable news networks like to bring her in as an expert on the talking head shows."

"Oh, yes, I know who you're talking about. Very staunch supporter of the administration."

"Except when the President isn't being liberal

enough to suit her," Stark said. "Like in the case of those prisoners who were just transferred to Hell's Gate."

"Are you saying that Alexis Devereaux is in Fuego?"

"She is, Chief, and so is Phillip Hamil."

"I feel like I should know that name, too."

"He's some sort of professor who turns up on the news shows, too. In the past he's advised the administration on U.S.–Arab relations."

Cobb lifted the hand that wasn't holding the phone and scrubbed it over his face. He felt a sudden weariness settling into his shoulders. "Would it be correct to describe these two as publicity hounds?" he asked.

"In my opinion it would be."

"We're going to have camera crews in Fuego, aren't we?"

"Maybe more than that," Stark said. "According to what I've been told, there are a number of men of Middle Eastern descent in town this morning, too. I saw a couple of them at the motel just a little while ago."

"It's not illegal to be of Middle Eastern descent," Cobb pointed out.

"Of course not. And it might not even mean anything. But I've got a hunch you may have a mob of angry protesters on your hands, Chief."

"That's racial profiling."

"It's common sense," Stark said, sounding slightly impatient.

Stark wasn't even a cop, Cobb thought, but he knew what law enforcement officers everywhere were aware of if they had half a brain: facts didn't lie, and a thirty-year-old Middle Eastern male was a hell of a lot more likely to have trouble in mind than an eighty-year-old grandma. Stopping and interrogating Grandma just because of some misguided notion of political correctness was nothing more than a waste of valuable time and resources.

"Where are you now, Mr. Stark?" Cobb asked.

"As a matter of fact, I'm out at the prison visiting with George Baldwin."

"Why don't you stay there for a while?" Cobb suggested.

"What, you think I'm going to cause trouble?"

"No offense, but you seem to have a history of trouble cropping up wherever you are, Mr. Stark. Most of your problems have been with the Mexican drug cartels, but we both know they have a lot of ties with Islamic terror networks. The friends of those fellows who are locked up in Hell's Gate, in other words."

"All I said was that there might be a protest, not some sort of terrorist incident."

"I can't rule anything out until I've investigated the situation," Cobb said. "I don't want your presence aggravating things."

"All right, I'll stay put," Stark said, although he didn't sound very happy about it. "How about letting me know what you find out?"

"Yes, I'll stay in touch. Good-bye, Mr. Stark."

Cobb broke the connection and slipped the handset into the pocket of his uniform shirt. He sighed as he reached for the key in the police cruiser's ignition.

So much for a peaceful Sunday.

Jerry Patel hadn't slept much the night before. A little while not long before dawn when sheer exhaustion had claimed him, that was all. And when he woke up he had wished for a few seconds that it was all just a dream . . . but of course it wasn't.

Other than that he had lain there in bed whimpering. Lara had tried to comfort him at first, but after a while she had given up in disgust.

She was nervous about what was going to happen, too, he knew, but if anything, she was more fierce in her dedication to their cause than he was. She had said, "It has to be done, Jerry. I know some of the Americans are your friends, but they must be taught that they cannot mock the Prophet."

Patel knew she was right. They were only doing what was necessary. The blood that would be spilled today and in days to come would be in a holy cause.

The face that looked back at him from the mirror on Sunday morning was gaunt and hollow-eyed, though. Maybe when all this was over, he could rest then.

Hamil and Fareed had given strict orders that everyone was to stay in their rooms until the time came for the operation to begin. So no one was moving around the hotel this morning except for Mr. Stark, who still seemed to have no idea what was going on. Patel had seen the big American walk to the café for breakfast, then get in his pickup and drive off.

In a way, Patel hoped that Stark had left for good, although he hadn't seen the man load any belongings into the pickup. Despite Stark's crimes against Islam and its allies in the past, he had been friendly to Patel. He seemed like a good man, not a devil.

Patel was at the counter in the lobby, puttering around, trying to stay busy and keep his mind off what was going to happen, when the door opened and the blond woman came in.

Alexis Devereaux wore a dark blue dress today, along with stockings and heels, and she was sinfully beautiful. Literally sinful, since Patel felt a sharp twinge of guilt to go along with the surge of lust she provoked in him.

She smiled and said, "I'm expecting a satellite truck and a camera crew to show up any time now, Mr. Patel. In fact, they should have been here before now. I'm afraid they've been delayed. When they get here, could you send them on out to the prison?"

"To . . . to the prison?"

"That's right. They're going to be doing a field report

for one of the news networks on the new prisoners who were brought out there last week and the conditions in which they're being kept. I'll be appearing on the broadcast as a legal expert."

"I . . . I see."

She frowned a little as she looked at him and asked, "Are you all right? You seem nervous, and you're sweating."

"My apologies," Patel said quickly. He used the sleeve of his white shirt to wipe away the beads of perspiration from his forehead. "I am perhaps becoming a bit under the weather, as they say."

"Oh, I hope not. Maybe you'll feel better later. Can you take care of that for me? About the TV crew, I mean?"

"Yes, of course," Patel replied without hesitation. Hamil wanted plenty of press coverage. Having a famous lawyer on TV from the prison was a good thing.

His hands were on the counter. Alexis reached out and rested her fingertips on the back of Patel's right hand for a second. Her touch was warm and made his pulse leap.

"Thank you," she said.

Patel knew the way she acted didn't mean anything. Alexis was just one of those women who were naturally a little flirtatious with men. But that didn't stop his heart from pounding harder and his mouth from going dry.

"Yes . . . yes, of course." He struggled to get the words out.

She lifted her hand—the hand she had used to touch him—and wiggled the fingers in a wave. As she walked out of the motel lobby, he couldn't tear his eyes away from the subtle sway of her elegantly clad rear end.

Behind him, Lara cleared her throat.

Patel jumped.

When he looked around, his wife was glaring at him.

"You want her, don't you?" Lara demanded. "That blond American bitch."

"What? No, don't be crazy."

Patel hoped his denial was convincing. Even with everything else going on, keeping his wife from being angry with him was still an important consideration.

He really *had* turned into an American, he thought gloomily.

"She's only important because of the publicity she can provide for our holy cause," Patel went on. "You know what Dr. Hamil said about her."

Lara sniffed and shrugged her shoulders.

"Perhaps. But you were still drooling over her."

He might have continued denying his wife's accusations, but at that moment the glint of the morning sun off a windshield in the parking lot caught his eye. A vehicle had just turned off the highway.

Maybe that camera crew Alexis Devereaux had asked him about, he thought.

A second later he saw that was wrong. The car that came to a stop in front of the motel office was a police cruiser.

Patel's eyes widened in instinctive fear.

The police car's lights weren't going, and the siren had been silent as the vehicle rolled to a stop under the canopy just outside the office. Patel reminded himself of those things and tried to remain calm.

Just in case, though, he said to Lara, "Go back into our quarters."

"I should stay out here."

"No!" His voice was sharp, and for one of the few times in their marriage it possessed a note of command. "Do as I say."

"Well . . . all right," Lara said grudgingly. She disappeared through the door behind the counter and closed it after her.

Patel took a deep breath as he watched the chief of police get out of the car. He knew Charles Cobb, but not well. In the three years that Cobb had been chief, he had gotten to know all the merchants in town, but didn't seem to be close to anyone.

Cobb wore his police uniform, but something about it wasn't right. Patel frowned as he tried to figure out what it was.

As Cobb opened the glass door and came into the lobby, Patel realized what had struck him as odd.

The chief wasn't wearing a standard service revolver or automatic in a holster with a flap over the butt, or any other sort of keeper.

No, the holster attached to the gun belt strapped around Cobb's hips was open at the top and cut down so that the gun would come out quickly with nothing for it to snag on. And the gun itself was a big revolver with wooden grips, like something out of an old cowboy movie.

It looked distinctly out of place on the black police chief.

Cobb smiled, but it wasn't a very friendly expression. He said, "Good morning, Mr. Patel."

"Chief," Patel said. "What brings you here on a Sunday morning?"

He was pleased by how steady his voice sounded. It wasn't easy to achieve that effect, that was certain.

"I'm not really sure," Cobb replied. "I've had a report of something, and I'm checking it out."

Patel held his hands out to the side and said, "Anything I can do to help you, I'll be glad to, Chief. You know that."

"Sure, sure," Cobb said, nodding. "Do you have any vacancies, Mr. Patel?"

A curious frown creased Patel's forehead. He thought that was a plausible reaction to such a question from the chief of police.

"As a matter of fact, the motel is full," he said.

"This late in the morning? Haven't most of your guests usually packed up and left by now?"

"I don't really have any control over when they check in and check out," Patel said. "I just serve the public."

"Of course. I've been told that you have a lot of guests of Middle Eastern descent."

Damn it! Everyone had been supposed to stay out of sight until the time came for the operation to begin. Obviously, some of the men had not been careful enough.

Maybe he could still keep the chief from getting too curious, Patel thought. He would play the discrimination card. That nearly always worked.

"I can't turn away anyone because of their ethnicity. That isn't legal." Patel couldn't resist adding, "I would have thought that *you* would know that, Chief."

Something sparked in Cobb's eyes. He said, "You mean because I'm black?"

Patel shrugged, spread his hands again.

"Your people have always suffered from prejudice."

"*My people* are the citizens of Fuego, black, white, brown, whatever color," Cobb snapped. "I think I'll run the plates of some of the cars parked out there."

"You can't—" Patel began.

"Yes, I can," Cobb interrupted. "I don't need a warrant or a court order to check license plate numbers."

He started to turn away from the counter but stopped abruptly as he swung around. A man stood in the doorway.

Patel had been concentrating on the chief and hadn't noticed the newcomer, either. At the sight of him now, though, Patel's heart started to thud in his chest even harder than it had when Alexis Devereaux touched him.

Fareed Nassir stood there with a look of undisguised hatred on his hatchet-like face and the burning desire to kill in his eyes.

CHAPTER 11

Patel was hiding something. Cobb was sure of that. The motel owner was trying to put up a good front, but Cobb could tell he was scared to death.

That was enough to convince Cobb that John Howard Stark might have been right about some sort of protest brewing.

Cobb could imagine a group of protesters turning into an angry mob and causing some real damage. He was old enough to remember what had happened at the American embassy in Iran nearly fifty years earlier. He was not going to let something like that happen on the streets of Fuego.

No, sir.

So he turned away from the counter with anger building inside him. Nobody was going to threaten his town, no matter what political axe they thought they had to grind.

As he did, he saw a tall, lean man standing in the doorway, silhouetted against the light outside. That sight alone was enough to surprise Cobb and make him stop what he was doing.

Then the man moved a step deeper into the lobby and Cobb saw his face.

That glimpse was more than enough to tell Cobb that right here was trouble on two legs.

Bad trouble.

His mind flashed back to a night many years earlier, when he'd been a rookie cop in Fort Worth and had walked into a convenience store on the south side. The clerk, a middle-aged Vietnamese man, had been standing at the counter with his hands pressing down hard on it.

In front of the counter had been a young black guy, about the same age as Cobb, wearing a hoodie with his hands shoved in the pockets.

As soon as the "customer" turned and looked at him, Cobb had known what was about to happen. He had seen the urge to kill in the man's eyes.

He had survived that night only because his reactions were fast. He'd grabbed a rack full of chips and shoved it right into the guy, knocking him backward.

That had given Cobb enough time to draw his weapon and yell for the would-be robber to get on the ground.

The man hadn't obeyed the order. He had fired through the hoodie pocket instead.

The shot went wild and hit a display of soft drinks in plastic bottles, spraying the sticky brown stuff all over the floor.

Cobb would have returned fire, but he didn't have to. The Vietnamese clerk reached under the counter, came up with a sawed-off shotgun, and blew a hole in the robber's chest big enough to drive a pickup through.

That was the only time in his career Cobb had come close to firing his weapon in the line of duty.

That was about to change, though, because he saw the

same look in the eyes of the man who had just come into the motel lobby, that same eagerness to kill.

The man's hand darted under the lightweight jacket he wore.

Cobb knew the man was reaching for a gun. Every instinct in his body screamed a warning at him. His muscles and nerves began to react automatically.

But he had to wait, had to actually *see* the gun before he could respond. That was what years of training and serving as a law enforcement officer had taught him. The habit was too ingrained to discard it now.

The man's hand came into view, and sure enough, it was holding a short-barreled automatic. The gun wouldn't be very accurate except at close range, but no more than ten feet separated the man from Cobb.

That was enough evidence for Cobb. His hand flashed down to the butt of the Colt.

It was a good draw, as fast and smooth as he'd ever made. A gunfighter's draw, just like the old days.

The tall man never got a shot off. Cobb fired from the hip and put two slugs into his chest. The bullets punched all the way through his skinny body and shattered the glass door behind him.

The shots were deafening in the relatively close confines of the lobby. As the man Cobb had just shot dropped his gun and collapsed, the chief swung back around toward the counter to see what Patel was doing.

The motel owner had clapped his hands over his ears and his mouth was wide open, as were his eyes. Cobb figured he was screaming but couldn't be sure because his own ears were ringing so loudly from the gun blasts.

The door behind Patel flew open and hit him in the back. The impact knocked him forward so that he fell across the counter. His wife—Lara was her name, Cobb remembered somehow in that desperate split second—lunged through the door, and Cobb suddenly found himself seeing the same thing that unlucky robber had seen in that Fort Worth convenience store so many years earlier.

He was looking right down the twin barrels of a shotgun.

He might have had a chance if he hadn't hesitated. Maybe it was because she was a woman. Whatever the reason, Cobb didn't pull the trigger.

Both barrels erupted in flame as the shotgun went off with an even more ear-slamming roar.

The world turned red in Cobb's face, then black.

Then nothing.

Patel thought his head was going to explode. The shotgun blast was bad enough, so loud and so close that it seemed to jolt his brain inside his skull.

The sight of the police chief's body lying on the tiled floor in front of the counter, gushing crimson blood from the stump of its neck, was even worse. Screaming, Patel forced himself to look away from it.

That was a mistake. His gaze landed on the dark, shredded lump of flesh and bone that had been Charles Cobb's head.

The double load of buckshot fired at such close range had blown the chief's head right off his shoulders.

Patel's knees buckled. He would have fallen if he hadn't caught hold of the counter and hung on to it with the desperation of a drowning man.

He was drowning, all right.

Drowning in horror.

Slowly, he became aware that somebody was shaking

him. He looked over and saw Lara standing beside him. Her mouth moved, but he couldn't hear what she was saying.

He couldn't hear anything except his own screaming and the gunshots.

Gradually, words began to penetrate his stunned brain. He heard her say, "—it!" Or maybe it was "Shit!" That would certainly be appropriate under the circumstances.

No, she was saying, "Stop it!" He realized that as she took hold of his shoulders with both hands and continued shaking him. "Stop it, Jerry! Get ahold of yourself!"

What Patel wanted to do was crawl under the counter, curl up in a ball, and stay there until all the bad things in the world had gone away.

He couldn't do that. Lara was right. He had to cope with what had happened, because this was just the beginning.

Hard though it might be to believe, things were only going to get worse.

As an example of that, several men appeared outside the ruined door, glass crunching on the sidewalk under their feet as they rushed into the lobby. Some of them carried pistols, the others automatic weapons. They jerked from side to side, searching for someone to shoot.

Patel and Lara both thrust their hands in the air to let the men know they were no threat.

One of them yelled, "Fareed!" at the side of the second body lying on the floor. The front of Fareed's shirt was sodden with blood, but other than that he looked a lot better than the police chief.

Equally as dead, though. His lifeless face was slack, and his dark eyes had begun to glaze over as they stared at nothing.

The men started shouting at Patel and his wife, some in English, some in their native tongues, demanding to know what had happened. Patel could only stutter, unable to get a coherent word in.

Phillip Hamil ran up outside, also carrying a small pistol. As the others had done, he pulled the door open to step through it, even though most of the glass had shattered and fallen out.

At a sharp word of command from Hamil, the other men fell silent. He looked at the motel owner and asked, "What happened here, Jerry?"

Patel swallowed hard, took a deep breath, and said, "The chief of police came in asking questions. Someone told him there were a lot of strangers staying here. He was going to check the license plates of the cars—"

"So you shot him?" Hamil sounded astonished. "All those vehicles were bought legally. And of course there are strangers at a motel. There always are!"

"No, no," Patel said quickly, pushing at the air with his hands. "I didn't try to stop him, but then Fareed came in, and when he saw the chief, he . . . he—"

"He pulled a gun," Hamil finished with a note of resignation in his voice. "Fareed always had trouble controlling his hatred for the Americans. I suppose he thought that since everything was about to begin anyway, he might as well go ahead and kill the chief."

Patel nodded, glad that Hamil seemed to understand.

"Who shot Fareed?" Hamil asked.

"The chief did. He . . . he let Fareed draw his gun first, then . . . I never saw anything like it. The chief's gun came out so fast, and he shot Fareed, and—"

"And you shot him with that shotgun," Hamil said, nodding to the weapon Lara had placed on the counter.

"No, I—"

"Don't be modest, Jerry," Lara broke into Patel's denial. "You were so brave."

She looked intently at him, and he knew what she wanted. She intended for him to take credit for killing

Chief Cobb. She didn't want to disgrace him and cast a slur on his manhood by admitting that she'd had to kill the chief herself.

After a second, Patel's shoulders rose and fell in an eloquent shrug. He couldn't bring himself to put the lie into words, but if Hamil wanted to believe he was some sort of hero, then so be it.

"You did the best you could in a bad situation, Jerry," Hamil said. "I know that. I'm proud of you. Both of you." He turned to one of the other men and added in English, "Go set off the flares to let the others know it's time to move in."

As the man hurried out, Patel said, "But the operation isn't scheduled to begin yet."

"We don't have any choice. People will have heard those shots. Some of them may be coming to investigate." Hamil paused and leaned his head to the side. "Although, this *is* Texas, where everyone is in love with their guns, so maybe they won't. But we were going to launch the operation in another half-hour anyway, so we're only jumping the gun by a little."

Jumping the gun, Patel thought. What a fitting expression for what was happening in Fuego this morning.

"There's something else I want to know," Hamil went on. "You said someone told the chief about a lot of strangers being in town. Who could have done that?"

"I don't know, unless . . ."

Hamil just waited in silence for Patel to go on.

"The only one I can think of is Mr. Stark," Patel continued after a moment. "Other than our men—and Ms. Devereaux—he was the only one around here this morning. I don't think Ms. Devereaux would have alerted the chief."

"No, even if Alexis was curious, she wouldn't have bothered saying anything to some hick lawman. Besides, she's probably expecting protesters—better visuals that way—and she wouldn't have suspected our men of being anything else." Hamil nodded. "No, I agree with you, it had to be Stark."

The man Hamil had sent outside reappeared on the asphalt in front of the office. He had an odd-looking cylindrical object in his hand. It was some sort of gun, Patel realized.

The man pointed the thing into the air. It went off with a thumping sound, followed a few seconds later by a distant report. The man reloaded and fired again.

The flares descending slowly to the earth were bright enough they would be visible even against the Texas sky, Patel knew. They were the signal for all the men in other locations in Fuego to converge on the motel, along with the men who were waiting outside town.

In a matter of minutes, there would be a small army in the streets.

Phillip Hamil put his gun away in a shoulder holster under his stylish jacket. He said, "John Howard Stark has been an enemy to our cause long enough. After today, he will never cause trouble for us again." He turned his head to look at Patel. "Where is he?"

"I don't know," Patel answered honestly. "He drove off earlier, after eating breakfast at the café."

"Did you see which way he went?"

"West, I believe. Out of town."

"Toward the prison," Hamil mused. "Stark told Alexis that he was friends with the warden out there, so there's a good chance that's where he is." A smile creased Hamil's face. "He's going to make it easy for us. All he has to do is stay right where he is, and we'll be coming to him."

CHAPTER 12

Kincaid was at the computer behind the library's main desk when the door opened and Warden Baldwin came in accompanied by a man Kincaid didn't recognize. The stranger was dressed like a cowboy, in boots, jeans, a faded blue shirt, and a straw Stetson. He was tall, and while he was getting on up in years, he still had an impressive width of shoulders and moved with the graceful ease of a younger man.

To Kincaid's experienced eyes, he moved like a man who was no stranger to trouble.

"Lucas, I didn't expect you to be here today," Baldwin said.

"Just getting a little extra work done."

Baldwin chuckled and said, "Some people might accuse you of brown-nosing. I know that's not the case, though. You're just a man who genuinely likes to work."

Kincaid shrugged. He didn't bother explaining that he didn't have anything better to do than work.

The warden turned to his companion and went on, "John Howard, this is Lucas Kincaid. He runs the library here. Lucas, my old friend John Howard Stark."

The name was familiar to Kincaid, but he couldn't

place it right away. He extended his hand and said, "Mr. Stark."

"Call me John Howard," Stark said as he gripped Kincaid's hand. "It's a pleasure to meet you, Lucas."

Kincaid nodded, instantly feeling a kinship with this older man.

"I thought the inmates usually ran the library in most prisons," Stark went on.

Baldwin grimaced and shrugged.

"Several of them work here, but regulations say that a member of the prison staff has to be in charge," he explained.

"Ah," Stark said. "Regulations."

Baldwin rolled his eyes.

"All those by-the-book officers we had back in 'Nam would've loved the way things are run today," he said with a note of bitterness in his voice.

"From what I hear, that's about the only kind of officers left in the military these days," Stark said. "Our last few Democratic presidents have fired all the ones who actually cared about getting things done and defending the Constitution. They all wanted yes-men who're willing to fire on American citizens."

"I hope and pray that if that day ever comes, enough of our guys will have the backbone to stand up and say no."

"I do, too, George," Stark said as he nodded slowly, but Kincaid thought the older man sounded like he wasn't convinced of it.

Baldwin put an affable smile on his face and said, "Well, we'll leave you to whatever you were doing, Lucas. Just don't work too hard on your day off."

Kincaid returned the smile, although the expression was smaller on his face, and said, "I won't."

Baldwin and Stark left the library. As the door swung closed behind them, Kincaid thought that there went a couple of tough old birds. If you were in a fight to the death, you could do a lot worse than to have those two at your back.

He thought as well about what Stark and Baldwin had said about the current state of the military, especially its upper echelons. He was afraid Stark was right when he was doubtful about the generals' ability to stand up to the politicians. Too many of the top brass had made it to their elevated ranks by compromising and playing politics. They would go along with their orders, no matter how unconstitutional those commands might be.

Kincaid had served with plenty of guys—and some gals—who had their boots planted solidly on the ground of freedom and would never pull a trigger on their fellow citizens. If it ever came to that, it would mean war . . . war within the military first, then war against whatever would-be Democrat dictator was currently occupying the White House.

The only good thing about the situation, Kincaid mused with a faint smile, was that the right side, including civilians, had most of the guns in this country, despite the best efforts of the mealymouthed liberals trying to do away with the Second Amendment . . . and they knew how to use those weapons.

Kincaid hoped fervently that such a bloody clash never came about, but he was confident that if it did, those on the side of freedom would win in the end.

And if they didn't . . . well, he hoped he never lived to see that.

An underground bunker . . . somewhere

"Sir, we've got some unusual satellite intel coming in."

"Put it up on the screen."

One of the giant screens in the room changed its feed in response to the young technician's fingers moving around on the touch screen in front of him.

The big screen displayed a satellite view of a town somewhere, surrounded by large swaths of green and brown. Although it wasn't readily apparent from this height, the green patches were fields under cultivation. Evidently wherever this was, the growing season was fairly long there.

Movement was discernible outside the town. Brown, irregular patches appeared to be dust clouds.

"Is this real time?"

"Yes, sir."

"Zoom in."

The soldier did so, and as the image moved closer to the ground and resolved, vehicles became visible. They were closing in on the town from the northeast and southeast.

"Looks like some sort of military maneuver. Classic pincers formation. Should we check with DOD?"

"Where is this happening?"

"Texas, sir. That town is called . . . let me see . . . Fuego."

That name meant something to the man in charge. He had known something was going to happen there, although he wasn't privy to the details. But he knew something was going to happen . . . and he knew his orders were to ignore it.

Those orders came from high up.

Very high up.

Almost as high as the chain of command went.

"Sir? Should I call the Department of Defense and see if they already know about this?"

"No."

The man in charge moved up closer behind the tech. The two of them were the only ones on duty on this Sunday morning.

It had been another Sunday morning, more than

eighty years earlier, when the Japanese fleet steamed toward Pearl Harbor and changed the world forever.

The world was going to change today, too, the man in charge thought as he slipped a small syringe from his pocket, took the cover off the needle, and plunged it into the technician's neck. The young man jerked in his chair, exhaled a startled "Ah!" and died.

The autopsy would show heart failure brought on by habitual drug use.

Such a tragedy, and to the rest of the world an unnecessary one, at that.

But to the man who withdrew the needle, put the cap back on it, and slid the now-empty syringe back into his pocket, it was an absolutely necessary death.

The world couldn't be told just how far up the chain of command what was happening today really went.

The American people had to be kept in the dark about what was really going on in their country.

What *used* to be their country, the killer thought as a thin smile tugged at his lips.

They had given it up willingly. Traded their freedom for cradle-to-grave government assistance. Government control. That was bad enough just on the surface.

But if they had known who really ran the government now . . .

Grasping the dead technician's shirt collar, the killer dragged him out of the chair in front of the console and dumped him on the floor.

Then he picked up a microphone attached to a wired intercom system—cell phones didn't work down here, because of all the shielding and because they were too easily hacked to start with—and said, "This is Colonel Mohammed Havas. I need medics. The man on duty with me in the command center has collapsed . . ."

* * *

Raymond was pacing back and forth agitatedly when Officer Chuck Gibbs walked into the police station.

"What's the matter, Ray?" Chuck asked.

The dispatcher stopped pacing and swung around to face the young officer.

"Have you seen the chief?"

"Not today," Chuck said. "He's supposed to take over patrol when my shift ends, though, so I'm sure he'll be here. One thing you can say for the boss, he's always punctual."

"He's not answering his cell phone or his radio," Raymond said. "Something's wrong."

Ray was a good guy, Chuck thought, and a good dispatcher. Anybody who thought he couldn't handle the job just because he was born with Down syndrome was full of crap.

But every now and then Raymond overreacted to something just like anybody else might. Chuck suspected this was one of those times.

"Why are you tryin' to get hold of him?"

"Because of the gunshots!"

"Gunshots?" Chuck repeated with a frown.

Raymond shook his head a little and said, "Didn't I tell you?"

"No, you didn't." Chuck was taking this more seriously now. "What's this about shots?"

"I got a couple of calls about them a little while ago. They said it sounded like somebody was shooting a pistol and a shotgun down at the other end of town."

"Right here in town?" Chuck pointed at the floor to emphasize what he was asking.

Raymond nodded impatiently and said, "Yes. If somebody was shooting outside of town, I wouldn't be as worried."

"No, I reckon not. How come you tried to call the

chief about it instead of me? I'm the one who's on duty this morning."

"I knew you were busy with that traffic stop out on the highway west of town," Raymond said.

The Fuego city limits included the highway, but not the land on either side of it. Because of that, the PD sometimes worked radar out there, as Chuck had been doing this morning.

"And I talked to the chief earlier and knew he was coming back here," Raymond went on.

Chuck smiled again and said, "He was out in the country doin' his usual Sunday morning gunfightin' practice, eh?"

Chief Cobb thought his officers didn't know about that . . . but they did, of course.

"Yes. So I thought he could check it out quicker and easier than you could."

"You were probably right about that," Chuck said with a nod. "But you couldn't get hold of him?"

"No. And then somebody else called and said there were some bright lights in the sky, and I know what that means."

"What does it mean?"

Raymond leaned forward over the counter and answered earnestly, "Fuego is being invaded by aliens."

Chuck would never laugh at Raymond. They were friends. They had gone to school together and had been in some of the same classes because kids like Ray were mainstreamed and had been for a long time.

Sometimes, though, it was difficult not to laugh. Chuck made an effort and controlled the impulse. Instead he said, "I'll go down there and check it out. Down around the McDonald's and the Dairy Queen and the motel, right?"

"That's right. And keep an eye out for the chief!"

"Will do," Chuck said with a nod as he went out.

It was a little after eleven o'clock now, he thought as he got back into his cruiser. The fast-food places were open by now. There was an open field behind the DQ, and sometimes jackrabbits and even coyotes came up in there, scrounging for food. The rednecks who hung out there—and Chuck could think of them that way because he was a redneck himself, and dang proud of it—had been known to grab guns from their pickups and take some potshots at the varmints, just to break the monotony of small-town life.

Chuck figured that was all it was, but he needed to be sure. As for the bright lights in the sky Raymond had mentioned . . .

Well, he didn't believe it was aliens from outer space, but he didn't have a clue what they might have been. They had mysterious lights down in Marfa, but those showed up at night, not on a Sunday morning.

Chuck did see something odd as he drove east along Main Street, though. Dust clouds were rising east of town. Somebody was out there riding ATVs around, he supposed. He hoped nobody wrecked out and broke a neck.

As he approached the edge of town, he spotted the chief's car parked at the motel. Maybe Raymond had finally been able to get hold of him after all. Chuck swung the cruiser off the street and into the motel parking lot. He would check in with Chief Cobb before he did anything else.

He was getting out of the car when he noticed a convoy of trucks approaching along the highway. They looked like military vehicles, complete with camo covers on the backs. That was strange, too. Fuego was just full of weird shit this morning.

Like those two guys standing beside the open back doors of a van about fifty yards away in the parking lot. Chuck had never seen them before, and they sure didn't look like they came from around here.

With his door still open and his left hand gripping the top of it, Chuck called over the cruiser's roof, "Hey, fellas—"

One of the men took a funny-looking object out of the van and pointed it at him. Chuck's eyes went painfully wide as he recognized the thing as a grenade launcher.

The sons of bitches were about to blow him up!

CHAPTER 13

George Baldwin led Stark into a fairly large room where a flat-screen TV mounted on one cream-colored wall was displaying an NFL pre-game show.

Half a dozen computers in individual workstations were arrayed along another wall, and an inmate in an orange jumpsuit sat at each computer while other prisoners perched on chairs and waited for their turns.

Square metal tables with chairs, all bolted to the floor, were arranged in a grid. Prisoners sat at most of those tables, some playing cards, some playing dominoes.

"Looks like a rec room," Stark commented. "Well, except for the guards."

Uniformed correctional officers were posted here and there around the room.

"That's what it is," Baldwin said. "Sunday's a free day, and men who have earned the privilege by good behavior can spend it here, even some of the lifers."

"Pretty lenient for a maximum security facility."

"I try to treat all the men with dignity and respect, even the ones who don't deserve it at first. Maybe someday they will."

"Not a bad policy," Stark said with a nod. He looked

around the room at the two dozen prisoners. "Some of these guys look a little familiar."

"You've probably seen them on the news." Baldwin nodded toward two men sitting at a table playing cards. "The little balding guy is Albert Carbona. One of the last of the old-time mobsters. The big fella with him is Billy Gardner. He was one of Carbona's top soldiers in the mob."

"I thought they were all Italian."

Baldwin shook his head and said, "No, organized crime was an equal opportunity employer." He pointed to a man sitting at one of the computers. "That's J.J. Lockhart."

This prisoner was a handsome man in his thirties or forties with a shock of wavy brown hair. Stark asked, "Why do I recognize that name?"

"He ran a gambling syndicate that covered Texas and most of the Southwest. That was just for guys who wanted to place an illegal bet in person. Lockhart also had an online gambling operation that raked in millions from all over the world. That's what finally landed him in hot water with the Feds."

Stark noticed another jumpsuit-clad prisoner who sat at a table gazing longingly at the computers. He said, "That fella looks like he can't wait for his turn at one of the computers."

Baldwin snorted. "He's going to have to wait a long time. That's Simon Winslow. Big computer hacker. Stole millions, leaked a bunch of government secrets. He's not allowed to touch a computer. I probably shouldn't even let him be in here. But if he gets within ten feet of one of those stations, a guard will make him back off."

"So you're sort of driving him crazy by letting him see the computers but not use them."

Baldwin chuckled and said, "I never really thought of it quite that way, but I suppose you're right. I'm not gonna waste any sympathy on the guy, though. He could've used his smarts to do something worthwhile with his life."

Simon Winslow was short, slender, and redheaded. He seemed out of place, surrounded as he was by inmates who were, for the most part, bigger and rougher-looking than he was.

One of the guards standing against the wall not far from Stark and Baldwin didn't look much tougher than Winslow. He nodded to the two visitors and said, "Good morning, Warden Baldwin."

"Cambridge," Baldwin said without any warmth. As they walked away, the warden added under his breath to Stark, "Kid's kind of a suck-up. Nobody really likes him, but he does a decent job."

Stark didn't doubt that. Baldwin ran a tight operation, always had. He wouldn't tolerate incompetence in anyone who worked for him.

Something poked at Stark's brain. He said, "What's the story on that fella Kincaid, the one who works in the library?"

"Lucas? Good man. Was an MP in Germany when he was in the service. I was glad to get him."

"He looks more like he ought to be a guard, instead of checking books in and out."

"When he applied, that's what I had in mind, too, but when he found out about the opening in the library, he asked for it. That sort of took me by surprise, but I was willing to give him the job. It's not one that most guys would want. He's qualified to handle any trouble that comes up, like any of the other guards."

"I noticed that about him right away," Stark said. "Those quiet, unassuming fellas are usually tougher than the ones who are full of bluster."

"Like you."

Stark grinned.

"You mean I'm full of bluster?"

"No, you're one of the men who keeps his mouth shut and does his job and doesn't make a big show out of being tough."

Stark shrugged.

"And modest, too," Baldwin added with a smile.

Before he could say anything else, the walkie-talkie clipped to his belt chirped. He unfastened it, raised it to his lips, and keyed the mic.

"This is Baldwin."

"Got a civilian at the front gate asking to see you, Warden," came a man's voice, accompanied by a faint crackle of static. "She says her name is Alexis Devereaux. Should we let her in, sir?"

Baldwin glanced at Stark, told him, "You called it, John Howard," then said into the walkie-talkie, "Escort her to my office. I'll be right there."

"I used to be a White House correspondent, you know. You probably remember." The man with the perfectly styled graying hair and dignified demeanor lowered his voice to a solemn timbre and intoned, "'This is Travis Jessup, reporting from the White House.' Remember?"

"Of course I do," Alexis told him, even though she really didn't. After a while all the TV newspeople began to look and sound alike whether they were black or white, male or female. They were useful idiots, always eager to quote Democrat talking points as fact and make the Republicans look as bad as possible, all the while maintaining a haughty, laughable façade of journalistic integrity.

Alexis was counting on Jessup to make her look good, though, so she wasn't going to say anything to offend him. She would use every weapon available to make her point, including the lapdog media.

She was just glad that Jessup and the rest of the TV

crew hadn't gotten lost. They had pulled up in their van equipped with a satellite dish while Alexis was waiting at the prison gate to be admitted to the facility.

The crew wasn't a big one: a producer/director, a sound technician, and a camera operator. Plus the on-air talent, Travis Jessup.

Actually, Jessup's name *was* familiar to Alexis, and after thinking about it for a couple of minutes, she remembered why.

As Jessup had mentioned, he had been the White House correspondent for one of the broadcast networks, until he had slipped up and reported a story about how one of the First Lady's old college friends had been indicted on criminal conspiracy charges in some financial sector scandal.

That had nearly been the end of Jessup's career. All it had taken was one angry phone call from the vengeful First Lady to the president of the network—who had been a member of the White House communications staff in the previous administration—to get Jessup fired.

For a while he had dropped out of sight since none of the other networks wanted to hire him, but then an election had come along and the administration had changed—although remaining Democratic, of course— and Jessup wasn't quite as persona non grata anymore, Alexis supposed. Recently he had started to show up again now and then on the air.

It was a little galling that they'd sent someone like that to cover this story, she thought as she waited impatiently. She should have had a major anchor, maybe even a morning show host, assigned to her visit to Hell's Gate. But she'd just have to make the best of it, she supposed.

The guard came back out of the little hut where he'd gone to talk to somebody on a walkie-talkie. He smiled through the open car window at Alexis and told her,

"The warden says you're to be escorted to his office, ma'am. He'll meet you there."

"Escorted by whom?" Alexis asked.

The guard pointed toward the prison. This gate was a good hundred yards from the main complex. She wondered if the open, sandy ground between the high, razor-wire-topped fences was actually covered with land mines. She wouldn't put it past these reactionary fascists.

The gate in the inner fence had opened and a black SUV drove through it toward the outer gate.

"You'll have to leave your car here," the guard went on. "The news van will have to stay outside the fence, too."

"Wait just a minute," Travis Jessup said in his booming voice. He stood just outside the open driver's side window of Alexis's rental car. "I'm not sure if that will work."

The producer/director in charge of the crew, a stocky, graying man who appeared to be in his late forties, said, "Yeah, that'll be fine, Travis, don't worry. I'll stay with the truck. Joel and Riley will go inside with you and Ms. Devereaux. Their equipment will be linked with the truck, and we'll get the signal out live."

"All right, fine," Jessup said.

The guard said, "Um . . . I just cleared Ms. Devereaux with the warden. I'll have to ask him about you TV folks before I can let you in."

"Well, you'd better get at it," Jessup said with a disapproving frown. "You can't stand in the way of the media. It's un-American."

"Yeah, yeah," the guard muttered as he retreated into the hut again.

When he came back out a minute later, he nodded and said, "Okay, you and you and you can go in with the lady."

As he spoke, he pointed to Jessup, the tall, skinny, bearded sound tech, and the cameraperson, a woman about thirty with her long chestnut hair pulled back in a ponytail.

"All your gear will have to be checked before you go in, though," the guard added.

All this red tape annoyed Alexis, but she knew the fastest way to get through it was to just put up with it. She got out of the rental car as the black SUV stopped inside the outer gate.

The two men who got out of the vehicle wore Kevlar vests over their uniform shirts and carried semiautomatic assault rifles with big clips. Alexis hated the sight of the evil-looking guns. As far as she was concerned they should have been banned ages ago, even for law enforcement personnel.

Once the inner gate had rumbled closed, someone pushed a button somewhere and the outer gate began to open. Alexis knew all such functions probably were controlled from a command center inside the prison. There would be cameras focused on her right now, but that idea didn't bother her.

She had always enjoyed being the center of attention and was pragmatic enough to admit it.

One of the armed guards told her, "Ma'am, if you and your friends would get in the SUV, we'll take you to the warden."

Alexis didn't bother explaining that the TV people weren't her friends.

The SUV had three seats, each separated from the others by a sheet of glass that Alexis assumed was bulletproof. The middle and rear sets of doors had no handles on the inside, just like the back doors of police cars.

The seats were more comfortable than the backseats of police cars, though. Alexis had been in one or two of those, having been arrested at protests during her younger days.

Now she preferred to try to mold public opinion

without resorting to such means. She would rather pro-
voke other people to go out and protest in the streets
and get arrested, rather than doing it herself.

Once everybody was inside the SUV, Alexis and Travis
Jessup in the middle seat, the soundman and the
cameraperson in the back, all of them having been
wanded with a portable metal detector and their equipment thoroughly examined, the vehicle swung around
and drove back through the gate.

By the time it reached the inner gate, the outer one
had closed again. Step by precautionary step, the visitors
made their way into the prison, and eventually Alexis
found herself being shown into a comfortably furnished
but not fancy office.

Jessup had been told he would have to wait in the reception room outside, which made the newsman stew
sullenly.

A man stood behind the desk when Alexis came in.
She recognized him from her research as George Baldwin, the warden of this private correctional facility that
bore his family's name, one of several in various parts of
the country owned and operated by the Baldwins.

"Ms. Devereaux," Baldwin said as he came around the
desk and extended his hand to her. "Welcome to Hell's
Gate."

"So even you use that derogatory name for this place,"
she said as she gave his hand a perfunctory shake.

Baldwin smiled and shrugged as he said, "I don't
know that the name is all that derogatory. I think of it
more as descriptive."

"It's only descriptive if that really is Hell on the other
side of that gap in the cliffs."

"Well, that's a good point. People in these parts have
been using the name for nearly a hundred and fifty
years, though, since long before there was a correctional
facility here, so I don't think we'll be breaking the habit."

He waved at a plush leather chair in front of the desk. "Won't you have a seat?"

"Thank you," Alexis said coolly. She sat down and crossed her legs, well aware of the effect that usually had on men—and a surprising number of women as well. "I suppose you know why I'm here, Warden."

Baldwin settled down in his chair and said, "Why don't you tell me anyway?"

"I want to inspect the conditions under which those political prisoners are being held."

"You mean the terrorists that were brought here last week."

"In the eyes of the world they're political prisoners," Alexis snapped.

Baldwin spread his hands and said, "That may well be true, Ms. Devereaux, but to speak plainly, I don't really care how the rest of the world sees them. They've all been charged with numerous counts of criminal conspiracy. Some of them are facing murder and attempted murder charges as well. They've tried and in some cases succeeded in killing American citizens, and they've damaged American interests here and around the world."

"Allegedly," Alexis said with a slight sneer on her face and in her voice.

"Point taken," Baldwin said. "Innocent until proven guilty, right? Due process and all. That's still the way we do things in this country." His voice hardened. "If you're on the proper side of the political aisle, anyway. Republicans and other conservatives don't always seem to get the same leeway, do they? Just ask the IRS and all the other agencies that have raised political harassment to an art form."

Alexis's voice wasn't cool anymore. It was downright cold as she said, "Don't try to change the subject by bringing up a bunch of old scandals that were phony to begin with, Warden. I represent a number of human rights organizations, and they want to know that the men being kept here are being treated fairly and humanely. Are you going to let me see for myself if that's true, or are you going to stonewall?"

"You're right."

His response took her by surprise. She said, "I am?"

"Yes, you are. My job is to keep those men here until their cases come to trial, and then it's up to the justice system to deal with them. This facility is professionally run, and we have nothing to hide. I'll have to ask you to cooperate with our security requirements, but within that framework I'll be glad to show you anything you want to see."

Alexis was a little nonplussed. She had expected more of an argument.

But Baldwin was giving up, so she wasn't going to turn down his surrender. She said, "Thank you. I've brought along some people from the media to document what I find."

"Of course you have," Baldwin said as he got to his feet.

She thought about acting offended at his comment but then decided it wasn't worth the effort. She stood up, too, and he started to usher her out of the office.

"Your visit wasn't exactly unexpected, you know," Baldwin commented.

"It wasn't?"

"No, I had a pretty good idea you'd be showing up sometime. I was told that you were in town."

As Alexis stepped out of the office, she saw a tall, muscular figure leaning against the wall of the reception room. He straightened from his casual pose and gave her a little smile and a nod.

"John Howard Stark," Alexis said. "Why am I not surprised?"

CHAPTER 14

For a split second, Officer Chuck Gibbs thought about drawing his service weapon and calling on the two men to lay down their weapons and surrender.

But every instinct in his body told him that wouldn't do a damned bit of good. He realized, too, that he shouldn't take cover behind his cruiser.

Not when the bad guys were armed with a freakin' grenade launcher.

Instead, he turned and ran as fast as he could.

Half a dozen years earlier, Chuck had played wide receiver and defensive back on the Fuego High School football team. He had run track, too. He was pretty fast.

He needed to be fast right now. The more space between him and that police car, the better.

He heard a *whoosh*ing sound behind him.

The world blew up.

That was what it seemed like, anyway. The pavement jumped under Chuck's feet and a wave of concussive force slammed into his back. The tremendous impact lifted him off his feet and threw him forward.

Chuck had no idea how long he flew through the air, cocooned by heat. It seemed like a long time.

Then the ground came up and hit him and even though he was mostly stunned, he was aware that he rolled over and over. That went on for so long he figured he'd been blown all the way to the other end of Main Street.

When he finally came to a stop, though, he lifted his head, blinked his stinging eyes, and saw that he was lying on the road less than a block from the blazing inferno that had been his police cruiser.

Clearly, the grenade's explosion had ignited the gasoline in the car's tank. The cruiser's body had blocked the shrapnel from the grenade, though, saving his life.

Chuck couldn't hear anything except a hum. The blast had deafened him, maybe permanently.

He wasn't aware that he was still under attack until he saw bullets chipping up the pavement a few yards away from where he sprawled.

The man who had fired the grenade launcher, along with his companion, had come around the burning cruiser and now ran toward Chuck, firing pistols as they charged.

Chuck's muscles didn't want to work at first, but his brain kept screaming at them that they were about to die. Reflexes, instinct, and training kicked in. Chuck reached down to his hip for his weapon, a 9 mm Glock.

Luckily, the gun was still in the holster where it was supposed to be. Chuck drew it as he rolled onto his belly. He gripped his right wrist with his left hand to brace it as he returned fire, just as he had practiced on the range.

Like a lot of young men in West Texas, Chuck had grown up taking potshots at jackrabbits and coyotes. At this moment he was scared almost to the point of hysteria, but muscle memory was his friend.

He drew a bead, squeezed the trigger, and saw one of the attackers jerk back as the slug from the Glock punched into his chest. The man stumbled and fell.

A bullet kicked up dust and concrete fragments close to Chuck's head. He rolled again, this time on purpose, and lunged to his feet. The Glock erupted again and again as he ran for the cover of a parked car.

More gun-toting men were coming down the street toward him. Chuck thought at first they were Hispanic, then realized they weren't from this part of the world at all.

His mind flashed back to news broadcasts he had seen, footage that came from countries in the Middle East where angry men who looked just like these yelled and waved burning U.S. flags and chanted about death to America.

The town was under attack by just such a mob.

Fuego was being invaded.

And Chuck was smart enough to know he couldn't stop an invasion by himself.

Behind him, only about ten feet away across the sidewalk, was the mouth of a narrow passage between buildings. He turned and dashed into it, feeling as much as hearing the bullets that whipped past his head. The welcome gloom of the passage swallowed him up. When he reached the end of it he cut left along the alley that ran behind the buildings.

He had to get back to the police station, he thought, and tell Raymond to call in all the other officers. Hell, they were going to have to get help from the Rangers or even the National Guard.

Fuego was at war again, and this time it wasn't with a neighboring town's football team.

Andy Frazier had a semi-private room in the hospital on the south side of Fuego, but the other bed was empty at the moment. The hospital was fairly small, and most patients who had anything seriously wrong with them usually wound up being transferred to hospitals in El Paso or Midland/Odessa.

Since nobody else was in the room at the moment, Jill had gotten onto the bed beside him, and they were making out. Jill rubbed her hand over his groin through the sheet, and Andy's hand was under her shirt, heading for her left breast, when the door opened and a big shape loomed there.

"I know what you guys were doin'," Ernie Gibbs said with a grin as Andy and Jill hastily put a little distance between each other.

"Gibby, what are you doing here?" Andy asked the team's starting right offensive tackle and backup defensive end. Also probably his best friend.

"Just wanted to see how you were doin'," Gibby said. His close-cropped hair was so fair it was almost white. "When are they gonna let you out of this place?"

"Tomorrow, maybe, the doctor says."

Jill slid off the bed and unobtrusively rearranged her shirt.

"When can you get back to school?"

"Don't know," Andy said. "Maybe in a week or so?"

"Your leg's not, you know, healin' up miraculously or somethin'?"

Andy shook his head and said, "No, I'm afraid not."

"Dang. That means we'll have to finish out the season with Pete Garcia at quarterback. He's a pretty good kicker, but he's no Andy Frazier at QB."

"Well, you'll all just have to do your best."

"I know." Gibby chuckled. "But hey, we already ruined McElhaney's perfect season, didn't we? I don't really care if we win another game."

"Oh, man, don't say that. We can still make the play-offs . . . if we don't lose another game."

"Yeah, I don't see that happening," Gibby said. "You need anything? Want me to sneak in a six-pack for you?"

"I'm sure that would go over real well."

"All right, then. I'll let you get back to what you were doin'." Gibby leered. "I'm sure Jill was takin' care of you real—"

Jill had started to blush, but evidently she forget about being embarrassed when something boomed in the distance, clearly audible even through the hospital room's closed window.

"What in the world was that?" she exclaimed.

"Sonic boom?" Gibby suggested with a frown.

Andy said, "That wasn't a sonic boom. You hardly ever hear those anymore, and anyway, that's not what it sounded like."

"Well, something blew up, that's for sure." As Gibby started toward the door, he went on, "I'll go find Chuck. He's on duty this morning. He'll know, if anybody does."

Gibby's older brother Chuck, who had also played football for Fuego High, was one of the town's half-dozen police officers. He was a good guy and had been known to turn a blind eye to some of the things the current team got into, like the time he'd caught them drinking out at the reservoir.

"I'll come by and see you tomorrow if I can," Gibby threw over his shoulder as he left the room.

Once the big lineman was gone, Andy said to Jill, "Go over there and open the window, would you?"

"What's wrong? Do you need some air?"

"Seems like I keep hearing something else," Andy told her.

She went to the window and raised it. Even under the circumstances, Andy couldn't help but notice how good her butt looked in the tight jeans.

She had a worried expression on her face as she turned back toward him.

"I hear it, too," she said. "Some sort of popping noise . . ."

Andy's heart suddenly began to pound harder. It was

like what he felt when the game was on the line, but even worse.

"That's not popping," he said. "Those are gunshots. A lot of gunshots."

Between the explosion and the gunfire, he knew something bad was happening in Fuego.

As one of the town's cops, Chuck Gibbs might well be right in the middle of whatever it was.

And Chuck's little brother Ernie—Andy's best friend Gibby—had gone to look for him. Big, good-hearted Gibby . . .

Who would probably waltz right into disaster before he realized just how much trouble he was really in.

Fuego had five churches: Catholic, Baptist, Methodist, Christian, and Church of Christ. Anybody who belonged to some other denomination had to go elsewhere to worship.

Even though church attendance had been dropping steadily ever since those running the government had decided that their so-called love for tolerance and diversity didn't extend to the Christian faith, resulting in official treatment that ranged from benign neglect to outright hostility and harassment, the churches in Fuego still put people in the pews every Sunday. Other folks might be willing to give up their religion, but not these West Texans.

Randall Harper, who was pastor of the First Baptist Church—which was also the *only* Baptist church in Fuego—was approaching the home stretch of his sermon about forgiveness. It was a little longer than some of his sermons. He didn't have to worry about wrapping up and getting everybody home by noon today, since the Dallas Cowboys didn't play until later in the afternoon.

Although that wasn't nearly as much of an issue these days, when the Cowboys had pretty much been mediocre for the past three decades. It was getting harder to find somebody who remembered when they were actually good. Tom Landry and Roger Staubach were just names in a football history book now.

Randall tried to force his mind back onto what he was saying. That was one of the hazards of being a veteran preacher. Once you'd written your sermon and practiced it a few times, you could deliver it without paying much attention. Under those circumstances, a fella's thoughts tended to stray.

The sound of an explosion somewhere not far off jolted Randall back to the here and now. He stopped in mid-sentence. Many of the people in the congregation had jumped at the sound. A loud murmuring started.

Randall caught the eye of one of the deacons standing at the back of the church by the doors and nodded to the man, hoping he would take the hint to go and see what was going on.

The man returned the nod and vanished through the sanctuary doors.

Randall lifted his hands and said, "It's all right, folks. Brother Winston's gone to see what that was. I'm sure it's nothing."

The church's music director and youth minister, Mark Corder, had gotten up from where he was sitting on one side of the platform and wandered over toward the pulpit.

"That didn't sound like nothing, Brother Randall," he said. "I hear something else. Sounds like trucks."

"The volunteer fire department truck, maybe?" Randall suggested. The explosion could have been the result of a gas leak, he supposed.

All he knew for sure was that he had lost control of this worship service. Everybody was talking worriedly now, and they weren't going to shut up until they found out what was happening outside the church.

Randall looked over at Mark and said, "Maybe we should sing a hymn or something—"

At that moment, the doors at the back of the auditorium burst open. Winston Cramer, the deacon Randall had sent to check on the situation, charged into the church yelling, "Run! Everybody run! Look out—"

A chattering sound ripped through the air, and Winston's body came apart in a grisly spray of blood and shredded flesh. The bullets tearing through him flung him forward to land facedown on the carpet runner between the sections of pews.

Screams filled the church as armed men poured through the doors behind Winston. Some had pistols, some had shotguns, some had automatic weapons. They opened fire on the congregation, slaughtering men, women, and children as those innocents leaped to their feet in fear-stricken panic. The invaders moved inexorably up the center aisle, splattering the pews on both sides with blood and shredded flesh.

Horrified, Randall gripped the sides of the pulpit and stared in shock at the terrible carnage. An odd thought flashed through his mind.

The First Baptist Church of Fuego had been founded in 1880, when bands of Apache Indians still strayed up out of the Big Bend now and then and raided the isolated ranches and settlements. Randall remembered reading in the church history that the first pastor had delivered his sermons with a six-gun lying on each side of the pulpit, flanking his Bible. The men of the congregation had brought their rifles to services with them, too, just in case of trouble.

Randall wished he had a couple of those six-shooters right now.

Not that they would have done much good against such an overpowering, heavily armed force.

All he had was his faith and the Word of God. He grabbed his Bible, held it aloft, and shouted, "Stop! Stop this madness! In the name of the Lord—"

One of the intruders raised his weapon from the family of four he had just cut down in a welter of gore. Fire flickered from the gun's muzzle as the man wielding it screamed, "Death to the infidels! Allahu akbar!"

Randall felt the bullets punching into his body. He staggered back as beside him Mark Corder's head flew apart from a hail of bullets fired by another of the killers. The Bible slipped from Randall's fingers and thumped to the platform.

As his knees folded up and he fell, he sent a last desperate prayer for his soul heavenward.

And as death claimed him, he added a prayer that God would take vengeance on these unholy monsters who had invaded His house and murdered His people.

CHAPTER 15

"You two know each other?" Travis Jessup asked as Alexis Devereaux glared at Stark. She seemed to be annoyed by the fact that he kept on smiling pleasantly at her.

"We've met," Stark said. "And of course I've seen her on TV many times."

"And me, too, of course," Jessup said. "You've seen me, haven't you?"

The newsman had introduced himself to Stark a few minutes earlier when Stark came into the reception room outside George Baldwin's office. He had stopped at a restroom along the way to the office.

Anyway, Alexis wanted to meet with Baldwin, not with him, Stark reasoned, so he didn't horn in on their conversation.

It was clear from her expression now that she wasn't happy he was here.

Stark had known who Jessup was, and Jessup had recognized Stark, too. Very few in the news media were fond of John Howard Stark. Most of them considered him a crazed, violent, right-wing vigilante.

The only exceptions were a couple of rogue cable

networks that dared to swim against the tide of liberal swill dished out by the rest of the media as "objectivity."

Stark meant ratings, though, and that was more important than ideology, so all the networks had covered his previous clashes with the Mexican drug cartels operating in partnership with Islamic terrorist organizations, as well as his part in the bloody fiasco at the Alamo caused by political correctness gone amok.

Because of that, Jessup ignored the fact that Stark hadn't answered his question and suggested, "Why don't we get the two of you to sit down together for a dialogue about the situation here at the prison? I'm sure it would be very instructive for our viewers."

"I don't think so," Alexis replied coldly. "Mr. Stark and I really don't have anything to say to each other. Besides, he's hardly an expert on prisons and the judicial system . . . other than being arrested a few times."

"But never charged with anything," Stark pointed out.

"Only because for some reason unfathomable to me, you have a few friends in high places."

Stark shrugged and said, "A few friends in low places, too, to quote Garth Brooks." He turned to Jessup and went on, "But Ms. Devereaux is right. I'm no expert. I wouldn't have anything to add to the discussion."

Alexis said, "Phillip Hamil is in town. You should find him and see if he'd like to come on with us."

"He is? That would be excellent. I've interviewed Dr. Hamil a couple of times. I'm sure he'd be glad to cooperate with us."

Stark didn't doubt it. Hamil struck him as a person who liked being the center of attention . . . just like Alexis.

It might be amusing to watch those two trying to upstage each other, he thought.

Alexis turned to George Baldwin, who had followed

her out of the office, and said, "I suppose we should go ahead and start our tour now, Warden."

"By all means," Baldwin said. "I'll be happy to show you around the prison."

Alexis's tone sharpened as she said, "I don't care about the rest of the place, just wherever you have those political prisoners locked up."

Baldwin looked like he wanted to argue again about whether the terrorists were actually political prisoners, Stark thought, but he didn't say anything.

Stark also noticed that Travis Jessup had made an unobtrusive gesture toward the two people with him. The tall, bearded man made some adjustment to the equipment he carried, and the attractive, ponytailed woman with the camera lifted it to her shoulder. Stark figured she was already recording, and so was the soundman.

From here on out, everything that happened would be documented.

In a firm voice, Baldwin said, "I'm certainly willing to show you what you want to see, Ms. Devereaux, but I think it's only fair that you let me show you the rest of the facility, too. After all, there's a lot more to Hell's Gate than just the one wing you're concerned with. There's also the story of what an economic boon this facility has been to the citizens of the county."

Alexis looked equally stubborn, but she said, "All right, if that's where you'd like to begin, perhaps you can tell me why Hell's Gate was scheduled to be closed until those prisoners were transferred here from Guantanamo and other, even more shadowy military prisons?"

Stark could tell that the question surprised his old friend. Baldwin's jaw clenched and a little muscle jumped in it for a second before he said, "I don't know where you heard that rumor—"

"It's not a rumor. The federal government's contract

with the Baldwin Correctional Facility wasn't going to be renewed when it expires next year. Without that contract, the prison would have to close. But now that you're housing those political prisoners here, the government is willing to keep the place open indefinitely. The government is paying you back for your shameful complicity in this matter."

"Any time a government contract is up for renewal, there are going to be negotiations," Baldwin said stiffly. "I assure you, nothing has been settled regarding any of this. And to be blunt, Ms. Devereaux, it's not really any of your business, either."

"But it's the business of the American people, isn't it? The government works for them."

"Does it?" Baldwin said. "As far as I can tell, the past few Democratic administrations have taken the view that the people work for the government, not the other way around."

Alexis wasn't happy that Baldwin had gotten that shot in, Stark thought. And Travis Jessup wasn't happy because Alexis hadn't let him get a word in edgewise so far. He was holding a microphone and looking like an eager little boy waiting anxiously for his part in the school play. Alexis was the one acting more like a crusading journalist, though.

"All right, go ahead and lead the way," she told Baldwin. "Just don't think you're going to get away with glossing over the truth."

"That wasn't my intention," Baldwin said as he held out a hand to indicate that Alexis should precede him out of the office.

She did, and he went with her, followed closely by Travis Jessup. The other two members of the news crew trailed Jessup.

Stark brought up the rear.

The woman with the camera lowered it. She wasn't

shooting at the moment. She hung back a little until Stark's long-legged strides caught up with her, and then she said, "You should be up there with the others, Mr. Stark."

Stark shook his head and said, "I'm not the story here. To tell you the truth, I'm not sure what the story *is*."

"The government's got those men locked up because they're Muslims."

"Nope. They're locked up because they're terrorists who have murdered American citizens and plotted to kill even more. They're fanatics who want to destroy this country."

The woman lowered her voice to a confidential tone and said, "Don't tell anybody, but I sort of agree with you. Not everybody in the media swears blind allegiance to the left, you know."

"Enough do that it's hard to get the truth out there. Getting harder all the time."

The woman shrugged and said, "We've got to eat. This is our job." She put out her hand. "I'm Riley Nichols."

"John Howard Stark," he said as he shook with her.

"My buddy up there with the sound equipment is Joel Fanning."

"He share your political opinions?"

Riley said, "Not hardly. Neither does Travis."

"You'd think anybody who nearly got his career ended by a Democratic First Lady wouldn't be as sympathetic to their cause anymore."

"You know about that, eh?"

"I remember reading something about it," Stark said.

"Well, even with what happened to Travis, he's still a true believer. For a lot of people in the media, liberal politics is their religion, you know. Their faith in the government rises above everything else. Unless, of course, a Republican happens to be running things, like the governor here in Texas. Then government can't be trusted."

"Must be hard for you, seeing things different than the people you work with."

"I've learned how to put up with it," Riley said with a grin. "A healthy application of scotch and a little mental elbow grease wipes away most of the stains."

The two of them had dropped back about twenty feet behind the others as Baldwin led the group along a corridor. Stark enjoyed talking to Riley Nichols and felt an instinctive liking for her. Not in any romantic way—she was half his age—but he sensed that they were kindred spirits in some respects.

But the conversation didn't continue because Travis Jessup looked back over his shoulder with an irritated expression on his patrician face and motioned for Riley to catch up.

The group had reached a door that Stark recognized, and as Baldwin opened that door, he said, "I'll start by showing you our library."

"That's not—" Alexis began impatiently.

Baldwin interrupted by saying, "You told me I could conduct the tour as I saw fit, Ms. Devereaux, as long as you get to see what you wanted to see. I want the American people to get a true picture of this facility, and that includes more than just locking up prisoners."

"Oh, all right," Alexis said in obvious annoyance. "Just get it over with."

They stepped into the library, first Baldwin, then Alexis, then the news crew, and finally Stark. On the other side of the room, behind the counter, Lucas Kincaid looked up from the computer where he'd been working and stared in surprise as the visitors entered.

Stark was a little surprised, too.

Because just for a second it had looked to him like Kincaid was scared.

And he had a hunch that not many things in this world scared Lucas Kincaid.

* * *

In this day and age, the only way to escape surveillance cameras entirely was to find a piece of wilderness isolated enough that nobody ever came there, pitch a tent, build a fire, and squat for the rest of your life.

But even then, a man wouldn't be completely safe. Kincaid had heard through some of his contacts that the intelligence agencies—which now answered only to the president, not Congress, since that august body had dissolved its oversight committees and abdicated yet another of its responsibilities to their dear Democratic leader—had such powerful satellite capabilities that they could zero in from space on an area no more than ten feet square.

They could spy on anybody on the face of the earth . . . and they did, if that somebody was deemed to be a political enemy of the man in the White House.

So Kincaid knew he was taking a chance on discovery, just by continuing to live his life.

But what was the point if you had to spend the rest of your days deep in hiding?

That wasn't living. That was just existing.

And it wasn't worth it.

It didn't hurt anything, though, to try to minimize the chances of being seen by somebody who would recognize him and want to kill him.

For that reason, he didn't want those people coming into the library with their camera. The last thing in the world he needed was to have his face plastered all over the news broadcasts.

Wasn't much he could do about it now, though. They were in here, coming toward the counter, and if he tried to duck and refused to be on camera, that would be even more suspicious.

So he kept his face blandly expressionless as the

group came up to him. Warden Baldwin said to the blond woman with him, "This is our library supervisor, Lucas Kincaid."

Kincaid wasn't worried about the name being recognized.

That wasn't the name he had used in the killing fields on the other side of the world. Over there he had still been known by the name he was born with.

"Lucas," Baldwin went on, "this lady is Ms. Alexis Devereaux."

The name was vaguely familiar to Kincaid, but he couldn't place it. He nodded politely to the woman and said, "I'm pleased to meet you, Ms. Devereaux."

"I wish I could say the same," she responded.

Her cold, sneering tone made Kincaid realize where he had seen her before—on TV, appearing as a liberal commentator on various news and opinion shows. Although in reality the line between "news" and "opinion" had long since disappeared where liberals were concerned, Kincaid reminded himself.

She didn't offer to shake hands, so Kincaid didn't, either, and was glad of it.

"Tell me, Mr. Kincaid," Alexis Devereaux went on, "are the inmates allowed to use this library?"

"Well, that's sort of what it's here for," Kincaid said.

"*All* the inmates?"

He had a hunch he knew what she was getting at, but he said, "All the ones who have library privileges. That's like any other privilege. It can be taken away for various reasons."

"Behavioral reasons," Baldwin put in. "There are other privileges that men who cause trouble lose."

"Have the new prisoners caused any trouble so far?" Alexis asked quickly.

Kincaid saw the warden wince at the way Alexis

pounced on that. Baldwin said, "As a matter of fact, they haven't—"

"So are they allowed to use the library?"

"Not at the moment. They're still confined to their own wing—"

"So they're being treated differently from other prisoners, simply because of their religion."

Alexis sounded pleased with herself for scoring that point.

"That's not exactly an accurate description of the situation," Baldwin argued. "Remember, those men have been here less than a week. We're still figuring out what our procedures will be for dealing with them. But security is our uppermost concern. Everything else has to come after that."

"So you're denying them access to books and the Internet and whatever other services the library offers," Alexis said, as if she hadn't heard anything that Baldwin had just told her.

The warden sighed in exasperation. He said, "Eventually we'll make some provision for those things, once the situation has settled down."

"When will that be?"

"That's not really up to me, is it? You're the one who brought a news crew in here to stir everything up."

Kincaid thought the warden's frustration must have gotten the best of him. Otherwise Baldwin wouldn't have made a comment like that. He was just playing into Alexis Devereaux's hands.

Once again, she pounced like a tigress.

"Stirring everything up? You think getting to the truth and telling it to the American people is stirring everything up, Warden?"

"We're not trying to hide anything here," Baldwin insisted stiffly. "Why don't we move on? I think we've seen everything here that there is to see."

Kincaid thought for a second that Alexis was going to argue. Maybe she thought Baldwin was trying to cover up something. Maybe she wanted to disagree just on general principles.

But she said, "All right. I'm sure there are plenty of other ways you're discriminating against those political prisoners, and I want to see them all."

Baldwin didn't say anything. Kincaid was sure that was difficult for him.

As Alexis and the warden left the library, the man with the microphone stepped in front of the camera and said, "We continue now with our tour of the notorious Hell's Gate prison. This is Travis Jessup, reporting from Texas."

The woman with the camera lowered it and said, "Okay, Travis, we'll pick it up at the next stop."

"Fine. Did you get everything here?"

"I did."

"So did I," said the tall, bearded man with the sound equipment.

The three of them started to follow Alexis and Baldwin. On their way out, the woman paused for a second and glanced back at Kincaid.

Normally he didn't mind if a good-looking woman glanced at him, although he wasn't really in the market for even a fleeting relationship right now, but what he saw in this woman's eyes bothered him.

He would have sworn that she looked at him with recognition.

But then she was gone along with the others, leaving only John Howard Stark in the library with Kincaid. He expected Stark to go with the group, but the big man ambled over to the counter instead.

"You looked like that took you by surprise," Stark commented.

"It did," Kincaid admitted. "I just came in to do a little

extra work on a day off. I didn't expect it to turn into anything."

"What I'm curious about," Stark said, "is why you didn't like having that camera pointed at you. What did you do to make you want nobody to recognize you, Lucas?"

CHAPTER 16

Blood pounded ferociously inside Chuck Gibbs's skull as he stumbled into the police station's back door. He had sprinted all the way there.

"Raymond!" he yelled. "Raymond, where are you?"

The dispatcher came out of one of the other rooms and looked confused and upset.

"Chuck, I tried to call you on the radio. There was an explosion, and people are calling about gunshots, and . . . and I couldn't find you or the chief—"

"It's all right, Raymond," Chuck broke in. He leaned over, rested his hands on his knees for a second, and tried to catch his breath. As he straightened, he went on, "Call everybody in. We need help. We've been invaded."

"It's aliens, isn't it? I knew it was aliens!"

"Listen to me." Chuck gripped Raymond's shoulders. "It's not aliens. It's worse. It's a bunch of crazy Arabs with guns. Not just guns. Grenade launchers. Who knows what the hell else they've got. But we have to stop them."

Chuck heard gunfire coming from down the street. Lots of gunfire. The sound sickened him, because he knew there was a good chance it meant some of Fuego's citizens were dying.

"Call for help, Raymond," he went on. "Call anybody and everybody you can think of."

"O-okay." Raymond swallowed and nodded. "I can do my job, Chuck."

Chuck slapped the dispatcher on the shoulder and said, "I know you can, buddy."

He turned and ran to the big, locked cabinet that served as the station's armory. The key was on his belt. He unlocked it and swung the door open.

Racked inside were several pump shotguns and a couple of AR-15s. Chuck knew he needed firepower, so he took one of the rifles and grabbed a couple of extended magazines for it as well. Then he took one of the shotguns and placed it on the counter.

Raymond had sat down behind the console and was on the radio, talking as quickly as he could as he told somebody that there was bad trouble in Fuego and they needed help. In his excitement and fear, he stumbled over some of the words, but he kept going, determinedly.

When Raymond paused, Chuck laid a hand on the shotgun and said, "This is for you."

"But I'm not supposed to handle guns. The chief said so."

"The chief's not here, and I'm making an exception to that rule. Listen to me, Raymond. If men try to come in here and you don't know them . . . if they have guns and they look like they're gonna hurt you . . . it's okay for you to shoot at them."

Raymond shook his head and said, "I don't know if I can do that. I might hurt them, and I don't want to hurt anybody."

"Neither do I, but if somebody's trying to hurt you, it's okay to stop them, even if it means hurting *them*. That's just the way it is. Understand?"

Raymond still looked doubtful, but Chuck didn't have time to stand around trying to convince him.

He needed to be back out there on the street, doing *something*. Anything to stop this madness.

But he had a sinking feeling that it was too big and had gone too far to be stopped now.

The scene of wanton slaughter that had taken place in the First Baptist Church had been duplicated in Fuego's other churches. At each house of worship, a truckload of the Prophet's followers had pulled up outside, and the heavily armed men had swarmed in to carry out their holy mission of death.

Phillip Hamil's forces had lost a handful of men. Some of the Americans had been armed. In this damned Texas with its concealed carry laws, some people even took their guns to church, Hamil thought as he listened to the reports from his lieutenants in the command post he had established at the motel. Those pitiful few defenders had put up a fight, but they were no match for Hamil's men.

Things were going well so far. The only real setback had been the destruction of the police car. One of his men had overreacted to the threat posed by a lone policeman and had blown up the officer's cruiser.

Hamil had had a use in mind for that car.

But there were other police cars in town, he was sure, and as long as none of them got blown up, his plan could proceed.

Hamil had picked a man named Raffir to take Fareed's place as his second-in-command. He told Raffir now, "Take men and capture the police station. We want to control any communications from there. Also, you're to seize any police vehicles and weapons you find."

"Yes, Doctor," Raffir said. "And the officers?"

"Kill them, of course," Hamil said offhandedly. His mind was already moving on to something else. One tiny, niggling detail annoyed him.

The police officer whose car was blown up had gotten away.

It seemed like wherever Chuck went in Fuego, he heard two things—gunfire and screaming.

He was sick with grief and fear. He wanted to throw up and then crawl in a hole somewhere and pull it in after him.

But he had his duty to perform. He had sworn to uphold the law and protect the citizens, and he was going to do his best to carry out those solemn tasks.

He had another worry gnawing at his guts as he trotted along an alley with the AR-15 held at a slant across his chest.

Three worries, actually.

His parents—and his little brother Ernie.

Chuck hadn't lived at home for several years. He had an apartment in Fuego's lone apartment complex. But Ernie did, since he was still in high school. He had talked for a long time about how he was going to move in with Chuck when he graduated. Chuck had tolerated the talk, but he didn't think it was ever going to happen.

He was still close to his family. He knew that on Sunday morning, his mom and dad would be at the Methodist church. Ernie, more than likely, was at home asleep.

Chuck had decided to head for the church first. He wanted to be sure his folks were all right. If he could find them, then they could try to reach the house and get his little brother.

He stuck to alleys and backyards as he made his way across town toward the church. He didn't want to get caught in a firefight with the invaders, not because he was afraid—although he was scared shitless, what person in his right mind wouldn't be?—but because he couldn't afford to let anything happen to him before he was sure that his family was safe.

He was about a block away from the church when he realized that the shooting had tapered off. That was a bad sign, Chuck thought as he heard pistol shots in the distance, usually one report followed quickly by another.

The classic double-tap.

Somebody was finishing off survivors.

That thought sent a stab of fresh pain through Chuck. He knew that a lot of people had to be dead already. People he was supposed to take care of and make sure nothing bad happened to them.

But it had happened anyway, on a beautiful Sunday morning in autumn, in a peaceful little town where folks should have been safe. Evil had come in with no warning and wreaked bloody havoc.

Maybe the universe really was a cold, chaotic place. Maybe the love and kindness in people's hearts was just an illusion, a wisp of smoke to be blown away by the winds of an uncaring reality.

Chuck tried not to think about that as he stopped at the rear corner of a house across the street from the church. He pressed his back against the wall and slid stealthily along it until he could get a look at the church.

He had to clench his jaw to keep from groaning. As it was, a tiny sound of grief and desolation escaped from him.

The doors of the Methodist church were wide open. Several of the invaders stood in front of them, guns tucked under their arms, laughing.

Chuck knew what that meant.

They had finished their bloody work inside.

In all likelihood, Chuck's mother and father were dead.

The hell with it, he thought. He brought the rifle to his shoulder. He could cut down most of those bastards before they knew what hit them. That would draw more of them, but he didn't care. He was ready to die . . .

As long as he could hit back at them first.

Before he could pull the trigger, the screech of rubber on pavement made him jerk his head to the right. A pickup careened around a corner a couple of blocks away. For a second Chuck thought it was going too fast to make the squealing turn and was about to roll over.

But then the tires caught and the vehicle lunged ahead, and to Chuck's shock, he recognized it.

The truck belonged to his brother, Ernie.

Through the windshield, he saw Ernie hunched over the wheel. The kid was trying to get away from something.

A second later, Chuck saw what his little brother was fleeing from. A bigger truck, a military-type truck, came around the corner after Ernie. The driver sawed at the wheel, trying to control the vehicle, as another man leaned out from the passenger door and fired an automatic weapon at the pickup. Chuck heard the bullets pinging against the tailgate.

He acted instinctively, bringing the AR-15 to his shoulder. He blasted two rounds through the truck's windshield, then dropped his aim to the front tires. As he kept up a steady fire, the truck's left front tire exploded.

The driver was already having a hard time keeping the truck under control. Now he either lost it from the blowout—or he was dead from those slugs Chuck had put through the now-shattered windshield.

Either way, the truck went over, crashing down on its right side, with any luck squashing the gunner on the passenger side into bloody pulp. It flipped, then flipped again before it smashed into the front of a hardware store, obliterating the business's big plate glass front window.

Chuck heard bullets whipping past his head and realized the guys who had been standing in front of the church had opened fire on him. He ducked and swung the rifle toward them, but he was outnumbered four to one. They had automatic weapons, too.

They were going to chop him into little pieces.

The pickup's engine roared. Ernie didn't slow down, but he veered hard to the right, up onto the sidewalk. The invaders must have realized he was rocketing toward them, because a couple of them appeared to forget about Chuck. They turned their guns toward the onrushing pickup instead.

From one knee, Chuck aimed and fired. His bullets punched into the men who were about to open fire on Ernie and knocked them down.

A second later, the pickup hurtled over them, crunching bones and mangling flesh, and then its grille slammed into the remaining two gunmen. One of them went down and the truck roared over him. The other flew through the air like a carelessly tossed rag doll.

That man landed in a heap.

Chuck shot him twice just to make sure he was dead.

Then, not seeing any more of the invaders in the vicinity, Chuck leaped up and burst out from his meager cover. He ran toward the pickup, which had slowed to a stop after ramming the quartet of invaders.

"Ernie!" Chuck yelled. "Ernie!"

His brother threw the driver's door open and leaned out to wave an arm.

"Chuck! Over here! Come on, before any more of those sumbitches catch up to me!"

Keeping an eye out for more of the enemy, Chuck ran around the front of the truck, jerked open the passenger door, and leaped inside. Ernie floored the gas and spun the wheel, and the pickup surged out onto the side street where the Methodist church was located.

"Mom and Dad . . . ?" Ernie gasped. As far as Chuck could see, he wasn't hurt, although the pickup was shot up pretty bad. It was still running, though.

"I'm pretty sure they're dead," Chuck said. The awful words sounded hollow in his ears. "I think those guys wiped out everybody in the church."

Ernie clenched a hand into a big fist and pounded the dashboard.

"No! It can't be true! It just can't!"

"What are you doin' here?" Chuck asked as he swapped the partially depleted magazine for a full one.

"I knew Mom and Dad were at church. I . . . I couldn't find you . . . I drove around all over town lookin' for you . . . Then I saw your police car all burned out—" Ernie had to stop and draw in a deep, ragged breath. "I figured you were in there, Chuck. I figured you were dead. So I thought I'd try to get to the folks—"

He started to cry, big tears running down his cheeks.

"What is this, Chuck?" he asked in a tortured voice between the sobs. "Who are those guys? Why're they doin' this to our town?"

"I don't know for sure, Ernie," Chuck said. "All I know is they're bad guys and we have to stop them."

"You and me? There's a whole freakin' army of 'em!"

"I know. So we need an army of our own." An idea had occurred to Chuck. "All the numbers of the guys on the team are in your phone, right?"

"Yeah, sure."

"Hand it here."

Ernie took the phone from his shirt pocket and handed it to his brother.

"What are you gonna do?"

"I'm going to call and tell them to get to the high school if they can. We'll meet in the field house. Let's head for there right now." Chuck took a deep breath in an attempt to calm his raging nerves. "We may need an army . . . but what we've got are the Fuego Mules."

CHAPTER 17

Lucas Kincaid was really good at controlling his emotions, Stark had to give him that.

But the tiniest flicker of startled reaction in the man's eyes told him that his guess about Kincaid's not wanting to be recognized was correct.

"I'm afraid I don't know what you're talking about, Mr. Stark," Kincaid said.

That answer didn't surprise Stark. He didn't expect Kincaid to admit anything. But Kincaid's denial didn't mean that Stark was convinced.

"So you didn't mind the warden coming in here with a reporter and a camera crew?"

Kincaid shrugged and said, "The warden does whatever he wants to do. He's the boss."

"Yeah, I guess."

Kincaid was dug in and braced now, Stark saw. He wasn't going to be giving anything up. Trying to get him to would just be a waste of time.

"All right. Reckon I was wrong, then." Stark smiled and lifted a hand in farewell as he left the library to catch up to Baldwin and the others.

They appeared to be on their way to the room where Stark and Baldwin had been earlier, the one Stark had described as a rec room—with guards.

When they got there, Baldwin explained to Alexis about the television, the computer access, even the domino tournaments that some of the inmates had organized.

"But the new Muslim prisoners aren't allowed to take part in any of those activities, are they?" Alexis asked. "They're probably not even allowed in here."

She was prettier than any bulldog he had ever seen, Stark thought, but once she got her jaws locked on something, she was just as stubborn.

"We don't know for sure yet just what our procedures regarding that will be," Baldwin replied. Stark could tell that he was struggling to remain patient. "Right now we have no plans to mix those inmates with the general population, but things can always change."

"So you admit that you're discriminating against them."

Baldwin grimaced, took a deep breath, and said, "Ms. Devereaux, if you were a Christian inmate locked up in a prison in a Muslim country, how do you think you'd be treated?"

Alexis rolled her eyes dramatically. Stark noticed that she made sure she was turned so the camera Riley Nichols held could catch the reaction.

"Don't start on that tired old cliché about how the United States is a Christian nation," she said in a scolding tone. "It never has been and never will be. The Founders didn't intend that. The Constitution is very clear on that point."

Stark smiled slightly. As usual, a liberal invoked the Constitution to support her own agenda, when most of the efforts of the past three Democratic administrations had been devoted to weakening and outright ignoring the Constitution.

That was one reason trying to have an honest discussion with a liberal about almost anything could be incredibly frustrating. They were totally blind to their own hypocrisy.

"I didn't say anything about the U.S.," Baldwin replied. "I simply asked how you think a Christian inmate would be treated in an Islamic prison."

"I don't see how that's at all relevant," Alexis told him with obvious sincerity.

Stark could have told his old friend just to give it up. Alexis wasn't going to change her mind about this or anything else.

She *couldn't* change her mind, because her ideology told her what to think.

Facts had nothing to do with it.

One of the inmates sitting at a table in the rec room stood up and approached the group. The man who had been at the table with him followed along like a big, friendly dog.

One of the guards moved to intercept them before they got too close.

"It's all right, Cambridge," Baldwin said. "I don't think Albert intends to cause any trouble. Do you, Albert?"

Stark remembered that the smaller man was Albert Carbona, the organized crime kingpin Baldwin had pointed out to him earlier. The big man, whose name Stark had forgotten, hovered over him like an unofficial bodyguard.

"Trouble?" Carbona echoed. He held up both hands, palms out, as if to demonstrate that he was harmless. "Why would I cause trouble for such a beautiful lady, Warden? And such a famous one, at that." He smiled at Alexis. "It's an honor to meet you, Ms. Devereaux. I've seen you on the television many times."

"All right," Alexis said, obviously wondering who this weaselly little man was.

Travis Jessup leaned in and asked, "Have you seen me on TV, too?"

Carbona ignored him and went on, "I used to ask my lawyers why they couldn't be as pretty as you were."

The big guy—Billy Gardner, that was his name, Stark recalled—added, "That's true, ma'am. I heard him say that."

"Thank you," Alexis said. She had been thrown for a loop for a second, but she looked like she'd recovered. "I've been told that I have many admirers among the incarcerated."

"Yeah, you do," Carbona said. The little wiggle his caterpillar-like eyebrows made as he spoke gave the innocuous words a lascivious edge.

"That's enough, Albert," Baldwin said, moving between Alexis and Carbona.

"No, wait a minute," Alexis said. She stepped to the side so she could look around the warden at Carbona. "Albert . . . can I ask you a question?"

Baldwin started to say, "I don't know if that's a—"

"You can ask me anything you want, dollface," Carbona interrupted. "You can even ask me for my number if you want—but they don't really do that in these joints anymore!"

"My God," Alexis murmured. "You're like something out of a 1940s movie, aren't you?"

"That's the best thing anybody coulda' said about me. Now, what is it you want to know?"

From the expression on Baldwin's face, it was clear that he realized he had lost control of this situation and decided to just let it play out. Stark felt some sympathy for his old friend, but at the same time it was hard not to chuckle.

Things grew serious, though, as Alexis said, "How do

you feel about all the new inmates here at Hell's Gate, these so-called terrorists?"

Carbona's bushy eyebrows drew down in a frown. He said, "I don't like 'em. Don't want nothin' to do with 'em."

"Because they're Muslims?"

"Because they want to tear down this country! My guys and me, we were crooks, sure, but we didn't want to overthrow the government and put a bunch of crazy ayatollahs or whatever you call 'em in charge."

"I don't think that's what the Islamic movement actually wants—"

"It ain't? I read, ya know? I get on the computer and I study up on current events."

Billy nodded and said, "He does. I seen him."

"And I've read plenty about how these Muslims want to scrap our legal system and replace it with that, what do you call it, sherry law."

Jessup leaned into the camera shot again and said, "That's sharia law."

"Yeah, yeah, whatever, it's the law accordin' to their religion. Not the Constitution and the Bill o' Rights or even the freakin' Magna Carter. Now, I ain't what you'd call the biggest fan of our legal system . . ." Carbona spread his hands to encompass their surroundings. "We haven't always gotten along that well, know what I mean? But it's *ours*. It's American. For the most part it treats everybody the same. Sure, it falls down on the job now and then, but we don't chop a guy's hand off for stealin' a loaf of bread. We don't think it's all right to *murder* a girl just because she smiles at some young fella her papa and her brothers don't approve of. You want a system like that runnin' things here in the good ol' U.S. of A., Ms. Devereaux? Because I gotta tell you, a system like that ain't gonna want a woman like you who's used to doin' things her own way."

Billy Gardner lifted his ham-like hands and began to clap them together slowly. As he sped up, some of the other inmates in the room joined in the applause. A bald, skinny prisoner with tattoos all over his head called out, "You tell it, Al Capone!" More cheers and yells of encouragement followed.

Alexis looked flustered and angry now. She said, "I think I've seen enough."

"You mean you don't want to see the rest of the prison?" Baldwin asked. Stark thought he sounded hopeful.

"I mean I want to see where those political prisoners are being kept." She looked at Riley and made a slashing motion across her throat. As soon as the camera was down, she added, "I've had enough of this bullshit runaround."

"That's too bad," Baldwin told her. "I can't allow you into the maximum security wing where the new inmates are being housed."

"I'll get a court order—"

"On what grounds? You don't represent any of those men. You have no standing in any of their cases." Baldwin paused and took a deep breath. Stark could tell that his old friend was trying to rein in his anger. "I'll tell you what I'll do. I'll take you to the entrance of that wing so you can see it, but that's as far as you go."

Alexis looked just as angry and stubborn as Baldwin did, but after a second she nodded and said, "All right."

Stark's eyes narrowed slightly. It seemed to him that she had agreed a little too easily.

Like she might have done if she planned on trying some sort of grandstand stunt.

But Baldwin had to be as aware of that possibility as

he was, so Stark figured there was no point in saying anything.

"Let's go," Alexis added curtly. She turned and stalked away.

Of course, she didn't actually know where she was going, so she had to pause and let Baldwin catch up and lead the way.

"So long, Ms. Devereaux!" Albert Carbona called from behind them. "You can come back and visit me anytime you want!"

As they walked along the corridor with its walls painted an institutional green, Travis Jessup leaned over to Riley and said, "That was really good TV, wasn't it? That was really good TV."

"Yes, Travis," she replied, shooting a glance and a flicker of a smile at Stark as he followed them. "That was really good TV."

Mitch Cambridge watched the warden and the others leave and wished his shift here was over so he could go with them. That Devereaux woman was some good looker, and Mitch wouldn't have minded getting on TV some more. He had tried to make sure he was standing where the camera angles would get him.

Not that Mitch wanted to be an actor or anything like that. He actually had an unusual ambition for a young man.

He wanted to be the warden of a prison.

If anyone had asked him, he couldn't have said why he felt that way. The desire had always been there, that's all.

Maybe his mother had watched some old prison movie on TV while she was carrying him.

Whatever the reason, he had decided to pursue prison administration as a career, and being a guard seemed to be the best way to start.

George Baldwin was lucky. For him, running a prison was just the family business, easy to get into.

Mitch had known he would have to work a lot harder.

He hadn't been a very impressive physical specimen in high school, sort of scrawny and geeky. But once he'd hit college and started majoring in criminology, he began working out as well, training intensively in mixed martial arts, building up his strength and speed and stamina.

He'd learned how to handle a gun, too. By now he was one of the very best at the range where he practiced.

Of course he had never actually shot at anything except a target, but he was confident that if there was trouble, he could handle himself, whether with guns or hand to hand. He still looked kind of scrawny in his uniform, but underneath it was some impressive muscular development.

"Hey, Mitch," Albert Carbona called. The mobster beckoned to him. "C'mere."

Mitch had tried to keep a professional distance between himself and the inmates, but it was hard not to like Carbona. He had to remind himself that the guy was responsible for who-knew-how-many murders and probably a ton of other human misery.

But at the same time he was like somebody's friendly, slightly goofy uncle, and Billy Gardner was like an older brother, overbearing at times but still a good sort.

As Mitch came up to the table where Carbona and Billy sat along with J.J. Lockhart, the mobster said, "We need a fourth for bridge. Why don't you sit down and play a few hands?"

"You know I can't do that, Mr. Carbona."

"Eh, why not? The TV camera's gone now. Nobody's gonna know—or care."

Mitch hesitated, then said, "Captain Frazier's somewhere here in the facility. He might come in any time."

"If he does, I'll put in a good word for you. I'll tell him Billy muscled you into it."

Billy said, "I wouldn't do that, boss."

"I know, I know, but Frazier don't have to know."

Mitch looked around and spotted another inmate sitting alone. He told Carbona, "Wait a minute," and went over to Simon Winslow. He jerked a thumb over his shoulder and told the computer hacker, "Some of the guys are getting up a game of bridge. Do you play?"

Winslow looked surprised that somebody was talking to him. He kept to himself all the time, which was a risk for a guy like him who couldn't take care of himself physically. But on the other hand, he didn't make any enemies, either.

"They want me to play?" Winslow asked, sounding like he couldn't believe it.

Mitch started to tell him that the others just needed a fourth player and didn't really care who it was, but he decided against that and said in a hearty voice, "Sure. You know how to play, don't you?"

"As a matter of fact, I do."

"Well, come on, then."

Winslow stood up and Mitch escorted him over to the other table.

"Here's your fourth," Mitch told Carbona, Billy, and Lockhart.

Carbona gave the hacker a dubious frown and said, "You're that computer guy. You got like a computer brain or something."

"Like an android?" Billy asked.

"No, like he's a machine."

"That's what I said, ain't it?"

Winslow said, "I know a lot about computers, but I don't have a computer brain. Just a regular old human brain."

"Trust me, pal," Carbona said. "Anybody smart enough to steal as much money as you did ain't got a regular brain."

Winslow smiled faintly. "I wasn't smart enough to keep from getting caught, though, was I?"

Lockhart said, "The young fella's got a point. Sit down, son. You can be my partner."

"All right," Winslow said with a nod.

Mitch drifted back over to his previous position next to the wall. He was pleased with how he'd handled that. He had been professional, but he hadn't angered Carbona, who wielded some influence inside these walls.

It was just too bad Captain Frazier or Warden Baldwin hadn't been here to see what he'd done.

But he was sure they'd have plenty of other opportunities to realize that he was somebody they ought to keep in mind when it came to advancement around here.

CHAPTER 18

In the county seat fifty miles away, the dispatcher in the sheriff's department who answered the call from Fuego about some sort of massacre happening there took it seriously.

"The PD there has that kid who's not right in the head working communications for them," the dispatcher said with a laugh. "He's probably imagining the whole thing."

"I don't know," the other dispatcher who was on duty said with a dubious expression on her face. "Maybe we should send a car to check it out, Helen."

The first dispatcher shook her head and replied, "You can send somebody if you want to, but I'm not gonna cause a panic and waste valuable resources just on the word of a retard."

The other dispatcher had been trying to motion with her eyes for her co-worker to shut up, but the warning hadn't done any good. Sheriff Jim Wallace, who had come up behind the first dispatcher without being heard, drawled, "I'm not much on all that sensitivity bullcrap, Deputy, but even I don't like that word."

Helen jerked around, swallowed hard, and said, "Sorry, Sheriff. I . . . I guess I wasn't thinking."

"Yeah, I'd say you weren't." Wallace leaned on the counter in the communications center. He was a tall, leathery, middle-aged man, just the sort who looked like what he was, a West Texas sheriff. "What's this about something going on in Fuego?"

"How'd you know where it was?"

"Because of what you said about their dispatcher. I happen to have met Officer Raymond Brady a few times. He works mighty hard at his job."

"Yes, sir, I'm sure he does."

"So what did he tell you?"

"That Fuego was being invaded by aliens." Helen frowned. "No, wait a minute. He started to say that, but then he changed it. He said they weren't aliens. They were Arabs."

"Arabs?" Wallace repeated with a frown of his own.

"That's right, Sheriff. Arabs with guns. He said they're killing people all over town."

Wallace rubbed his jaw. What he had just heard sounded pretty unlikely, but with the way the world was today, who was to say what was impossible? Plenty of things had taken place in the past fifteen or twenty years that he never would have dreamed would happen . . . like hardworking Americans allowing a bunch of freeloaders and starry-eyed dreamers to elect Democratic presidents again and again and again, just so the dreamers could give away stuff and the freeloaders could rake it in.

"If there's the slightest chance somebody's gone on a shooting spree over there, we have to check it out," Wallace said. "Better send two cars. Send an ambulance, too. I know the volunteer fire department over there has one, but they may need help if people are hurt."

"What are you going to do, Sheriff?" the other dispatcher asked as Wallace turned and headed for the door.

"I'm gonna go have a look for myself," he told them over his shoulder without looking back, as he grabbed his Stetson from a rack and went out.

The call came in to the office of Texas Ranger Company E in El Paso a little before noon. Sounding scared, the young man on the other end of the line identified himself as Officer Raymond Brady from the Fuego Police Department.

"We need help!" Raymond bleated. "We need the Rangers! There are men with guns everywhere! They're shooting anything that moves!"

The Ranger who'd answered the phone tried to break in and calm him down, but Raymond just kept repeating frantically, "Send help, send help!"

The Ranger might have thought this was a prank, but the highly efficient Caller ID and GPS locator built in to the Texas Department of Public Safety's communications system pegged the call as coming from the police department in Fuego, some 150 miles away.

He still wasn't sure he believed the bit about a mass shooting—until he heard a crash of some sort, followed by the distinctive chatter of automatic weapons and then a dull boom that could only be a shotgun.

And then the line went dead.

The Ranger was on his feet a second later, running into the office where Lt. Dave Flannery was on duty on what should have been a sleepy Sunday morning. Flannery was one of two lieutenants assigned to Company E, serving under the command of Major Neal Burke.

He looked up in surprise from the computer where

he'd been working when the other man burst into the room.

"We've got a mass shooting in Fuego, east of here," the Ranger reported.

"I know where Fuego is," Flannery said as he came to his feet. "You're sure, Tommy?"

"I got a call that originated at the PD there. The caller identified himself as one of their officers and requested help. Then—" Tommy paused and took a deep breath. "Then I heard a bunch of shooting, Lieutenant. It sounded like a war."

"Good Lord," Flannery muttered as he came out from behind the desk, moving fast now. "Mobilize the SRT. I'll take command of it myself."

"What about Major Burke?"

"Let him know what's going on—*after* we've got the wheels rolling on the SRT."

"He won't like not being the one to make the call," Tommy warned.

"I don't care," Flannery snapped. "Just make the calls. Call the airport and tell them to start warming up the engines on the choppers, too."

"Yes, sir."

Flannery stood there alone for a moment after the other Ranger rushed out to follow his orders. He had been a Ranger for several years and a DPS officer before that and had worked on plenty of major cases. He had seen some bad things, too, things that sometimes still haunted him.

But he had never taken part in the sort of action this sounded like it might be. He had trained with the Special Response Team, of course. The SRT was part of the Rangers' Special Operations Group and included not only Rangers but also officers from the Highway Patrol and the Criminal Investigation Division. The Rangers had a SWAT unit as well, but it was headquartered in

Austin. There was a Special Response Team assigned to each of the six Ranger companies around the state.

They would be the first state law enforcement officers into any active shooter situation.

From what he had just heard, there were a *lot* of active shooters in Fuego.

The two DPS helicopters carrying the SRT could be there in less than two hours.

Flannery hoped they wouldn't be too late.

Maria Delgado had just gotten back to the governor's mansion from the late mass when her personal cell phone buzzed.

Not too many people had that private number. When she checked the screen, she saw the call was from Texas Attorney General Ellis Flynn.

"What is it, Ellis?" Delgado asked as she answered the call. She didn't believe in wasting time on pleasantries. That came from growing up in a household where her mother, a single parent, had worked twelve to fourteen hours a day and instilled that same work ethic in her children.

Her brusque attitude annoyed some people, but nobody could deny that she threw herself wholeheartedly into the job of governing the Lone Star state.

"Maria, I've just heard from the DPS that we may have a mass shooting incident on our hands."

"Oh, Lord," Delgado breathed. It was more a prayer than anything else. "Where?"

"Some little town out in West Texas called Fuego."

"I think I've seen it on maps. Don't know that I've ever been there."

"It's not much more than a wide place in the road. The Ranger office in El Paso got a call from a police dispatcher there about people being killed."

"How many shooters?"

Flynn hesitated, then said, "That's just it. According to what we know at the moment, there are multiple shooters. Dozens, maybe more. Like a military operation."

Delgado's hand tightened on the phone. She looked out the window of the room where she was standing at a beautiful autumn day in Austin.

The world she had known all her life couldn't be about to come crashing down . . . could it?

Quietly, she said into the phone, "Is this it, Ellis? Is Washington making the move?"

Over the past few years, she and several governors from other Republican-leaning states had had discussions about the direction the country was taking, and they were all convinced that sooner or later a Democratic president, emboldened by the slavish devotion of the media and a certain percentage of the population, would use the Department of Homeland Security in an attempt to seize complete federal control of their states, removing Republican governors and other elected officials by force if necessary.

That terrible day of reckoning was coming. Delgado knew it in her bones.

And there was a strong likelihood Texas would be first on the list for such an action. Even though the Democrats had been trying to take it over for many years, so far the state had resisted at the ballot box. Texas had even elected an Hispanic Republican woman governor and a black Republican attorney general, and those were particular slaps in the face to Washington and the growing Democratic dictatorship.

Such a threat to one-party rule couldn't be tolerated indefinitely by the so-called progressives.

Flynn said, "No, it doesn't sound like it. Supposedly the shooters are Arabs."

"Arabs," Delgado repeated. "Islamic terrorists?"

"That would be my guess. But it's just a guess," Flynn emphasized. "Right now there's a whole lot more we don't know than we do know."

"All right." The governor massaged her temples with her free hand. "Do you think I need to be on the scene?"

"No, ma'am, I don't," Flynn answered without hesitation. "Not as uncertain as the situation is. And if somebody does need to go out there later on, probably it should be me. Right now we just need to monitor things and wait to find out more."

"How are the Rangers responding?"

"They have a Special Response Team in the air right now."

"We'll pray that's going to be enough . . . and that they get there in time to do some good."

"Yes, ma'am."

"Keep me informed, Ellis. And thank you for the heads-up." Delgado paused. "It's been a long time since anything this bad has happened in Texas, hasn't it?"

"That's right. And I wish I could say it'll be even longer before things go really bad. Unfortunately . . ."

"I know," Delgado said softly. She broke the connection, lowered the phone, and looked out the window again.

The beginning of the end, she thought.

Unless we're really lucky.

But Texas wasn't going to go down without a fight. She lifted the phone again, punched in a number.

A number that she alone knew.

The phone on the other end rang twice before a man answered it, growling, "Yeah?"

"Get ready, Colonel," Delgado said. "I'm going to need you."

CHAPTER 19

Raymond's father had said that Raymond wasn't the sharpest knife in the drawer. That he wasn't playing with a full deck. That his elevator didn't go all the way to the top.

Raymond's father was an A-hole.

He had thought that many times, although every time he did, he felt embarrassed for even thinking such a bad word and guilty for feeling that way. A-hole or not, the guy was still his dad, and he wasn't like that *all* the time. Just most of it.

But when he wasn't, he could be pretty good. Sometimes he ruffled Raymond's hair and said, "Hey, sport, how ya doin'?" just like a dad on one of the old black-and-white TV shows Raymond liked to watch on the satellite.

And one time they had gone all the way to El Paso to watch a baseball game in person. Raymond went to all the high school games he could, in all the different sports, but this was a real professional baseball game. Minor league, but still.

Sometimes when he wasn't off working somewhere on an oil or gas rig, Raymond's dad sat down and watched

TV with him. He'd say things like, "Good Lord, are they still showing this? It was ancient when I was a kid." Or, "Wait a minute, the boxes are gonna start coming faster and faster on that conveyer belt. It's a hoot."

Best of all was when his dad would come into his room at bedtime, make sure he was tucked in good, and lean over to kiss the top of his head and say, "Have a good night's sleep, big guy."

Raymond never felt better than at times like that, and he sure wished he could figure out how somebody could be such an A-hole most of the time and then do something so nice.

He never could understand it, though. He guessed that was just the way people were.

All he knew right now, as he knelt behind the counter in the police station and thumbed more shells into the shotgun, was that he was glad his father was up in Oklahoma on a job.

That way he wouldn't get killed by the bad guys, the way Raymond figured he was about to, any minute now.

After Chuck had left, Raymond had called the other four officers in the department. Two of them didn't answer, the calls going straight to voicemail.

He knew one of the men sang in the choir at the Baptist church, so that was probably why he'd turned his phone off. Raymond didn't know where the other officer could be.

But he got hold of the other two men and told them to get to the station as fast as they could. As it turned out, both of them were already on their way in, having heard the shooting and realized that all hell was breaking loose.

Then he had called the sheriff's department and finally the Rangers, and he'd been talking to them when somebody had driven a pickup through the parking lot and crashed it into the front of the station.

The wreck made Raymond drop the phone. He saw men with guns climbing out of the pickup, and he remembered what Chuck had said about using the shotgun if anybody tried to hurt him.

These men were shooting at him, so he figured that counted. He crouched, grabbed the gun, and pointed it at the invaders. He pulled the trigger but nothing happened.

Then he remembered how Chief Cobb had showed him how the shotgun worked. Even though the chief told him not to touch any of the guns, he showed them to Raymond sometimes and told him about them. The chief liked to teach him stuff, and Raymond enjoyed learning.

He wished the chief was here now.

But Raymond was alone, so he pushed the safety lever the way the chief had showed him and pulled the trigger, and this time the shotgun made a terrible racket and jumped so hard it flew right out of Raymond's hands and landed behind the counter.

He dived after it as more bullets tore into the communications console and sparks flew everywhere. When he tried to grab the gun again, he was clumsy and it slid away from him. Then he got his hands on it and pumped it just as a man came around the end of the corner with a gun in his hand.

Raymond fired from the floor.

The load of buckshot slammed into the man's groin and abdomen and threw him backward. Raymond let out a sob of horror as he saw all the blood.

But he stood up and kept shooting, pumping the shotgun as he swung the barrel from left to right, spraying buckshot across the shattered front of the police station.

The other men who had gotten out of the pickup dived for cover. Raymond ducked back down. A box of shells sat on a shelf below the counter. He fumbled some of them out and started reloading.

That's what he was doing while he thought about his dad and how glad he was the A-hole was nowhere near Fuego this morning. Then he said a prayer because he knew he was going to die and he figured it wouldn't hurt to let God know he was on his way to Heaven.

Leaving pretty soon now.

Then the shooting started again.

Officer Lee Blaisdell slammed on the brakes and brought his cruiser to a skidding stop as he saw the damage to the side of the police station where the entrance was. The front end of a pickup was partially inside the building where it had crashed through the doors and taken out part of the wall, too.

Several men had taken cover behind the wrecked pickup and were firing into the station. Blaisdell didn't know who was in there, but it was pretty easy to tell who the bad guys were here.

He pulled his Mossberg riot gun out of the clips that held it and floored the gas again, aiming the cruiser at the pickup.

The men were too busy shooting to notice him coming. He didn't open the door and roll out onto the pavement with the riot gun until he was almost on top of them.

It was like something out of a movie—but it hurt a hell of a lot worse.

The impact against the ground jolted all the way down to his toes. For a second he couldn't get his breath.

But he squeezed the riot gun harder and hung on to it for dear life, because he knew his life probably depended on it.

He looked up in time to see the cruiser slam into the back of the pickup with a metal-grinding roar. One of the invaders was caught between the two vehicles. The collision practically pinched him in half and made his eyes pop right out of their sockets.

That was like a movie, too, a grisly special effect that made guys gasp and girls scream.

Lee watched a lot of movies. Played a lot of video games. Was a cop because it was a job. A job that actually had some insurance with it, crappy though it might be. The country's health care system still hadn't recovered fully from the train wreck that had almost destroyed it nearly a decade earlier, but Lee had a pregnant wife and some coverage was better than nothing.

Right now, though, he felt more like a soldier than a cop. This was war, sure enough. He pushed himself up onto his knees and fired a round from the riot gun into one of the guys beside the pickup.

As that man flopped to the ground, another one jumped onto the crumpled hood of Lee's cruiser and launched himself at Lee with a high-pitched yell. Lee didn't have time to shoot before the man plowed into him and knocked him over.

The back of Lee's head hit the pavement and he saw stars for a second. When his vision cleared, the guy's face was right in his, inches away, spit flying as the man screamed at him in some foreign language. His eyes were filled with crazy hate as he locked his hands around Lee's neck and started trying to choke him to death.

Lee still had hold of the riot gun with one hand, fingers wrapped around the weapon's breech. He twisted the gun, poked the muzzle against the cheek of the man trying to kill him.

The man's face darkened with rage and got even crazier. His mouth moved and Lee supposed he was still screaming, but he couldn't be sure because all he could hear was the roaring of his own blood inside his brain as he groped with his other hand for the Mossberg's trigger.

The man tried to jerk his head away from the gun. He squeezed harder on Lee's neck. Lee swung the gun back in line. His fingers brushed something. One finger hooked around, caught the trigger, pulled . . .

Blood and bone fragments and chunks of gray matter sprayed across Lee's face as his attacker's head blew apart. The choking hands spasmed, loosened, fell away from his throat.

Yelling hysterically, Lee shoved the corpse off himself and rolled the other way.

He didn't have his uniform on today. He wore jeans and a flannel shirt. Desperately, he used the shirtsleeves to wipe away the gore on his face.

Nobody else was shooting at the moment, but he heard brakes squeal somewhere nearby.

Lee took deep, gasping breaths and tried to get himself under control. He could be in danger again. He looked around and saw one of Fuego's other police cars stopped at a slant about twenty yards away. Martin Corey, at fifty the oldest member of the department, crouched behind the open driver's door and pointed his service revolver at Lee.

"Stay on the ground!" Martin shouted. "Stay on the ground!"

"Martin!" Lee called. "It's me. Lee Blaisdell. Don't shoot!"

Martin straightened slightly and lowered the gun.

"Lee?"

Engines roared somewhere not far off. Lee had the

sinking feeling that they didn't mean help was on the way. He scrambled to his feet and said, "We gotta get inside. Somebody's holed up in there."

Martin trotted over to him. Stocky, with graying brown hair and glasses, he didn't look like much of a cop. He made no bones about the fact that he was just putting in his time until retirement, when he planned to sell his house, buy a motor home, and travel around the country with his wife. He had told Lee about it many times.

After today, he might not have a chance to do that.

First things first, though, Lee reminded himself. If you got in a hurry, it was game over. He motioned for Martin to follow him and trotted toward the police station.

Pausing in the gaping hole knocked out by the pickup, he called, "Hey! Anybody in here?"

"Who . . . who's there?" came a voice from behind the counter.

"Raymond! Is that you? It's Blaisdell and Corey!"

Raymond Brady stood up holding one of the shotguns from the weapons cabinet. He was crying but he didn't appear to be hurt. They were tears of relief.

"I thought I was gonna die," he said.

"Not today, buddy," Lee told him. He hoped he could keep that promise. "I think more bad guys are on the way. Do we fort up in here, or do we take off and stay on the move, make ourselves harder to hit?"

"I have to stay here," Raymond said. "I'm on duty."

"I don't think we have to worry about rules like that right now," Lee said.

Another worry had wormed its way into his brain, and it helped him make up his mind. He had left his wife Janey at home, out by the high school, when he heard the shooting start. He'd told her to stay there with the door locked.

Now fear for her safety clawed at him. He had to get to her, make sure she was all right. He said, "We have to go, all of us. Martin, we'll take your cruiser."

"Okay," Martin said. He looked stunned and confused. "Do . . . do either of you know what's going on here?"

"Hell," Lee said. "Hell's come to Fuego, Martin."

CHAPTER 20

The high school looked deserted and peaceful, Chuck thought, as Ernie wheeled the pickup into the parking lot and circled the school toward the football stadium and the field house next to it.

Another pickup and a couple of cars were parked at the field house already. Some of the team members lived close by and had gotten here in a hurry.

The streets were empty. Everybody was hunkered down in their homes, scared because of all the gunfire, waiting anxiously to see what was going to happen.

Chuck wished he knew. He figured it wasn't going to be anything good.

Ernie stopped next to one of the pickups and said, "That's Brent's F-150. I think Pete and Spence are here, too."

"Not everybody on the team will show up," Chuck said as they got out of the pickup. "Some of them, their parents won't let 'em out of the house, and not all of them will be able to sneak out."

He felt bad about putting high school kids in danger, but on the other hand, these were West Texas kids. Most of them owned guns and had grown up hunting. They worked on farms and ranches, some because their families owned the places, others for summer jobs. A few of them had probably worked as roughnecks in the oil patch during the summer. Sure, they spent a lot of time on their phones and tablets, like kids anywhere, but they had a core of toughness about them.

And Chuck needed help no matter where it came from.

Lord knows he needed help.

Half a dozen young men came out of the field house to meet Chuck and Ernie. A couple carried shotguns, and the other four had hunting rifles.

Brent Sanger, the starting running back on the varsity team, said, "Man, we're glad to see you guys, Chuck. What's this all about? What's all the shooting?"

"It's a terrorist attack," Ernie blurted before Chuck could say anything. "They're shooting up the town!"

The boys looked at Chuck, who nodded grimly.

"That's right. The shooters appear to be Middle Eastern, so we're talking about Islamic terrorists."

"What do they want in Fuego?" Pete Garcia asked. "This is nothing but a wide place in the road!"

Chuck had been thinking about that very thing. He said, "Yeah, a wide place in the road that's just a few miles away from the prison where a bunch of their buddies are locked up now."

Looks of comprehension appeared on the faces of the football players. Brent said, "You think this attack has something to do with that?"

"It's got to," Chuck said. "Nothing else makes sense." He took a deep breath. "I think they intend to take over the town and then attack the prison. But first they'll try to round up everybody they haven't already killed and keep them corralled to use as hostages if need be."

"We have to stop them."

Chuck nodded and said, "That's what I had in mind."

"I wish Andy was here," Ernie said.

Chuck looked over at him with a puzzled frown and asked, "Andy Frazier? How come?"

"Because he's the quarterback," Ernie said as if the answer were obvious. "The quarterback always knows what to do."

"See if you can find some crutches," Andy told Jill.

"You know you can't get out of bed," she argued. "Not with a broken leg."

"We may have to move around some. I want to be sure I can do it."

For the past half-hour, they had been listening to the gunfire that came from various locations around town. Out in the corridor, hospital personnel rushed around and talked in loud, frightened voices.

When Jill had stepped out and asked a couple of nurses what was going on, they had ordered her to get back in the room and stay there. They hadn't offered any explanation for the commotion.

Whatever was going on, it had to be pretty bad. Andy and Jill had seen an ambulance leave the hospital with its lights flashing and siren blaring, but it hadn't come back yet.

"I need to go home," Jill said. "My parents and my little sister . . ."

"The nurses told you to stay in here."

"I know." She sighed. "And I don't want to leave you, Andy. I really don't. But I'm afraid something really bad is happening, and I . . . I have to be sure they're all right."

Andy understood how she felt. His dad was out at the prison today, so Andy was pretty sure he was all right. Hell's Gate had plenty of security.

But his mom was home alone, as far as he knew. He should have been there in case she needed help, he thought. If it hadn't been for this stupid broken leg—

"Find me some crutches," he said again. "We're gonna get out of here. You've got your car. We'll go by my house and get my mom, then we'll head for your folks' house."

She gazed at him, clearly wanting to believe what he was saying.

"You really think we can do that?"

"I don't think we've got any choice," Andy said.

He reached down to the IV attached to the back of his hand and pulled it free, wincing at the sharp pain. That made the equipment start to ding, but he didn't figure anybody would come to check it for a while . . . if ever.

Jill eased the door open, looked up and down the corridor, then glanced at Andy and said, "I'll be back."

"Just like the guy said in that old movie," he told her with what he hoped was an encouraging smile.

While she was gone, he sat up better and then swung his legs off the side of the bed. The one in the cast stuck out in front of him. He was going to have a heck of a time getting around, he thought, but if he took it slow and easy he could manage.

Thankfully, the leg didn't hurt all that much. But that might be because he was still pumped full of painkillers, he reminded himself. Once they wore off . . .

He would worry about that when it happened, he decided.

Right now there were more pressing problems.

When he looked out the window he saw smoke rising here and there in town. Fuego was looking and sounding more like a war zone all the time.

His nerves grew tighter as the minutes dragged past. He had hoped that Jill would be able to find a supply closet or something and grab a pair of crutches without having to ask anybody. If she had to talk to the nurses, they would probably argue with her.

A couple of loud reports somewhere in the hospital made Andy jump. He almost slid off the bed and had to dig his fingers into the sheets and hang on to keep from slipping. That could have been bad, he thought.

But it seemed like everything on this Sunday morning was turning bad.

The door swung open. Andy's breath caught in his throat.

It was just Jill. And to his great relief, she had a pair of crutches in her hands.

"I got some," she said. "Andy, did you just hear—"

"Yeah," he said as he reached for the crutches. "That sounded like shots."

"And they were close. Like, here in the hospital."

Jill's face was pale with fear, despite her healthy tan.

"There's an emergency exit at the end of this hall," Andy said. "I think it lets out into the parking lot. We'll go that way so we don't have to go past the nurses' station and the lobby."

She nodded. He positioned the crutches under his arms, then swung his weight onto them as she stood ready to grab him if he started to fall.

He wished he had something other than a stupid hospital gown to wear. At least they had let him keep his underwear on.

It was bad enough having to make a run for it on crutches. He didn't need his bare butt sticking out in the wind, to boot.

Andy had had to use crutches his freshman year when he hyperextended his knee, so he knew how to maneuver on them. As he started toward the door with Jill hovering beside him, he said, "Check the corridor."

She opened the door, looked, and then nodded to him. She held it open wider so he could get through.

They moved out into the hall, which was deserted at the moment. That struck Andy as odd, but right now he would take any lucky break they could get.

He and Jill had just turned toward the emergency exit marked with a red sign over it, when a harsh, accented voice called, "You two! Stop! Stop there!"

Andy's head jerked around as Jill grabbed his arm in fear. A man had come around the corner where the nurses' station was located and now strode toward them.

Andy had seen enough movies to know that the thing the stranger was pointing at them was an automatic weapon.

Quietly, he said, "Jill, get behind me and make a run for the door."

"No! I won't leave you—"

A middle-aged man stepped out of one of the patient rooms as the gun-toting stranger stalked past. This man had a straight-backed chair in his hands, and he swung it high as he tried to bring it crashing down on the intruder's head.

The man with the gun must have heard him, though, because he swung around and the weapon belched fire and noise. Bullets thudded into the chair-wielder, who must have been visiting a patient, and knocked him backward. He dropped the chair and collapsed as blood welled from his wounds.

"Run!" Andy told Jill. He moved as fast as he could on the crutches, knowing he had to try to get away, too, since she wouldn't desert him.

They were both going to get shot in the back, he thought.

But when the automatic weapon went off again, the slugs smashed into the wall just above the emergency exit. One of them hit the sign and shattered it.

Andy and Jill froze. They had no choice. All the

gunman had to do to chop them to pieces was lower the barrel a little.

"Stop there," the man said again. "Come with me."

More men appeared as the two young people made their way slowly toward their captor. More men with guns appeared and began forcing patients and visitors out of the rooms.

They were gathering up everybody in the hospital and taking them somewhere, Andy thought.

Like animals being led to slaughter.

The glass doors at the hospital's main entrance slid aside for Phillip Hamil as he approached them.

Just like any obstacle moved out of his way sooner or later, he thought. There might be setbacks now and then, but in the end he would emerge triumphant. It was Allah's will.

With his personal bodyguards trailing him, he strode into the hospital, where Raffir met him along with several other men. A machine gun hung on its sling from Raffir's shoulder.

"The hospital is secured, Doctor," Raffir reported. "All the captives are being held in the cafeteria."

Hamil nodded in satisfaction.

"Did we suffer any losses?" he asked.

"None," Raffir replied with a smirk.

"Excellent. How many of the infidels did you have to kill?"

"Only three or four. And none of the medical personnel, as you instructed."

"Very good. Some of our men have been wounded already. I'll have them brought here."

Taking over the town's medical facility was an important component of the plan, Hamil knew. Not the most important part, certainly, but still, he was glad to hear that this part of the operation had been successful.

"What about the police station?"

"Also secured, Doctor. But . . . we lost four men."

Hamil frowned.

"The Americans put up that much of a fight?"

"They were lucky," Raffir declared. "But in the end our forces took the station."

"And executed the infidels, I hope."

When Raffir hesitated, Hamil knew his new lieutenant had something displeasing to report. But after a second, Raffir forged ahead bravely.

"They fled. We found no one inside the building except one of our men . . . dead."

Hamil's jaw tightened in anger. He asked, "How many of the Americans were there?"

Raffir shook his head and said, "I can't say for sure, Doctor. None of the men who led the initial assault survived, and by the time the others got there, the Americans were gone."

Anger turned to fury and welled up inside Hamil. In an icy but controlled voice, he said, "You sent only four men?"

"The others were only a few minutes behind them. A whole truck full—"

Raffir stopped short and gulped. Perhaps he read in Hamil's eyes the desire to kill him as an example. That was the first impulse Hamil felt.

But he forced down the urge and said, "All right. At least there will be no more communication between the authorities and the outside world."

He squared his shoulders. Time to move on.

"Take me to the prisoners."

Raffir led him to the cafeteria, where approximately eighty people stood in a frightened, huddled mass on one side of the big room. Half a dozen armed men guarded them.

Hamil strode in front of them. He felt hatred emanating from them, along with their terror.

It was good that they hated him, he thought. The more righteous a man was, the more the infidels hated and feared him. He wore their loathing like a badge of honor.

Raising his voice slightly, he said, "I want hospital medical personnel on one side of the room, patients and visitors and other hospital staff on the other. Doctors, nurses, technicians, move over there, please."

He pointed to the other side of the room.

Nobody moved at first. Then a tall, fair-haired man in scrubs stepped forward. He said, "What are you going to do with us? Why are you doing this?"

Hamil moved closer to him, read the little name tag pinned to the green scrubs.

"Dr. Conley," he said.

"That's right."

"You are a doctor here?"

"Of course I am. I was working in the ER this morning."

"Doctor, you need to take your people and move over to the other side of the room. You need to do that . . . right . . . now."

Conley looked like he wanted to argue, but instead he turned and gestured vaguely, saying, "Come on, folks. It'll be all right."

One by one the medical personnel parted from the others. They were probably starting to realize that their expertise was valuable to the invaders. They straggled past the watchful, impassive guards and gathered on the other side of the room.

That left the patients, visitors, cafeteria staff, and maintenance workers where they had been when Hamil came in. Many of them glared defiantly at Hamil, none more so than a young man with one of his legs in a cast. He balanced on crutches and kept one arm tightly around the shoulders of the pretty American girl beside him.

Raffir eased up beside Hamil and asked, "What do we do with the others, Doctor?"

Hamil smiled.

"Allah will be pleased by their deaths," he said.

CHAPTER 21

Sheriff Jim Wallace took his foot off the gas and let the SUV slow as he spotted the flashing lights up ahead. As he came closer he saw that a Fuego PD cruiser was angled across both lanes of the highway. A man sat behind the wheel with the driver's door open. He appeared to be talking on the radio.

Maybe now he'd get some answers, Wallace thought. He had been trying to contact the Fuego police station on his radio ever since he'd left the county seat. He hadn't been able to raise anyone, and calls to the station's landline hadn't gone through, either.

The roadblock confirmed that something bad had happened in the little town. Clearly, the local authorities were trying to keep people out.

That wouldn't apply to Wallace, though. They would tell him the story, or he'd raise holy hell with Charles Cobb.

Wallace liked the Fuego police chief. Always had. Cobb had a solid background as a law enforcement officer. He had a sly sense of humor, too, that Wallace appreciated. And he never acted like the fact that he was black earned him any special privileges. Wallace tried to be as color-blind as possible, in both his personal and his professional life, and Cobb was the same way.

Wallace brought his SUV to a stop. Leaving the engine idling, he opened the door and stepped out.

The Fuego cop lifted a hand and gave him a friendly wave. Wallace couldn't see the man that well yet, but so far he didn't recognize him.

As Wallace came closer, the cop hung up the radio mic and started to get out of the car. He said, "Everything's under control, Sheriff."

Wallace definitely didn't know the man. He looked Hispanic, which certainly wasn't unusual anywhere in Texas. Wallace wondered how long the fella had been working for the Fuego PD.

"We had reports of a shooting," Wallace said.

"Yeah, there sure was."

The sheriff's mouth was a grim line as he asked, "Anybody hurt?"

"Just a few hundred infidels."

It took a second for the odd answer to penetrate Wallace's brain. By the time it did—by the time he realized this man in a cop's uniform wasn't Hispanic at all but something else entirely—by the time Wallace reached for the service revolver on his hip . . .

Two more men stood up from behind the car and opened fire on him. Wallace felt the tremendous hammer blows of the slugs that spewed from the automatic weapons. They threw him backward, filled him with an incredible heat that blazed up like the sun.

When that heat burned out, it left nothing behind but a bloody husk that had been a lawman.

Lt. Dave Flannery wore a Kevlar vest and leg protectors over the gray SRT uniform. A helmet was strapped on his head, and goggles covered his eyes. He had a

9 mm Glock holstered at his waist, a couple of flash-bangs attached to his belt, and an AR-15 in his lap.

He leaned forward to ask the chopper pilot, "How far out are we?"

The pilot worked for the Highway Patrol. He glanced over his shoulder and said, "Just a couple more minutes, Lieutenant. You can see Fuego up ahead."

He pointed, and Flannery looked through the canopy. The little town looked peaceful from the air . . . but wisps of gray smoke rose here and there, as if things had been on fire earlier and were dying down now.

"Still no luck raising the Fuego PD?" he asked.

"No, sir. I talked to the sheriff's office in the county seat. They said the sheriff himself had come over here to check out the reports of a shooting, and they had a couple of other units on the way, too."

Flannery nodded. He looked around at his companions in the first chopper.

There were six men counting himself. Three others were Texas Rangers, and the remaining two were Highway Patrol officers. Flannery knew all the Rangers well but was acquainted with the troopers only from joint SRT training exercises.

The other six members of the twelve-man Special Response Team were in the second helicopter. They were divided evenly: two Rangers, two state troopers, two investigators from the Department of Public Safety's Criminal Investigation Division.

It seemed pretty likely there was going to be a crime that needed investigation, but first the scene had to be secured. Flannery didn't know if twelve men would be enough for that, but he was counting on assistance from the local authorities.

More Rangers were on their way, too, but they wouldn't arrive for at least an hour and a half.

"Where do you want me to land, Ranger?" the pilot called back to him.

"The high school parking lot ought to be a good place," Flannery replied. "It should be empty since today's Sunday."

"You got—Shit!"

The pilot's startled exclamation made Flannery lean forward to look out the canopy again. He saw something streaking toward them through the air, rising at an angle from the ground.

The pilot threw the chopper hard to the left and down. The thing flashed past them, and a split second later Flannery heard an explosion behind them.

As the helicopter continued to turn, Flannery caught a glimpse through the side door of flaming debris falling through the air. Horror washed through him as he realized the second chopper had been blown out of the sky.

"That was a missile!" the pilot yelped. "It missed us but got the other guys!"

Flannery had expected to find trouble here in Fuego, but he'd never dreamed they would encounter such an explosive welcome in the form of a surface-to-air missile.

Grief and anger at the deaths of his fellow lawmen in the other chopper threatened to overwhelm him for a second, but he forced those emotions down. He had to think clearly, because he and the rest of the men were still in danger.

"Continue evasive maneuvers," he barked at the pilot. "Find a place to set us down."

"Yes, sir. Looks like there's the high school—Incoming!"

Another SAM targeted the chopper. The missiles didn't appear to be laser-guided, so there was a chance the pilot could dodge them. Flannery and the other men were thrown hard against their restraints as the chopper heeled over.

The next instant something blasted close by. The helicopter gave a big lurch.

"We're hit!" the pilot cried. "It got our stabilizer!"

Indeed, the chopper was beginning to spin out of control. Flannery's stomach twisted.

"Can you get us on the ground?"

"I can try! One way or another, we're gonna be on the ground in less than a minute!"

The cruiser turned out to be too easy a target, but on foot, Lee , Martin, and Raymond had covered less than two blocks in the past half-hour. At this rate it would take them the rest of the afternoon to reach Lee's house.

Fear for his wife and their unborn child threatened to consume him. He couldn't do Janey and the kid any good if he was dead, though, so every time one of the trucks full of gunmen rumbled near, he and his companions scurried for cover.

Lee knew what the invaders were doing. They were patrolling the town, making sure it was secure. From time to time he heard bursts of automatic weapons fire. More than likely, some of the citizens were trying to defend themselves . . .

Only to find that they were outnumbered, outgunned, and doomed.

Every one of those bastards was going to rot in Hell, he thought. Lee wasn't a very religious man. Sometimes he wasn't sure he even believed in Heaven.

But he believed in Hell, all right, and no matter what happened in this world, that was where those invaders were going to wind up.

That was scant comfort, but it was better than nothing.

They were crouched behind a wooden fence around somebody's backyard when Martin said, "You hear that?"

Lee listened, heard a faint *whup-whup-whup* sound that seemed to be coming closer.

"Those are helicopters," Raymond said.

The kid was right, Lee thought.

And maybe choppers meant that help was on the way.

Even if that was true, Lee still wanted to get home. He motioned for the other two to follow him and led the way around the fence.

He paused, looked to the west, and saw two helicopters approaching.

Something flashed through the air. The first chopper banked violently to the side, and the second one blew up in midair in a massive fireball.

"No!" Martin said.

"The sumbitches got missiles," Lee said. His sense of despair got even worse at that realization.

What the hell were they up against, anyway?

The second chopper looked like it was trying to turn around and flee, but then another missile caught its tail. The explosion was smaller this time. The helicopter appeared to be badly damaged, anyway. It spun around and around so much that just looking at it made Lee a little queasy.

Steadily losing altitude, the chopper went out of sight. If it went down, the crash would be over by the high school, Lee thought. Since he and his companions were headed in that direction, they might be able to check it out later.

There might be survivors.

Officer Chuck Gibbs looked around the locker room in the Fuego High School field house.

Counting himself and his little brother, Fuego's "army of liberation" numbered fourteen—and some of them were barely old enough to have driver's licenses.

They were all husky, athletic young men, though, and they all had guns. That had to count for something.

They were desperate, too. They knew that their lives and the lives of their families might well depend on their being able to drive the invaders out of Fuego.

Chuck had his doubts about whether that was possible, but they couldn't just roll over and give up. That probably wouldn't get them anything in the long run except a couple of bullets in the back of the head.

No, they had to fight back, even if it was futile. He went around the room, taking a quick inventory of their armament. Shotguns, hunting rifles, even a couple of .22s not good for much more than plinking at cans or jackrabbits.

That would have to do.

"All right, we can't stay here," Chuck told them. "They're gonna be patrolling the town, looking for pockets of resistance, mopping up on anybody they find. So what we're gonna have to do is stay on the move. If we see a bunch of them we can hit, we do it hard and fast and then get the hell out of Dodge. Find a place to hunker down again. Don't take chances. And follow my orders."

"Yeah, well, who put you in charge?" Spence Parker asked. He played wide receiver, the same position Chuck had played several years earlier, and he was an arrogant little snot whose father owned the bank. Chuck happened to know that he had knocked up a couple of girls and gotten away with it. He didn't like Spence, but the kid had an AR-15 of his own and Chuck was glad to have him on their side.

"I'm the oldest," he said as if he were explaining something to a little kid. "And I'm a cop, so I have experience in dangerous situations. If you don't want to accept that, you can go home, Spence."

"I didn't say that," Spence replied sullenly. "I was just making sure everything's clear, that's all."

"It's clear. We're in deep shit, that's what's clear." Chuck decided it wouldn't be fair to pull his punches. "And all of you should know, too, that there's a very good chance none of us are gonna live through this. But we may be the only ones left fightin' for our families and our town, and I'm willing to risk it."

"So am I," Ernie said, and several others of the young men nodded.

"All right, then." Chuck was about to tell them that they'd go see if they could find any of the invaders, when he heard a sound that struck a chord of hope inside him.

A helicopter. Maybe more than one.

And they were coming toward Fuego.

Chuck figured choppers had to be bringing help from outside. Maybe even the Army. The others heard them, too, and muttered excitedly among themselves.

"Let's go have a look," he said. "But be careful. Keep your heads down."

Chuck led the way out of the building, checking first to make sure none of the enemy were in sight. When he was sure it was clear, he motioned for the others to follow him.

They ran along the front of the field house. When they turned the corner, Chuck spotted the two helicopters flying toward town.

Then he saw a plume of smoke, a streak of light, and the first chopper darted out of the way.

The second helicopter blew up.

"Whoa!" Ernie said.

Burning pieces of wreckage plummeted to earth in the distance. The other helicopter started to swing around, then a second missile homed in on it and blew part of the tail off. The chopper began to spin wildly.

The young men tilted their heads back to watch as the

out-of-control helicopter passed above them. Dropping steadily, it disappeared beyond the field house and the rise of the grandstand on this side of the football stadium.

"Come on!" Chuck called as he broke into a run.

The gates in the chain-link fence around the stadium were locked except for the one beside the ticket office, which was left open so that recreational runners could get into the stadium on the weekends to use the track around the football field. Chuck headed for that gate.

He heard a terrible, metal-rending crash, but it didn't sound like the helicopter had blown up on impact. He ran underneath the stands and then up a ramp. Ernie and the others trailed behind him.

The chopper had gone down on the field, about the east 40-yard line. The skids had torn up the turf. It looked like the pilot had tried to put it down without crashing, but the helicopter had tilted over and the rotor had ripped a great gouge in the field before being torn loose from its mooring.

The helicopter's cabin was still largely intact, but as Chuck looked through the shattered windows, he saw flames leaping wildly.

The wreck was on fire, and that meant the gas tank might blow.

And there might still be somebody alive in there.

Chuck shoved his rifle into Ernie's hands and said, "Stay here."

Then he vaulted over the railing along the front of the stands and dropped to the grass behind the home bench area. He ran toward the crash.

Pounding footsteps made him look back. Ernie lumbered after him. His hands were empty because he had given the rifle to somebody else.

"Damn it, Ernie—"

"I'm not lettin' you have all the fun, Chuck."

There was no time to argue. Chuck sprinted up to the wreck and yelled over the crackle of flames, "Hey! Is anybody alive in there? Hey!"

A faint voice answered him. Chuck couldn't make out what the man said, but the response was enough to tell him that somebody had survived the crash. He grabbed the door handle and tried to wrench it open.

"Let me," Ernie said as he shouldered Chuck aside.

Ernie was four inches taller and sixty pounds heavier. He could bench-press way more than his brother ever could. Chuck didn't argue. He just stepped back and let Ernie haul the door open with a tortured squealing of hinges.

Chuck got inside first. A quick look told him the pilot was dead. A large piece of windshield had cut his head halfway off, and he was covered with blood.

But several of the passengers were struggling to get out of their restraints. One man hung limply in his with his head at an odd angle on his shoulders. Chuck figured the crash had broken his neck.

The other five were alive, though. Injured, some of them, but alive.

Chuck had a folding KA-BAR knife in his pocket. He took it out and started using the razor-sharp blade to saw through the seat and shoulder belts holding the men in their positions.

The fire was spreading, and the suffocating heat from the flames filled the chopper.

The man Chuck was trying to free had a bloody mouth, like something had come loose during the crash and slapped him across the face. He said thickly, "Officer . . . you better get out of here . . . This thing . . . is liable to blow—"

"Not without you guys," Chuck said.

This attempted rescue wasn't motivated solely by

humanitarian reasons. Whoever these men were, they would swell the forces of what Chuck was already thinking of as the resistance.

He got the first man loose, helped him up, practically shoved him out the door into Ernie's arms.

"Get him away from here!" Chuck ordered. Ernie turned and trotted away with the man over his shoulder like a sack of potatoes.

By the time Chuck got the next man loose, Ernie was back at the door. He had carried the first man to the sidelines and dropped him there. He took the second one and started off.

Another man had succeeded in freeing himself, and he was working on one of his companions. That just left one more, and Chuck cut him free.

They all clambered out except for Chuck and staggered away from the burning chopper. He knew he should go, too. He was already pushing his luck, because logic said the gas tank should have blown by now.

But he saw several rifles lying around and knew he and his allies would need all the weapons they could get. He grabbed the rifles and started pitching them out through the open doorway.

Ernie ran halfway out from the sidelines where everyone else was gathered by now and shouted, "Chuck, get outta there! Come on!"

Chuck saw what looked like an ammunition locker and grabbed it. Grunting under the weight, he carried it to the door and threw it out. That was the last of it, he thought. That was all he could do.

He felt the blast's concussion as it slammed into his back, but he never felt the searing wave of fire that engulfed him.

He was dead from a broken neck before the flames ever touched him.

CHAPTER 22

The takeover of Fuego was virtually complete by one o'clock in the afternoon, less than two hours after the first shots had been fired by Charles Cobb.

In that time, the death toll was already closing in on a thousand. Each of the five churches in Fuego had been transformed into a charnel house. The massacre in the hospital cafeteria added to the rivers of blood being spilled for the glory of Allah.

During their sweep through the town, the invaders had killed many more, ruthlessly cutting down any citizen who tried to put up a fight. Those who surrendered were rounded up and marched to the football stadium on the edge of town. The grandstand there was the only place large enough to hold all of the prisoners. They huddled there on the metal bleachers, terrified, under the watchful eyes, and the guns, of their captors.

Phillip Hamil stood under the scoreboard at one end of the field and surveyed the cowering infidels. Already his men were placing explosives under the stands. If anyone from outside tried to interfere with his operation, those worthless Americans would pay with their lives. Hamil intended to make sure everyone understood that, too.

The wreckage of a helicopter continued to burn in the middle of the football field, sending up a pall of black smoke. It was the second of two aircraft his men had shot down with surface-to-air missiles bought on the black market. The first had been blown to bits in midair. The pilot of this one had tried to save it but failed. Hamil saw one body that had been thrown clear lying on the scorched turf next to the wreck.

He was confident the others were still inside, burned to a crisp by the blaze.

The policemen who had escaped from the station were still unaccounted for, but Hamil wasn't worried about them. However many they were, they were as nothing, bits of chaff in the wind of Islamic vengeance.

No, there was no one left in Fuego who could stop him, Hamil thought with a smile as he turned to gaze toward the red cliffs in the distance to the west. From where he stood at this moment of triumph, he couldn't see the prison, but he knew it was there.

And Hell's Gate was where he was going next.

Colonel Mohammed Havas was in his quarters at the underground installation where he was posted. He had been relieved of duty for the rest of his shift because of the shock of the "heart attack" that had claimed the satellite technician.

Before anyone arrived after the call for help he made, Havas had used his considerable computer skills to erase anything in the surveillance that might serve as a warning and replaced it with innocuous footage. As far as the Department of Defense, the NSA, and Homeland Security were concerned, nothing unusual was happening in Fuego, Texas, today.

The world would know soon enough that that wasn't true. Today was the first real stroke of the Sword of Islam against the godless West in far too long.

The phone the colonel used to make his call was one of the most secure in the world. The only phone more secure was the one he was calling. He listened to it ring on the other end, in a house on Pennsylvania Avenue in Washington.

A voice familiar to Havas answered. If he hadn't recognized the voice, he would have broken the connection without saying anything, taken out his pistol, and put a bullet through his brain.

But as it was, he said simply, "The first part is complete. Judgment has begun."

BOOK TWO
The Battle of Hell's Gate

CHAPTER 23

The sally port leading to the maximum security wing of the Baldwin Correctional Facility was all steel and bulletproof glass reinforced with thick wire mesh inside it.

A narrow, concrete-walled corridor led to the entrance, which could be hermetically sealed like a watertight door between compartments on a ship.

Beyond that first door, which had a square window of bulletproof glass set into it, was a small reception area manned by four heavily armed corrections officers. There was an intercom so someone outside the sally port could communicate with the guards.

To get into the cell block itself, visitors had to pass through the first door, go past the guards, through a second, equally impregnable door, then a maintenance area and kitchen, and finally into the long, double-level cell block.

At the far end of the cell block, a door opened into a small exercise yard that from the outside looked like a concrete cube with several skylights set into it. When the inmates were allowed into the exercise yard, they could see the sun, but they wouldn't feel the touch of the breeze on their skin for the duration of their stay in Hell's Gate.

George Baldwin explained all this to Alexis Devereaux, albeit in not quite so poetic terms, while Riley Nichols filmed the exchange and Travis Jessup interjected an occasional comment or question so he'd be sure to get at least a little screen time.

Alexis looked more and more outraged as Baldwin spoke. When he paused, she said, "This is shameful. Human beings shouldn't be treated like this."

Watching from down the corridor, Stark wasn't sure the terrorists ought to be considered human beings. They were mad-dog killers whose only goal in life was to destroy his country and wipe out his way of life. Getting three meals a day, a bunk to sleep in, and medical care was about all they deserved.

More than they deserved, really, but despite all the America-bashers both at home and abroad, the liberal blame-America-first crowd, Stark liked to believe that the nation still had a core of goodness.

"You have a right to your opinion, Ms. Devereaux," Baldwin said, "but I disagree. These inmates are being treated very similarly to the previous occupants of the maximum security wing. They're not being discriminated against in any way, other than the fact that some of our security procedures are slightly different. And to be honest with you, that's as much for their protection as anything else. You heard what Mr. Carbona said. Many of the inmates would like nothing better than the chance to strike back against these terrorists."

"Alleged terrorists," Jessup put in.

"Not my call," Baldwin said. "I just keep 'em locked up. The courts will decide what they did or didn't do."

Alexis said, "Do you know why those prisoners want to harm the Muslim inmates?"

"Gee, I don't know," Baldwin said dryly. "Because they're Americans?"

"That's exactly right."

Baldwin looked a little surprised. He said, "It is?"

"Yes. And all too many Americans are still racist, xenophobic bigots."

Stark couldn't resist. He said, "We cling to our guns and our religion, too. Because those are rights the Constitution guarantees us." He paused. "You can look it up."

Riley had swung the camera around to catch him when he started talking. Now, as both Alexis and Jessup glared at her, she turned back to them.

"Warden Baldwin, I demand to be allowed into the maximum security wing so I can see for myself the conditions under which these political prisoners are living," Alexis said.

"And I repeat what I said earlier, that's not going to happen. No civilian personnel are allowed beyond this sally port."

"What about when attorneys representing the inmates need to talk to them?"

"We make an exception for that. We have a special room where they can meet."

"It's probably bugged and has surveillance cameras in it, too," Alexis said.

"It's not bugged, but there *are* cameras. Believe me, those lawyers want us to be able to keep an eye on them while they're talking to their clients, in case there's any trouble. We also allow inspectors from the state bureau of prisons and from the Justice Department. In fact, I went over everything about this setup with representatives from the Attorney General's office before the prisoners were transferred here, and they signed off on our plans. You can check with Washington if you don't believe me."

Alexis didn't have anything to say to that. Before she could think of another question intended to embarrass or annoy Baldwin, a burly, brown-haired man approached quickly along the corridor and said, "Excuse me, Warden, I need to talk to you for a minute."

"All right, Captain Frazier," Baldwin said. He nodded to Alexis. "I'll be right back, Ms. Devereaux."

Baldwin and Frazier withdrew along the corridor until they could talk in low voices without being overheard. Stark watched them with interest. He had heard an undercurrent of worry in the guard captain's voice, and a concerned frown appeared on Baldwin's face as he listened to what Frazier had to say.

Stark wondered what was going on.

After a few moments, Baldwin turned to catch Stark's eye and inclined his head in an indication that Stark should join them. Stark did so, aware that the other visitors seemed very curious about this development, whatever it was.

"John Howard, this is Bert Frazier," Baldwin said. "Bert, my old friend John Howard Stark. He's had some experience with trouble."

"Pleased to meet you, Bert," Stark said with a nod. "Is that what we've got, George? Trouble?"

"Something's happened in Fuego. Some of my men spotted smoke coming from the town, too much smoke to be harmless."

Stark frowned and said, "I told you it looked like a bunch of protesters were showing up. You think maybe there was a protest that turned into a riot? That crazy bunch could've set some cars or buildings on fire."

"Yeah, I wouldn't put anything past them, either. But here's the really worrisome thing. One of the men at the gate thought he heard some explosions. And he swears he saw one occur in midair."

"How reliable is this fella?" Stark asked.

Frazier answered that. He said, "Reliable enough that I'd bet my life on him. *Something* is happening in town, and I don't like it. My wife is there, and my kid's in the hospital."

"Yeah, I saw him get hurt in the game the other night," Stark said. "I hope he's doing okay."

"I'm sure he is. But I'm worried about my wife and about what it might mean for the facility out here."

"There's only one road to the place," Baldwin said as he rasped his fingertips over his chin. "And it runs through Fuego."

"If you're thinking what I'm thinking, boss, I'd better go check it out."

Baldwin nodded curtly.

"You go ahead, Bert. Take a man with you. Check on Lois while you're there. And let me know right away what you find out."

"Yes, sir."

Frazier turned and hurried away.

"What was that about?" Alexis wanted to know when Stark and Baldwin turned back to the little group.

"Nothing I can discuss right now," Baldwin said, "but it isn't anything for you to be concerned about, Ms. Devereaux."

"I'm concerned about everything that goes on here when it involves the mistreatment of prisoners placed in your care."

"Nobody has been mistreated," Baldwin said with what Stark thought was remarkable patience. "There haven't been any incidents since the new inmates have been here, and there won't be. I won't allow any."

"But you won't allow me to go in there and ask those men if you're telling the truth."

"That's right, I won't."

"Then how will anyone know if you're lying? How will America know?"

"America will just have to take my word for it, at least

for the time being," Baldwin said. "Now, Ms. Devereaux, I'm afraid that's all the time I have for you today."

She stared at him as if she couldn't believe what he had just said.

"You're kicking us out?" she said.

"No, I'm telling you that other matters have come to my attention and I need to deal with them." Baldwin gave her an obviously forced smile. "Running an institution like this is complex and requires a lot of time. So if you'll come with me I'll escort you back to the gate—"

Travis Jessup had started talking into his microphone in a low voice, doing a wrap-up for the broadcast, when Alexis interrupted both him and Baldwin by declaring, "I'm not going anywhere. Not until I get what I came for."

"Which is?" Baldwin asked tightly.

"I want to talk to at least one of those men in there," she said as she gestured toward the sally port and the maximum security wing beyond it. "If you won't let me in there, you can bring one of them out here."

"Security considerations—"

"Surely you're not afraid of what *one man* might be able to do," Alexis interrupted in a scathing tone. "You can put him in chains, surround him with guards, whatever you want to do. But I'm going to talk to him, or I'm not leaving here."

"I can have you removed from the grounds."

"If you do, all of America will see it on TV tonight."

Stark felt sorry for his old friend. George Baldwin was a tough, well-organized administrator, but he wasn't used to dealing with situations like this. Handling the media required a person who was skilled in public relations, and that wasn't Baldwin's strong suit.

Stark sympathized because it wasn't his strong suit, either. He missed the days when straight talk still meant something in this country.

"If I allow this—"

"You're not going to stick us in some grim little room where the prisoner will be intimidated, either," Alexis said. "I know. I want to interview one of the prisoners in the library. There were some comfortable chairs in there."

"You said I could put the inmate in chains and surround him with guards," Baldwin reminded her.

"You can, but that's no reason we can't sit down together comfortably and have a discussion."

Stark could practically see the wheels turning in Baldwin's brain. The warden was sifting through everything and weighing it, trying to decide what the best and quickest way would be to get Alexis Devereaux out of his hair.

Obviously it would be to cooperate with her, and Alexis had to know that.

"All right," Baldwin said. "We'll go back to the library, and I'll have one of the new inmates brought there. As for the meeting itself, you'll follow my instructions to the letter, do you understand?"

Alexis smiled and said, "Of course. I don't want to be unreasonable."

Stark could tell it cost Baldwin considerable effort not to curse at that comment, or guffaw with derisive laughter.

"Is there any particular prisoner you want to talk to?"

"How could there be? The government has never released their names. The public doesn't know who they are."

"I'll just pick somebody, then."

"That's fine. And once he's assured me that he and his companions have been treated fairly and with respect, I'll be glad to leave."

"Not as glad—Ah, never mind," Baldwin said. "Let's go."

CHAPTER 24

Mitch Cambridge had just gotten off his lunch break and was coming out of the employees' cafeteria when Captain Frazier walked by. Mitch was going to say something, but Frazier beat him to it.

"Cambridge," the captain snapped. "Come with me."

Mitch fell in alongside Frazier, who didn't slow down.

"Where are we going, Captain?"

"We're making a run into town," Frazier said. "Draw a vest and an AR-15 from the armory. Get a vest for me, too."

Mitch's heart slugged harder. He said, "Is there some sort of trouble?"

"Are you questioning my orders, Cambridge?"

"No, sir," Mitch replied instantly. "I just thought there must be something wrong—"

"Maybe, maybe not." Frazier came to a stop. Weariness was in his eyes, along with worry, as he said, "That's what we're going to find out. Some of the outside guys saw smoke coming from the direction of Fuego, and one of them thought he saw and heard an explosion in the air toward town. Something's going on, and the warden wants me to find out what it is."

"And you want me to go with you. I'd be honored, Captain—"

"Just get the gear like I told you, and let's go."

A few minutes later, they drove out through the main gate in one of the prison's vans. Frazier was at the wheel, while Mitch sat in the passenger seat. Mitch tried to control his nerves as he gripped the assault rifle he had gotten from the prison's armory. The vest he wore felt heavy and hot.

He wasn't afraid, exactly, although uncertainty always had a little fear mixed in with it. He was pleased by the trust in him Captain Frazier had displayed by picking him to come along, although he knew luck had played a part in that by putting him right there in front of the cafeteria when Frazier had come along the corridor.

But if Frazier didn't think he could do the job, the captain would have kept walking and found somebody else.

This day wasn't working out too bad, Mitch thought.

"Do you have any idea what might be going on in town, Captain?" Mitch ventured to ask.

"If I did, we wouldn't be going to see," Frazier said without taking his eyes off the two-lane blacktop in front of them.

"Well, sure, but I thought you might have some inkling—"

"I don't."

The flat, hard sound of Frazier's voice warned Mitch that now might be a good time to shut up.

He didn't need to be running off at the mouth, anyway. That would just make the captain think that he was nervous.

And he wasn't.

Not really.

Frazier narrowed his eyes and leaned forward a little to peer through the windshield.

"What the hell is that?" he muttered.

Mitch looked down the road, too, and saw what had caught the captain's attention.

Clouds of dust had started to rise from the ground on both sides of the blacktop. The terrain was flat, hard-packed sand, dotted with clumps of hardy grass and the occasional short, gnarled mesquite tree. Vehicles could drive on it without much trouble, and from the looks of the dust, a number of them were coming this way.

"Captain," Mitch said slowly, "that can't be good."

Frazier hit the brakes. As the van skidded to a halt, he said, "There should be a pair of binoculars in the glove box. Get out and take a look, Cambridge."

Mitch opened the glove compartment and found the binoculars. He swung the passenger door open, set his rifle on the floorboard, and stepped out.

When he raised the glasses to his eyes and peered through the lenses, it took him a moment to get oriented. Looking through binoculars had always thrown him a little that way.

Then he located one of the brownish-yellow clouds and followed it down to its base, lowering the binoculars slowly until he could see what was kicking up all that dust.

Cold fear stabbed into him. No point in denying it, what he saw scared him.

"Captain," he said, "there are trucks coming toward us. They look like . . . army trucks."

From behind the wheel, Frazier asked, "Some sort of military maneuver we weren't told about? That doesn't make any sense."

Mitch tracked the glasses along the line of vehicles advancing toward Hell's Gate.

"It's not just trucks. I see pickups and SUVs and

vans. Even a few cars. That's not the Army, Captain. At least . . . not the U.S. Army."

A couple of pickups spurted out in front of the formation and veered onto the road. Mitch's heart began to hammer faster as he saw that they had something mounted on the roofs of their cabs. Men stood in the pickup beds as the trucks raced toward the prison van.

Those were machine guns on the roofs, Mitch realized.

And with that, he knew that he and Frazier were in deep shit.

He leaped back into the van and said, "Captain, get us out of here! They've spotted us!"

"What the hell are you talking about?" Frazier demanded.

"They've got guns—machine guns—on top of their pickups. We're under attack, Captain. We're under attack! We've got to get back to the prison!"

Mitch knew Frazier would balk at being given orders by a mere guard. Sure enough, the captain hesitated, and in that moment the onrushing pickups came that much closer.

Close enough to open fire.

The range was still a little long, though. The .50 caliber slugs chopped up the blacktop about twenty yards in front of the van. Frazier yelled a curse, took his foot off the brake, and slammed it down on the gas as he cranked the wheel hard to the left.

The van lurched into a wide turn that took it across the road's other lane and onto the gravel shoulder. The tires spun for a second, then gained traction. As the van skidded back up onto the road and sped toward the prison, Mitch heard pinging sounds.

Those were bullets hitting the back of the van, he knew.

He cursed and prayed under his breath as Frazier

kept the van's accelerator floored. The needle on the speedometer crept past 75, 80, and then on to 90.

"Get on the horn to the prison!" Frazier shouted over the roar of the engine. "Let 'em know we got trouble!"

Mitch fumbled with the microphone clipped to the dashboard. He had radio training, but fighting off the sheer terror that threatened to engulf him forced all other thoughts out of his head for a moment. He struggled to remember what to do.

Then the training kicked in. He set the dials on the radio correctly, keyed the mic, and said into it, "Hell's Gate, Hell's Gate, this is Officer Mitch Cambridge. Captain Frazier and I are under attack by a large, armed force that is advancing on the facility. Repeat, Captain Frazier and I are under attack—"

Movement in the side mirror caught Mitch's eye. He saw to his horror that one of the pickups had almost caught up to them and had now swung out off the road to get a better shot at them. The muzzle of the machine gun swept toward the van.

He dropped the mic and grabbed the rifle at his feet. More slugs hammered against the side of the van. Mitch twisted on the seat, rolled down the window, and stuck the AR-15's barrel outside. He opened fire on the pickup.

He couldn't tell if any of his bullets hit the speeding vehicle, but the pickup veered farther off the road. Mitch kept shooting as it swung back toward them again.

At least one of his shots was lucky. The pickup's windshield exploded. He poured more lead into the cab and was rewarded by the sight of the pickup careening out of control. The men in the back yelled and jumped around frantically, but there was nothing they could do as the pickup's front wheels hit a small dry wash and the vehicle flipped into the air. The men in the back were thrown clear, but Mitch couldn't see if they landed safely.

He hoped they hadn't.

He hoped they had broken their damned necks.

The prison's main entrance was visible up ahead. Mitch grabbed the microphone again and yelled, "Open the gate! Open the gate!"

Then his heart sank as he realized that the guards couldn't open the gate. Not with a large enemy force bearing down on the place. In fact, they would be hardening their defenses right now in response to his earlier message.

The electrified outer fence was topped with razor wire. A few feet beyond that was a concrete barrier designed to stop any vehicles that broke through the fence. There were barriers around the entrance as well, located close enough together that only one vehicle could pass through at a time, and there was a reinforced steel gate that could rise from its housing belowground to block that opening.

It would take an army to break into Hell's Gate.

Unfortunately, that seemed to be what was descending on the place.

And he and the captain were stuck on the outside with the bad guys, Mitch thought.

The other pickup moved up on the van's left. Machine gun slugs pounded the side panel. When Mitch glanced back he saw light poking through scores of bullet holes on both sides of the van. It was a miracle none of them had found the gas tank so far.

In a matter of seconds, though, the pickup would draw even enough that the machine gun could fire directly into the driver's side window, and when that happened, the hail of .50 caliber slugs would chop the two of them into bloody, quivering chunks of meat.

Before that could happen, Frazier hauled the wheel over and sent the van drifting into the pickup. The back end of the van hit the pickup's right front fender in a jolting, metal-screaming collision. The pickup veered away, and the van squirted ahead again.

"Hold it steady, Captain!"

Frazier exclaimed, "What the hell?" as Mitch started squirming the upper half of his body through the open window. He sat on the sill with the slipstream tearing at him and braced his elbows on the van's roof as he fired the assault rifle across it.

He knew he was making a better target of himself, but they had to fight back somehow. Their chances of surviving were pretty slim anyway.

Might as well go out with a bang.

He targeted the men handling the machine gun. Not really thinking about what he was doing, letting instinct and long hours of practice take over, he fired five shots.

One man's head blew apart in a grisly explosion. The other went spinning out of sight into the pickup's bed as blood spurted from his wounds.

That put the MG out of action.

But the passenger in the pickup had a handheld automatic weapon, and he blazed away with it. Mitch brought his rifle's muzzle down to try for a shot, but the angle was bad.

Then the van suddenly slowed, and the pickup jumped ahead. That gave Mitch the chance to fire through its rear window. Glass flew as the window shattered, and the inside of the windshield turned red as blood splashed all over it. The pickup's front wheels turned sharply, probably from the mortally wounded driver slumping over the steering wheel, and the vehicle rolled, turning over several times before it came to a stop beside the road and burst into flame.

The van was still slowing down. Mitch slid back onto the front seat and saw Captain Frazier leaning over the wheel with an agonized expression on his face. He gripped the wheel tightly, pushed himself up, and found the gas pedal again. His foot had slipped off it a moment earlier, and Mitch knew why.

The front of the captain's shirt was bloody.

"I'm hit, kid," Frazier grated. "But I'm gonna get you back to the prison."

"They won't let us in," Mitch said.

"They'll open the gate enough for you to get through . . . on foot. That won't take . . . but a second."

"Captain—"

"Shut up. You fought good . . . You're a good officer . . . Cambridge. What's your . . . first name again?"

"It's Mitch, sir."

"Keep up . . . the good work . . . Mitch. You'll probably be . . . runnin' the place . . . one of these days." Frazier's lips drew back from his teeth in a grimace of agony as he hunched forward over the steering wheel again, but he kept the gas floored and steered the van straight toward the prison entrance. "Tell my kid—"

That was as far as he got. He slumped forward again, and his hands slipped from the wheel. His foot slid off the gas.

Mitch knew the captain was dead. He reached over, grabbed the wheel, and got his left foot on the gas. The prison entrance was only about a hundred yards away now.

And sure enough, the gate was opening. The guards inside were going to give him a chance to get through on foot, just as Frazier had predicted.

The van weaved back and forth on the blacktop as Mitch tried to steer from the passenger side. Frazier's head flopped loosely on his shoulders. Mitch glanced in the side mirror. The line of enemy vehicles was still several hundred yards away.

He might have a chance.

He let off on the gas, jammed his foot on the brake, spun the wheel. The van's rear end swung around, and the van slid sideways along the road toward the gate. It came to a stop no more than ten yards away.

More fire came from the attackers now. Mitch heard the bullets striking the van as he piled out through the passenger door and made a run for the narrow gap. What sounded like angry hornets buzzed past him. Guards in armor and helmets yelled at him from inside the gate, urging him on. The opening was right in front of him.

Something struck him in the back and knocked him right through the gap. He hit the ground and lay there gasping for breath as pain filled his body.

But he realized after a second that the bullet had caught him in an area where the vest protected him, and he didn't think it had penetrated. The impact had knocked the breath out of him and might have even broken a rib . . .

But he was alive.

The narrow opening in the gate rumbled closed.

The steel barrier started to rise a couple of feet in front of Mitch.

He had to get over it. He forced himself up, got his hands on the top of the barrier, flung a leg over it. With a grunt of effort, he heaved himself forward and toppled over the thick steel wall, which continued rising to a height of six feet.

He was safe for the moment, Mitch realized. Somehow, against all odds, he had survived.

But Hell's Gate was still under attack, and before this was over, it was possible none of the people inside the prison would make it through what was to come.

CHAPTER 25

Lucas Kincaid was about to leave for the day when he heard the voices of people coming along the corridor outside the library's open door.

He hoped they would go on past, whoever they were, but as he recognized Warden Baldwin's gruff tones, he figured he was about to be paid another visit.

Sure enough, Baldwin came in with that Devereaux woman, the news crew, and John Howard Stark.

"We're going to have to borrow your library, Lucas," Baldwin said. "I hope you don't mind."

"It's your library, Warden, not mine," Kincaid said. "With all due respect, sir, I just work here."

Baldwin shrugged, and Kincaid got the feeling the warden was saying that he was lucky to be just an employee. And that was true as far as it went. Kincaid's responsibilities ended when he left the prison. Baldwin actually lived here, his quarters being located in the administration wing.

Although the personal lives of the people he worked with didn't mean much to Kincaid, he had heard that Baldwin was a widower, and his children were grown and gone. His entire life revolved around this prison.

"We're going to be conducting an interview in here," Baldwin said, although he certainly didn't have to explain his intentions to Kincaid. "You're welcome to stick around if you want, but we won't actually need your help."

Kincaid gave in to curiosity and asked, "What sort of interview?"

"Ms. Devereaux wants to talk to one of the new inmates."

Kincaid was surprised Baldwin was going to allow that, but again, Baldwin was the warden and could do whatever he wanted.

"I'll stick around," Kincaid said, once more acting on impulse. He thought this might be his only chance to lay eyes on one of the terrorists, since it was unlikely they'd ever be allowed to use the library.

It was possible he might even know the guy, he thought wryly. He had helped Company men and American contractors take down more than one terror cell.

Of course, that would mean he was running the risk of being recognized in return.

He was willing to chance it. The odds against anybody in Hell's Gate realizing he had been at Warraz al-Sidar were pretty damned high.

Those odds had been even more on his side before somebody got the bright idea of transferring all those fanatical bastards here. This prison had been a good, anonymous place for him to hole up until that happened.

Now he might have to start giving some thought to moving on, finding some other isolated spot, where nobody would think to look for a man wanted by the authorities at the highest level.

All because he hadn't been able to turn a blind eye to what was going on. All because he had tried to do the right thing . . .

"Will those chairs be all right?" Baldwin asked Alexis Devereaux as he gestured toward a pair of dark blue wing chairs.

"Can that one be turned so that I can look directly at the inmate?" she said.

"Sure." Baldwin adjusted the chair himself. "How's that?"

Alexis looked at the woman with the camera—Riley Nichols was her name, Kincaid recalled—and asked, "Will that work?"

"Sure," Riley said.

Kincaid had caught her sneaking glances at him. That was worrisome. She was in the news business. If she had a good memory for faces, she might recall that she had seen his somewhere, even though he had changed some in the past year.

Kincaid lowered his gaze to the floor and half-turned away from her. He wasn't going to make it easier for her to recognize him.

John Howard Stark came over to the counter while Baldwin continued talking to Alexis Devereaux and Travis Jessup. Quietly, Stark said, "We're sort of intruding on your bailiwick, aren't we, Lucas?"

"It's fine," Kincaid said. "Like I told the warden, he has the right to do whatever he wants."

"You don't feel a little territorial?"

Kincaid grunted. "About a prison library? Please."

In a way, though, Stark had a point. Kincaid's apartment was just a place to eat and sleep. It wasn't really home.

He could never go back to his actual home in Louisiana. Even being next door, so to speak, in Texas probably wasn't wise if he wanted to keep his family safe. At least he was on the other side of Texas from them, and this was a pretty big state.

He had reconciled himself to the fact that he would never see them again. It wasn't easy . . . but it was best.

So maybe Stark was right. This library was his territory. The closest thing to a home he had right now.

And it was being invaded by a loudmouthed, liberal lady lawyer. Soon a cold-blooded killer whose only real goal in life was to massacre innocent Americans was going to be brought in here as well.

Both of them were threats to the America where Kincaid had grown up.

And to be honest, he didn't know which type posed the biggest danger in the long run. He thought maybe it was easier to fight an avowed enemy from without than it was to combat the liberal rot from within.

The real enemies of the United States know how to exploit the country's weaknesses. How to burrow deep within the system. How to do things that appeared innocuous, even benevolent, when all the while they were designed to bring down everything good about the nation and make it impossible for the American way of life to carry on. And they would do it all with smiles on their faces, promising to make things better. We're from the government, and we're here to help you.

That was the true evil, the true threat facing the United States.

And Kincaid didn't like having it in his library, but there wasn't a blasted thing he could do about it.

"What about that inmate, Warden?" Alexis asked with an impatient note in her voice.

"I already made the call," Baldwin said. "A security team should be bringing him in here in a few minutes."

True to Baldwin's prediction, only a couple more minutes had passed when they heard footsteps in the corridor. A pair of guards wearing protective gear and helmets and carrying shotguns appeared in the doorway.

"Ready to bring the prisoner in, Warden," one of them said to Baldwin, who nodded for them to go ahead.

The guard who had spoken nodded in turn to someone out in the corridor, then he and his companions came into the library and flanked the entrance. Another guard backed in, shotgun at the ready.

A prisoner in an orange jumpsuit followed him, shuffling awkwardly because of the leg irons clamped around his ankles. His wrists were manacled together, too, and a chain ran from those cuffs to a ringbolt set into a wide leather belt strapped around his waist. He had to hold his hands close together in front of him with only a couple of inches of play in any direction.

The man had a close-cropped dark beard touched in a place or two with gray. His hair was equally dark, but long, hanging down over his ears and almost touching his shoulders. His face was thin enough that Kincaid figured he had gone on a hunger strike sometime in the past, while being held at another facility.

Three more shotgun-toting guards came into the library after the prisoner. The room was getting a little crowded.

The prisoner's eyes immediately found Alexis Devereaux. He must have read the sympathy in her eyes, because he said in English with a slight British accent, "I appear to be completely harmless, don't you think?"

"You certainly do," she assured him. She turned to Baldwin and snapped, "Is it absolutely necessary to treat this man in such a degrading fashion?"

"He's a highly dangerous prisoner," Baldwin said. "He masterminded an attack on one of our embassies that killed more than a dozen Americans."

The prisoner said, "They were war criminals executed by men fighting for the freedom of our people."

"As I recall, the suicide bombers who actually carried out the attack were women and children," Baldwin said.

"Allegedly." The answer was cool, arrogant.

"He's right," Alexis said. "He's presumed innocent until proven guilty. Have you forgotten that, Warden?"

"I haven't forgotten anything."

With a smirk, the prisoner said, "You haven't introduced us, Warden. You seem to have forgotten that."

Baldwin grunted. Kincaid heard the contempt in the sound.

"Ms. Devereaux, this is Abu Rahal."

"And I know, of course," Rahal said, "who Ms. Devereaux is. Your efforts on behalf of political prisoners worldwide are well-known and much appreciated, *madame.*"

"You're welcome," Alexis said, all but preening under the praise.

Baldwin reached out as if he were about to take hold of Rahal's arm, then stopped himself with a vaguely repulsed look, like he had realized he was about to touch something unclean.

He turned the movement into a gesture toward the chairs.

"Sit down," he instructed Rahal.

"I would be more comfortable if my hands and feet were free."

"Well, nobody else in here would be."

"Speak for yourself, Warden," Alexis said. "I don't mind if Mr. Rahal's restraints are removed."

"That's not going to happen," Baldwin said. "Let's get on with this. I want this over with."

"So that you can send this man back to his confinement?" Alexis asked.

"So that we can quit running this security risk. Sit down, Rahal."

The terrorist shuffled over to one of the chairs and carefully sat down. Alexis took the seat opposite him.

Riley Nichols moved closer, keeping the camera trained on Rahal while Travis Jessup intoned a low-voiced introduction.

Then Alexis leaned forward with a sincere smile and said, "Thank you for agreeing to speak with me, Mr. Rahal."

"It is my pleasure," he said, "although I was given no choice in the matter."

Instantly, a look of professional concern appeared on Alexis's face. She said, "Were you threatened or in any way coerced to come here and speak with me?"

Baldwin said, "There were no threats—"

"I asked Mr. Rahal, not you," Alexis cut in coldly.

Kincaid thought the warden looked like he could chew nails right about now, but somehow Baldwin controlled his temper and didn't say anything else.

"My continued illegal imprisonment is coercion enough, don't you think?" Rahal asked. "The rest of the world knows that the United States is holding me and my fellow fighters for freedom without any right to do so. Sooner or later those who persecute us will be held accountable for their crimes. Judgment is coming for them."

"Some might say that sounds like a threat."

Rahal shook his head. "I make no threats. Islam is a religion of peace. We seek only justice and respect."

"Have you been mistreated since you've been brought here to Hell's Gate?"

Rahal's face twisted for a second. Kincaid saw the hatred there before Rahal was able to control it and restore the blandly pleasant mask he wore.

"I am a devout man. Is it not mistreatment to force me to live in a place called Hell's Gate? When I pass from this world, my destination will be Heaven, not Hell."

Where ninety-nine beautiful virgins would be waiting for him as a martyr, Kincaid thought. He had heard that bullcrap over and over. Some of the foot soldiers in the fanatical Islamist movement probably even believed it.

Not the leaders, though. They didn't care what awaited them on the other side, if anything.

All that really mattered to them was their hate and their lust for inflicting pain on America.

"Are you allowed to conduct your religious practices? Can you pray as your faith demands?"

"We are allowed to practice our religion . . . although it is difficult, surrounded by infidels as we are."

"Is there anything you'd like to say to America?"

Rahal glanced at the camera and asked, "This is going out live?"

Alexis had to glance at Jessup for the answer to that question. Jessup looked at the soundman, who was in touch with the truck outside. The tall, bearded man nodded, and Jessup said, "Yes, this is going out live to the entire country, Ms. Devereaux."

She smiled and said, "If you have a message for the country, Mr. Rahal, now is the time to deliver it."

"Very well." Rahal took a deep breath. "I do have something I want to say . . . you filthy American whore."

Alexis gasped in surprise. Rahal ignored her and leaned forward to stare into the camera with a cold, hate-filled glare.

"When I said judgment is coming to America, I meant it will be delivered with a sword! All unbelievers will die, cut down by the righteous wrath of Allah's warriors! We will gut you like the pigs you are and sing praises to God for the rivers of your blood we spill! America will die and its corpse will rot! Allahu akbar! God is great!"

As soon as Rahal's rant had started, John Howard Stark had stiffened and started to take a step toward the prisoner. Kincaid leaned over the counter and touched the big Texan's arm. When Stark glanced at him, Kincaid shook his head.

He understood how Stark felt. He wanted to go over there and shut up that evil, raving lunatic, too.

But maybe this was a good thing, Kincaid mused. Maybe all the people who were sympathetic to the terrorists would see for themselves just how crazy they were.

The guards reacted to Rahal's tirade, too, moving in with their weapons ready in case the man tried to fling himself across the intervening space at Alexis Devereaux.

The stunned expression on Alexis's face was priceless. She had devoted herself to defending Rahal and his fellow terrorists, and now, without warning, he had thrown her sympathy back in her face and called her a filthy whore.

The abrupt 180-degree change in Rahal's attitude had even rendered Travis Jessup speechless, something that couldn't have happened very often. He stood there with his mouth hanging open as if he couldn't believe what he had just heard.

"Mr. Rahal . . ." Alexis began tentatively.

"Shut up, bitch. In my religion, women know their place. They know to keep silent."

"But . . . but I've always tried to help you! I've always been on your side."

Rahal smiled thinly and said, "Then you are a fool."

"Get him out of here." Baldwin barked the order to the guards. "Put him back where he came from."

A couple of the guards moved in, grabbed Rahal's arms, and jerked him to his feet.

"Don't," Alexis said. "Don't hurt him. Don't retaliate against him on my account."

"You really are slow to understand, aren't you?" Rahal said to her. "To me, you are nothing but an American sow, fit only for raping before your throat is cut."

"Out!" Baldwin bellowed. "Get him out!"

The guards hustled Rahal out of the library. Alexis still sat there looking like someone had slapped her across the face, but after a moment she blinked a couple of times, swallowed, and looked at Riley Nichols.

"You cut the camera when he started talking like that, didn't you?" Alexis asked. "You didn't allow that to go out live?"

"Why, I thought you wanted the live feed, Ms. Devereaux," Riley said in apparent innocence.

Kincaid heard the faint tone of mockery in the woman's voice. She had known very well what she was doing. Suddenly he liked Riley, even though the way she had looked at him earlier, as if she were trying to recall where she had seen him before, was worrisome. She was not only good-looking, she was smart as well.

Plenty smart enough not to agree with all of Alexis Devereaux's liberal claptrap.

"No!" Alexis practically wailed. "The country shouldn't have seen that. The man is obviously deranged. He's not a true representative of Islam—"

"He represents the part that wants to kill us and destroy our country," Stark spoke up. "And that's a whole lot bigger percentage than people like you want to admit."

"No! You heard what he said. Islam is a religion of peace."

"He also said he and his friends were going to put us all to the sword," Stark pointed out. "Hard to reconcile that with claims of being peaceful. Which was the lie you wanted to hear, Ms. Devereaux . . . and which was the truth?"

"I've had enough of this," Alexis snapped. Clearly, she had gotten over her shock. She stood up and went on, "I'm leaving."

Baldwin said, "No offense, ma'am, but I don't think any of us will be sorry to see you go."

Alexis scowled at him, then told the news crew, "Come on," and stalked out of the library with the others trailing her.

Riley Nichols gave Kincaid another of those unreadable glances over her shoulder as she left.

Baldwin looked at Kincaid and Stark, shook his head ruefully, and said, "Your visit has been more eventful than I intended, John Howard."

"That's all right, George," Stark said. "As you pointed out, things seem to happen that way."

Baldwin just grunted and followed the others out of the library, leaving Kincaid and Stark there alone.

Kincaid leaned on the counter and frowned in thought. He said, "You know, there's something about that performance that bothers me."

"Rahal's, you mean . . . or Ms. Devereaux's?"

"Both, actually, but I was talking about Rahal's. Ms. Devereaux's attitude just kind of makes me sick at my stomach. I'm thinking about the way Rahal suddenly changed his tune. Before he was mouthing the sort of feel-good platitudes that the Left always likes to hear from Muslims . . ."

"And then he was foaming at the mouth and revealing the way he really feels about us."

"Exactly," Kincaid said with a nod. "Did he just get tired of putting on an act? He wasn't able to keep the truth inside anymore?"

"Or was he thinking that everything is about to change and there wasn't any reason to lie?" Stark asked.

From the look on the big Texan's face, Kincaid could tell that Stark was starting to see things the way he did.

What was about to happen that had prompted Rahal's sudden change of attitude?

And how did he know?

Kincaid didn't have any answers to those questions, but the sudden, strident blare of a siren made both him and Stark straighten and go tense as their muscles instinctively readied for action.

"Is that—" Stark began.

"The alarm," Kincaid confirmed. "I don't know what's going on, but it's bound to be trouble. Bad trouble."

CHAPTER 26

Stark was glad Lucas Kincaid was with him as they left the prison library. Not only did Kincaid know his way around the place, but also he would be a good man to have at your side if all hell broke loose.

Or rather, *when* all hell broke loose, because Stark knew that generally such occurrences were inevitable.

Going all the way back to his service in Vietnam, Stark had been a good judge of character. He'd had to be in order to survive that jungle hellhole. Put your trust in the wrong man and you were as good as dead.

That had held true in all the fracases in which Stark had found himself in recent years, too.

He trusted Kincaid and was confident that the man would have his back, and vice versa.

As they hurried along a cement-walled corridor, Stark asked, "Is that siren what goes off when there's a breakout, like in the old prison movies?"

"Yeah, but that's not necessarily what it means. It's just an alarm. Could be for bad weather or something like that."

"The sky was just about clear when I drove out here today, and there weren't any storms in the forecast."

Stark paused. "But out here, a thunderstorm can blow up without much warning and spin off a tornado. Not many windows in here to let a fella keep an eye on the sky."

He didn't believe for a second, though, that the alarm was weather-related, and judging from the way Kincaid said, "Uh-huh," neither did he.

Kincaid led them to what appeared to be a command center for the correctional officers who worked here at Hell's Gate, and from there they followed the sound of angry voices to the prison's main entrance hall.

Alexis Devereaux had her hands balled into fists and planted against her hips as she confronted George Baldwin. It was an oddly inelegant pose for her, but she appeared to be so furious that she didn't care.

"You can't keep us locked up in here," she told Baldwin. "We're not some of your damned inmates."

"I told you, I can't allow you to leave until I know what the situation is out there," Baldwin responded. "As long as you're on the grounds of this facility, your safety and the safety of your companions is my responsibility."

"At least tell me what's going on," Alexis demanded.

"I wish I knew," Baldwin muttered. He noticed Stark and Kincaid and waved them over. "John Howard, I'm sorry to have to say this, but you can't leave right now."

"That's all right, George," Stark assured his old friend. "If there's something I can do to help . . ."

Baldwin drew Stark and Kincaid over to one side, ignoring the glare that Alexis directed at him as he did so. Lowering his voice so that only the two of them could hear him, he said, "It looks like the prison is under attack."

"By who?" Kincaid asked.

"A damned army, from what Cambridge told me. I sent him and Bert Frazier to check out the trouble in Fuego, but they didn't make it that far. They ran into a bunch of trucks and pickups headed this way. There's an armed force about to—"

From outside came the roar of an explosion, loud enough to make most of the people in the room jump. A panic-stricken Travis Jessup ran toward the glass entrance doors, but a couple of guards blocked his way. He looked out past them and yelled, "They're shooting out there! The prison is being invaded!"

Kincaid looked at Stark and said, "Rahal knew this was coming. That's why he acted like he did."

The tall, bearded sound technician said, "Yes, he did." He reached under the bush jacket he wore to pull out a pistol, which he pointed at George Baldwin and fired.

Phillip Hamil had hoped to get closer to the prison before his force's approach was discovered, but fate had intervened. Since Hamil was not one to question the workings of fate, he assumed Allah had a good reason for allowing the encounter with the prison van.

It didn't really matter anyway, he told himself. The infidels would have known soon enough that their day of judgment had arrived.

The men in the pickups and cars, the quicker, more maneuverable vehicles, struck first, charging the fence and the guard installations and peppering them with machine-gun and small-arms fire.

That served its purpose, which was to draw out as many of the guards as possible. As they gathered at forward positions to fight off the attack, Hamil ordered the big guns brought up. They were D-30 122 mm Howitzers, Soviet armament captured in Afghanistan forty years earlier, and despite their age they had been well-maintained, and functioned flawlessly.

Disassembled and shipped to Mexico by circuitous routes, the guns had been smuggled into the United

States over a period of months by the cartel allies of Hamil's cause. They had been put together again in remote, camouflaged locations hidden away as much as possible from satellite surveillance.

It helped that the organization had tendrils in the NSA and the Department of Defense, the same as it did in every other area of the federal government. Not sleeper agents, not exactly, because they were active operatives working against American interests under the cover of being part of the government. Not many dared question the fact that so many Muslims were now part of the military and most governmental agencies. To do so would be politically incorrect, not to mention career suicide in a Democratic administration, which was all Washington had anymore.

If any hint of what the organization had planned was about to come to light, there were agents in place to snuff it out right away. Hamil always smiled when he thought about how the Americans were already teetering on the brink of annihilation—and most of them had no idea of their peril.

Who had time to think about such things when there was so much celebrity gossip to keep up with?

Because of the Americans' unwitting complicity in their own destruction, Hamil now had these big guns mounted on the backs of heavy trucks, and as they rumbled up and took their places and their crews began the process of loading the guns and zeroing in on the prison, he was filled with a vast sense of satisfaction.

One of the men called to him, "We're ready, Doctor!"

Hamil nodded solemnly and said, "Then in the name of Allah . . . fire!"

The plastic gun—because that was what Kincaid was sure it was, probably taken apart before Joel Fanning came into the prison and then put back together while the sound tech was in the bathroom or something—popped as it went off. The report wasn't loud, wasn't threatening, but the rubber projectile the weapon fired would have killed Baldwin if it had hit him in the right place.

Luckily for the warden, Kincaid had reacted with instinctive, blinding speed and rammed his body into Baldwin's, knocking him aside.

The rubber bullet still struck Baldwin, but it thudded into his shoulder rather than ripping into his throat and maybe severing the jugular. Baldwin grunted in pain, stumbled, went to a knee.

Fanning tried to bring the gun to bear on Kincaid, but he was too slow. Kincaid swept his left arm up, caught it under Fanning's right forearm, and thrust it toward the ceiling.

At the same instant, Riley Nichols snap-kicked the side of Fanning's left knee, breaking it. Fanning started to yelp in pain, but the sound barely got started before the side of Kincaid's right hand slashed across his throat, crushing the larynx and causing him to gasp futilely for air as he collapsed to the floor.

Fanning's struggles lasted only a few seconds before a grotesque rattle came from his ruined throat. His body went lax.

"You—you killed him!" Alexis Devereaux cried in shock and horror.

"That's what he had in mind for us," Kincaid replied curtly. "He was working with that bunch out there."

He turned to Baldwin but saw that Stark was already helping his old friend. Stark helped Baldwin to a chair and pressed a handkerchief to the blood welling from the warden's shoulder wound.

More explosions hammered the prison. Kincaid felt the floor tremble under his feet. He scooped up the plastic gun Fanning had dropped and ran over to the entrance. The sliding doors there were thick, bulletproof glass, and through them Kincaid saw a holocaust of smoke and fire as shells screamed in and pounded the compound's outer perimeter.

The fence was already a tangled mess of wire. The concrete barriers designed to stop car and truck bombs were no match for artillery. They had been reduced to rubble.

A lot of good men were dead out there, Kincaid knew, but then he shoved that thought out of his mind.

If any of them were going to survive this attack, they had to act now.

He swung around to look at Stark and Baldwin and said, "We need to fall back to a more secure position."

Baldwin's rugged face was pale and drawn. The handkerchief Stark was holding to the wound was already soaked with blood. But Baldwin nodded and said, "Yeah, this part of the prison wasn't designed to stand up to an onslaught like that." He paused, then added bleakly, "I'm not sure any of it was. That's a damned artillery barrage!"

"What is going on here?" Alexis Devereaux screamed.

Travis Jessup stood to one side, microphone dangling forgotten in one hand as he blubbered in fear.

Riley was the only one of the visitors other than Stark who seemed to be keeping her head. She had the camera running, in fact, documenting the desperation in the prison's reception area.

"I can tell you what's going on here, Alexis," she said coolly. "Abu Rahal's buddies have come to get him out of jail."

"You don't know that," Alexis responded in a shrill, strident tone. "You can't make such an accusation. That's racial profiling—"

"Why don't you just shut the hell up, you stupid bitch?

You couldn't see the truth if it came up and bit you on the ass—which it's probably just about to do!"

Kincaid grinned. His admiration for Riley Nichols had just gone up yet another notch.

"The lady's right," Stark said. "This is a terrorist attack, plain and simple. I don't know how they got a blasted army together in the middle of West Texas, but those are fanatical Islamic terrorists out there, and their goal is to kill all of us and free their friends. That's the only explanation that makes any sense."

Alexis had been opening and closing her mouth like a fish. She struggled to regain control of herself with a visible effort and then said, "It can't be. It must be right-wing nutjobs! A militia! The—the Tea Party!"

"Now she's hysterical," Kincaid said dryly. "But we won't leave her for them to find. Let's go."

Baldwin looked at Kincaid with narrowed eyes and said, "You know what you're doing, son. You're in charge." He lifted his weak voice so the handful of other guards in the room could hear. "Kincaid is in charge, understand?"

Kincaid hesitated. He didn't want to be in command. He hadn't come to Hell's Gate to do anything except lie low and hope that someday the forces that were after him would forget about him.

That wasn't likely to happen, but after today it might not matter.

The explosions were creeping closer to the front of the prison as the enemy's guns got the range.

"Mr. Stark, help the warden," Kincaid said. He looked around, spotted a guard he recognized, a young man who appeared disheveled and shaken. "Cambridge! Are you all right?"

Cambridge nodded and stood up a little straighter.

"Yes, sir," he said.

"You've traded lead with those bastards. How many of them are there?"

Cambridge shook his head slowly and said, "I don't know. A lot. They've got machine guns and no telling what else."

"All right, we'll talk about it later. For now, you take Ms. Nichols, Ms. Devereaux, and Mr. Jessup and head for the maximum security wing. Mr. Stark, you and the warden go with them."

Alexis protested, "I don't have to do what you tell me."

Riley lowered the camera, took hold of Alexis's arm, and steered her toward the door leading back deeper into the prison.

"Right now you do, if you want to stay alive," Riley said.

Cambridge urged the still-sobbing Travis Jessup after them.

Stark had Baldwin on his feet again. Baldwin asked, "Why the max security wing, Lucas?"

"Because if we're going to make a stand, that's where we have the best chance of doing it," Kincaid said.

"That's where the prisoners they're after are being held."

"I know, but it's also the best place for us to defend."

"What are you going to do?"

"Round up as many guards as possible, break open the armory, and get ready for a gunfight. A *big* gunfight. And then we'll move as many of the prisoners as we can, too."

"Thank God you said that, son. The inmates are my responsibility. We can't just leave them behind to be slaughtered. And you know that bunch is going to kill every American they find in here, inmates, guards, who-ever."

Kincaid nodded and said, "I know."

He had dealt with that kind before. They wouldn't

leave any infidels alive behind them. They believed in a scorched-earth policy.

Another explosion rocked the prison as everyone fled. In a matter of moments, Kincaid thought, the softening-up would be over, and then a howling horde of fanatics would come pouring into the prison bent on red-handed slaughter. They used modern technology, but at heart they were the same medieval barbarians they had been a thousand, fifteen hundred years earlier. Their basic nature, the urge to kill those who didn't believe as they did in as bloody a manner as possible, never changed.

The Americans in Hell's Gate wouldn't go down without a fight, though.

CHAPTER 27

The word was slow to get out, but by the middle of Sunday afternoon it was becoming obvious that *something* had happened in the town of Fuego, Texas.

There had been a few frantic calls from townspeople to relatives, frightening tales of armed men in the streets killing anything that moved. Those calls had been cut ominously short.

The county sheriff had disappeared, along with several deputies dispatched to Fuego to investigate reports of a disturbance.

The Texas Rangers had sent in a Special Response Team in a pair of helicopters, neither of which had radioed back in. No one had heard from the Ranger commanding the SRT, either.

The news media had gotten wind of the puzzling situation, of course, and sent their own choppers to investigate. They had relayed back video footage of empty streets and several burned buildings that a quick Internet search identified as the locations of Fuego's churches. What appeared to be a perimeter of armed guards had been established around the town.

Several hundred people were visible from the air,

huddled together in the stands at the football field next to the high school. They were being guarded as well.

It didn't take long for the pilots of the news choppers to realize they shouldn't be flying over the town. Nobody had started shooting at them yet, but that could change at any second.

They banked and flew away from Fuego as fast as they could.

A short time later, Air Force jets arrived to establish a no-fly zone over the town. The order came directly from the Pentagon.

In less than an hour, the question was on the lips of practically everyone in the country.

What the hell was going on in Texas?

The house was located in the rugged Palo Pinto Mountains, fifty miles west of Fort Worth. The only way to get there was by following a winding gravel road barely wide enough for one vehicle for more than a mile. Flanking the primitive road on both sides was an impenetrable tangle of brush, briars, poison ivy, stinging weed, live oaks, and post oaks.

The house was low and rambling and appeared to be built of logs, but that was only the outer layer, to make it look rustic and help it blend in with its surroundings.

Under the logs were thick concrete walls reinforced with steel beams.

Inside, the rustic, hunting-lodge look continued in some of the rooms, including the living room with its massive stone fireplace. But other rooms were sleek and high-tech. Hidden satellite dishes provided access to the rest of the world. Surveillance cameras covered every inch of the hundred-acre property, which had a good creek running through it to provide water. Generators powered several freezers filled with more than a year's worth of food, but enough game roamed the hills that a man who was a good shot could live for a long time just by hunting and cultivating a small, hidden garden patch.

Colonel Thomas Atkinson was a good shot.

He lived quietly here, reading, writing, watching old movies and television shows. He cherry-picked what he wanted from modern life and disdained the rest. Some people might think that made him hypocritical, but it just seemed practical to him.

And he didn't give a rat's behind what people thought of him, anyway. If they wanted to figure he was a crazy survivalist whacko, then so be it. He knew the truth.

He hadn't turned his back on the world, but he only ventured out into it when he had to.

Today might be one of those days, he thought as he stood on his front porch, a tall, rangy man whose deceptively lean form possessed a wolfish speed and strength. His graying fair hair was cut short, as was his beard.

Atkinson held a cup of coffee in one hand and a buzzing cell phone in the other. The phone's display told him who was calling.

He brought it to his ear, thumbed the button to open the connection, and said, "Hello, Governor. I take it you know more about the situation than you did when you called earlier?"

"That's just it," Governor Maria Delgado said. "I don't know nearly enough. But something definitely has happened in Fuego. Something very bad."

"I was watching the news a little earlier. Sounds like the town's been taken over by terrorists. Washington's established a no-fly zone."

"Yes, and Homeland Security is going to throw up a cordon around the town."

"Did they ask you if they could do that?" Atkinson inquired dryly.

The question brought a disgusted snort from the governor.

"Washington doesn't ask permission for anything anymore, Colonel, you know that," she said. "It was established a long time ago that the Constitution no longer means anything. The president's word is law . . . as long as he's a Democrat."

"Dictatorship," Atkinson growled. The word put a bitter, sour taste under his tongue. "Too many people just don't realize it yet."

On the other end of the connection, Delgado sighed. Atkinson could practically see her rubbing her temples in weariness.

"That problem will have to be dealt with another day," she said. "Right now we have what may be an army of Islamic terrorists that has invaded and captured a town, for what purpose we don't know."

"Sure we do," Atkinson said. "Fuego commands the only approach to Hell's Gate."

"You've been doing your research."

"I believe in being prepared—just like the Boy Scouts."

Atkinson was about as far from being a Boy Scout as you could get. Career military, busted in the ranks time and again for brawling, insubordination, and ignoring direct orders. More than once, he had been perched on the razor's edge of a dishonorable discharge. Only one thing had saved him.

He got things done.

Eventually he had learned to control the demons raging inside him and operate within the system just enough to thrive. His record of success in hot spots all over the world had been enough to elevate him to the rank of colonel without his ever having to kiss ass or mouth politically correct platitudes like so many other officers had done.

Then the day had come when he'd walked away from all of it to retire to his native Texas, here in these rugged, tree-covered mountains, a place that was isolated yet within less than a two-hour drive from an international airport. Atkinson could get anywhere in the world from here and did so whenever a suitable job came along.

It was almost inevitable that a maverick governor like Maria Delgado would eventually have a need for his services. Over the past couple of years they had become friends as well.

Delgado knew that when it all hit the fan with the Feds, Atkinson was one person she could count on—and the feeling was mutual.

"You need boots on the ground out there, don't you?" he went on.

"Yes. How soon can you assemble your team and be ready to move if I need you to?"

Atkinson thought for a moment and then said, "We can be in position by nightfall."

"All right. By then we ought to have a better idea what's going on there and what Washington's reaction to it will be. If they're not going to do anything . . ."

"Yes, Governor?"

"I'll be damned," Maria Delgado said, "if I'm going to let a bunch of crazed, fanatical barbarians massacre innocent Texans and get away with it."

Atkinson chuckled and told her, "That's exactly what I thought you were going to say."

He broke the connection and started making the calls he had to make.

The broadcast networks had interrupted regular programming—even NFL coverage—in order to present special reports on the apparent violence in Fuego, even though details were still pretty sketchy. One pundit, looking properly solemn as he was interviewed by a news anchor, said, "It's a terrible shame, but I'm afraid as long as we have such a pervasive gun culture in this country, tragic incidents like this one are inevitable. When you have a bitter political minority that believes the only response to their continued lack of power is to pick up a gun—"

"Wait a minute," the token conservative on the panel—who was probably there mostly because she was an attractive woman—interrupted. "Are you saying that whatever has happened in this little town in Texas, Republicans are to blame?"

"Texas *is* one of the last Republican strongholds in the country." The response was delivered with a smug smirk.

"What about the speculation that this is a terrorist incident, that the shooters are in fact Middle Eastern—"

"If you want to resort to pandering to the right-wing extremists in this country and indulge in such blatantly bigoted racial profiling—"

"The call to the county sheriff's office from the local police dispatcher said the men doing the shooting were Arabs!"

"That's just a rumor, and I don't think we should give it any credence. Muslim leaders here in this country and around the world have assured us time and again that they want only peace. It's the homegrown terrorists we have to worry about, the gun nuts, the Bible-thumpers, the anti-government fanatics—"

"Like every mass murderer who went on a shooting spree in the past twenty years."

"Exactly!"

"All of whom, if they had any discernible political leanings at all, were left-wing Democrats."

In the booth, the director blurted, "Cut to a commercial!" then leaned back in his chair and cupped a palm over his forehead in distress.

"I should have shut her up one exchange earlier," he moaned to one of his assistants. "Letting that out on the air might cost me my job!"

"But wasn't what she said true?" the assistant asked. "Haven't all the mass shooters been Democrats?"

"That doesn't matter! The head of the network news division used to work at the White House!"

But a few minutes later it was all moot. At every network, broadcast and cable, except for one, the orders came down from corporate offices. For the time being, there was a total news blackout on the situation in Fuego.

Nobody had to ask where those orders originated. Nobody would come right out and say it . . .

But they came from Washington.

From the White House.

Phillip Hamil felt nothing but contempt for the man brought before him. One of the guards kicked the back of the infidel's right knee. The man gasped in pain as his leg buckled. The guard kicked him again, this time in the other leg.

The American wound up kneeling in front of Hamil—as was only proper.

Sooner or later, all Americans would kneel before the warriors of Allah . . . or else they would die.

Of course, many of them would die anyway, whether they knelt or not.

The biggest problem with America, as Hamil saw it, was that it had too many Americans in it.

He and his fellow holy warriors would do something about that. Today had been a good start.

For the moment, though, Hamil could make use of this man. He said, "What's your name?"

One of the guards prodded the American in the back

of the head with a machine gun muzzle to make him answer quicker.

"It . . . it's Lomax," the man said. "Bob Lomax."

"You work for the cable network whose logo was on the side of the truck where we found you?"

"That's right," the stocky, graying infidel answered. "I'm a . . . a news producer."

"Well, I have some news for you, Mr. Lomax," Hamil said with a faint, mocking smile. "Can you guess what it is?"

Lomax swallowed hard and said, "You and your friends have taken over the town?"

"That's right. And you're going to play a very important part in our plan."

"Me?" Lomax's voice was weak and terrified.

"Yes, of course." Hamil gestured to his men. "Help Mr. Lomax to his feet."

Finding the cable news van with its satellite transmission equipment was a stroke of luck. Hamil's men had brought along their own communications equipment, but what was in the van was even better. State of the art. Hamil was glad the vehicle hadn't been blown up as his men were blasting their way into the prison. As soon as he'd heard about it, he had ordered that the van and its occupant be brought to him.

When Lomax was standing again, shakily, Hamil went on, "You're going to help us get our message out to the American people, Mr. Lomax. You see, we're the ones who have been wronged here, and people will understand that once we've explained the truth."

"O-okay."

"You can broadcast live to the entire country, can't you?"

"I can send a live feed to New York. It . . . it's up to

somebody there to push the button that actually broadcasts it."

"I'm sure your associates in New York will cooperate." Hamil didn't mention that several executives at the very network under discussion had connections to his organization. "Do you need any special equipment besides what's in your truck?"

Lomax shook his head and said, "N-no, that's it. The truck has its own power source. I can bounce a signal off the satellite with it just fine."

"Very good," Hamil said with a nod. He turned away and added over his shoulders to the guards, "Bring Mr. Lomax and his van. We're going to the football field."

Only one network had the feed, but that didn't matter. The others became aware of it within seconds and their anchors began talking about it, even though being scooped and upstaged like this had to rankle.

In the White House, an aide charged into the President's living quarters but skidded to a halt when he saw that the nation's chief executive already had the TV on, tuned to the right channel.

A solemn-faced newsman was saying, "—warn you that we don't know exactly what you're about to see, but we take you now to Fuego, Texas, for this live statement."

The scene changed. A sleekly handsome man stood in the open with a football stadium behind him. There were no graphics on the screen except for the network's logo in the lower right-hand corner.

"My name is Dr. Phillip Hamil," the man on the screen said.

That came as no surprise to the President. Phillip Hamil had attended more than one state dinner in the White House. The President considered him a friend.

"Recently a great injustice has been done to my Muslim brothers," Hamil continued. "After being unjustly imprisoned by an oppressive, imperialist American government, some of them for many years, these political prisoners, these freedom fighters, have been incarcerated in a facility known by the unholy name of Hell's Gate. This is a slap in the face of all devout, peace-loving Muslims, and so we have been forced to take action to address this wrong."

The President's aide said, "I don't understand it. We arranged it so they could be tried in civilian courts. That's what they wanted. Some of them were probably going to be acquitted, for God's sake! Then they could sue the U.S. for millions of dollars."

"Some things are more important than money," the President said.

The aide stared at him in surprise.

On the TV, Hamil went on, "A group of my Muslim brothers and I, known from this day forward as the Sword of Allah, have occupied the town of Fuego, Texas, which is near the infamous prison where our other brothers have been locked up. This is a peaceful occupation. The citizens of Fuego are cooperating with us."

The aide said, "There are rumors that they've killed hundreds of people there."

The President lifted an elegantly manicured hand and motioned for quiet.

"At this time we are in the process of liberating the prison and freeing those political prisoners. When this is accomplished we will leave as peacefully as we came. In the meantime, to assure that there will be no interference with our efforts in this holy cause, the citizens of Fuego have volunteered to serve as living shields. They have gathered here, in this stadium you see behind me, and any efforts by the American authorities to prevent the Sword of Allah from completing its quest will result in a terrible tragedy."

The aide couldn't hold it in. He blurted, "Good Lord! He just threatened to kill all those people if anybody tries to stop them! He's probably planning to blow up that football stadium!"

The President turned his eyes away from the TV screen just long enough to give the aide a steely-eyed glare. He said, "You should know better than that, Dan. Our Muslim brothers wouldn't do such a thing. Islam is a religion of peace."

"But sir, he said—"

"Dan . . . you're starting to sound like a Republican."

The aide's eyes widened, his face turned pale, and he swallowed hard. There was no mistaking the threat in the President's voice.

On TV, Phillip Hamil was saying, "—accordance with sharia law, all legal and security matters in Fuego are now under control of the Sword of Allah. In the name of religious freedom, we demand the cooperation of all local, state, and federal authorities. All outside military and law enforcement personnel are therefore banned within a ten-mile radius of Fuego until we have achieved our aims, which are holy and legitimate. Any infringement of this ban will result in drastic action for which the followers of Islam are not responsible. Control of the region will be returned to those authorities when the will of Allah is done."

He paused, then concluded, "*Allahu akbar!* God is great!"

The satellite feed went dead.

The President picked up a remote and muted the TV sound as news anchors and pundits began blathering excitedly. He said, "The Pentagon has already issued a no-fly order around the town, correct?"

"Yes, sir. And Homeland Security has established a

perimeter, but I'm not sure if it's as far back as what Dr. Hamil just demanded. We didn't know exactly what they were going to want."

"See to it that the perimeter is pulled back to the full ten miles. In addition, I want everything in the *next* five miles beyond that evacuated. Use the Army if we have to."

"Some people will say that you're capitulating to terrorists."

The President waved that objection away as if it were unimportant.

"Would those people ever vote for me anyway, no matter what I did?"

"No, sir. But after the Casa del Diablo affair, you need to be careful about using the military here at home."

The President's head lifted, and an arrogant, supercilious sneer appeared on his face.

"Elections have consequences, Dan. We learned that ten years ago. I'm the President. I can do anything I damned well please, and fifty-one percent of the people who bother to vote will still love me and vote for me. So what else matters?"

What else indeed?

One thought kept nagging at the back of the aide's brain as he hurried to do his master's bidding, though.

Those people down in Texas, the ones at the prison and the ones in the little town . . .

They were on their own.

CHAPTER 28

Texas Ranger Lt. Dave Flannery came swimming back up out of darkness, a clinging black oblivion that seemed to have had him in its grip forever. He winced as light struck his eyes, then tried to say something and grimaced again because of the pain in his mouth and across his face.

He remembered seeing a piece of debris flying across the helicopter's cabin at him just before he blacked out during the chopper's crash landing. Obviously that debris had knocked him unconscious.

"The lieutenant looks like he's comin' around," somebody said. The words sounded hollow and far away to Flannery. Too many loud noises had partially deafened him. He could only hope that his hearing would get back to normal as time passed.

Squinting against the light, he looked around and saw to his surprise that he was sitting in a gully, with his legs stretched out in front of him and his back propped against a dirt bank about ten feet tall.

Quite a few people were clustered around him, including a couple of men in khaki police uniforms, a slender, brown-haired woman who looked like she might be pregnant, and a big, blond teenage kid whose eyes were red and swollen from crying.

"What . . ." Flannery forced out through his painfully swollen lips. "Where . . ."

"Take it easy, Ranger," the lean, sandy-haired cop said as he hunkered on his heels in front of Flannery. "You're all right for now. Something clouted you a good one across the face, but other than that you don't seem to be hurt."

"Who . . . are . . . you?"

"Officer Lee Blaisdell, Fuego PD." He inclined his head toward the other cop, who was young and, Flannery now realized, looked like he might have Down syndrome. "This is Officer Raymond Brady, our dispatcher."

"Where are . . . the rest of your officers?"

Talking was getting a little easier for Flannery now that he was using his mouth more, but he felt a warm trickle of blood on his chin, too, as it oozed from his cracked, swollen lips.

"I'm afraid we may be the only ones left," Blaisdell said, "except for one other fella who's down at the end of this arroyo keepin' an eye out for those murderin' bastards."

"Where . . . are we?"

"About half a mile northeast of Fuego High School. That's where we pulled you and some of your men out of that helicopter that crashed in the middle of the football field."

"I . . . remember. You say you have . . . the other members of the SRT?"

"The Special Response Team? We got five of you out of there, Lieutenant. The pilot and one of your men were already dead. And I'm sorry to say, another one died of his injuries on the way out here. But there are four of you left who aren't in too bad of a shape, three cops, and six members of the Fuego High School Fighting Mules football team." Blaisdell clicked his tongue and shook his head. "Thirteen fellas to take back a town from a whole army of terrorists. That's pretty unlucky odds no matter which way you look at it."

The brunette said, "There are fourteen of us. You're forgetting about me, Lee. Fifteen if you count Bubba here."

She smiled and pointed at her stomach.

"Dadblast it, Janey—" Lee Blaisdell began.

She ignored him and said to Flannery, "I'm Janey Blaisdell, Lieutenant. And you might not think it to look at me, but I'm a better shot than Lee here."

"I wish I could say I'm pleased to meet you, Mrs. Blaisdell," Flannery said. "But under the circumstances . . ."

"I know," she assured him. She held out a half-full bottle of water. "I'm sure you're probably thirsty."

"I don't know if I can drink with my mouth like this. And I'll get blood on the bottle—"

"I don't reckon any of us are too worried about a little blood right now," Lee said. "There's liable to be a lot more spilled before this is over."

Lee spent the next fifteen minutes explaining to Lt. Flannery as much as he knew about what was going on in Fuego. One of the other Rangers had told Lee what Flannery's name was while the lieutenant was still unconscious.

While he was kneeling down doing that, Janey stood beside and a little behind him and rested her hand on his shoulder. They had been doing that a lot ever since Lee had rushed into the little rental house with Raymond and Martin right behind him. Touching each other, reassuring themselves that the other one was still alive and unharmed—at least for now.

After all the terrible things that had happened, it was a little hard to believe that both of them were still all right.

Lee didn't have any illusions about things staying that way, though.

While he and Janey were still hugging each other, they had heard the explosion from the nearby football field and since Lee wanted to get out of Fuego anyway and that was on the way, they had gone to check it out.

By the time they'd gotten there, the helicopter was burning, Chuck Gibbs was dead, and half a dozen players from the football team were standing on the sidelines with some unconscious lawmen, not knowing what to do next.

Somebody had had to take charge. Lee didn't particularly want the job, but he figured he was the one to do it.

A whole convoy of vehicles might attract attention, he'd decided. So they had piled the unconscious Rangers in the back of Ernie Gibbs's pickup, along with the weapons the football players had taken from the chopper before it blew up, and everybody had climbed in the back with them except Ernie, Lee, and Janey, who sat between the two men while Ernie drove.

The kid struggled to hold back tears of grief over his brother's death, but he was keeping himself pulled together as well as could be expected.

Lee told Ernie to head for the arroyo where they were hiding now. He was familiar with the place from all the times he had hunted jackrabbits out here. They had followed a dirt road for a quarter-mile or so, then Ernie had driven through a barbed-wire fence and headed across country.

The hole in the fence was liable to attract attention, and the pickup left tracks on the ground that could be followed, but those things couldn't be helped.

Maybe the bloodthirsty sons of bitches who had taken over the town would be content with the havoc they had already wreaked. Maybe they wouldn't come looking for any stragglers who had gotten away.

Lee was going to cling to those hopes, even though logically he considered them unlikely.

Now Flannery had regained consciousness and Lee was more than willing to turn over command to him. He said as much to the Ranger.

"You're in charge, Lieutenant. What do you think we should do?"

Flannery frowned in thought and said, "We need to get in touch with somebody who can help us. Did you get any radios out of the chopper before it blew up?"

Lee looked at the kids. A couple of them shook their heads, and Spence Parker said, "No, we just grabbed guns and threw them out. That's what Ernie's brother told us to do."

"What about cell phones?" Flannery asked. "You've got to have cell phones."

"Already thought of that," Lee said. "Nobody's getting a signal. My guess is that bunch took out the towers somehow. They want to control all the communications in and out of town. Classic military strategy."

"You served?" Flannery asked.

Lee grimaced slightly and said, "Uh, no, not really. But I've played a lot of war-themed video games, and not just first-person shooters, either."

Lee thought he heard Flannery mutter something that sounded like "Lord help us." He tried not to take offense. Sure, he wasn't some ex–Navy SEAL or anything, just a small-town cop who'd barely made it through the community college classes to get certified, but he thought he had done all right so far.

He was alive, wasn't he? A lot of folks weren't. Maybe that was just the luck of the draw, but it was something to consider, anyway. He had gone up against those terrorist bastards and survived.

It might be a different story next time, though.

"There's communications equipment at the police station, right?" Flannery asked.

"Well, yeah, sure, but I don't think we can reach it. Even if we did, the enemy is bound to be in control of it."

"Who *is* the enemy? Do any of you know?"

"Not for sure," Lee said.

"They're Arab terrorists," Ernie put in. "That's what Chuck told me."

"I've seen some of 'em close up." Lee tried not to shudder when he remembered how he'd blown that fella's head off with the Mossberg. "Too close for my taste. They all looked Middle Eastern to me."

Flannery nodded and said, "I think there's a good chance that's what we're facing, all right. How many of them?"

"A lot. Dozens. Maybe hundreds. Maybe even more. It's a small army, Lieutenant. And before you can ask me what they want, I don't know. Maybe just to kill a bunch of Americans. They've been doing a pretty good job of it so far."

"No, it's got to be more than that," Flannery said as he shook his head. "It must have something to do with the prison."

Janey said, "Of course it does. The government just took a bunch of terrorists out there and locked them up. Didn't it ever occur to them that something like this might happen? What were they thinking in Washington?"

"They were thinking about how they can get re-elected next time, so they can continue transformin' America into something it was never meant to be," Lee said. "That's all they ever think about in Washington. You can't expect any common sense from that bunch, Janey, you know that."

"Yeah, but it's like they—" Janey paused, her eyes widening in realization. "It's almost like they expected something like this to happen. Wanted it to happen."

"Let's don't get ahead of ourselves," Flannery warned. "Right now let's see if we can think of some way to strike back at them, weaken their hold on the town."

Lee doubted if that was going to be possible. He'd been giving some thought to continuing to flee. Getting as far away from Fuego as possible. It wasn't like they could do any real good here, and he had a couple of very important people to consider: his wife—and their unborn child.

They could all get back in Ernie's pickup and head for the interstate highway, which was about fifty miles away. If they went across country and avoided the roads, he didn't think anybody would stop them.

He was about to suggest that when Pete Garcia, one of the football players who had been standing guard at the mouth of the arroyo with Martin, came running toward them and called urgently, "They're coming! The bad guys are coming!"

CHAPTER 29

Colonel Tom Atkinson walked into a truck-stop restaurant next to the Interstate and found half a dozen men and two women waiting for him. They were seated in a circular booth in a corner, casually dressed, drinking coffee and talking. Not many people would have looked twice at them.

Nobody would have dreamed what they were capable of when they needed to be.

Atkinson slid in beside the attractive black woman on the right end of the circle and said, "You folks made good time."

"When you call, Colonel, we come a-runnin'," one of the men said. He was in his thirties, with a roundish, deceptively friendly face to go with his southern drawl.

"I appreciate that, Sergeant Porter."

"This is about what's going on in that little town south of here, isn't it?" asked one of the other men. His half-Japanese ancestry wasn't very visible in his features, but if you knew him you could see it in the slight slant of his eyes.

"That's right. The governor wants us to take a look around and be ready to go in there if we need to."

"Oh, we'll need to," the black woman said. She nodded toward the flat-screen TV hung on the wall behind the restaurant's counter.

Atkinson looked at it and saw that the camera was focused on a large mob of people clogging a street somewhere, yelling angrily and waving anti-American signs.

"Somewhere overseas?"

"Chicago," the woman beside him said. "There have been similar demonstrations in Boston, New York, Philadelphia, Houston, San Francisco, and Los Angeles. All within the past hour."

One of the other men, burly and bald with a little goatee, said, "Right now the over/under on how long it takes for them to turn into full-fledged riots is forty-five more minutes."

"These demonstrations didn't spring up simultaneously," Porter said. "Some of the signs mention the Sword of Allah. That's what the bunch that's taken over Fuego is calling itself."

Atkinson nodded and said, "I heard about Dr. Hamil's broadcast. I didn't see it myself, but I can't say I'm surprised that he's part of this. He's been apologizing for Islamic terrorism for years now. I always figured he was tied in with some of the terror networks. His buddies in Washington refused to open their eyes and see that for themselves, though."

"Demonstrations like this take time to put together. They were prepared. They knew exactly what was going to happen today. Anybody with any common sense ought to realize that."

"You're talking about Washington, Porter," the other woman said. "The ones who aren't actually trying to undermine the country are willfully blind to anything done by the ones who are."

A waitress approached the table. Atkinson told her to bring him coffee. He didn't have much of an appetite right now.

Besides, if they were going into action, as they very well might be, he didn't want a bellyful of food weighing him down.

Once he had his coffee, Atkinson said, "No bet on the over/under. Those so-called peaceful demonstrations are going to turn ugly, sooner rather than later. And they'll have exactly the effect they're supposed to have: they'll scare all the liberal politicians and make them think we have to give the terrorists whatever they want, just to maintain a false illusion of safety and security."

"What the hell happened to this country?" Porter said, his voice edged with dismay and disbelief. "How did things get like this?"

"Media and popular culture made an alliance with the Democrats," Atkinson said. "As for the rest of us . . . hell, boy, we were just voices crying in the wilderness. That's all. Just lonesome voices crying in the wilderness."

The President spoke to the nation from the Oval Office a few minutes before three o'clock. He knew exactly what he was going to say, and he was calm as he faced the camera and waited for the red light to come on.

The Vice President, the Secretary of State, the Attorney General, and the majority leaders of the House and Senate were on hand, out of camera range. There were no representatives from the permanent minority party in the room . . . but hey, who needed Republicans to do anything, anyway, the President thought. He had enough votes locked up in both houses of Congress to cram through any legislation he wanted.

Lately he hadn't even gone to that much trouble. Why bother passing laws when he could just issue an executive order or have one of his agencies write a new regulation to accomplish whatever his goal happened to be this week?

It went against security protocols for this many top-level members of the government to be in the same place at the same time, especially on an impromptu basis like this when the Secret Service hadn't had time to put the usual precautions into action.

However, the President wasn't a bit worried.

He knew they were in no danger.

The red light came on, and with practiced ease he put a solemn, concerned, but confident expression on his face. He said, "My fellow citizens."

Not "My fellow Americans," as previous presidents had traditionally opened their statements to the country. That was too nationalistic, too . . . patriotic.

"I wanted to let you know that the government is aware of the events taking place today in the town of Fuego, Texas. At this point we have few details, and it is not the policy of this administration to engage in rumor-mongering."

No, when this administration wanted to lie to the American people, it just lied straight-out, as the previous several administrations had—all of which lying had been given a pass by the media and enough members of the public to keep them in office. The President knew *that* quite well, too.

"It appears that there has been some sort of civil disturbance in Fuego, fueled by the spontaneous protest of what is considered a grievous wrong by certain segments of our population. As a free and open society, we must always allow for the expression of dissenting points of view."

Unless it was a point of view that disagreed with the opinions of the ruling elite, in which case it would be silenced and quashed as quickly and brutally as possible—all for the common good, of course, as the President and his cronies constantly assured themselves.

"However, when dissent takes the form of violence, the authorities have no choice but to step in and put a stop to it. But only after careful consideration of everything that is involved and in a manner designed to protect the rights of everyone, including any citizens who are upset by the unjust treatment of their brothers."

The Vice President frowned and shuffled his feet a little. That "unjust treatment" phrase bothered him, as the President had known it would. That was like the government admitting that it had been wrong to throw all those terrorists who wanted to destroy the country behind bars. That idea made the Veep uneasy.

But he wouldn't do or say anything about it. The President was confident of that. The man craved power too much to rock the boat, even the illusory power of the vice presidency, which was about as much use as a bucketful of warm spit, as an ancient legislator had once termed it.

The President, you see, knew his political history, whether he respected it or not.

"Because of this need for caution, I have directed the Department of Homeland Security to establish a ten-mile perimeter around the town of Fuego—"

Making it sound like his own idea, rather than giving in to Phillip Hamil's demands.

"—and the Air Force is enforcing a no-fly zone over the town while our investigation into this matter continues. Both the Attorney General and the Secretary of

State are taking leading roles in this investigation, and they will be reporting directly to me as we work out the best way to proceed. Rest assured that this matter *is* being dealt with, and it is absolutely no threat to the sovereign security of our nation. Thank you, and good afternoon."

No "God Bless the United States of America," either.

But at least he hadn't said anything about Allah.

This time, he thought to himself with a secret smile.

The day was coming, though, when the infidels would discover just who they had elected in return for promises of free . . . well, free *everything*.

But for now, things were proceeding according to plan, and by the time the authorities got around to actually doing anything about what was going on in Fuego and at Hell's Gate, it would all be over.

Lee stood up and turned to see what Pete Garcia was talking about, but Flannery said, "Help me up, damn it."

The lieutenant lifted a hand. Lee clasped his wrist and hauled him to his feet.

Together they hurried to meet Pete, the Mules' placekicker and backup quarterback. Over his shoulder, Lee told his wife, "Janey, you stay back."

She looked like she wanted to argue, but she nodded and then bit worriedly at her lower lip.

"What is it, Pete?" Lee asked.

"There are jeeps coming, Officer Blaisdell," the young man replied. "There are guys with guns in them."

"How many?"

"I couldn't really tell, the way they were packed in there—"

"How many jeeps?" Lee interrupted.

"Oh. Uh, two. That's all I saw."

Lee nodded.

"Can't be any more than four or five men in each vehicle," he said.

"That means we outnumber them," Flannery put in. "Do we have guns enough to go around?"

"We do," Lee said. He turned his head and looked along the arroyo, which had a bend in it a couple of hundred yards away. "Are you thinkin' what I'm thinkin'?"

"Ambush," Flannery said.

"Yeah." Lee licked his lips, cupped his hands around his mouth, and called, "Martin!"

Martin Corey and the boys at the mouth of the arroyo looked at him. Lee waved for them to come on in. They did so, breaking into a trot as they hurried along the sandy bed of the dry wash.

"Everybody climb into the pickup," Flannery ordered. "Where's my rifle?"

"In the truck bed," Lee told him. "That's where all the weapons the kids recovered from the helicopter are."

As the others began clambering into the back of the pickup, Ernie Gibbs came over to Lee and asked solemnly, "Are we gonna fight now?"

"Yeah, we're gonna fight now," Lee told him. "Are you all right, Ernie?"

Grim-faced, the big young man nodded. "My friends call me Gibby. Sometimes Chuck called me that, too."

"All right, Gibby. Get in the truck and drive up there past the bend. We're gonna wait around there for them."

"Hold on," Flannery said with a frown on his face. "That's not going to work. They'll follow the tire tracks into the arroyo, all right. They're obviously out looking for anybody who got away from town. But if they've got any sense at all, they won't go charging blindly around that bend into a trap."

Spence asked, "How do we know they have any sense? They're just a bunch of sheet-wearing camel jockeys."

"I haven't seen any sheets or camels," Lee said. "Just guns. A bunch of guns."

"From everything we know about them, they're not amateurs," Flannery said. "They'll stop before they get to the bend and send some men to check it out. That's when some of us will hit them from behind."

Flannery pointed to an area where part of the bank had caved in, leaving chunks of sandstone as large as boulders scattered around, and went on, "We'll be hiding over there."

Lee understood now what the Ranger was getting at. He said, "Then when the shootin' starts, the rest can open up from farther along the arroyo, and we'll have the bastards in a cross fire."

"Exactly," Flannery said as he jerked his head in a nod. "I'll stay back here. The ones who stay behind will be running the biggest risk of discovery."

"I'll stay, too," Lee said without hesitation.

"Lee, no," Janey said. "It'll be safer around the bend."

"I'll be fine," he told her, wishing that he felt as confident as he was trying to sound. "We need a couple more volunteers."

"I'll do it," Spence Parker said.

"And me," one of the Rangers put in.

"All right," Flannery said. "Let's get busy. We don't have much time."

Lee knew that was true. He could already hear the growling of the jeeps' engines as the vehicles approached the arroyo.

The four men remaining behind took rifles from the back of the pickup and ran over to the big sandstone slabs. Erosion had softened and rounded the rocks, but they were still large enough to provide some cover. Lee and his three companions knelt behind them as the pickup, with Gibby at the wheel, Janey beside him, and everybody else packed into the back, roared off around the bend.

As they waited, Lee looked over at Flannery and said, "I know we're lawmen, but we don't have to read 'em their rights before we open fire on those sons o' bitches, do we?"

"The only right they've got is for us to blow their damned brains out," Flannery said.

CHAPTER 30

Only a couple more minutes passed before the jeeps appeared at the mouth of the arroyo. They had slowed down, and now they stopped as they entered the dry wash.

The terrorists were being careful, Lee thought, checking the place out before they drove in any farther.

Lt. Flannery had been right. Men that cautious wouldn't have just driven blindly around the bend without doing some reconnaissance first.

Lee glanced over at his companions. Flannery looked a little shaky, which wasn't surprising considering that he had been knocked out for a good while. Anybody hit hard enough to be unconscious for that long was at risk for brain damage.

The other Ranger, whose name Lee didn't know, seemed to be okay. Spence was obviously scared—the kid had probably never had to deal with anything worse in his life than the righteous wrath of the daddy of some cheerleader he was messing around with—but he noticed Lee watching him and gave a nod to indicate that he was all right.

Lee's hands were a little sweaty on the rifle he

gripped. In the fight at the police station, he hadn't really had time to be scared or even think that much about what was going on. He had just reacted and done what he had to in order to save his life.

Now he had a chance to ponder what was about to happen, and he was scared, too. Not so much for himself, although that was certainly part of it, but more for Janey and for little Bubba, as they jokingly referred to the baby growing inside her.

What would happen to them if he didn't make it through this fight?

What would happen to everybody who was left if the monsters who had invaded Fuego weren't stopped?

Why didn't somebody come to help them? The outside world couldn't have just *abandoned* them, could it? Surely help was on the way from somewhere.

Lee wished he could believe that, but some instinct told him that might not be the case. He and the others might truly be on their own, outnumbered by a brutal, bloodthirsty enemy.

He forced himself back into the moment. He and his companions could only fight one battle at a time.

And that battle was imminent, because the jeeps were on the move again, rolling forward slowly as the armed men riding in them watched the arroyo's banks. They were alert to the possibility of an ambush.

But they were looking too high, Lee realized. They didn't see him and the other three men hunkered behind these rocks.

Lee kept his head down as the jeeps went past. He didn't catch more than a glimpse of the men in the vehicles, but that was enough to tell him they were the same sort he had encountered back in town. Terrorists of Middle Eastern origin, no doubt about that.

He wondered briefly whether they were in the country legally or had been smuggled in, most likely across the Mexican border. Such things were more common than most people realized. In fact, a year or so earlier a group of Islamic terrorists had come too damned close to setting off a suitcase nuke in downtown San Antonio.

Of course, it was possible these killers were the home-grown variety. Despite all the bad things some folks said about the country, the United States was still the most welcoming nation in the world—sometimes to its own detriment. Some of these terrorists might well have been born here, sons and grandsons of legal immigrants who repaid their adopted land's generosity and hospitality by raising their offspring to hate America and want to see it destroyed.

We are all immigrants, the liberals liked to say, and there was some truth to that.

But the Irish, the Italians, the Germans, the Poles, and all the other various countrymen who had come to the United States in the past two and a half centuries had not done so with the express intent of remaking the country into a new version of their own homeland. They had come to America to take part in it, to become the building blocks of a new culture that for a time had been the strongest and most vital in the history of the world.

Too many of the immigrants in the past fifty or sixty years hadn't wanted that. And some of them actually wanted to bring it down.

It was entirely possible that was what the people of Fuego were facing today, Lee thought as the jeeps rolled on toward the bend in the arroyo.

The vehicles slowed again and then stopped. Lee heard the gunmen calling to each other in their native language, whatever that was.

Carefully, he rose enough to peer over the rock that sheltered him.

The jeeps had halted about ten yards short of the bend. A couple of men had hopped down from one of the vehicles and were now proceeding warily on foot, the automatic weapons in their hands held ready.

The other members of the bunch were visibly tense as they waited for their scouts to have a look around the bend.

Lee glanced over at Flannery. The Ranger gave him a curt nod.

It was time.

Lee, Flannery, Spence, and the other Ranger all stood up. The terrorists hadn't thought to have somebody keep an eye out behind them, so no one noticed as the four men aimed their weapons. The range was about eighty yards, not easy shots, but not that difficult, either, for experienced shooters.

Flannery didn't give an order.

He just opened fire.

The other three men did likewise. Lee had settled his rifle's sights on the back of a man sitting in one of the jeeps, and he didn't hesitate in pulling the weapon's trigger three times, fast but controlled. The rifle was a semiautomatic, and the three shots ripped out in less than two heartbeats.

Without waiting to see what effect those three rounds had, Lee shifted his aim and fired three more, then did that again.

Only then did he pause and look to see that half a dozen of the terrorists had toppled off the jeeps and now lay sprawled on the ground.

The other two men who had still been with the vehicles had jumped off and were now using the jeeps for cover as they opened up with their machine guns. The two who had been about to reconnoiter around the bend now came running back, the weapons in their hands spraying lead as well.

Lee and his companions ducked quickly as bullets smacked into the sandstone boulders.

With a full-throated roar from its engine, the pickup came around the bend, sand spitting up from its tires. The football players in the back opened fire with hunting rifles and shotguns, a couple of them shooting over the top of the cab and the others in the back leaning out to the sides. Martin and the other two Rangers joined in, but Lee didn't see Raymond.

That was all right. The kid didn't need any more blood on his hands.

To Lee's surprise, he saw Janey extending her arm out the pickup's passenger window. She held the service weapon he had given her earlier, and it jumped and spit as she fired it at the terrorists.

The barrage killed three of the men in a matter of seconds, knocking them off their feet to land in bloody heaps next to their comrades.

The lone survivor broke away from the jeeps and tried to run in blind terror, but Gibby slammed the pickup's grille into his back, knocked him down, and ran over him.

Then backed up for good measure.

Lee and the others left the boulders and trotted over to join their companions. Flannery and one of the other Rangers checked the bodies to make sure all the terrorists were dead.

They were. The odds against the Americans had just gone down by ten men.

Unfortunately, that wasn't enough to mean much.

"Everybody all right?" Flannery asked. He got nods and a chorus of assents in response.

Lee went over to the pickup and said to Janey through the open window, "I figured you'd stay back there around the bend where it was safe."

"You did, did you?" she asked. "Well, you should have known better."

He tried to keep a tight rein on the anger he felt welling up inside him.

"You weren't just risking your own life, you know," he said.

"You think I don't know that?" she snapped at him. "But what kind of life is Bubba going to have if we don't stand up—all of us—and fight back against the monsters who want to destroy us?"

Lee didn't have any answer for that.

Flannery leaned against one of the jeeps as he seemed to be dizzy for a second, but then he recovered and said, "We've got more weapons now, and a couple of jeeps, to boot. Officer Blaisdell, you know where people live around here, don't you?"

"Sure," Lee said. "There are some farms and ranches around. Plus some oil and gas camps. Are you thinkin' we need to recruit some more folks?"

"You need an army to fight an army," Flannery said. "Do you think they'll fight?"

Lee couldn't help but grin.

"They're good Texans," he said. "They'll fight." He glanced at Janey and thought about what she had just said. "Ain't nothin' like a bunch of Texans for standin' their ground."

Inside Hell's Gate Prison, George Baldwin said, "Where is it we're going again, John Howard?"

Stark had an arm around Baldwin's waist, helping him along a concrete-walled corridor. He worried that his old friend was going into shock because of the loss of blood from that shoulder wound.

In the movies and TV, people got shot in the shoulder all the time without its seeming to bother them all that much, but somebody could bleed out from a wound like that just as they could from any other injury.

Mitch Cambridge was leading the group. Alexis Devereaux, Travis Jessup, and Riley Nichols followed him, then Stark and Baldwin. They had run into several other guards along the way, and Cambridge had sent them to find Lucas Kincaid and help him get ready to defend the prison.

"We're going to the maximum security wing, George," Stark said.

"Why there?"

"Kincaid thinks it'll be the easiest place for us to defend, and I agree with him. From what I saw, I don't think we're going to be able to keep those fellas from getting into the prison."

"The inmates . . ."

"Kincaid's going to round up as many of them as he can," Stark said. He couldn't keep the grim expression off his face. There was only so much Kincaid could do to get the other inmates to safety.

It was likely there would be a bloodbath inside Hell's Gate before the day was over.

They came to the recreation room, and Stark was surprised to see that several inmates were still there, along with a couple of guards. Albert Carbona, the old-time mobster, saw Baldwin and exclaimed, "Mother of God, Warden, you been shot!"

One of the guards asked in a nervous voice, "What's going on? We heard all sorts of commotion."

"The prison's under attack," Cambridge told the man. "It . . . it looks like terrorists are trying to take it over."

"Terrorists!" Billy Gardner, Carbona's massive bodyguard when they were both still on the outside, gaped at the newcomers. "You mean like . . . blow stuff up and kill a bunch of people, that kind of terrorists?"

"There ain't any other kind," Cambridge snapped. He

frowned, looking like he was in way above his head here and knew it, but after a second a new determination came over his face. "Come on. You're all coming with us. We're headed for the max security wing."

Stark approved of that decision. Sending the prisoners— Carbona, Gardner, J.J. Lockhart, and Simon Winslow— back to their cells might well be the same as signing their death warrants.

And none of them, as far as Stark knew, had been sent to Hell's Gate to be executed.

"Wait a minute," one of the other guards said. "Who put you in charge, Cambridge? The rest of us all have more experience than you. Warden?"

Baldwin stood a little straighter. He said, "Mitch has already fought those bastards and lived to tell about it. Do what he says."

That was enough to make the guards cooperate. They, along with the four inmates, fell in with the group and hurried through the corridors toward the maximum security wing.

Stark was glad somebody was leading the way who knew where he was going. Even though he had gone along when Baldwin had shown the wing to Alexis Devereaux and the news crew, he might not have been able to find it again, even with his good sense of direction.

Cambridge took them right to it, however, slapped the button on the intercom to communicate with the guards inside the sally port, and said urgently, "Let us in!"

A helmeted guard looked through the bulletproof, steel-mesh-reinforced glass in the door's small window, staring at the desperate group in surprise.

"What's going on out there?" a voice crackled over the intercom. "Warden, is that you?"

"Help me, John Howard," Baldwin muttered. Stark tightened his grip and moved forward so that Baldwin was in the forefront of the group.

"The prison is under attack," Baldwin said. His voice was weak but still held an undeniable note of authority. "We're going to fort up, here in this wing. Reinforcements are on the way."

"Under attack?" The guard inside the sally port sounded like he couldn't believe it. "We heard some sort of racket and felt the ground trembling but never dreamed . . . Hell, Warden, we'd just about convinced ourselves it was an earthquake!"

"Believe me, there's nothing natural about this disaster." Baldwin took a deep breath and winced as it hurt him. "Protocol is out the window now, boys. Are all the inmates in lockdown?"

"Yes, sir."

"Keep them that way. Under no circumstances are any of them to be let out."

Trembling, Travis Jessup said, "Why . . . why don't you just let them go? That's what their friends are here for, isn't it? They just want to turn those other terrorists loose."

"Political prisoners," Alexis said, stubborn in her mind-set even now. "They're political prisoners."

Jessup ignored her and went on, "If you just turn them loose, maybe the others will go away and leave us alone."

Riley said, "That's not going to happen, Travis. Even if they get what they want, they're going to kill us all. That's just . . . what they do."

"Ms. Nichols is right," Stark said. "Our only chance to survive is to hold them off until help gets here. This place gives us the best chance of doing that."

"You heard the man," Baldwin said.

"Yes, sir," came the response over the intercom. A motor came to life, and the sally port's massive outer door began to slide back.

Baldwin motioned for everybody else to go through

first. He and Stark hung back to be the last ones into the maximum security wing. As they entered haltingly due to Baldwin's injury, the warden said, "Do you really think help is on the way, John Howard? The way the country is now?"

"I'd like to think so, George," Stark said. "But to tell you the truth . . . I just don't know."

CHAPTER 31

As Lucas Kincaid hurried through the prison, he heard an occasional muffled explosion, as well as the rattle of small-arms fire.

The thick walls couldn't keep all the sounds of the battle going on outside from reaching into the building.

That unholy racket gnawed at Kincaid's guts. He knew that good men were fighting and dying out there, sacrificing their lives to slow the terrorists' advance into the prison compound.

Unfortunately, there weren't enough guards to stop the attack. Kincaid knew that sooner or later the terrorists were going to penetrate into the prison, and more than likely it wouldn't take them long to crush any opposition.

Before that happened, he and the others who were trapped in here had to be ready to defend the maximum security wing. Their only chance to survive was to hold out until help arrived from outside—if it did.

Unfortunately, Kincaid had seen with his own eyes how the top brass, for the most part, whether military or law enforcement, liked to dither around and consider every angle—most important, how this problem was going to affect their own careers—before taking any action.

It was just that sort of politically correct navel-gazing that had prompted him to disobey orders at the village of Warraz al-Sidar. He'd had to go off-book in order to save lives.

That deadly firefight had uncovered something that landed him in hot water with some really bad guys. Powerful guys with friends in high places. *Very* high places. That was why he had been lying low ever since.

Hell's Gate had three distinct areas as far as the inmates were concerned: minimum security, general population, and maximum security. The minimum security cell block served as a buffer between the administrative area, where the library was located, and Gen Pop. As Kincaid came running up to the guard station at the entrance to minimum security, he found several officers he knew waiting there with guns drawn.

"Kincaid!" one of them exclaimed. "What the hell is going on out there?"

"The prison's under attack," Kincaid said. "Round up as many weapons as you can and get the inmates over to the max security wing. That's where we're going to mount a defense."

"Wait just a damned minute, *librarian*," one of the other guards said. "You're telling us to release the inmates *and* give them access to guns?"

"That sounds pretty crazy, Kincaid," said the first guard who had spoken.

"Look, there's no time to argue about it. There's a whole army of terrorists out there, if you want to take it up with them. But I'd rather save as many lives as we can."

Several of the guards looked like they were starting to agree with him. The others still appeared stubborn.

"Where's Warden Baldwin?" one of them asked.

"He was wounded by an assassin who got into the

prison posing as a member of the news crew that was here today," Kincaid replied, trying not to give in to the impatience he felt. "He put me in charge. I want a couple of you to come with me to the armory and help me gather more weapons."

"I think you've gone nuts," the most obnoxious of the other men said. "I'm not gonna get in trouble on your say-so."

"Fine," Kincaid snapped. "Whatever happens— whoever dies—it's on your head, then." He looked at the other men. "I still need two volunteers."

A couple of them stepped forward.

"We'll come with you," one said.

"Then let's go."

As Kincaid continued toward the armory, he thought that the guy who'd been complaining actually was right: his plan was crazy. A lot of the inmates, even the ones in minimum security, couldn't be trusted. They might try to seize the opportunity to arm themselves and take over the prison.

But if the terrorists found them locked in their cells, they would massacre the inmates, slaughtering them a cell at a time by firing through the bars with automatic weapons, simply because the prisoners were Americans.

Was that worse than the chaos that might be unleashed by letting the prisoners out of their cells? Kincaid thought it was.

And whether he liked the responsibility or not, he was the one making that call.

When he and the two men accompanying him reached the armory, he swiped his pass to unlock the outer door, then keyed the day's combination into the keypad on the inner door. He hoped he remembered it correctly.

"Take as many rifles and as much ammunition as you

can carry," Kincaid told his companions as the doors slid open. "Head straight to the maximum security wing."

He loaded himself down with rifles, pistols, and a couple of boxes of ammunition, then trotted toward the cell block where the general population was kept. There were a lot more hardened felons here, men who wouldn't think twice about shooting a correctional officer, no matter what the situation.

This hand was going to have to be played a little differently, Kincaid thought.

The alarm that had started going off as soon as it was obvious that trouble was imminent was still clamoring shrilly throughout the prison. Kincaid had gotten to the point that he wasn't paying much attention to it anymore.

The guards at the entrance to the main cell block certainly were, though. As Kincaid approached he found himself being targeted by eight men with riot guns leveled at him.

Kincaid slowed. Bristling with armament as he was, he wouldn't be surprised if the guards opened fire on him.

"Stand down!" he called to them. "You men know me. I'm Officer Lucas Kincaid."

One of the guards lowered his shotgun slightly, but the others didn't relax.

"Kincaid, what is all this crap? Alarms going off, explosions outside, we can't raise the command center—is somebody trying to stage a breakout?"

"You could say that," Kincaid replied. "The best anybody can figure right now is that a bunch of terrorists are trying to free the new inmates in maximum security."

That news drew an outburst of curses from several of the guards. One of them declared, "I've been saying all along that if the government wanted to put those crazy bastards here, they should have brought in the Army to guard them! It's like the politicians just dangled them out there and dared their friends to come after them!"

It seemed to Kincaid that somebody had made a comment like that more than once recently, and the more he thought about it, the more he believed there might be something to the theory. The idea that somebody at the Justice Department might have helped set this up should have been ludicrous, but ever since the Democrats had started running the show totally in Washington, anything was possible.

Twenty years earlier, for example, nobody would have believed that the Attorney General of the United States would set up an operation to sell guns to the Mexican drug cartels that would be used to murder American law enforcement officers—and get away with it, to boot, receiving a pass from the media, who called it just another phony scandal, and inattention from a majority of the voting population.

Kincaid thought about John Howard Stark, who was somewhere else in the prison right now. Some of the guns used by Stark's cartel foes in his battles against them might as well have had that former Attorney General's fingerprints on them.

And nobody but a few people—too few to do any good, obviously—even gave a damn.

But as disturbing as that was, it wasn't the issue right now. Kincaid said, "I don't care how it happened, we've got to deal with it. Leave the weapons you have here, go to the armory and get more, and then head for the maximum security wing. That's where we're making our stand."

"What about the inmates?"

"I'm going to unlock their cells and let them go," Kincaid said.

The guards gaped at him in disbelief.

"You can't do that!" one officer exclaimed. "If that bunch gets their hands on guns—"

"They'll have a chance to put up a fight," Kincaid interrupted. His voice was hard and flat. He didn't like what he was about to do, but he didn't have any choice. "They're our first line of defense."

Looks of horror appeared on the faces of a couple of the guards as they realized what Kincaid was talking about. The others still just looked confused.

"When the inmates realize their doors and the cell block doors are unlocked, they'll come pouring out through here," Kincaid went on. "They'll head for the main entrance. If I'm right, they'll run into the terrorists on the way."

"What if they get past the terrorists? You're talking about turning loose a bunch of murderers, rapists, and God knows that!"

"If any of them get past the terrorists, it won't be very many. They'll be outnumbered and outgunned."

Another man said, "That's a death sentence you're giving them, Kincaid. That's cold."

"I know. But the minimum security inmates are on their way to the max wing, and there are guards and other innocent people there, too. I'm trying to save as many of them as I can."

He was like a general in the old war movies, he told himself, ordering a company to hold the line while the rest of the regiment pulled back. He was sacrificing good men—and to be honest, quite a few bad ones—to save as many others as he could. There was a certain brutal nobility to it.

Not for the ones who were going to wind up dead, though.

Kincaid pushed that thought out of his brain and snapped, "Get moving. If you've got a problem, take it

up with the warden when you get to the max security
wing. He's waiting there."

The other officers still hesitated. One of them asked,
"How are we going to let the inmates out?"

Kincaid had considered that, too. He said, "I'll wait
until you guys have had a chance to get well on your way,
then I'll use the manual override to unlock all the cell
doors at once."

"Those bastards'll explode out of there once they realize what's happened," one of the guards warned.
"You'll have to get out of here quick to keep them from
catching you."

"That's exactly what I intend to do. And if I don't
make it . . ." Kincaid shrugged. "When you get to the
warden, tell him what I did. He probably won't like it,
but it's the only chance any of us have."

The grim realization that he was right put an end to
any arguments from the other men. They set their riot
guns and pistols aside so that the escaping inmates
could claim them and use them against the terrorists.
Kincaid planned to leave the weapons he had brought
along, too.

"For a guy who works in the library, you've got balls,
Kincaid," one of the men said as they prepared to depart.

"I've done a few things in my time besides shelving
books," Kincaid said with a faint smile.

Once the men had trotted up the corridor and then
turned into another corridor that would eventually lead
them to the maximum security wing, Kincaid stepped
over to the control panel in the guard station. He looked
at the video feeds that covered the cell doors. Inmates
stood at most of the barred openings. They had heard
the alarms, the shooting, the explosions. They knew
something was going on. Speculation was probably flying
around like crazy in there.

Chances were that none of those men were prepared

for the truth of what they would soon be facing, Kincaid thought. He knew a lot of them. Nearly every man in there had committed some sort of violent felony. Many were repeat offenders who had spent more of their lives behind bars than they had been out. Some were lifers, reptilian, sociopathic killers who up until now really had been wastes of perfectly good air.

But maybe for the first time, they were about to serve a purpose that had some decency to it, whether they were aware of it or not.

The other guards had had time to get clear. Kincaid took a deep breath and pushed the manual override button that unlocked every cell in the block. The shouts that went up as the inmates heard the clunking of the mechanisms and realized they were free blended together into an animalistic howl.

Kincaid unlocked the main doors into the cell block and started to step out of the guard station, then thought better of it and paused long enough to grab one of the pistols left behind by the other officers. Carrying the weapon, he broke into a run along the corridor.

Even through thick steel walls and bulletproof glass, he heard the frenzied clamor growing louder behind him as the inmates passed through the series of doors leading into the cell block.

He turned the corner into the other corridor, heading left and skidding a little because he was hurrying so much.

As he did, a startled shout sounded behind him. Kincaid's head jerked around as he looked back over his shoulder.

He was surprised to see that some of the terrorists had already made it this far into the prison. Half a dozen men were at the far end of the corridor, maybe fifty yards away. They hurried toward him, and as they did, the ones in the lead lifted the automatic weapons they carried and opened fire.

There were no doors or alcoves in the concrete walls, no cross corridors for another thirty yards, no place to take cover. Kincaid knew that.

All he could do was dive desperately to the floor as a hail of bullets sizzled through the air above his head where he had been an instant earlier.

CHAPTER 32

On the other side of the sally port leading into the maximum security wing was a fairly large reception room, and to one side of it was the small visitors' room where inmates could confer with their lawyers.

That room was divided in half by a sheet of bullet-proof glass with a counter and bench butted up against it opposite each other. Inmates and visitors talked to each other through an intercom system, but no physical contact was allowed.

Stark assisted George Baldwin into that room and then helped him sit down on the bench. He looked around, saw Riley Nichols watching worriedly from the doorway, and said, "You think you can find something else to use as a pad for the warden's wound?"

"I know I can," she said. She started unbuttoning her functional khaki shirt.

Stark frowned a little at that until he saw the lacy camisole Riley wore underneath the shirt. That actually made for a nice contrast, he thought, tough and all business on the outside, frilly and romantic underneath.

He wondered if her personality was the same, not that he had any romantic interest in her himself.

She pulled the camisole up and ripped a large piece of fabric from the bottom of it. She folded that into a pad and handed it to Stark, who used it to replace the blood-soaked handkerchief Baldwin had been holding to the wound.

Riley ripped strips of cloth from the undergarment as well and said, "We can use these to tie the dressing in place. Move over a little. I can do it."

After watching her swift, efficient movements for a moment as she worked on Baldwin's wound, Stark asked, "You've done things like this before, haven't you?"

"I had some medical training while I was in the Marines."

Stark grinned. "You were a leatherneck, too, Ms. Nichols?"

"Semper fi, Mr. Stark."

That explained some things, Stark thought. It must have driven Riley crazy, working for a liberal news network and having to be around people like Alexis Devereaux all the time, but sometimes folks didn't have much choice in the matter.

Years and years of any economic recovery being stifled by Democratic policies designed to expand their base and erode the middle class had left America a nation of people who had to take any job they could get, just to survive. And anybody who worked a full-time job was extremely lucky.

"Let's stretch him out on this bench," Riley suggested. She lifted Baldwin's feet while Stark took hold of the warden's shoulders. They maneuvered him into a reclining position so he could rest easier.

Baldwin's face was pale and his eyes were closed. His chest rose and fell, so Stark knew his old friend was still alive. Baldwin's breathing was irregular, though. He really did need qualified medical attention, and the sooner, the better.

But they all needed a lot of things right about now, Stark mused, most notably some reinforcements from outside.

"I'll keep an eye on him," Riley said. "You should help that guard set up our defenses."

Stark nodded. He said, "Give a holler if you need me."

He went out into the reception room and found Mitch Cambridge directing the other guards to move the desks and a couple of filing cabinets into a line facing the entrance.

"I know this furniture won't provide much cover if the terrorists make it this far," Cambridge told Stark, "but I figure it's better than nothing."

"You're right. That sally port's your main line of defense, though. If they breach both doors . . ."

Stark's voice trailed off, but the grim import of his words was clear.

"If they breach both doors, we'll have to try to keep them from getting on into the cell block. I'm going to put marksmen on the upper level. Luckily the entrance isn't very wide, so only a limited number can come through it at one time."

"They could throw grenades or fire rockets through it," Stark pointed out.

"If they do that, they risk injuring or killing the men they came to rescue," Cambridge said. "I'm hoping they won't take that chance. A smaller force can hold off a much larger one if you limit the number that can come at you."

"Gates of fire," Stark murmured.

"Thermopylae, exactly."

"Those Spartans wound up getting killed, you know," Stark said.

Cambridge shrugged.

"I think this strategy is still our best bet."

"Long odds are better than no odds at all," Stark agreed.

One of the guards posted in the sally port between the two doors called, "Somebody's coming!"

Stark heard the despair in Cambridge's voice as the young man said, "Already?"

He and Stark hurried through the inner door, which was still open. They peered through the reinforced glass in the outer door's window and saw a large group of men in bright orange jumpsuits hurrying along the corridor.

"Those aren't terrorists," Stark said.

"I know," Cambridge said, and now relief was evident in his tone. "I recognize most of them. They're inmates from the minimum security area."

"And there are more guards with them," Stark pointed out. "Kincaid must have sent them."

Cambridge reached for the controls that opened the outer door, then hesitated.

"What if it's a trick?" he asked. "The terrorists could be right behind them, forcing them along at gunpoint and using them as shields."

"Wait until they get here," Stark suggested. "That won't take long, and we ought to be able to tell then."

He was right. The newcomers began crowding up against the entrance to the maximum security wing. The press of inmates parted to let one of the guards through.

"Hankins!" Cambridge said through the intercom.

"Is that you, Mitch?" the guard called Hankins responded. "Let us in. Kincaid said to tell you he sent us."

"Have you seen any of the terrorists?"

"Not yet." Hankins looked nervous, and some of the inmates were obviously flat-out scared, with good reason. "We heard a lot of shooting outside, though."

Cambridge glanced at Stark, who nodded. Cambridge

pushed the right buttons, and the outer door began to rumble open.

As soon as the gap was wide enough, inmates and officers surged through. Stark was glad to see that none of the inmates had tried to take weapons away from the guards. Evidently they were smart enough to realize that their best chance for living through this lay in cooperation.

Some of the guards were carrying extra weapons. Stark reached out and took one of the semiautomatic rifles. The guard looked like he didn't want to hand it over to a civilian, but Cambridge nodded for him to go ahead.

"Got any extra magazines?" Stark asked.

The guard gave him one, and Stark slid it into his hip pocket.

"Think I'll go take a look around," he told Cambridge.

"Wait a minute," Cambridge objected. "We were supposed to rally here, not go wandering around the prison."

"I'd like to know how close the enemy is. Right now we don't have any idea how long we've got to get ready."

"That's true, I suppose," Cambridge said. He frowned. "Can you find your way back here?"

"Well, now, that's a good question," Stark admitted. "I tried to pay more attention this time and take note of all the landmarks." A grim smile touched his mouth under the mustache. "Worse comes to worst, I'll just follow the sound of gunfire."

"You're liable to get trapped on the wrong side of these doors with hundreds of terrorists."

"I'll take my chances," Stark said.

He knew it was a wild, grandstand play, the sort of thing he had done when he was a youngster in the jungles of Vietnam. He wished he had some of his fellow Marines from those days with him now. Rich Threadgill was crazy as a loon, but there was nobody better to have at your side in a fight.

Maybe this foolhardiness was the cancer talking, Stark mused. In remission or not, he knew it was still lurking inside him like a time bomb. One of these days it would kill him, if he wanted to wait that long. Maybe it was whispering in the back of his mind that he didn't want to go out that way if he had a choice.

Or maybe it was just strategically smart for him to scout out the enemy. The chances of any of them pulling through this were small enough already without the terrorists taking him and his companions by surprise.

"All right, go ahead," Cambridge said. "But this door is going to be closed and locked behind you, and it takes a little while to open it. If you come hotfooting back with a bunch of killers right behind you, I may not be able to help you."

"I understand," Stark said. He gave Cambridge a nod and then turned and started along the corridor at a trot.

He reached a corner, turned, and was gone.

As soon as Kincaid hit the floor, he grabbed his right wrist with his left hand to steady it and began squeezing the pistol's trigger. The 9 mm semiautomatic blasted twice.

Both slugs punched into the chest of the first man in the group of attackers. He stumbled and fell, and the two men right behind him tripped over him.

Kincaid shot each of them in the head.

Even crazed terrorists were taken a little aback by being splattered with blood and brains from their comrades' exploding skulls. They slowed their charge and then stopped.

Kincaid knew they would recover from the shock in a matter of seconds and then come rampaging down the corridor toward him, and there was still no place for him to go.

But he had done some damage, had killed three of the bastards, and he still had rounds in the gun's magazine. He was ready to start firing again . . .

That was when a riot gun roared and two more of the terrorists went down, shredded into bloody rags by a double load of buckshot. More shots slammed against the concrete walls and set up a deafening racket.

Kincaid realized the front ranks of the enemy force had halted right where the corridors intersected. Some of the inmates must have made it out of the cell block by now, and obviously they were armed. They had started shooting at the first thing they saw.

Which, to Kincaid's great good fortune, had been the terrorists.

His luck was only momentary, though. Either the inmates would overrun this bunch of terrorists and wipe them out, or else the terrorists would drive the inmates back into the cell block.

Either way, he would be left facing a bunch of armed men who wanted to kill him.

Unless he reached the next cross corridor while the two groups of killers were busy with each other.

He rolled over and surged to his feet, ready to make a run for it.

That good luck deserted him even faster than he thought it might. Several of the terrorists noticed him fleeing, broke off their battle against the inmates, and started to pursue him. A gun went off and the bullet whipped past Kincaid's ear.

He saw movement ahead of him and started to bring up the pistol, figuring that the way things were going he was trapped between two groups of terrorists, but it was John Howard Stark who stepped around a corner and smoothly brought an AR-15 to his shoulder.

"Get down, Lucas!" Stark barked.

Kincaid hit the deck again. Stark fired four swift shots over him. Guns clattered to the tile floor behind Kincaid.

Stark lowered the rifle and called, "Come on!"

He didn't have to tell Kincaid twice. Kincaid was up and running again in the blink of an eye. He didn't look behind him.

He didn't have to look in order to know that Stark had drilled the terrorists who were giving chase to him.

Stark covered him until Kincaid reached the corner. Together, the two men ducked into the narrow service corridor that crossed the main corridor.

"What are you doing here?" Kincaid asked as his pulse hammered inside his head. "You're supposed to be at the maximum security wing with the others."

"Thought I'd do a little scouting," Stark replied. "Find out how far into the prison those terrorists had made it."

"Now you know."

"Yeah," Stark said. "That was the main cell block where they were fighting somebody, wasn't it?"

"That's right."

"We've got guards holed up in there?"

"No," Kincaid said. "I turned the inmates loose and left guns for them."

They had been trotting quickly along the service corridor as they talked. Now Stark slowed, pausing to look over at Kincaid.

"I know," Kincaid said. "You don't have to tell me. That's wrong on so many levels. I used those men as cannon fodder."

"You did what any military commander who wanted to win a battle would do," Stark said. "You devised a strategy to slow down the enemy's advance and whittle down his numerical superiority."

"I did what every enlisted man and noncom has

cussed the brass for, ever since war was invented. I saw men as pawns, instead of human beings."

"If that was true, what you did wouldn't be gnawing at your guts right now. You know as well as I do the ones who really don't regard any of us as human beings. It's those terrorists. We're just godless infidels to them. The more of us who die, the better. We're trying to stop that."

Kincaid drew in a deep breath and nodded.

"I suppose you're right, Mr. Stark. But I still don't think I'm cut out for command."

"Some of the best generals who have ever lived have thought the same thing. We'd better get moving again. And make it John Howard, all right?"

"Sure," Kincaid said. "Where to now, John Howard?"

"We know the terrorists have reached the main cell block. Those inmates will keep them busy for a while, but I don't think they'll be able to stop that bunch. I think we should head back to maximum security and let everybody there know that they'll be having company soon."

"Sounds good to me."

"Just one thing . . . you better lead the way." Stark grinned. "I hate to say it, but it was pure dumb luck that put me in the right place at the right time to help you. No matter how hard I try, I still get turned around in this place!"

CHAPTER 33

After the broadcast from Fuego, Phillip Hamil had left his men firmly in control of the town and driven out to Hell's Gate to see how the assault on the prison was going.

Raffir met him where the compound's main gate had been. Now the fence and the building on the other side of it had been blasted into rubble. Gaping shell holes were visible here and there along the fence line and inside the fence.

The entrance to the main building was in ruins as well. Hamil could see it from where he stood next to his car and listened to Raffir's report.

"We haven't yet reached the maximum security wing where our brothers are being held?" Hamil interrupted with a frown of disapproval.

"It has been more difficult than we anticipated, Doctor," Raffir answered. "We were able to break through the outer line of defense and kill many of the infidels—"

He waved a hand to indicate the numerous corpses littering the area, looking like heaps of torn, bloody clothing once the men of the Sword of Allah were finished with them.

"—but the resistance inside the prison has been stronger than we expected," Raffir went on. "Not only have the guards been fighting us, but we've received reports over the walkie-talkies from squadron leaders that the inmates are taking part in the battle as well."

"The American prisoners are trying to stop us?" Hamil asked. This news surprised him. "I assumed the prison authorities would abandon them in their cells while they cowered before our unstoppable might."

"I know." Raffir sighed and shook his head. "All the men were looking forward to slaughtering every one of them in the name of the Prophet."

Hamil grimaced and waved a hand.

"It doesn't matter. The inmates can only slow us down. They cannot prevent us from achieving our glorious goal. Have you heard anything from our man who was inside the prison before our holy jihad began?"

Once again Raffir shook his head.

"We've had no communication with him since we let him know the attack was about to begin."

"The infidels may have discovered that he was one of us and murdered him," Hamil said. "Just as they have murdered so many of our people. Our innocent loved ones."

It was one of the great ironies of politics that many, many more Muslim lives had been lost to the Americans in the past twenty years under Democratic administrations than when the supposedly war-mongering Republicans were in power. From time to time the Democrats still beat the drum of blaming George W. Bush for every evil in the world, from natural disasters to the trouble in the Middle East that had spilled over onto American soil. And their followers continued to swallow that scenario without hesitation, swilling at the trough of lies like pigs.

The stupidity of the American "progressives" would

be amusing if they weren't so . . . well, stupid. One could only feel sorry for them.

Not that Hamil did, of course. The stupider, the blinder the Americans were, the better for his cause. Let them continue electing Democratic presidents and members of Congress. That only made his work of destruction easier.

"Let me know when we reach the cell block where our brothers are being kept," Hamil instructed his second-in-command. "I want to be there when we carry out Allah's will and liberate them from their unjust captivity."

"Yes, sir," Raffir answered crisply.

"Have you seen any sign of Alexis Devereaux and the newspeople who were with her?"

Raffir shook his head.

"I'm sorry, Doctor. We have not encountered them. Do you have orders regarding them?"

Hamil had to be careful. He couldn't allow his men to see him extending any mercy to infidels. He especially didn't want them to believe that he was concerned about Alexis because she was a beautiful woman.

In truth, her beauty hadn't really entered into his thinking. True, he wouldn't mind bedding her if the opportunity ever arose, but the real reason he hoped she would survive this bloody chaos was because she was useful. No matter what the situation, she could be counted upon to find a way to blame her fellow Americans for what had happened and bellow that ridiculous opinion at the top of her strident lungs.

So it would be fine if things worked out so that she lived, but if they didn't . . .

"If they're captured, Ms. Devereaux should be brought to me," he said. "I don't care what you do to the others. But if they're all killed in the fighting . . ." Hamil shrugged. "Such is the will of Allah."

* * *

Alexis had never been so scared in her entire life . . . and she had spent most of her adult years around dangerous gun nuts, Bible thumpers, teabaggers, hillbillies, rednecks, birthers, tax protesters, healthcare reform dodgers, climate change deniers, and other right-wing whack jobs, doing her best to expose them as racist, misogynist, homophobic bigots who posed the real threat to the country and to the progressive agenda that would transform the United States into a universal, government-controlled, centrally planned paradise of tolerance and diversity if only all the stupid, obstructionist Republicans could be done away with somehow.

It had been a hazardous, thankless job, but somebody had to do it.

The really odd thing was that none of *those* horrible people had ever tried to hurt her or even really been rude to her, and now here she was with her life apparently being threatened by peace-loving Muslims who had never wanted anything except the respect that their religion deserved.

She didn't believe it—she *couldn't* believe it—and yet she heard the explosions and the gunfire and the way the people around her were talking about how they were going to have to make a stand here and fight off the terrorists for as long as possible.

That was insane. This was all a trick. A right-wing conspiracy. It had to be.

Alexis wished she was back in Washington or San Francisco or anyplace where people were normal.

Riley Nichols came over to her and said, "I know this is probably a foolish question, Ms. Devereaux, but do you know how to use a gun?"

"A gun?" Alexis repeated in disbelief. "I've never even *touched* a gun, let alone fired one!"

Riley sighed and said, "Then it's a good thing millions of Americans *haven't* minded touching a gun over the past hundred years or so, or else we'd be speaking German or Japanese or Russian right now."

"I don't understand," Alexis said with a frown and a shake of her head.

"No, you wouldn't." Riley turned away, adding over her shoulder, "Maybe the best thing you can do to help is just stay out of the way."

Alexis's chin jutted out in anger. She said, "You can't talk to me that way. I can have you fired, you know."

"Lady, if you think I'm worried about my job right now—" Riley stopped and blew out an exasperated breath.

"How's Warden Baldwin?" Alexis asked. "I know you were helping take care of him earlier."

Riley looked a little surprised that Alexis would ask about the warden. She said, "He's resting fairly comfortably at the moment, and I think the bleeding from his wound has finally stopped. He's lost a lot of blood, though. He needs to be in a hospital."

"Well, surely we can appeal to the humanitarian instincts of those so-called terrorists everybody keeps going on about—"

Alexis stopped in mid-sentence as Riley began to laugh.

"What's so funny?" Alexis asked with an angry glare.

"Humanitarian instincts. It's hilarious that you think those monsters have any humanitarian instincts."

"You don't have to be uncivil and resort to name-calling," Alexis sniffed.

"Yes, because the real threat is that somebody might get their precious little feelings hurt, rather than a horde of barbarians trapped in the Middle Ages who'd like to behead everybody who doesn't pray exactly the same way they do. *Those* guys are perfectly fine with you."

"You are *never* going to work in Washington again."

"Yeah, I'll lose some sleep about that . . . assuming we get out of here without those buddies of yours raping us to death."

The two women might have continued to argue, but just then Mitch Cambridge hurried up to them and said, "You ladies need to pull back now. Somebody's coming up the corridor toward the cell block, and we're not sure who it is yet."

"I can fight," Riley told him without hesitation.

"You may have to before this is all over," Cambridge said. He looked at Alexis. "What about you, Ms. Devereaux?"

"Don't waste your breath," Riley told him before Alexis could say anything. "Ms. Devereaux is still convinced this whole thing is some sort of right-wing trick."

"I never told you that," Alexis said, not adding that Riley was correct.

Riley shrugged and said, "You didn't have to tell me. I know how your kind thinks."

"My kind? That's a—"

Alexis stopped short and frowned, momentarily stymied as to how to respond.

"What, a racist thing to say? We're both white. Misogynist? Both women. Homophobic? It's pretty common knowledge that you've slept with half the male lobbyists and politicians in Washington, and I know *I'm* straight, so that doesn't really apply, either. What progressive buzzword does that leave you, Alexis?"

"You're . . . you're mean!" Alexis sputtered.

"Ah, hurt feelings again. The last refuge of the liberal."

Cambridge held up his hands and said, "Ladies, enough. You need to back off now. There may be bullets flying around here soon, and I promise you—they don't discriminate against anybody. They'll kill you just as dead no matter what you think."

Stark and Kincaid hadn't encountered any more of the terrorists on their way back to the maximum security wing. When the sally port at the entrance to the wing came into sight at the far end of the long corridor, Stark felt a little relief as he realized that everything looked as it had when he left. There hadn't been any trouble here—yet.

The outer door was closed. As the two men trotted toward it, the door began to slide to one side with a rumble of the engine that drove it.

"You said this wing has its own power supply?" Stark asked.

Kincaid said, "Yeah, the doors, lights, and everything else run off generators. So the terrorists can't hope to do any good by cutting our power. They can't get to it."

"Where are those generators located?"

"Underground, in a sub-basement under this wing. They'd have to know exactly where the generators are and then tunnel a long way to get to them."

That knowledge eased one of Stark's worries.

Of course, there were still plenty more.

They were about halfway down the corridor, which was fifty yards long, when a strident yell sounded behind them. That shout was followed by gunfire. Bullets smacked into the walls behind them as both men instinctively put on a burst of speed.

Stark looked over his shoulder and saw that half a dozen terrorists had reached the far end of the corridor. They had opened fire at the sight of the two men heading for the entrance to the maximum security wing.

The outer door had opened almost all the way before the shooting started.

Now it lurched to a halt and then started to grind back the other way.

Stark and Kincaid were about to be caught in what amounted to a deadly shooting gallery.

Cambridge had just started the door closing when Riley appeared at his side, exclaiming, "No! You can't do that! They'll be trapped out there!"

"I warned Mr. Stark this might happen," Cambridge said. "I told him he might get stuck on the wrong side of the doors. Now get back beyond the inner door, Ms. Nichols!"

Riley ignored the order and said, "Damn it, the least you can do is give them some cover!"

Without any warning of what she was about to do, she turned and snatched an AR-15 out of the hands of an unsuspecting guard.

"Hey!" Cambridge yelled as Riley darted through the entrance's narrowing gap.

She brought the rifle to her shoulder. During her time in the service, she had carried a weapon similar to this and fired it many times. She knew what she was doing as she aimed down the corridor.

Kincaid and Stark must have realized what she was about to do. They veered to their right, giving Riley a narrow firing lane. She settled her sights on the charging terrorists and started shooting.

Slugs ripped into the group of men and blunted their attack. One man yelled in fear and tried to turn back. Riley put a bullet in the back of his head.

Cambridge slid out of the sally port, dropped to one knee beside Riley, and opened fire with his pistol. The corridor was ten feet wide, so the bullets missed by only a short distance as they whipped past Stark and Kincaid.

Under the circumstances, though, a matter of inches was as good as a mile.

"Keep going, John Howard!" Kincaid called to Stark as they neared the entrance. "Get inside!"

He turned back and crouched as the pistol in his hand spat lead, too. Several of the terrorists were down, but more had appeared to swell the ranks of the attackers.

Stark hesitated, but only for a second. He was the biggest of the four Americans on the wrong side of the door, and the gap was barely big enough for him to get through it now. He had to turn sideways to fit his shoulders through it as he ducked into the sally port.

"Now you two, go!" Kincaid shouted to Riley and Cambridge. "I'll hold them off."

Cambridge's pistol was empty—for the moment, anyway. Grimacing, he straightened, whirled toward the door, and gasped in pain as a bullet ripped a bloody furrow across the outside of his upper left arm. He was able to stay on his feet, though, and stumbled past the closing door.

"Go, go!" Kincaid yelled again at Riley.

"Not without you!" she told him as she fired the last shot in her magazine.

Snarling, Kincaid twisted toward her, grabbed her arm, and shoved her through the narrow gap. She reached back through, snagged his shirt collar, and tugged him toward her. Taken by surprise, Kincaid fell through the opening and tumbled to the floor, taking Riley with him.

A few last slugs from the terrorists screamed through the gap, then the door thudded shut. Bullets continued to strike it, but small-arms fire would never penetrate that barrier.

Kincaid was lying on top of Riley. He wasn't a huge guy, so she wasn't having any trouble breathing. In fact, under different circumstances this arrangement might be downright pleasurable, she thought.

To one side of the room, Cambridge cursed bitterly as Stark examined the wound on his arm. Riley barely heard him as she and Kincaid lay there catching their breath.

"Are you . . . all right?" Kincaid asked after a moment.

"Yeah. How about you?"

"Those guys are terrible shots—thank goodness."

"They're not much on strategy, either," Riley said. "They spot an enemy, they just chase after him, yelling and shooting."

"Five hundred years ago, they would have done the same thing, only they'd be waving scimitars."

"Yeah, the more things change . . ."

This was one of the craziest conversations she'd ever had, Riley thought. Lying on a hard floor with a ruggedly good-looking man, their faces only inches apart, weapons scattered around them, talking about blood-thirsty fanatics . . .

She glanced past Kincaid's shoulder, saw hate-twisted faces leering down at them through the reinforced, bulletproof glass of the door's window, and gasped.

"Damn!" she said.

Kincaid rolled smoothly off her, picked up the pistol he'd dropped, and came to his feet. He stood at the window, glaring defiantly through the window at the terrorists who had their faces pressed to the glass.

It was quite a contrast, Riley thought as she stood up and moved beside him.

Behind her, Stark told Cambridge, "You'll be all right. That graze probably hurts like blazes, but it's not bleeding too bad."

"You're right about the hurting like blazes part," Cambridge said. "We need to pull back and close the inner door." When Riley and Kincaid ignored him, he went on, "Hey, you two. Come on. We're falling back."

The terrorists were still raging impotently on the

other side of the outer door. Their mouths twisted and spittle flew against the glass as they spewed their hatred.

She was looking at an ancient evil, Riley thought, an ugly thing that had come down through the ages like some atavistic horror and still threatened mankind.

It wasn't Islam, per se—she didn't hate Muslims and had absolutely no desire to see all of them wiped off the face of the earth. She believed that everybody was free to worship as they wanted—or not worship—as long as they didn't hurt anybody else. She knew that some Muslims even believed the same way.

But an ever-expanding core of fanatics existed who believed that the only way for them to worship their God was to eradicate everybody who didn't have exactly the same brand of faith that they did. That hatred wasn't limited just to the so-called infidels, either, which explained why different Islamic sects had been slaughtering each other for hundreds and hundreds of years.

It was like Baptists and Methodists going to war and trying to kill each other over the question of whether to sprinkle or dunk when it came to baptisms.

Crazy.

She put a hand on Kincaid's arm and said, "Come on, Lucas, we need to go. We can't do any good here."

"Nothing's going to do these lunatics any good except a bullet in the brain," Kincaid grated. "I just hope we get the chance to make some more of them all better."

CHAPTER 34

By late afternoon, the cordon was in place around the town of Fuego and Hell's Gate prison. Air Force jets continued to enforce the no-fly zone. Roadblocks had been set up on all roads leading into town, and heavily armed personnel from the Department of Homeland Security patrolled the open countryside in armored vehicles to make sure no one tried to sneak through that way. Real-time satellite feeds from the nation's defense network covered the area and were monitored continuously. The intel from those feeds was passed on to the DHS troops so they were able to intercept anyone who tried to get to Fuego. Most of those were reporters, but there were some civilians who had loved ones in the town and wanted to find out if they were still alive.

Everyone who was intercepted was detained. They would be taken to various black sites and interrogated, since anyone who attempted to defy the orders of the President was regarded as a terrorist—especially if it could be determined that they had ever expressed any conservative political views in social media or elsewhere, even in face-to-face conversations with friends.

Coverage of the crisis in West Texas had preempted

almost all the programming on broadcast and cable networks. Well-groomed news anchors with nary a hair out of place reported solemnly that there was nothing to report. Equally well-groomed pundits speculated not only on what was happening but also on the causes, and eventually all of them reached the conclusion that it was all the fault of the Republicans, especially George W. Bush. He had set the stage for this catastrophe, they all agreed with self-satisfied nods.

The White House had no comment except to say that the investigation into the matter continued. Well-placed leaks, however, indicated the conclusion that the incident had begun as a totally justified protest by peaceful Islamic-rights advocates.

In the governor's mansion in Austin, Maria Delgado snatched up the cell phone on the desk in her study as it began to ring. Without making any small talk first, she asked, "What have you found out, Tom?"

"Unfortunately, not much yet," Colonel Atkinson replied. "Sergeant Porter and I managed to penetrate the DHS perimeter without much trouble and we're on our way to Fuego now. We're close enough to see some smoke." He paused. "It doesn't look good, Maria. In fact, it looks like a war zone, and I think it's gonna just be worse the closer we get."

Delgado massaged her temples, but that did nothing to make her headache go away. She said, "You're on foot?"

"That's right. Between our camo and the stealth gear we're using, it's going to be hard for the sats to pick us up. I assume the government's monitoring the area using NSA and DOD satellites?"

"Washington doesn't tell me anything, you know that. But I'm sure you're right, Tom."

She could practically see the grin on Atkinson's face as the colonel said, "It's a good thing Texas has its own encrypted communications satellite, then, isn't it? At least once Porter and I get to Fuego, you'll have a secure comm link in there."

He was right about that, Delgado thought. The remaining liberals in the Texas House and Senate would pitch a hissy fit, as would the media, if they found out how she had used some of the state's surplus funds to put what was disguised as a privately owned industrial satellite into space. Texas was one of the few states left in the country where the economy hadn't been completely crushed by progressive Democratic policies and punitive regulations, so she had decided that she might as well put some of that revenue to good use.

The communications satellite was just one of the measures she had taken to prepare for the clash with Washington that she regarded as inevitable. Although she didn't like the secrecy this effort involved, it was necessary to keep all her plans from being short-circuited.

The liberals and the media were really *good* at those hissy fits. They had raised the outraged reaction to a high art form eagerly embraced by the segments of the country who wanted to keep their benefactors in power. Even in a holdout state like Texas, they could cause a lot of trouble.

"Whatever you find in Fuego, let me know, Tom," Delgado told Atkinson. "I'm putting my trust in you. If we need to pull the trigger on the emergency measures we've talked about in the past—"

"Don't worry, Governor. You'll be my first and only call."

Atkinson broke the connection.

Delgado set the secure phone down and sent a silent prayer heavenward for the maverick colonel and Sgt. Porter.

* * *

The sun had started to drop toward the western horizon as Lee Blaisdell looked around at his motley "army." He and Lt. Flannery and the others had rounded up about forty more people—mostly men but a few women, too—from outlying farms and ranches in the area. That gave Lee and the Ranger a force of approximately fifty fighters to take on hundreds of terrorists.

But Sam Houston and the Texican army had been badly outnumbered at San Jacinto, too, Lee reminded himself. He recalled that much from Texas History class when he was in seventh grade. Those ol' boys had put Santa Anna's much larger army to rout and captured the Mexican dictator himself, winning Texas its freedom and ushering in almost a decade as an independent republic.

A lot of people thought Texas might have been better off staying a republic rather than joining the United States, and the way things had gone in recent years, Lee was beginning to think maybe that opinion had some validity.

You couldn't go back and change the past, though, and even if you could, it probably wouldn't be a good idea. Best just to deal with the here and now, no matter how bad it was.

They had the two jeeps and the weapons they had captured from the terrorists. The new recruits were in pickups for the most part, although there were a couple of old cars in the convoy that was forming up. People were armed with everything from double-barreled shotguns and antique but functioning revolvers to modern assault rifles and 9 mm pistols. One old fella even had a black powder cannon that he had built himself. They had lifted it into the back of a pickup and fastened it down, then loaded a supply of black powder and a crate full of three-inch cannonballs, too.

"All right," Lee said as he addressed his assembled force. "Nobody's cell phone works, so we can assume the terrorists disabled all the towers somehow. But the radio at the police station ought to work, so we need to take that objective. The best way to do that is to distract the enemy with most of our force and lure some of them away. Then a smaller group of us can hit the station and get control of it without the rest of the terrorists knowing what we're doing. We need to let the outside authorities know what's happened in Fuego and find out when help is going to get here."

"It's not gonna get here," Spence Parker said. "If it was, it would've already been here. They've all abandoned us."

Lee had a hunch the football player might be right, but he didn't want to admit that out loud. Not even to himself, really, because that would mean giving up hope.

"We don't know that," he said. "And I sure as hell don't intend to roll over and surrender to the same bastards who wiped out half the town. I don't reckon any of you want to do that, either."

He got a few shouts of agreement in response to that. When the group had settled down again, he went on, "Half a dozen of us are going to the police station: me, Lieutenent Flannery, Raymond, Gibby, Spence, and one of the lieutenant's men. The rest of you will circle around and approach the other end of town. I don't figure you'll have to look for the enemy. They'll come to you. Hit them as hard as you can for a few minutes and then get the hell out of there. While you're doing that, the rest of us will be taking over the police station."

"How will you know when to attack the place?" one of the men asked.

"We'll hear the shooting," Lee answered with a grim smile. "Any other questions?"

Silence and a lot of determined looks were all he got in return. He jerked his head in a curt nod, satisfied that they were doing all they could to free Fuego from the grip of the invaders.

"Let's move out," he said simply.

As the others were climbing into their vehicles, Janey came over to Lee and said, "I wish you'd let me come with you."

"You know that's not a good idea," he told her. "I'd be worrying about you and watching out for you, and before you know it, one of those sumbitches'd shoot me."

"But I could watch your back."

"The fellas with me will do that. Listen, Janey, the one thing that'll give me the best chance of comin' through this alive is knowing that you're safe." Lee took a deep breath. "That's why I told Martin to drop you off at the Simmons farm with the rest of the ladies before the fellas go on to town."

Janey's eyes widened. Lee saw the familiar spark of anger and indignation in them.

"You . . . you damn sexist!" she sputtered. "You think women can't fight?"

"I know you can. I've seen you do it."

"There are women in combat in the military now, you know."

"I know," Lee said. "I got no problem with that. But they ain't fightin' side by side with their husbands and boyfriends, either. They'd be tryin' to take care of their fellas, and their fellas'd be tryin' to take care of them, and it'd just be a bad situation all the way around. You know I'm right about this, Janey."

"Blast it," she muttered, and he knew that was her way of admitting that he was indeed right.

"C'mere," he said.

He drew her into his arms and kissed her. Her head tilted up naturally so that his mouth found hers. Their kisses had always been passionate, but this one had an extra urgency because they didn't know when—or if—they would see each other again.

"You be careful," she whispered when their lips drew apart.

"I intend to be," Lee said. "Bubba's gonna need his daddy while he's growin' up."

"Damn right he will."

Lee grinned, patted her on the butt, and turned away while he could still force himself to let her go. Without looking back, he strode over to Gibby's pickup, where the passenger door was standing open. He stepped up into the cab, paused there standing in the door, and circled his arm over his head, signaling the others to fire up their vehicles.

It was time to start trying to take back their town.

CHAPTER 35

The guards' command center in the maximum security wing contained several video monitors so that an officer could sit at the console and cycle through the live feeds from various cameras to keep an eye on the entire wing. Whoever was watching the monitors couldn't see everything at once, however.

One of the cameras was mounted at the far end of the corridor leading into the wing. Kincaid suggested that they keep its feed up on one of the monitors all the time, since that's where an attack would come from. Stark and Cambridge agreed. The three of them had formed a triumvirate of sorts to take charge of the wing's defense.

The terrorists had pulled back around a corner, out of sight of the camera. Kincaid had no doubt that they would be back, though, as he sat slumped in a chair at the console.

The killers had come too far, spilled too much blood, to turn back without achieving their goal.

Behind him, the door into the command center was open. He heard a lot of yelling going on but didn't pay much attention to it. Some of the terrorists locked up here had started shouting insults at the regular minimum security inmates who were crowded into the wing's open areas. The American prisoners had responded angrily, of course, and the pointless argument was still going on.

Kincaid heard a quiet footstep behind him and looked over his shoulder to see that Stark had entered the room.

"Everything under control out there, John Howard?" Kincaid asked.

"Yeah, as much as it's likely to be," Stark said as he took one of the other chairs. "Thought we should have a talk, Lucas."

"What about? The weather? Football? Please tell me you don't want to talk politics."

Stark grunted and said, "I've got a bad taste in my mouth already. Talking about politics would just make it worse. I was thinking more along the lines of you telling me what it is you're hiding out from."

Kincaid tried to control his reaction, but he couldn't keep from shooting a surprised glance at the older man.

"What do you mean, hiding out?" Kincaid asked, pitching his tone as if that were the craziest idea he had ever heard.

"You've been up to your neck in trouble before. I can tell that just by being around you. I know how to recognize a good fighting man when I see one."

Probably from looking in the mirror, Kincaid thought, but he didn't say anything.

"Not only that," Stark went on, "but Riley knows your face from somewhere. She was talking to me a little while ago, and I could tell she was trying to find out how much I know about you. I acted like I didn't know what she was talking about, but I sort of do. You're hiding something, Lucas, and if we're going to be fighting side by side . . .

probably dying side by side . . . I think I've got a right to know."

Kincaid could have disagreed with that and argued, but he realized suddenly that he wanted to tell somebody about it. He didn't know if that would ease the burden of carrying around the truth, but it might.

Keeping his eyes on the monitor that showed the corridor, Kincaid sighed and said, "All right, John Howard. I'll tell you the truth if you're sure you want to hear it. It isn't a very pretty story."

"I didn't expect it to be."

"First of all, my name isn't really Lucas Kincaid."

"That doesn't surprise me, either."

"But it's the only name you're going to get from me," Kincaid said. "It's not important to what happened, anyway."

"Fair enough," Stark said. "Is the law after you?"

"The law?" Kincaid repeated. A bleak laugh came from him. "You could say that. But it's more like the outlaws are after me." He straightened in his chair. "I might as well start at the beginning. I used to be in the Army. I was a Ranger, served in Iraq and Afghanistan. I was a pretty good shot, so they made me a sniper. That brought me to the attention of the Company and the other black-ops contractors over there."

"You worked for the CIA?"

"I worked *with* the CIA," Kincaid said. "I guess you could say I was part of a task force that went after highly specialized targets."

"Terrorist leaders."

Kincaid shrugged. He said, "All I knew was that they were bad guys and needed to be taken out. One of them was holed up in a compound in a Pakistani village called Warraz al-Sidar. We couldn't go after him in any conventional way because of . . . political considerations."

Stark grimaced. Kincaid knew exactly how he felt.

"Dealt with the same thing in Vietnam," Stark said. "Go on."

"A group of us went in to take the compound and eliminate the target. I didn't know until later that the guy who put together the mission was considered to have gone rogue. He'd been specifically ordered to leave this particular target alone. I don't think even the brass knew why, but they issued the hands-off order anyway."

"So you were disobeying orders without knowing it."

"Yeah. I guess I should've asked more questions. But I didn't, and we went in, fourteen guys, and the mission was FUBAR right from the start. It was pretty obvious why, too. They knew we were coming."

Stark frowned darkly. He said, "Somebody tipped them off. You were betrayed."

"Set up, even," Kincaid said. "And I found out why— but I'm getting ahead of myself. We found ourselves in deep, really deep, and it didn't take much figuring to know we weren't gonna get an extraction. We were supposed to be wiped out."

"But instead you fought your way clear."

Kincaid shook his head and said, "No, we took the compound and eliminated the target."

Stark gave a low whistle of admiration.

"They didn't plan on you doing that, I'll bet."

"No, they sure didn't. Only four of us made it. And more unfriendlies were on the way. So we cleared out. We had to get back across the border into Afghanistan alive. We knew that was our only chance. But before we left the compound I picked up some little USB drives that were in their command center. Nobody got around to wiping them, I guess because they didn't consider us a real threat."

"Something was on those drives," Stark guessed. "Something embarrassing."

"On one of them. The rest was just organizational stuff. But on one of them was an email archive . . ."

Kincaid took a deep breath again.

"It showed that this guy we'd gone in after, this terrorist mastermind, had been in close contact with a number of operatives in the United States. Operatives holding positions in our own government."

Stark stared at Kincaid for a moment, then said, "You're telling me that officials of our own government have been working directly with one of the leaders of the Islamic terrorist movement?"

"That's exactly what I'm telling you," Kincaid said in a flat voice. "Did you ever stop to wonder why there are dozens of Muslims holding high positions in the State Department, the Justice Department, the departments of Defense and Homeland Security?"

"Well, you can't refuse to hire somebody because of their religion," Stark said dryly. "That would be discrimination."

"Technically, sure. And I'm certain there are plenty of Muslims working for the government who are perfectly loyal Americans, whose only sin is being pissy little liberal bureaucrat toadies like the white people and the black people and the brown people they work with. But high up, a lot of them take their real orders directly from al-Qaeda or the Taliban or some other terrorist group. And I mean *really* high up, in some cases. As high as you can go."

"You're talking about . . ."

Kincaid cocked his head to the side and said, "It's no coincidence that everything the guy did while he was in office just made things worse here and weakened the country."

"Son of a—"

"Speaking of that," Kincaid said with a faint smile, "the emails confirmed that he really *wasn't* born here. The so-called nutjobs were right about that all along." Kincaid blew out his breath. "But he's long since gone from office, thank goodness. Unfortunately, the ones who followed him have been almost as bad."

"Did they know they were working with the terrorists? The fella who has the job now . . . ?"

Kincaid shook his head.

"Honest dupes, as far as I know. But it doesn't really matter. The pattern had already been established. The fanatical left wing of the Democratic party has strengthened their hold to the extent that all the Islamic undercover operatives have to do now is nudge things in the right direction from time to time. And the media is in the tank for the Democrats to such an extent that they could probably talk a majority into believing that none of it is important, even if the truth came out."

"But the Islamic cabal in Washington doesn't want it to come out anyway," Stark said.

"No, they do not," Kincaid agreed. "They don't want to take a chance. I realized that when I and the three guys who got out with me made it back to where we should have been safe, but people kept trying to kill us anyway."

"The bad guys had figured out what you uncovered in Warraz al-Sidar and sent assassins after you."

"Yep." Kincaid's tone hardened. "Death squads killed my friends, even though I hadn't told them anything about what was on the USB drive. They weren't any threat to the cabal. I'm the only one." He paused. "I used intelligence contacts I'd made, got to Germany through back-channel routes, and finally reached the States. I was considered a deserter by then, so the Army is looking for me, too. If they get me, I'll be given a DD and buried in some black-site federal facility where I can be eliminated at leisure. That's why I've been lying low."

"By working in a prison library."

Kincaid laughed humorlessly. "Would you have thought that a guy in possession of dangerous intel like that would be working in a prison library?"

"Well . . . probably not," Stark admitted. "You're wrong about one thing, though. You're not the only threat to the cabal anymore, not since you've told me about it."

"Yeah, and I'm sorry about that. But for all practical purposes . . ."

"We're not getting out of here alive anyway."

"That's the way it looks to me."

Stark sat there frowning in thought for a few seconds before he asked, "Why haven't you gone public with this?"

"Who would believe me? Hell, the media and a majority of the American public haven't been able to see the truth when it was right in front of their eyes for the past two decades! Besides, the personal destruction machine went into overdrive on me already. The Army spread the story that I and some of my buddies had gone berserk and massacred a bunch of innocent civilians in that village. That's probably why Riley recognized me. My face was plastered all over the news for a few days. I've changed my appearance some since then, but she's got a good eye, obviously."

"Have you told her any of this?" Stark asked quietly.

"How can I? That would just put her in danger, too. But then . . ."

"Yeah, there's that whole not-getting-out-of-here-alive thing," Stark said. "I can tell that something's sprung up between the two of you."

"Even though we've only known each other for a few hours?"

"Sometimes that's all it takes," Stark said. "If I'm right,

you might want to consider telling her the truth. Get it out in the open so there's no secrets between you."

"Yeah, maybe—" Kincaid suddenly stiffened. "Or maybe it's too late to worry about it," he went on as he looked at the movement on the monitor. "Here they come again . . . and they're really packing heat this time!"

CHAPTER 36

Lee and Gibby were in the kid's pickup. Spence, Flannery, Raymond, and the other man from the Ranger SRT rode in one of the jeeps "liberated" from the terrorists, with Spence at the wheel.

That was a good choice of driver, Lee thought as the two vehicles split off from the others. Spence had been in trouble with the law more than once for racing on the highway.

Every now and then, being an arrogant hothead came in handy.

"How're you holdin' up, Gibby?" Lee asked his companion.

"I'm all right," Gibby answered with a look of solemn determination on his face. "I know if Chuck was here he'd be tellin' me to keep it together. He taught me an awful lot, Officer Blaisdell."

"I know he did," Lee said. "He was a good guy and a good cop. I always enjoyed working with him."

"We're gonna pay those bastards back for what they did. They may not have pulled the trigger, but it's their fault Chuck's dead."

"It sure is."

After a minute or so of silence, Gibby went on, "But things are never gonna be the same. They came into our town. Into our *town*, where we live, and ruined it. What kinda world is it where things like that happen?"

"I don't know, Gibby," was all Lee could say. "I just don't know."

"This country's been lucky, really lucky. And now the people runnin' things . . . it seems like they're trying to just piss it all away."

"Yeah, it does," Lee agreed. "But you got to remember, the people up in Washington, the people in the media . . . they're not the whole country. There are still folks like you and me . . . like Chuck . . . out here willin' to fight for what's right. As long as that's true, I think we've got a chance. I hope so, anyway."

Gibby nodded slowly and said, "Yeah, me, too."

Lee stiffened and leaned forward on the seat as he spotted a cloud of dust rising, off to their right. It angled toward them on an interception course.

"We got company," he told Gibby as he pointed through the side window. "I figured when those two jeeps didn't come back, somebody might come looking for them."

"What do we do now?"

"Keep going," Lee said grimly. "We can't let anybody stop us from getting to town."

A gray van came into sight, cutting across country like Gibby's pickup and the jeep were doing. Lee figured it was full of terrorists, but he and the others couldn't open fire on it yet. There was a possibility the van was being driven by a civilian trying to get away from the hellhole Fuego had turned into.

The van veered to the right and slowed so that Gibby's pickup started to draw even with it. About twenty yards separated the two vehicles. Lee looked over, saw the face of the man driving, and recognized it as Middle Eastern.

Even then Lee hesitated. Like any law enforcement officer, he knew that while racial profiling wasn't politically correct, it was also a viable tool for spotting trouble. But it wasn't a hundred percent accurate. He didn't want to start shooting at somebody who wasn't really the enemy.

Any doubts about that vanished a moment later when the driver of the van floored the gas and sent the vehicle lunging ahead. As he swung the van back to the left, bringing it in front of Gibby's pickup, the rear doors flew open and gun barrels jutted out.

"Right, Gibby!" Lee yelled as he caught a glimpse in the side mirror of the jeep turning sharply left.

Gibby jerked the wheel and the pickup careened to the right as the men in the back of the van opened fire. With the jeep going the other way, that opened a gap between it and the pickup. The automatic weapons fire from the van passed between the two vehicles.

Flannery and the other Ranger in the jeep returned the fire. The terrorists in the van shot back at them. For the moment, Lee and Gibby in the pickup seemed to be forgotten.

"Gibby!" Lee said over the roaring engine. "How are you at drivin' backward?"

A grin split Gibby's big face as he must have realized what Lee was getting at. He slammed the brakes, spun the wheel, and hauled the pickup into a spinning turn that ended with it facing back the way it had come from.

Then Gibby threw the transmission into reverse and brought his foot tromping down on the gas again.

Dirt spurted as the pickup raced backward across the flat, hard-packed dirt. Lee was on the side facing the van now, and as Gibby began to catch up to it, he opened fire with the semiautomatic rifle he had brought along, concentrating his shots on the van's tires, front and rear.

After several rounds, the front tire shredded. That

corner of the van dropped sharply and dug into the ground. Momentum did the rest as the van flipped and rolled across the brush-dotted landscape.

By the time the van came to a stop, it was already burning. As a couple of men tried to climb out of it, that fire exploded into a ball of flame that engulfed the vehicle. The terrorists who had tried to escape ran crazily away from it, covered with flames as they burned alive.

It was more mercy than they deserved, but the Rangers cut them down as the jeep pulled up nearby.

A column of black smoke was already rising from the wrecked and burning van. Lee called to the others, "They'll be able to see that in town. Let's go before any more of them come looking!"

The pickup and the jeep took off again, headed for Fuego.

A short time later they approached the town from the west, the direction closest to the police station. The rest of their force would come in from the east and try to draw off the terrorists.

If anybody could make the radios in the station work, it was Raymond, Lee thought. That was why he had brought the dispatcher along. Gentle, slow-thinking Raymond probably wouldn't be much good in a fight, but he was a natural genius when it came to communications equipment.

One time somebody in the café had called Raymond an idiot savant. Lee had been ready to deck the guy, but luckily Janey had been with him and had explained what the term meant before a fight broke out.

The terrorists had probably clamped down so tight on the town that any moving vehicles would draw attention. That was why Lee told Gibby to slow down as they got closer. He didn't want their tires kicking up a lot of dust.

When they were still a mile from the edge of town, Lee signaled a halt.

The six men got out to stretch their legs. Spence asked, "How long do we wait?"

"As long as we have to," Lee said. "We'll know when to make our move."

Flannery squinted at the western sky. He seemed to be feeling better now and was steadier on his feet. "We've got, what, an hour, hour and a half of daylight left?" he asked.

"Yeah, about that," Lee replied.

"Might have been easier to wait until after dark to go in."

The Ranger had a point, Lee thought. In his eagerness to do something, to fight back against the invaders, that idea hadn't occurred to him.

But it was too late now. The others were on their way to launch their feint at the eastern end of town, and there was no way to communicate with them.

That was one of the most frustrating things about this whole deal. People were used to their iPhones and iPads and 5G and 6G networks and constantly being in touch with the rest of the world from the time they woke up in the morning to the moment they went to sleep at night. And even while they were sleeping, emails and texts kept going through, so that when they woke again, new communications would be waiting for them.

Now they were alone, cut off from everybody except the people they could see and hear right in front of them.

It made a fella feel small and insignificant, that was for sure.

"We'll have to do the best we can," Lee said, trying not to sound annoyed. Flannery's comment had gotten on his nerves, because he knew that the Ranger really ought to be in charge, not him. Flannery had been shaken up, though, so Lee had sort of been drafted into the job.

Now, for better or worse, the survival of the rest of Fuego's citizens might be up to him.

Before he could say anything else, the rattle of distant gunfire came through the air, followed by a small explosion.

"That'll be our boys gettin' their attention," Lee said. "Come on."

They piled into the pickup and jeep and headed swiftly for town.

Lee had already told Gibby and Spence to go to the supermarket on the western edge of Fuego and park behind it, where the vehicles would be hidden. There were a few houses farther out, but they appeared to be empty and deserted, Lee thought as the two boys drove past them.

That was ominous. It meant the terrorists had rounded up everybody in Fuego. Lee wondered what had been done with them. Had they all been killed already, or were they being held prisoner somewhere?

Maybe he and the others would try to find out, but first things first: taking control of the police station and trying to get a message to the outside world.

They reached the supermarket without incident. Gibby and Spence stopped beside the loading dock at the back of the big building. As everyone got out of the vehicles, they could hear the sounds of the battle going on at the other end of town.

"Weren't the others supposed to cut and run so the ragheads would chase them?" Spence asked. "That sounds like they're still fighting down there."

"Yeah, but we can't worry about that now," Lee said. "Let's get to the police station."

The station was a couple of blocks away. Lee led his men along a side street so they could come up behind it. As they trotted along the empty street, he saw the bodies of several dogs lying here and there. Fresh anger welled up inside him at the sight. He knew the dogs must have rushed out to protect their owners and their homes as the invaders made their sweep through town. Those monsters didn't hesitate to kill innocent people, so gunning down some loyal dogs would have meant less than nothing to them.

Lee hoped the Devil had a special place in Hell lined up for those bastards.

Then the rear parking lot of the police station came into sight. Lee knew the front of the building had been blasted apart in the earlier attack, but the back looked deceptively normal. It was empty at the moment. The police cars that were usually kept there were gone.

Lee's heart pounded heavily as he paused to look at the building. He couldn't seem to get his breath. He swallowed hard and said quietly to the others, "All right, spread out a little as we go across the parking lot. Raymond, you stay behind us, you hear?"

"I can fight," Raymond said.

"I know you can, but I need you to work the radio once we get in there, okay?"

"Okay," Raymond said. "But if you need me to fight, you just tell me."

"I reckon you'll know, buddy," Lee muttered.

He held the rifle at a slant across his chest and started across the parking lot, keeping his eyes on the building as he ran. The shoes and boots of the others slapped on the concrete as they joined him.

They were still fifteen yards from the back door when armed men boiled around both rear corners of the building and opened fire, catching Lee and his companions between the two forces.

This was a trap, Lee thought in wild despair, and they had waltzed right into it!

CHAPTER 37

Stark leaned forward to look at the monitor where Kincaid was pointing. He saw a man kneeling at the corridor's far corner, holding something.

Stark's guts went cold when he recognized the object as a rocket launcher.

The terrorists were about to try blasting their way in.

But the man seemed to be having some sort of trouble with the weapon. Maybe it was malfunctioning.

Whatever the reason, it gave the defenders a very narrow window to fight back.

"Open the doors!" Stark told Kincaid.

"But—"

Kincaid stopped short, evidently realizing what Stark had in mind, and pushed buttons on the console. The inner and outer doors of the sally port began to roll to the side.

"John Howard, if he fires that thing—"

Stark didn't hear the rest of Kincaid's warning. He didn't have to. He knew what the former Army Ranger was getting at. Stark was putting himself in close proximity to a potential explosion as he ran to the sally port's inner door, taking his rifle with him.

"That's enough!" he called to Kincaid.

The doors stopped opening. The gap was only a couple of inches wide.

This ought to be Kincaid making the shot, Stark thought as he brought the rifle to his shoulder. Kincaid was the marksman, the sniper.

But Stark had made some difficult shots himself in his lifetime. He aimed through the tiny openings in both doors and set his sights on the terrorist with the grenade launcher, who seemed to have gotten whatever the problem was squared away. The man lifted the weapon . . .

Stark fired.

One round, sizzling through the narrow gaps, along the corridor, and into the terrorist's forehead an inch above his right eye. As his skull exploded from the bullet's impact, he went over backward and his finger jerked and fired the grenade.

It went into the ceiling above him and exploded.

"Close the doors!" Stark yelled at Kincaid over the blast. He heard debris slamming against the outer door and felt the floor shake under his feet.

The ceiling caved in at the other end of the corridor. A huge cloud of dust and smoke billowed up, filling the corridor and obscuring the damage from the explosion. It rolled down the hallway toward the sally port but was blocked by the doors, which thumped shut just as it got there.

As Stark stepped back into the command center, Kincaid said, "That was one hell of a shot!"

"One hell of a lucky shot," Stark said.

"I don't know about that. It looked like you knew what you were doing."

"Well, the important thing is, they've blasted their way

through that outer door. And the damage that grenade did pretty much blocked the corridor for now."

"They'll be able to dig their way through it pretty quick," Stark said.

"Maybe." Kincaid picked up his rifle, which he had leaned against the console. "But not if we make it difficult for them."

Stark nodded. He knew what Kincaid meant, and it was a good idea. The longer they could hold off the terrorists, the better chance there was that help would arrive.

Stark just wished he could believe wholeheartedly that the government really did want to help them.

But he had seen for himself how the authorities had turned their backs on him when the drug cartels attacked his ranch.

He had been there inside those ancient, hallowed walls when the government sided with the Mexican army against the modern-day defenders of the Alamo.

He'd had to fight the law enforcement and political establishments almost every step of the way as he tried to protect his new home down in Shady Hills from being overrun by ruthless, drug-smuggling killers.

If the events of the past decade had taught him anything, it was that the Powers That Be in this country were more likely to side with the enemies of the people. Good, honest, hardworking Americans had been abandoned in favor of the electoral, urban-dwelling majority that wanted to be coddled, given free stuff, and told what to do. And most of the time when those traditional Americans tried to protect themselves, the government cracked down on them.

If by some miracle he and Kincaid and the others trapped here in Hell's Gate survived this terrorist attack, they might well find themselves facing legal charges for fighting back.

That was how insane things had become in this country under liberal Democrat rule.

Now that the smoke and dust had settled in the corridor, Stark and Kincaid could see the pile of debris blocking the far end of the passageway. Kincaid pushed the buttons to open the sally port doors again. When they had slid back about three inches, he stopped them.

Then he took his rifle and went to the inner door.

"I'll take the first shift, John Howard," he told Stark. "But I may have to call on you later."

"I'll be here," Stark said. "It's not like there's anywhere else I can go."

Mitch Cambridge had come up behind them in time to hear Stark's comment. He said, "Actually, Mr. Stark, that may not be true."

Stark and Kincaid both turned to look at the young guard in amazement. Kincaid asked, "Mitch, are you saying . . . ?"

"Yes, I am," Cambridge replied with a nod. "There's a way out of here."

Phillip Hamil had heard the explosion from deeper in the prison and felt a thrill go through him. That sound meant his men had blasted through the doors into the maximum security wing, and soon his imprisoned brothers would be free. Hamil strode in that direction, wanting to be there when the liberation took place.

Raffir met Hamil before he could get there. The second-in-command trotted along a hallway with a worried look on his narrow face.

"Raffir!" Hamil said sharply. "Are not our men on the verge of triumph?"

Raffir stopped and shook his head with obvious reluctance.

"I had a man about to blow down the outer door with an RPG," he said, "but one of the Americans killed him and caused the grenade to detonate so that the explosion blocked the approach to the maximum security wing."

Fury filled Hamil as he digested this unwelcome news. It was getting late in the afternoon. They should have breached the sally port by now and be busy killing the infidels for the greater glory of Allah and the Prophet.

"Then clear away the debris and try again," he snapped at Raffir. "We have more grenades. We have more men."

That was true. There were always believers willing to martyr themselves. That was why Islam would always emerge victorious in the end. The infidels cared about life on this earth. Hamil's men cared only about the glories that awaited them in Heaven.

Raffir nodded and said, "That was my first thought as well, Doctor. I sent men to move the collapsed ceiling. But . . ."

"Well, what is it? Spit it out, man."

"An American marksman killed them all," Raffir said. "They weren't even able to retrieve the body of the first man we sent, the one with the RPG."

The fury that filled Hamil turned cold. He said, "So the bodies of our brothers are simply lying there in the open, where the infidels can gloat over them?"

"I tried sending more men, but they were shot down as well. So I came to find you and see what you wanted to do next."

"What do I want to do next?" Hamil took a deep breath and roared, "I want to destroy the infidels!"

He struggled to get control of himself. Raging at Raffir wouldn't accomplish anything.

After a moment, in a calmer voice, Hamil said, "I may have something to use against the Americans. Two prisoners from town. When I heard about them, I had them brought out from Fuego. First, though, I have to establish contact with them."

"Many of the guards carried walkie-talkies," Raffir suggested. "Some of them in the maximum security wing should still have them. And we've gathered up plenty from dead bodies. We can find the right channel to contact the infidels."

Hamil nodded. This might work out after all.

"Bring me one of the walkie-talkies," he said. "And have the American boy and girl brought to me as well."

Andy had trouble believing that he and Jill were still alive. They should have died back there in the hospital cafeteria with all the other patients and visitors.

The terrorists had questioned the hospital staff before they opened fire on the huddled, terrified prisoners, just to make sure there was no one among them they could make use of somehow.

When they found out that he was the son of a guard captain from the prison, he had been pulled aside from the others. He had struggled to hang on to Jill, and the guy in charge of the killers had shrugged and said to bring her along, too.

As Andy walked slowly out of the cafeteria on his crutches, with Jill stumbling along beside him and gunmen all around them, he'd heard the shooting start behind them. He heard the screams cut short and felt tears roll down his face. He knew people were dying back there, people who had gone to church with him and watched him play ball and led simple, honest lives . . .

Until today when everything had been ripped cruelly away from them.

Guilt had filled Andy as well. He was thankful, as well as amazed, that he and Jill were still alive, but a part of him felt like they should have died back there with the others. It wasn't fair that a whim of fate had saved them, at least temporarily.

They had been taken out of the hospital and put in the back of a van. A couple of men with automatic weapons guarded them, but to be honest, they didn't need much guarding. With a broken leg, Andy couldn't put up a real fight, and he couldn't imagine Jill wrestling a gun away from one of those murderers and opening fire with it. That just wasn't gonna happen.

Time had dragged by. The back of the van grew uncomfortably warm in the sunny afternoon. Andy wasn't going to complain, though. Not when he was alive and had no real right to be.

Every now and then he heard an explosion or a burst of gunfire. The terrorists seemed to have taken over the town for the most part, but obviously there were still pockets of resistance.

Finally, past the middle of the afternoon, another man came up and talked to their captors in a rapid, guttural language that Andy didn't have a hope of understanding. Then the man had gotten behind the wheel, started the engine, and driven off with Andy, Jill, and the guards in the back.

From the glimpses that Andy caught through the van's windows, he soon figured out that they were headed for the prison.

"What are they going to do with us, Andy?" Jill asked in a small, frightened voice as she pressed herself against his side.

"I don't know. Maybe . . . maybe try to trade us for

something they want. They know my dad works at the prison."

"I think they're going to kill us."

"If they were gonna do that, they'd have done it already," he said, trying to sound confident.

He wasn't, though. He didn't know if he and Jill were going to survive for the next five minutes, let alone until this ordeal was over.

It didn't take long to reach the prison. The van drove in, bumping over something several times along the way. Andy didn't know what those bumps were. He wasn't sure he wanted to know.

The van came to a stop, and a moment later the rear doors swung open. The two guards hopped out and swung around to cover the prisoners with their automatic weapons, while more men reached in and grabbed hold of Jill's blue jean–clad legs. She screamed and tried to kick as they hauled her out of the van.

A man holding a pistol used the gun to gesture at Andy and ordered in a harshly accented voice, "Get out now."

"I'll move as fast as I can, okay?" Andy said. He nodded toward the cast on his leg. "I'm gonna be a little slow, though."

"Come," the man growled.

Awkwardly, Andy scooted over to the rear door and swung his legs out. He wished he was wearing something besides the hospital gown and his boxers. This was as humiliating as it could be.

Once he was out of the van and had the crutches tucked securely under his arms, he was marched toward the prison through something he had never seen before: a battlefield. Bodies and, well, *pieces* of bodies lay scattered on the ground. Shell holes gaped in the pavement.

Some of the outbuildings were just rubble. The front of the facility's main building showed heavy damage as well. In Andy's online history textbook, he had seen images of destruction from World War II, and that was what Hell's Gate looked like today.

Jill said, "Andy, your dad . . ."

"I know," Andy said, his voice bleak. He had no way of knowing right now whether his father was dead or alive, but the chances of Bert Frazier having survived this battle had to be pretty small. Andy knew his dad would have been right in the middle of the fighting, trying to do his job.

Jill started to sob from fear and horror. Andy couldn't say or do anything to comfort her. They were both powerless right now.

They were taken into what had been an anteroom off the prison's main lobby and allowed to sit down. They waited there, under armed guard, listening to the faint sounds of shooting going on elsewhere in the prison.

At last a tall, lean man came in and said to the guards in English, "The doctor wishes to see these two."

Andy had no idea who "the doctor" was. Under normal circumstances that designation might be comforting, but these were anything but normal circumstances.

Somehow, knowing that "the doctor" wanted to see him and Jill sent a chill through him.

That feeling didn't go away as they were taken through the prison, Andy moving slowly on his crutches, until they were brought into an office where a well-dressed, darkly handsome man stood in front of a desk.

This was Warden Baldwin's office, Andy recalled. He had been here before with his dad.

The man waiting for them certainly wasn't George Baldwin, though. He smiled at them and said, "Mr. Frazier,

Miss Hamilton, my name is Dr. Phillip Hamil. I am very pleased to meet you. You two young people are going to help me and my friends achieve our goals and bring glory to the name of Allah."

All Andy had to do was look at the cold, reptilian hatred in the man's eyes to know that he and Jill had just had a death sentence pronounced on them.

CHAPTER 38

With the parking lot behind the police station in Fuego being empty, there was no place to take cover as the jaws of the trap started to close on Lee Blaisdell and his companions. He and Flannery, along with Spence and Gibby, opened fire because that was all they could do.

The other Ranger didn't have a chance to do even that much. He grunted and went down, drilled through the neck. Blood fountained from the wound.

That was the fate that awaited the rest of them—but suddenly a pickup roared around the corner of the building and plowed through one group of terrorists, crushing some of them beneath its wheels and sending others flying through the air from the devastating impact.

The driver and the other man in the cab had more than just running down the killers in mind. They fired pistols from both windows into the other group of terrorists, who scattered to avoid being run over.

That gave Lee and his companions time enough to aim their weapons and cut them down one by one. In less than half a minute, approximately two dozen terrorists lay dead or dying on the parking lot's concrete pavement, and the pickup containing the unexpected rescuers skidded to a halt.

The passenger door popped open. A tall, lean man with graying fair hair and a close-cropped beard stepped out. Sunglasses covered his eyes. He wore camo fatigues and combat boots and was unquestionably American.

"Looks like we got here just in time to give you boys a hand," he said in a Texas drawl. He jerked his head toward the pickup bed and went on, "Hop in. We need to get out of here while we've got the chance."

"Wait just a minute, mister," Lee said. "I don't know who you are, but we've got to get into that police station and see if we can make any of the radios work."

"If it's a comm line you want, I've got a sat phone with state-of-the-art encryption," the stranger said. "What I don't have is a lot of time. By the way, I'm Colonel Thomas Atkinson. Retired."

He added that last in a dryly amused way. He might not be on active duty anymore, but he was still every inch a soldier, Lee thought. And he had to make a decision, right now on the spur of the moment, about whether he was going to trust Atkinson.

"All right," he said to the men with him. "Let's go."

"I agree," Flannery said. "I've heard of Colonel Atkinson."

They hurried over to the pickup. Atkinson held out a hand toward Raymond and said in a gentle voice, "Why don't you ride inside with Sergeant Porter, son? That'll give me a chance to talk to these other fellas."

Raymond looked at Lee, who nodded.

"You go ahead and do what the colonel says."

"Is he the boss now?" Raymond asked.

Lee longed to surrender all the responsibility to somebody else, but at the same time, he had been running things reasonably well so far, he thought, so he said, "We'll see."

Atkinson grunted. Lee realized after a second that the sound was a laugh.

"Head for open country, Sergeant," Atkinson said through the open window to the driver, who looked more like a small-town lawyer or high school football coach than a noncom. He had handled the pickup with great skill, though, and was a good shot. The terrorists he had gunned down testified mutely to that.

As the pickup bounced over the curb and out of the parking lot, Lee introduced himself to the colonel.

"I'm Officer Lee Blaisdell, Fuego PD," he said.

"How many are left from your department, Officer Blaisdell?"

"I don't really know," Lee admitted. "Me and Raymond, he's our dispatcher, and one other officer. I know one officer is dead, and I haven't seen the chief or any of the other fellas since all this started, so I don't feel very optimistic about them."

"Unfortunately, I'd agree with you." Atkinson looked over at Flannery. "And you are . . . ?"

"Lieutenent David Flannery, Texas Rangers. Out of the El Paso office. I brought a Special Response Team in here earlier today by chopper." Flannery grimaced. "For all I know, I'm the only one left, although a couple of my men were with another force of defenders earlier this afternoon."

"And you two look like football players," Atkinson said as he glanced at Gibby and Spence.

"That's because we are," Spence said. If he was intimidated by Atkinson, he didn't show it. "But we can still fight."

"I don't doubt it, son." Atkinson turned his attention back to Lee and Flannery. "Tell me everything you know about what's going on here and what you're doing about it."

"First—and with all due respect, Colonel—I'd like to know what *you're* doing here," Flannery said.

"Fair enough. The governor sent me and my team to find out what the situation is here and advise her on what she should do next."

"You're talking about Governor Delgado?"

"She's the only one Texas has got right now."

Lee said, "You're not with the federal government?"

Atkinson's snort eloquently conveyed his contempt for that idea.

"I'm a Texan," he said, "and you may not be aware of it, but Texas is about that far—" He held up his thumb and forefinger, a short distance apart. "—from saying to hell with the federal government. We still believe in a little thing called the Constitution down here, even if most of the people in Washington don't."

"That's good to hear . . . maybe," Lee said. "But what can the governor do?"

"Tell me what we're looking at here, and maybe we can figure something out."

Lee glanced over at Flannery, who said, "Go ahead, Lee. You've been on the ground here right from the start."

"All right," Lee said. Colonel Atkinson was the first person who had offered any real help since the attack began, so Lee decided he might as well trust the man.

As Sgt. Porter stuck to back roads in town and then took off across country when he reached the edge of Fuego, Lee told Atkinson all he knew about how the attack had taken place around the middle of the day. Atkinson asked questions about the enemy's strength and capabilities, and Lee answered them as best he could.

When he was finished, the colonel thanked him, then said, "You may have to go over all that again with the governor, Lee. Once she hears it, I can't imagine that she'll let this stand."

"What can she do about it?" Flannery asked.

"You might be surprised," Atkinson replied with a faint smile. "For now, we need to hole up somewhere. What about this farm where you say the women were supposed to wait?"

"I can tell your driver how to get there," Lee said. He was relieved that Atkinson had suggested going to the Simmons place. He wanted to see Janey again and assure himself that she was all right. "By the way, you fellas *did* steal this pickup in town, didn't you?"

"I'm afraid we did. Are you going to arrest us, Officer?"

"I'll let it pass . . . this time," Lee said with a weary smile of his own.

While they were on their way to the Simmons farm, Atkinson told Lee and the others about everything that had happened outside Fuego that day, from the attack on the prison to the official response—or non-response—from Washington.

"You mean to say the Feds just threw a ring around the whole area and are going to leave us in here to stew?" Lee asked.

"Muslims are rioting in major cities across the country in support of Hamil and his bunch," Atkinson said. "The President's afraid to do much because he doesn't want to make things worse, I suppose. He doesn't want to go down in history as being blamed for an American jihad. Although when you get right down to it, our government's been sympathetic to the extremist Islamic movement for a long time. Remember Benghazi? Remember the Muslim Brotherhood?"

"I've heard of that stuff in history class," Gibby said.

"Well, it's not history to some of us, son. We lived through it. We couldn't believe what was happening then, what this country was becoming without most people even seeming to care. And somehow it's just gotten worse." Atkinson paused. "It wouldn't surprise me if there were people pretty high up in Washington who knew what was going to happen in Fuego today. But anybody who said that in public would be crucified by the press as a paranoid conspiracy nut."

"Yeah, but you know the old sayin'," Lee said. "You're not paranoid if they're really out to get you."

Atkinson grinned.

"Truer words were never spoken, son. Truer words were never spoken."

They were following a narrow dirt road now. The sun had dipped below the horizon, but its lurid glare remained, shining through the geographic formation known as Hell's Gate in the distance. In that reddish light, which would soon vanish, the Simmons farmhouse came into view.

Everything about the place looked normal, Lee thought as the pickup followed the lane toward it. But the police station had looked relatively normal, too, before it erupted with terrorist gunmen, he reminded himself. There was no telling what waited for him up there . . . the welcoming embrace of his wife . . . or bloody, unspeakable horror.

Lee swallowed hard. His hands were slick with sweat on the rifle he gripped. One at a time, he wiped them on his uniform trousers.

"Back there at the police station, they knew we were comin'," he said. "I hadn't really thought about it until now, but they had to know, otherwise they couldn't have set up that trap for us. That means they've got eyes in the sky."

Atkinson nodded and said, "Yes, it's likely that someone is feeding them satellite intel. One more reason to think that the NSA and DOD have moles in them."

"How can we fight something that big?" Flannery said. "How can we fight those terrorists if they have people in our own government helping them?"

"We don't give up," Atkinson said. "We try to remember that most Americans—even the ones who've been taken in by all the leftist bullshit propaganda—are still decent people. We keep hoping that there'll come a time when they realize what they've allowed our enemies to do to us from within, and then they'll rise up and put things right."

"Do you really believe that, Colonel?" Lee asked. "Or is it already too late?"

"I guess we'll find out over the next few years, Lee . . . starting now."

The men were all on edge, with their weapons ready to fire, as the pickup drove up to the old farmhouse and stopped in front of the porch. The house seemed to be deserted. The front door was closed, and curtains were pulled over all the windows.

Then someone jerked the front door open, and the screen door banged back as a slender shape burst out onto the porch.

"Lee!" Janey cried.

Lee vaulted out of the pickup bed and ran to meet her. At the bottom of the porch steps, he swept her into his arms and brought his mouth down on hers. The kiss jolted Lee to the core of his being as all the relief packed into both of them flowed into it.

Finally, Janey pulled back a little and whispered, "You're all right."

"I'm fine," Lee told her. He was vaguely aware that several other people had come out onto the porch from inside the house, but nearly all of his attention was focused on his wife as he held her close to him. "Nothing's happened here?"

"No, not . . . here."

Her hesitation warned him that something was wrong. He frowned and said, "Janey, what is it?"

"Some of the others . . . they're back from town already, Lee," she said. "They have news." She took a deep breath. "Bad news."

CHAPTER 39

Kincaid stood looking at the hatch Mitch Cambridge had uncovered earlier in one of the wing's maintenance areas.

"There was always the possibility that the wing would need to be evacuated for some reason, but nobody could go out through the sally port," Cambridge had explained to Kincaid and Stark when he first showed them the hatch. "It was even more likely that the warden would need to get officers in here without going through the main entrance, like in a case where the inmates rioted and took over the wing."

"I thought the procedure there would be to pump tear gas in through the ventilation system and storm the place, as long as no hostages were in danger," Kincaid said.

"Yes, but if there were hostages, or if you couldn't use tear gas for some other reason, you'd need a way to get armed men inside. Anyway, even with the tear gas, if you sent in men wearing gas masks, they'd be able to round up the prisoners pretty quickly."

Kincaid had nodded in understanding and said, "Yeah, I suppose so. Where does it go?"

"It leads to a tunnel with several branches. You can get

to administration from here, or to minimum security or
Gen Pop."

"How do you know about this?" Kincaid asked with a
frown. "I've been working here for a while, and I never
heard anything about secret tunnels."

That had put a grin on Cambridge's face.

"That's because they're secret," he said. "No, seriously,
the warden and the guard captains know about them,
but the thinking was that regular correctional officers
didn't need that information unless it became necessary
to use the tunnels."

"Which leads me back to the question I just asked you:
how do *you* know about them?"

"I've studied this prison, everything about it. One of
these days I'm going to be a warden, either here or in
some other facility like it, and I want to know everything
there is to know about running it. So I went back and
looked at everything I could find about it online and
checked out all the physical records in the county clerk's
office. I found some plans in the permitting office that
mentioned those access tunnels, as they're called. But I
figured out what they're really for."

Kincaid had been surprised by the amount of ambition
the mild-looking young guard possessed, but Cambridge's
career goals wouldn't mean anything if he and the others
didn't survive this siege.

The information Cambridge had uncovered just
might help with that.

Stark had said, "The important question is, will folks
fit through them?"

"Sure. The tunnels are four feet wide and eight feet
high. Room to spare."

"The problem is that the terrorists seem to be in control of the rest of the prison," Kincaid said. "Wherever we
come out, we're liable to run right into them."

"Might be able to wage a little guerrilla war against

them that way," Stark mused, "even if it's not an actual escape route."

That comment had been percolating in the back of Kincaid's mind ever since. It would be sort of fitting, he thought now, if he and his fellow Americans became the insurgents in this war.

Stark was posted at the sally port at the moment, to pick off any of the terrorists who tried to clear away the debris at the far end of the corridor. For the time being, that was working, but Kincaid knew it wouldn't last. Sooner or later the terrorists would risk using explosives to blow the junk out of the way.

Kincaid and Stark had been communicating by walkie-talkie, shifting around the frequencies so the enemy wouldn't be as likely to listen in on their conversations. As Kincaid stood there contemplating the hatch and trying to figure out their next move, the unit clipped to his belt suddenly crackled and an unfamiliar voice said, "Warden Baldwin or whoever is in charge of the infidel forces inside the maximum security wing. This is Dr. Phillip Hamil, leader of the Sword of Islam."

That showed how confident the guy was, identifying himself bold as brass like that, Kincaid thought. He grabbed the walkie-talkie, lifted it to his mouth, keyed the mic, and said, "What do you want?"

"To whom am I speaking?" Hamil wanted to know.

"That doesn't matter," Kincaid said. "Spare the rhetoric and tell me what you want."

"Is Ms. Alexis Devereaux unharmed?"

That question took Kincaid by surprise. He said, "As far as I know."

"Bring her to the inner door of the sally port, please. Right now. And you and anyone else in there who is in charge should see what's about to happen."

Those casual words made Kincaid go cold inside. He

didn't know what the terrorist mastermind was up to, but it couldn't be anything good.

"Wait a minute," Kincaid said quickly. "Don't do anything crazy."

"I assure you, I'm absolutely sane."

Kincaid had serious doubts about that, but he didn't say so. Instead he told Hamil, "I'll get Ms. Devereaux. Just hang on."

He ran out of the maintenance area, which was at the far end of the maximum security wing, and hurried toward the sally port. The guards and inmates he passed watched him with worried frowns. They could guess from his haste that something was up.

He came to where Alexis Devereaux was sitting on the floor with Riley Nichols and Travis Jessup, looking very unhappy about her plight. Kincaid paused and said, "Ms. Devereaux, come with me."

"I don't have to follow your orders," Alexis snapped. "I'm a civilian, in case you haven't noticed. I shouldn't even be in here."

"If you hadn't been in here in the first place trying to stir up trouble—" Kincaid stopped short. He knew he was wasting his breath. He went on, "Look, you have to come with me. The leader of the terrorists called me on the walkie-talkie. He told me to bring you to the sally port."

Clearly, Alexis was confused. She said, "What . . . How would he know about me?"

"He sounded like he might be a friend of yours. At least he asked if you had been hurt. His name is Hamil. Dr. Phillip Hamil."

Alexis gaped at him.

"That . . . that can't be true," she said. "Phillip Hamil is a good, decent man—"

"Who's the leader of the Sword of Islam, the group responsible for what's happened today. Now, are you coming or not?"

Riley got to her feet and said, "Hell, yes, we're coming."
She extended a hand to Alexis.

After a moment, Alexis gripped the other woman's hand and climbed awkwardly to her feet. They hurried along the wing toward the guard station and command post. Travis Jessup stayed behind, muttering to himself in fright.

Mitch Cambridge was at the console in the command center. He stood up as Kincaid and the two women came in.

"Mr. Stark and I heard Hamil on the walkies, too," Cambridge said. "Ms. Devereaux, do you have any idea what he wants?"

"No, and I still refuse to believe that Phillip Hamil would have anything to do with this atrocity," Alexis said. "This madman has to be someone pretending to be him. You'll see."

"That's right," Kincaid said. "Let's see what he wants."

They went through the reception area where Stark stood with the barrel of his rifle sticking through the door's narrow opening. He had his eye to the sights, watching the far end of the corridor.

"Nobody moving around down there," he reported.

Kincaid's walkie-talkie was still set to the same channel. Figuring that the terrorists would be monitoring it, he said, "Hamil, do you hear me?"

"I hear you," Hamil's voice came back.

Alexis's shocked gasp was enough to tell Kincaid that she'd recognized the voice.

"Ms. Devereaux is here with us," he said. "What do you want?"

"Well, first of all, I'd ask that you don't shoot me when I step out into the open."

"It'll be tempting," Stark muttered, "but I'll hold my fire."

"You'll be safe," Kincaid said into the walkie-talkie.

"Very well. I won't be coming out first. Someone else will be."

Kincaid, Cambridge, Alexis, and Riley watched through the windows in the sally port doors. Stark kept his rifle's sights lined up. A figure moved clumsily into view at the end of the corridor, on the other side of the pile of debris. He was visible from about the waist up.

Even with that limited perspective, Kincaid could tell that the man was young, no more than a boy. He was on crutches and wore what looked like a hospital gown. And even though Kincaid couldn't see his face that clearly at this distance, he knew the kid had to be scared out of his mind.

"Good Lord," Cambridge said. "That's Andy Frazier."

"The football player who broke his leg the other night?" Stark asked.

"They've taken him out of the hospital in Fuego," Kincaid said. "But why bring him out here?"

The answer wasn't long in coming. Two men with hoods obscuring their features moved up alongside Andy, one on each side. They grasped his arms to hold him steady.

Another man appeared behind the youngster. He lifted a walkie-talkie to his mouth and said, "Can you see me in there?"

"We see you," Kincaid said. "Why don't you let that kid go? He can't do you any harm."

"Of course he can't. No infidel can stand against the glory of the Prophet and the might of the Sword of Islam. But he can do us some good. He can help us show you the fate in store for all of you if you don't cooperate and give us what we want."

Hamil raised his other hand. In it he gripped a long, wicked-looking knife.

Alexis screamed.

Hamil said, "I'm truly sorry you have to witness this,

Alexis, but you know it never would have happened if not for American arrogance."

With that, he tossed the walkie-talkie aside, used that hand to grab hold of Andy Frazier's hair, and jerked the young man's head back while he lifted the knife.

Stark fired. He didn't have a shot at Hamil because Andy was in the line of fire, but he took out the man holding Andy's left arm.

It wasn't enough. Hamil moved with blinding speed, stroking the razor-sharp blade across Andy's throat, cutting deeply so that blood geysered from the hideous wound as the boy spasmed.

Stark shot the other terrorist. Andy fell forward, collapsing across the pile of rubble. Then he rolled backward and fell out of sight.

Hamil was gone. He had already ducked back behind cover.

Alexis screamed hysterically, covered her face with her hands, and turned away from the window. She would probably never be able to get the sight she had just witnessed out of her head.

Kincaid knew he might not.

Riley was crying, but she was cursing, too. She said, "How . . . how could he . . . how could anybody—"

"Because we're less than nothing to them," Kincaid said in a flinty voice. "The way Hamil sees it, he just earned himself another reward in Heaven by murdering that kid."

He was surprised to hear the walkie-talkie crackle again. Hamil's voice came over it.

"I regret that young man had to die to illustrate the injustices to which your country has subjected my people. He had a friend with him, a young woman named Jill. If you listen closely, you can probably hear her screams as my men deal with her."

Hamil paused but left the channel open, and sure

enough, Kincaid heard faint screams in the background. He had to close his eyes for a second as his emotions threatened to spiral out of control.

"This can end right now," Hamil went on after a moment. "Release my brothers who have been unjustly imprisoned. No more innocents have to die. Ms. Devereaux and those with her will be allowed to leave in peace."

Oddly enough, Kincaid believed that. Hamil was clearly such a megalomaniac that he would welcome Alexis's eyewitness testimony being broadcast around the world. That would just make him a bigger hero in the Muslim countries.

Breathing a little hard through his nose, Kincaid lifted the walkie-talkie and said, "Those murderers you call your brothers aren't going anywhere, Hamil. They're going to stay behind bars where they belong. And before this is over, I'm going to kill you."

Hamil just laughed.

"Such bravado," he said. "You should be rewarded for that, my friend, whoever you are. Here. I have something for you."

An arm appeared and tossed something around the corner, over the rubble, so that it bounced several feet along the corridor toward the sally port.

Kincaid gritted his teeth and swallowed the sickness that tried to well up in his throat.

The object lying there in the corridor, features twisted in agony, was the head of Andy Frazier.

CHAPTER 40

Martin Corey limped out of the Simmons farmhouse before Janey could say anything else to Lee about what had happened in Fuego. The bloody rag that he had tied around his left thigh explained the limp.

"They were waiting for us, Lee," Martin said in a hollow voice. "The bastards knew we were coming."

"They knew about us, too," Lee said. "It was a trap all the way around." He gestured toward Martin's leg. "How bad are you wounded?"

"This?" Martin waved a hand at the makeshift bandage. "Hurts like hell, but the bullet missed the bone. Once we got the bleeding stopped, I was all right. It'll heal. I may limp for the rest of my life . . ." He laughed. "But that probably won't be too long, will it?"

"Don't talk like that, Martin," Janey told him. "We'll find a way out of this." She looked at Lee again. "Maybe we should all load up and leave. Just get out of this part of the country and never come back."

Colonel Atkinson had climbed out of the back of the pickup with the others and now leaned against its fender, his attitude appearing casual when it was probably anything but. He said, "I wouldn't recommend that, Mrs. Blaisdell."

"Who's this?" Janey asked Lee. "I don't remember ever seeing him around town before."

"This is Colonel Atkinson," Lee explained. "He, uh, works for the governor."

"Governor Delgado?"

"Yep. She sent him and some other folks in to take a look around and figure out what needs to be done."

Atkinson straightened and came over to them. He nodded to Janey and said, "Pleased to meet you, Mrs. Blaisdell. I wish it were under better circumstances."

"So do I," Janey said curtly. "What did you mean, it wouldn't be a good idea to get out of here? Do you think the terrorists would stop us?"

"Probably not. I'd say there's a good chance they know where you are right now. They could come after you if they wanted to. You're insignificant to them right now. What you'd have to worry about is running into the cordon set up by Homeland Security."

Janey shook her head and said, "I still don't understand. Wouldn't they help us?"

"I reckon maybe I get it," Lee said. "From what you were sayin' earlier, Colonel, it sounds like some of the people runnin' things in the government don't want the truth about what's happenin' here getting out to the public."

"Exactly," Atkinson said. "Those Homeland Security agents might 'help' you right into a lockup somewhere. I'm talking about the kind of place where they throw you down a hole and nobody ever sees you again."

Janey looked back and forth between the two men and said, "That's crazy! Nobody could get away with such a thing in this country."

"Just like the Democrats couldn't get away with their candidates receiving more votes in some precincts than there are registered voters?" Atkinson asked with a cocked eyebrow. "You wouldn't think that could happen, either, but it has in every national election for more than a decade now. I hate to tell you this, Mrs. Blaisdell, but this isn't the country you think it is. Not anymore."

A look of hopelessness appeared on Janey's face. She asked, "Then what can we *do*?"

"Fight back," Atkinson said.

Martin said angrily, "How are we going to do that? We had close to forty men, and less than a dozen of us made it back from Fuego. The rest were all killed or captured. Half the town's been wiped out, and all the rest are prisoners. We might be able to come up with fifty or sixty more people if we scoured every farm and ranch in the county, but that wouldn't be enough to make a dent in those terrorists."

"That's why you need help from outside."

"But you just said the government won't help us!" Martin exclaimed.

Atkinson held up a finger.

"I said the federal government won't help you. I didn't say anything about the State of Texas."

"What are you talking about?" Flannery asked. "I can see the governor ordering the rest of the Rangers in, but there aren't enough of us to recapture the town. Maybe if she called in all the DPS troopers, too . . ."

Flannery's voice trailed off as Atkinson shook his head.

"No offense, Lieutenant, but I'm not talking about law enforcement personnel," the colonel said. "I'm talking about soldiers. One of the first things Governor Delgado did when she took office was to get me on her team. I was placed in charge of putting together a military force that can respond to dangerous situations when the feds either can't or won't."

"Or situations where the feds *are* the enemy?" Lee guessed.

"I won't comment on that, Officer. You'll have to draw your own conclusions. But I can tell you that the call went out earlier today. Men are gathering from all over the state. Some are law enforcement, some are ex-military, some are what used to be called soldiers of fortune."

"You mean mercenaries," Martin said.

"No. Mercenaries work for anybody who pays them. The sort of man I'm talking about sells his fighting skills, all right, but not necessarily to the highest bidder. He wants to put his talents to what he considers a good use."

"How many men are we talking about?" Lee asked.

"Upwards of a thousand . . . but they won't all be able to get here. I'd say there's probably a well-armed force of four or five hundred heading this way already. Enough to do the job."

Flannery said, "Homeland Security won't let them through."

"What Homeland Security doesn't know, they can't do anything about," Atkinson said.

"How can you get a force that big into Fuego without anybody knowing?"

Atkinson glanced at the sky.

"It'll be dark soon," he said. "I think we can figure something out. Right now, though, we need to get on the horn to the governor. Lee, you need to tell her everything you've told me. If she's going to commit that many men . . . if she's going to take action that the federal government will regard as a slap in the face, with God knows what consequences . . . she has to know that it's necessary."

"It's necessary, all right," Lee said. "Even if those terrorists got everything they wanted, you reckon they'd leave any of us alive behind them?"

"Not a one," Atkinson replied grimly. "When you get

right down to it, killing infidels means more to them than anything else."

Night fell, and an uneasy peace descended on Fuego. The Sword of Islam remained in firm control of the town. In the football stadium next to the high school, the hundreds of prisoners—hostages was probably a better term to describe them—huddled together on the bleacher seats because they were cold and scared. At this time of year, the days were often still warm, even downright hot, but the dry West Texas air cooled quickly once the sun went down.

More prisoners had been brought in a short time earlier, the survivors from what had sounded like a fierce, if short-lived, battle. Among them were several members of the Fuego High School Fighting Mules, who had known moments of both victory and defeat in this stadium.

Tonight, all of them had to be wondering if they had played their final game.

In the rest of the world, most eyes remained focused on Fuego and on Hell's Gate prison, several miles out of town. The cable channels were full of the story. There wasn't much new to report, but that had never stopped network talking heads from talking. Everybody had an opinion.

The White House was saying very little except that the area remained under military quarantine. The Texas governor had no comment at all, deferring all questions to the federal government. That was unusual for the normally outspoken Maria Delgado, but with everything else that was going on, no one paid much attention to it.

In major cities across the country, martial law had been declared because of riots by Muslim protesters in support of the Sword of Islam. The local mayors and police departments had to make do with the resources they had on hand, because so far, requests for assistance from the National Guard had gone unanswered, leading a few conservative commentators to wonder if the administration actually sympathized with the rioters.

Such an idea was roundly and loudly condemned as racist hate speech by those on the left, of course.

As far as what was going to happen next, no one really knew . . . but the whole world seemed to be holding its breath as it waited to find out.

In the motel on the eastern edge of town, Jerry Patel was drunk. Had it really been only forty-eight hours since the man called Fareed had walked into the office, said the word "Judgment," and started this seemingly never-ending horror show in motion?

Surely that had been at least a week ago, Patel thought as he stared into his glass of whiskey. It seemed more like a month.

He was a terrible Muslim, he told himself. He shouldn't be drinking like this. He would never know the delights of Heaven that Dr. Hamil had promised to all those who took part in this holy war against the Americans.

He wondered if he got in his car and drove away, would they let him go? Or was he trapped here, trapped in his own way just like the infidels who had been marched into the football stadium at gunpoint?

A car stopped in front of the office. Patel looked up, his vision fuzzy from the alcohol. It took him a second to recognize the man who got out of the car as Dr. Phillip Hamil.

Patel was sitting behind the counter. He pushed himself shakily to his feet as Hamil stalked into the office.

"Doctor," he said. "Wha . . . what can I do for you?"

Hamil stopped and frowned at him.

"Are you drunk, Jerry?" he demanded. "Have you really turned into that much of an American, that you have to take refuge from reality in a bottle?"

"I . . . I didn't expect it to be like this."

"How did you expect it to be? Did you think we would walk in here, tell the godless American devils our demands, and they would just give us what we wanted?"

"I didn't know so many people would . . . would have to die."

Hamil nodded solemnly and said, "It's true, many of our brothers in arms have martyred themselves for our sacred cause."

"No, I was talking about—"

Patel stopped short and looked ashamed.

"I know what you were talking about," Hamil said in a quiet but cold and dangerous voice. "You've grown weak, Jerry. You think of the infidels as people, not as enemies of Allah to be destroyed in any way possible."

Patel shook his head emphatically. That made him sick, so he had to struggle not to throw up.

"I understand, Doctor, I truly do," he was able to say after a moment. "I've done everything that was asked of me."

"Yes," Hamil admitted, "you have. Despite your moments of weakness, you have been a most excellent servant of the Prophet, Jerry. No one will forget that."

"Th-thank you, sir. If there's anything I can do for you . . ."

"No, I just came back to get a few hours of sleep. Nothing seems to be happening right now." Hamil's mouth twisted in a grimace. "All this should have been over by now. Our brothers should have been freed. It took us too long to subdue the Americans here, I suppose, and then the ones inside the prison have proven to be more stubborn than I expected. Tomorrow—"

Hamil stopped. A fresh determination came over his face.

"Tomorrow is too long to wait," he went on. "The Americans need another reminder tonight." He turned back toward the door, then paused and looked at Patel. "Thank you, Jerry."

"Me? For what, Doctor?"

"For showing me how easy it is for a normal person to become discouraged."

"Oh. Well, I . . . I'm glad . . . I guess."

"I don't want the Americans going to sleep tonight thinking that they can wait us out. I want their dreams to be haunted by the inevitable results of their own evil."

Hamil had looked weary when he came in, but he seemed filled with renewed energy now as he walked out of the motel office, Patel thought.

That probably portended something bad for someone.

Something very bad.

The broadcast from Fuego came just before ten o'clock, local time. Hamil had waited a little while before putting his new plan into action. He wanted as much news coverage as possible.

When the video feed went live from the football stadium, the camera showed one end zone. Phillip Hamil stood there alone.

"Earlier today," he began, "our humanitarian plea that our illegally imprisoned brothers be freed was ignored by the Americans still in partial control of the facility known as Hell's Gate. They have been given warning of the dire consequences that await if they continue their lawless, godless actions. To demonstrate our determination to triumph in our righteous cause, we were forced to give them an example of what their refusal has caused."

Hamil nodded to someone offscreen, then added,

"Do not look away. This is a reminder of what America has brought on itself."

But all across the country, people did look away as video footage shot with a cell phone was cut into the broadcast. The grisly, sickening spectacle of Andy Frazier's beheading went out to the entire nation.

That video lasted only a little more than a minute. With a solemn expression, Hamil faced the camera again and continued, "The responsibility for this young man's tragic death rests solely on the shoulders of the American government and the American people. You have the power to prevent such things in the future by realizing that the Sword of Islam is blessed by Allah and that the Muslim people and their beliefs must be respected. In case you stubbornly refuse to understand this . . ."

Again he nodded to someone off-camera.

The camera swung slowly to reveal six figures standing to one side of the end zone, their hands tied behind their backs, hoods over their heads. Men with scarves wrapped around their faces to disguise them stood behind them with automatic weapons.

Hamil walked along the line of captives, and as he did so he pulled the hoods off them one by one. With each terrified face that he revealed, he announced the prisoner's name.

"Brent Sanger . . . Peter Garcia . . . Kevin Caldwell . . . Theo Morris . . . Jack Conley . . . Steve Brashears." Hamil reached the end of the line. "These young men are all members of the Fuego High School football team. Their only concerns should be their team, their schoolwork, their girlfriends. And yet earlier today they took up arms against the holy cause of Islam. They are responsible for the deaths of valiant freedom fighters who even now receive their just rewards as martyrs in Heaven. I call on them to kneel and ask forgiveness."

Close-up after close-up of the prisoners appeared on

TV screens all over the country. Their faces were pale with fright, streaked with tears, and yet stubborn defiance still shone in their eyes. Hamil's mouth thinned into a grim, angry line when he saw that.

Not one of the prisoners knelt. Hamil confronted one of them and asked tautly, "Don't you want to live, boy?"

"When I hit my knees it's to pray, not to beg for anything from scum like you, mister," the young man said.

With an effort, Hamil controlled his rage. He turned to the camera again and said, "There can be no forgiveness for infidels."

He strode away from the captives. The gunmen who had gathered into a group behind the ballplayers opened fire.

In control rooms across the country, directors tried to cut away so they wouldn't be accused later of showing this mass execution on live TV. But no matter how quickly buttons were pushed and switches were thrown and keyboards were tapped, enough footage went out over the air to produce indelible images.

Images of innocent young men screaming in agony as scores of bullets ripped into their bodies . . . images of bright red blood spurting into the air and splashing across the green turf . . . images of bodies literally shredded into pieces by the storm of lead . . .

When the carnage was over, Hamil said into the camera, "America, you have until dawn to turn over our brothers now being held in Hell's Gate prison. If that does not happen, then you—all of you—will be responsible for the deaths of more of the people of Fuego." He gestured, and the camera followed the movement to show the hundreds of prisoners in the stands. Then it went back to Hamil, who said, "Their blood will be on your hands. Remember . . . you have until dawn."

Then the feed from West Texas went dark.

Hamil knew that all over the country, people would

be crying and wailing over what they had just seen. Some would be in their bathrooms getting sick. Others would be cursing him in the most blasphemous terms.

None of that mattered to him. The only thing he cared about was knowing that he had just won. By morning the American government would be glad to cooperate with him to prevent another such atrocity.

Because Americans were weak. They didn't understand that sometimes a righteous cause required payment in blood.

Hamil looked at the heaps of bloody, quivering flesh that had been six young men, heaved a sigh of satisfaction, and whispered, "Allahu akbar."

CHAPTER 41

Even though day and night didn't mean much in the maximum security wing, Stark and his allies knew that night had fallen because the skylights in the exercise area had grown dark. Some of the lights in the wing had been turned off as well, at Mitch Cambridge's suggestion. They didn't have an inexhaustible supply of fuel for the generators, and they didn't know how long they would be trapped in here, so it was wise to lessen the load on the power supply as much as possible.

One area where they hadn't skimped was in the lighting and video coverage of the approach to the wing. Whatever the terrorists tried next would come from that direction.

Stark was walking along the wing when someone hailed him. He looked over and recognized Albert Carbona, the old mobster, along with Billy Gardner, Carbona's former bodyguard, and J.J. Lockhart and Simon Winslow.

"What can I do for you, Mr. Carbona?" Stark asked as he came up to the four men.

"Mr. Stark, we been thinkin'," Carbona said. "Now, don't just say no without considerin' my proposition."

"It sounds like you think that might be exactly what I'll say."

"I'm just askin' you not to be narrow-minded. My friends here and I, we got a lot to offer."

"I'm listening," Stark said.

Carbona said, "We think you should give us guns."

That came as no surprise to Stark. He'd had a hunch that was where this conversation was going.

"That's not my decision. Lucas Kincaid is in charge since the warden is wounded."

"Yeah, turns out the guy is more than just a librarian, right? Who'd'a figured? By the way, how's the warden doin'? Mr. Baldwin's a right guy, ya know?"

"He's resting as comfortably as possible under the circumstances," Stark said. "He needs some real medical care, of course."

"Yeah, I hope he gets it soon. But what about our idea?"

Stark shook his head and said, "I don't think Kincaid is going to agree to arm you."

"Why not?" Billy Gardner asked. "When it comes to those damn terrorists, we're all on the same side, ain't we?"

J.J. Lockhart put in, "And we may wind up having to protect ourselves, Stark. We can't do it with our bare hands."

Lockhart actually had a point, Stark thought. If the terrorists ever made it in here, the defenders would need every able-bodied man fighting as hard as he could.

"I'll talk to Kincaid," he said. "But I don't make any promises."

"That's all we ask," Carbona said. "Just think about it."

Stark nodded and started to turn away, but Simon Winslow stopped him by saying, "Mr. Stark, do we know what's going on in the outside world?"

"All we know is that there was some bad trouble in Fuego. But I don't have any details."

354 William W. Johnstone

"You don't have any communications?"

Stark shook his head and said, "Nobody's phones work, and the computer network is off-line. They've blocked it somehow."

Winslow smiled.

"I might be able to do something about that," he said quietly.

Stark recalled that Winslow's specialty was computers— and that was putting it mildly. He had used his hacking skills to steal millions of dollars. Or was it billions?

If anybody could get them connected again, it was Simon Winslow.

"All right, come with me," he said.

"What about our request?" Carbona asked.

"I'll talk to Kincaid."

"Fair enough. Thanks, Mr. Stark. Tell him he's got my word that we won't double-cross you guys. And anybody in my line of work can tell you, Albert Carbona's word is his bond."

Oddly enough, Stark found himself believing the mobster. He nodded to Carbona and led Simon Winslow toward the guard station where Kincaid and Cambridge were.

When they came in, Stark noticed Alexis Devereaux and Riley Nichols sitting together in a corner of the room. Alexis was still crying, and Riley had her arm around the older woman's shoulders. Even though it had come out that Riley despised Alexis, she was still trying to comfort her. That was the sort of person Riley was, Stark supposed. Compassion came first.

Funny how those on the left always insisted that conservatives were heartless bastards who wanted to starve the children and push Grandma off a cliff. And yet studies had shown again and again that conservatives not only donated more money to charity, they spent more time volunteering and actually helping people than liberals did. Most conservatives he'd known were quick to help somebody who was really down on his luck. Even when they didn't have much themselves, they had a generosity of spirit that drove them to do whatever they could to lend somebody a hand.

That came from the way they'd been raised, Stark reflected. Them, and the generation before them, and the one before that, and right on back up the line to the Greatest Generation. And yet a liberal wouldn't believe that a conservative could ever do anything good, even if he saw the evidence of it with his own eyes.

It was a real shame that the so-called champions of tolerance were so filled with hate for anybody who disagreed with them.

Stark led Winslow over to the control console where Kincaid and Cambridge were sitting and talking quietly. One of the other guards was posted at the sally port with a rifle to shoot anything that moved down at the other end of the corridor.

"What's up, John Howard?" Kincaid asked as he looked at Stark and Winslow.

"Simon here thinks he might be able to get the computers working again," Stark said.

Cambridge said, "It's against the rules for Winslow to touch a computer—" He stopped short and then laughed humorlessly. "I guess the rules don't really mean much anymore, do they?"

Winslow said, "Look, the last thing on my mind is trying anything criminal. I mean, I'm worried about surviving here. Maybe it would help if we could get in touch with the outside world."

"Somebody in the main office has taken all the computers off-line," Kincaid said.

"I'll bet that's what they want you to think," Winslow said with a smile. "I guarantee they've left themselves a back door to gain access. And if they can program it, I can find it and crack it."

Kincaid frowned and asked, "You think?"

"I *know*."

Kincaid looked at Cambridge and shrugged.

"Might be worth a try," Kincaid said. "Simon's got a point. It wouldn't do him any good to try to steal anything if he's not alive in the morning to benefit from it."

"I say we give him a chance," Stark put in.

Cambridge thought about it for a few seconds and then nodded. He stood up and waved Winslow into the chair where he'd been sitting.

"Go to it, Simon. Find out what's happened in Fuego and see if you can get in touch with the authorities. We need to know if any help is on the way."

"Give me a few minutes," Winslow said as he sat down and pulled a keyboard to him. "A half-hour, tops."

While Winslow's fingers were moving too fast on the keys for Stark to follow them, Stark turned and went over to Riley and Alexis. The lawyer was still sniffling, but she'd stopped sobbing. Her eyes were red and swollen.

"Is . . . is *it* still out there?" she asked Stark.

He knew she was talking about Andy Frazier's head. He said, "We can't very well go and get it."

"Somebody . . . somebody should *do* something."

Somebody should do something, thought Stark. The motto of the liberal. Somebody—meaning the government, most of the time—should do something—with the taxes all those evil rich people had been forced to pay—about something, anything, whatever. Some folks don't have insurance? Well, let's wreck the insurance industry and cripple health care for everybody, just so long as we *do* something about it. Somebody with mental health issues so dangerous he should be locked up for his own protection, as well as everybody else's—almost without exception a Democrat, at that—gets hold of a gun and kills a bunch of people, so let's pass a bunch of new laws that will do absolutely nothing to prevent such tragic occurrences, laws that criminals will laugh at and ignore, laws that won't accomplish anything except to inconvenience honest, law-abiding citizens, and oh, by the way, make it easier for the government to come and take any legally owned guns away from those honest, law-abiding citizens should they decide to, but we have to do it anyway because . . . somebody should *do* something.

These days, folks with half a brain in their heads didn't know whether to laugh or cry over what had happened to the country.

"I'm sorry, Ms. Devereaux," Stark said quietly. "It's a terrible, terrible thing your friend did."

"You can't blame that on Phillip—"

"Oh, for God's sake," Riley said. "You saw him with your own eyes, Alexis. You watched while he cut that poor kid's throat. We all did."

Alexis started crying again. Between sobs, she choked out, "But . . . but Islam is a religion of peace."

Stark and Riley exchanged a despairing glance. Stark shook his head.

"All right, guys," Simon Winslow announced. "I'm in. There was a back door, just like I thought."

Stark turned to go back to the console. Riley stood up, leaving Alexis crying this time, and joined him. Kincaid and Cambridge were already looking over the inmate's shoulders. As Stark and Riley came up, Riley laid a hand on Kincaid's shoulder. Stark noticed that and thought that if they lived through this, Kincaid needed to do whatever it took to hang on to that woman.

Unfortunately, given everything that Kincaid had told Stark about his past and the people who were after him, that might not be possible.

Somehow, Winslow had pulled up a live news feed from the football stadium in Fuego and put it on one of the monitors. The five of them leaned forward to watch it.

And as they did, as they watched six fine young men, six innocent young men, murdered in cold blood, expressions of horror slowly etched themselves on their faces.

Stark looked at Phillip Hamil's face, saw the smirk of arrogance and satisfaction on it, so proud of the wanton slaughter, and one thought burned through Stark's brain.

Somehow, before this was all over, that son of a bitch needed to die.

CHAPTER 42

At the Simmons farm, Lee Blaisdell had spent quite a while talking to Governor Delgado on Colonel Atkinson's shielded, encrypted satellite phone. He could tell that everything he told her shocked her to the very core of her being.

Then Lee had handed the phone back to Atkinson, and the colonel had had a long conversation with the governor, one that, judging by Atkinson's expression, was pretty upsetting at times. When that talk was over, Atkinson motioned for Lee and Flannery to follow him outside.

Janey tagged along. Lee didn't try to send her back. He wanted to keep her with him as much as possible, wanted to feel her hand warm in his.

Besides, whatever the colonel had to tell them, Lee figured it would be a good idea to get Janey's take on it, too. She was probably smarter than he was, and he didn't have a problem admitting that and seeking her advice.

Atkinson walked out a short distance from the farmhouse. Millions of stars burned brightly in the chilly night sky overhead.

"Governor Delgado and I agree that we have to make

a move, and it can't wait," Atkinson said. "While we were talking, something else happened. The governor had to step away from the phone for a few minutes to watch the news coverage on TV. It seems that Phillip Hamil, the leader of the Sword of Islam, has executed some of his hostages."

"No!" Janey exclaimed. "My God, how . . . how could anybody . . ."

In a flat, grim voice, Atkinson went on, "He took a young man out to the prison and beheaded him so the defenders could see it."

"Do you know who it was?" Lee asked. He knew that whatever Atkinson said, the answer was going to sicken and horrify him.

"A high school boy named Andy Frazier."

Janey put her hands over her face and started to sob.

"I guess you know him," Atkinson went on.

"Yeah, we do," Lee said, trying to keep emotion from choking his voice. "He was the quarterback on the high school football team. A really good kid, too."

"Well, it gets worse," Atkinson said. "Hamil had six more members of the team machine-gunned at the stadium, in front of millions of people on live TV. The guy's totally insane now. He may think he's doing God's work, but he's really just a mad-dog killer."

"Six more kids," Lee murmured.

"Is . . . is this nightmare ever going to end?" Janey managed to say between sobs.

Atkinson nodded curtly and said, "Yes, ma'am, it is. Before morning, in fact. Hamil issued a deadline. If those terrorists in Hell's Gate aren't released by dawn, he's going to kill more of the hostages. He's hinted that he's got that whole football stadium wired to blow."

Flannery asked, "How can you stop him? Even if you have a force of men on the way, they can't fight their way in past that federal cordon. Even if a few of them get through, the others will be wiped out or captured."

"That's why they're not going through the cordon," Atkinson said. "They're going over it."

"How are they going to do that?"

The colonel took a cigar from his shirt pocket and put it in his mouth. He didn't light it. Instead he asked around it, "Ever hear of HALO?"

"The old computer game?" Lee asked with a frown.

Atkinson shook his head.

"It stands for high altitude, low opening. Our men will be coming in by parachute."

"What about the no-fly zone?" Flannery asked.

"That's where the high altitude part comes in. The planes will be so high up they'll be able to escape detection."

Lee said, "You've got the resources to do something like that?"

"This is Texas," Atkinson said, grinning around the cigar. "We find a way to get things done."

Flannery frowned and said, "The feds won't like this when they find out about it."

"Well, it'll be too late to do anything about it by then. And right now, I don't think the governor gives a damn what the feds like or don't like."

"This is a chance to hit those bastards without them knowin' that it's comin'," Lee said. "When's this gonna happen?"

"It'll take a while to set up," Atkinson said, "but that's all right. If everything goes according to plan, the drop will be about an hour before dawn. We'll be there in time to stop Hamil."

"We?" Janey repeated.

"I'm not going to miss out on the finish," Atkinson said.

"Neither am I," said Flannery. "Anyway, if we launch

an attack of our own, it'll serve as a distraction to help the paratroopers get down safely."

"Exactly what I was thinking. So you're in, Lieutenant?"

"I'm in," Flannery said grimly.

"So am I," Lee declared.

Janey took hold of his arm and said, "Don't you think you've done enough already, Lee?"

He shook his head and said, "I'm sorry, Janey, but I don't. Not by a long shot."

The argument continued most of the night, with Lee insisting that he had to go along with the small force led by Colonel Atkinson, while Janey tried to persuade him not to risk his life again.

When she played the pregnancy card, the "leave your son to be raised without a father" card, that had almost been enough to sway him.

But then he said, "What kind of world would it be if folks won't stand up for what's right?"

"*This* kind of world!" she said. "Look around you, Lee. Relatively speaking, do you see anybody but a handful of people who even worry about what's right and what's wrong anymore? Most of them are too busy wondering what the government's going to give them this month!"

"That doesn't change things," Lee insisted stubbornly.

"All right!" Janey said as she threw her hands in the air. "I give up. Go and get your head shot off! See if I care. But you can bet I'll tell Bubba what a reckless fool his daddy was."

Those words hurt, sure enough, but as Janey stomped off, Lee told himself it didn't matter. Nothing really worthwhile came without pain and sacrifice.

And Lee couldn't think of anything more worthwhile for a fella to do than to stand his ground against evil.

Before even the faint flush of gray in the eastern sky

heralding the approach of dawn appeared, Atkinson gathered the men at the farm. They all carried as many guns and as much ammunition as they could. There was no point in holding anything back. One way or another, this was going to be the end.

Lee was about to climb into Gibby's pickup. The big youngster had been freshly devastated by the news of Andy's death, along with those of the other members of the team who had been executed by the terrorists. In less than twenty-four hours, Ernie Gibbs had lost his brother, his best friend, and half a dozen more friends and team-mates. It was entirely possible that Gibby's parents were dead in Fuego, too. How could any young man cope with that much loss?

Gibby was behind the wheel, though, apparently ready to go. Lee paused with the door open and asked, "You okay, Gibby?"

"No, sir," Gibby answered without hesitation. "I don't figure I ever will be again. But takin' the fight to those terrorists is the only thing I can still do for Chuck and Andy and everybody else."

"I reckon you're right about that," Lee said.

He was about to climb into the cab when he heard his name called behind him.

He turned and Janey rushed into his arms, threw her arms around his neck, and kissed him. The kiss shook Lee right down to his toes.

"You come back safe and sound," Janey said when she took her mouth away from his. "Don't you dare do anything else, you hear me, Lee Blaisdell?"

Lee grinned and said, "I hear you. Don't worry about that. I hear you loud and clear."

Letting go and stepping away from her was one of the hardest things he'd ever done.

But there were monsters waiting in Fuego, monsters that had to be exterminated if there was ever going to be any justice in the world. It was up to Lee and the men with him to see that it was done.

A few minutes later, the heavily armed convoy started toward town. The drivers steered by starlight, since the headlights on all the vehicles were dark.

Earlier, Atkinson had said, "If the terrorists have a pipeline into the NSA and Department of Defense and can access their satellite intel, they'll be able to use infrared to see that we're on the move. So they may be ready for us."

"That's what we want, isn't it?" Flannery had asked. "We want them concentrating on us instead of watching the skies."

"That's right. But it does put us in sort of a precarious position."

"Not as precarious as those poor folks in that football stadium," Lee had said. No one could argue with that.

So none of them had any doubt that they were doing the right thing as they headed for Fuego. They would do whatever was necessary to break the terrorists' hold on the town.

At the same time, Lee was going to do his level best to stay alive, too. For Janey, and for their child. No way he was gonna go and get himself killed when he hadn't even had a chance to say hello to that little rascal.

The lights around the football field were visible for a long way in this mostly flat West Texas terrain. That was their destination for two reasons. The terrorists would expect them to head for there, since that was where the hostages were being kept, and so that would serve the purpose of being a distraction. Not only that, but maybe when the force sent by the governor arrived and launched the real attack, Lee and his group would be in position to free some or all of those prisoners . . . perhaps without getting themselves and everybody else blown up in the process.

Atkinson and Sgt. Porter were leading the convoy in the pickup they had stolen in town the previous afternoon. Porter brought the vehicle to a stop when they were about a mile from the stadium. Lee and Flannery joined the colonel next to the pickup.

Atkinson was chewing on a cigar again. He said, "All right, we'll spread out in a line to advance from here. I want at least fifty yards between each vehicle."

"That's spreading out, all right," Flannery said. "Spreading pretty thin."

"They'll have to devote more resources to stopping us that way," Atkinson explained. "Also, a lucky shot won't take out but one vehicle. And they'll make some lucky shots, I think we all know we can count on that. We won't all come through this alive, gentlemen. But then, that's true of life itself, isn't it?"

"Are we ready to go?" Lee asked tensely. "I'm ready to get this over with."

"Patience, Officer. I'm just waiting for a signal—"

As if on cue, the satellite phone buzzed. The colonel took it out of his pocket and said, "Atkinson . . . Yes, I understand . . . Thank you, Governor. We'll do our best."

He broke the connection, stowed the phone away, and looked at the men gathered around him in the starlight.

"The planes have successfully penetrated the no-fly zone at high altitude. The drop will be in approximately seven minutes. From that high, it'll take about three minutes for our men to reach the ground. So we have to keep those bastards busy for the next ten minutes or so. Let's go!"

CHAPTER 43

Lee's heart pounded in his chest as he got back in the pickup with Gibby and stuck one of the AR-15s out the open window. Engines rumbled as the vehicles in the convoy began spreading out, following Atkinson's orders. It didn't take long until everyone was in position.

Atkinson and Porter led the way. The sergeant's foot tromped down on the gas, and the pickup spurted forward. All the other drivers in the long line followed suit, and the sound of engines turned into a deep-throated roar.

The terrorists would hear them coming, thought Lee, and even in the starlight, they could probably see the big cloud of dust that rose from the wheels.

Lee saw a flash through the windshield, and off to the right an explosion bloomed redly in the pre-dawn darkness. That was a rocket or a bazooka or some sort of artillery round. No telling what sort of armament the sumbitches had, Lee told himself. They certainly had plenty of money behind them, so they could buy whatever they wanted.

Middle Eastern oil money. Some of our so-called allies, Lee thought bitterly.

Then he put that out of his mind. He saw more flashes up ahead and knew he was looking at muzzle flashes. The terrorists had set up a defensive line to keep them from getting to the stadium.

Suddenly, Porter flicked his pickup's lights on. That was the signal for everybody else to do the same. The lights would give the terrorists something to aim at, but for a few moments the unexpected glare would blind them first.

Lee leaned out the window and opened fire with the semiautomatic rifle. On the other side of the seat, Gibby kept his right hand on the wheel and stuck his left out the window with a pistol in it, firing as he drove.

Lee tried to keep his shots low. He didn't want any of his bullets ranging into the stands around the football field. There were enough gaps between the bleacher seats that slugs might go through them and hit some of the hostages.

There was no road where Gibby drove. The pickup bounced and careened over the open ground. That played hell with a fella's aim, but under these conditions nobody could hope for any real degree of accuracy, anyway. They were just here to make a lot of racket, at least at this point in the attack.

Another explosion sent one of the pickups flying into the air. It landed in a fiery rollover crash. As the rest of the line raced past it, Lee knew that the men in that truck couldn't have survived. Atkinson had warned them there would be more casualties to go with all the people who had already been murdered by the terrorists. He'd sure been right about that.

Lee's mouth was dry, and so was the magazine in his rifle. He swapped it out and kept shooting. They were only about a hundred yards away from the perimeter established by the terrorists, and closing fast. Lee heard bullets thudding into the pickup around him. The windshield shattered, spraying glass back across him and Gibby. Lee didn't even have time to throw an arm up to protect his face. He felt the sting as the shards cut his face, but none of them found his eyes.

That was all that mattered. He could still see to shoot.

The pickup gave a great shudder and lurched to a stop. Steam billowed up from the bullet-pierced radiator.

"Grab a rifle, Gibby!" Lee shouted. He flung the passenger door open and rolled out of the cab. As he stood up, he used the open door for cover and continued shooting at the muzzle flashes he saw.

There seemed to be as many of them as there had been stars in the sky earlier, the last time he had held his wife in his arms and tasted the sweetness of her kiss.

Phillip Hamil had slept the sleep of the just. The hundreds of deaths he had set in motion didn't haunt his dreams. He knew that his bloodthirsty god approved of them.

The alarm on his phone went off an hour and a half before dawn. He had to look good for the cameras, so he had showered and was shaving when the knock came on the door of his motel room.

Hamil frowned when he opened the door and found Jerry Patel standing there. The motel owner looked sick and hungover and scared. He said, "There's shooting."

"Where?" Hamil asked curtly.

"Out by the football field, I think. I thought you would want to know—"

Hamil stepped out onto the concrete sidewalk in front of the rooms and listened. He heard the gunfire, punctuated by grenade blasts.

"The Americans are attacking again," he snapped. "The men monitoring the satellite feeds must have been warned. Why wasn't I notified?"

"I . . . I'm sure I don't know, Doctor. Maybe—"

Hamil waved away Patel's stammering response. He said, "It doesn't matter. I'll go find out what's going on."

He knew there had been no new developments at Hell's Gate. Raffir would have called him if there were. But something was happening here in Fuego in advance of his dawn deadline, there was no doubt about that.

He shooed Patel away and went back into the motel room to finish getting dressed. When he emerged a couple of minutes later and started toward his car, he wasn't quite as dapper as he would have liked, but history was sometimes messy, he reminded himself.

He had just reached the car when some instinct made him look up. His eyes widened as he saw large black shapes blotting out part of the stars. It took him only a second to realize what they were.

Parachutes.

And those weren't his men dropping into Fuego.

Those damned Americans! He couldn't believe they were attempting such a double cross. He had been assured that there were enough sympathizers—indeed, enough active agents—within the federal government that no one would interfere with whatever the Sword of Islam did.

Someone would pay for this treachery, Hamil thought as he jerked the car door open. He would take particular pleasure in beheading the dog himself, if that was at all possible.

In the meantime, what was happening at the football stadium wasn't as important as the situation at the prison. As Hamil started his car, he thumbed a button on his cell phone. When one of his lieutenants at the stadium answered, he said, "Blow up the place! Now!"

The man sputtered a little, but Hamil knew he would do as ordered. He broke the connection, tossed the phone on the seat beside him, and gunned out of the parking lot.

He hadn't gone a block when two black-suited, body-armored soldiers landed on the street in front of him with black parachutes billowing down around them. Hamil's foot came down hard on the gas as the Americans tried to right themselves and bring their weapons to bear. He didn't give them time.

He hit one man straight on, full force, and clipped the other with the car and sent him spinning away. That slowed Hamil down for a second, but then he accelerated again and sent the car screaming down Main Street and out the other end of town. He veered hard onto the road leading to Hell's Gate.

He would rain down bloody vengeance on the Americans, he thought as his hands tightened their grip on the steering wheel and the speedometer needle climbed past ninety miles per hour.

But behind him, it was justice that continued to descend on Fuego.

Everything was ruined, Jerry Patel thought. His faith had deserted him. The Sword of Islam was going to fail. At the very best, he would spend the rest of his life in prison.

He stood there in the dimly lit motel office and looked down at the gun he had placed on the counter in front of him. It was a revolver, a Smith & Wesson .38. He had bought it years earlier to keep in the office in case of an attempted robbery. He had fired it a few times on the range, then hadn't touched it for a long time. He was fairly confident it would still work, though.

He picked it up and wondered if he could find the courage to do what needed to be done.

He put it back down.

Behind him, his wife said anxiously, "Jerry, what are you doing?"

He jumped a little, said, "Lara!"

"Were you going to kill yourself?" she asked. Her voice sounded cold and angry to him.

"I . . . I . . . The Americans are attacking the football stadium. Dr. Hamil left. It's all going wrong, Lara. It's going to fail."

"You pathetic coward," she said. "Allah can never fail."

"No . . . but we are just men. We can make mistakes."

"*I* made the mistake when I married you. I never dreamed you would turn out to be such a weakling."

Her words cut him to the bone. He had thought they were happily married for a long time. Now he realized that had all been a lie.

At least something happened then to distract her. She exclaimed, "What's that?" and hurried past him to the big window that looked out on the parking lot. Patel came out from behind the counter to join her. He muttered a curse as he saw the big black shapes floating down onto the parking lot like giant bats.

"American soldiers," he said.

"Take the gun," Lara said. "Go out there and fight them."

"I . . . I . . ."

"You dog!" She wheeled around, went to the counter, and picked up the revolver. "If you won't fight them, I will!"

As she started toward the office door, Patel moved hurriedly to stop her.

"Lara, no!" he said as he clutched her arm and tried to turn her toward him. "You can't—"

The gun went off.

Patel felt as if a huge fist had punched him in the belly. The slug's impact doubled him over, unhinged his knees. He collapsed as searing pain filled his body.

He didn't lose consciousness, though. He was still awake and aware as he watched his wife rush out of the office in her nightgown and bathrobe, crying, "Help me! Help me!"

In the glow of the lights scattered around the parking lot, Patel saw the soldiers disengaging themselves from their parachutes. They turned toward Lara as she hurried toward them, no doubt seeing only a hysterical woman who represented no threat.

Then she proved them wrong by taking the gun from the pocket of her robe and opening fire. One of the soldiers fell. She had taken them by surprise.

But only for a second. Then their automatic weapons came up and flame danced from the muzzles and Lara fell backward as dozens of bullets tore through her body. She hit the parking lot pavement hard and didn't move again.

Inside the office, on the tile floor, Patel sobbed, both from the pain of his own wound and his grief at his wife's death. He couldn't help but wonder, though . . . had she pulled the trigger by accident when he grabbed hold of her?

Or had she meant to kill him because of the disgust she felt for him?

He died without knowing the answer.

Lee heard Colonel Atkinson shouting, "Go! Go! Go!" He and Gibby lunged out from the cover the stalled pickup had given them and raced through the predawn gloom toward the stadium, firing as they ran.

Over the past few minutes, Lee had heard shooting erupt in other parts of town and knew the main thrust of the attack was under way. The paratroopers were reaching the ground and engaging the terrorists. Something blew up, sending a pillar of flame into the sky several hundred yards away.

It made sense that Hamil had sent the main body of his force out to Hell's Gate to try to take the prison, leaving only enough men in Fuego to keep the town under control. He couldn't have expected an airborne assault from the State of Texas. But that was what he was getting.

The threat of the explosives planted under the bleachers remained, though. Lee and the men with him needed to get in there, kill the terrorists guarding the prisoners, and get all those innocent folks out of the stadium before something awful happened.

Lee emptied his rifle again, switched out the magazines. He had just put the last full mag in the weapon, he reminded himself as he motioned for Gibby to follow him. He ran toward the field house, knowing there was a gate there leading into the stadium.

Bullets sang through the air around them. Men yelling and chanting in their native language ran around firing wildly. They wanted to die and be martyred.

Lee obliged as many of them as he could.

Then he and Gibby were past the field house, past the ticket office, running along the open area underneath the stands. Lee looked up, saw the bundles of explosives attached here and there.

If those suckers were to go off now, there wouldn't be enough of him and Gibby left to bury, he thought.

He spotted one of the terrorists running up a ramp that led to the seats. The man had an automatic weapon in his hands, and Lee didn't doubt for a second that he was crazy enough to start mowing down the prisoners. Calling to Gibby, "Watch my back!" he went after the would-be mass murderer.

Lee heard the machine gun chattering and people screaming before he reached the top of the ramp. As he emerged into the open, he saw the terrorist spraying bullets into the crowd as he shrieked out his hatred.

Lee fired without taking the time to aim, but instinct guided his shots. The pair of slugs from his rifle ripped through the terrorist and drove him back against the railing that ran along the front of the stands. The man flipped up and over it, falling out of sight.

Then Lee saw something that made the blood in his veins turn to ice. Farther along the walkway at the front of the bleachers, a man was down on both knees, leaning forward with his head pressed to the planks. He was facing toward Mecca, Lee realized, which meant he was praying. This sure wasn't the time and place for that, Lee thought, unless the fella figured he was about to die . . .

The man raised his head and lifted something in his right hand. Lee's eyes widened as he saw a little red light blinking on the object.

It was a freakin' detonator!

Lee didn't stop to think. He brought the rifle to his shoulder, took the tiniest fraction of a second to aim, and squeezed the trigger. The rifle kicked against his shoulder as it went off.

The bullet went in the back of the terrorist's head, shattered his skull, bored through his brain, and destroyed his nose as it exploded out through a fist-sized hole in the middle of his face. His thumb had almost reached the button on top of the detonator, but his hand opened automatically as all his nerves spasmed in death. The little cylindrical object dropped from his fingers and rolled toward the edge of the walkway.

A hand reached down to pluck the detonator from the planks. Colonel Thomas Atkinson gripped it tightly. He had reached the top of another ramp just in time to grab the detonator.

The colonel nodded to Lee and grinned for a second, as if to say, job well done.

Then he shouted, "Let's get these people out of here!"

All of Lee's muscles seemed to turn to water as he thought about how close they had come to being blown sky-high. He had to lean against the railing to steady himself.

Gibby appeared and asked, "Are you all right, Officer Blaisdell?"

"Maybe," Lee said. "Maybe."

He heard only scattered gunfire now. Governor Delgado's special force had done its job. The Battle of Fuego—the Second Battle of Fuego, he corrected himself—appeared to be just about over.

And this time the good guys had won.

But most of the terrorists were out at Hell's Gate, and they could still get what they wanted.

Unless there was somebody there to stop them.

CHAPTER 44

"All right," Stark said as he stood beside the hatch. "Down you go."

Kincaid and Cambridge were poised beside the opening, each armed with a rifle and two pistols. Stark didn't care much for the idea of just the two of them going out there, but this sort of operation called for a small, fast-moving force. Using Cambridge's knowledge of the labyrinthine network of tunnels, they could pop out, do some damage to the terrorists, and disappear again before any of the enemy knew what had happened.

That was the plan, anyway.

In the meantime, Stark would be in charge of the defense here in the maximum security wing. He had been involved in the defense of the Alamo from the Mexican army a few years earlier, so trying to hold off an overwhelming force was nothing new to him.

"It's four a.m. now," Kincaid said. "We'll be back by six . . . if we're coming back."

"All right, but don't blame me if you're later than that and I don't give up hope," Stark said. "Things like this have a way of not going exactly according to plan."

Kincaid laughed. "That's the truth," he said. "Good luck, John Howard."

"Same to you boys," Stark said.

Kincaid and Cambridge climbed down through the hatch and disappeared into the tunnel. Stark closed the hatch behind them and fastened it securely. They had worked out a simple, primitive, but effective signal that could be given by tapping on the underside of the hatch. If whoever was guarding the hatch on this side didn't hear that signal, it would stay closed to prevent the terrorists from following Kincaid and Cambridge back here and getting into the wing that way.

When the two commandos were gone, Stark stepped out of the maintenance area and motioned for Simon Winslow to come over.

"Do you know the opening of 'Louie, Louie'?" Stark asked the computer hacker.

Winslow frowned and asked, "What? I'm afraid I don't know what you're talking about, Mr. Stark."

Stark tried not to sigh at how culturally deprived this kid was. He knew everything there was to know about computers but didn't know how the most iconic garage rock song of all time began.

Stark used his knuckles to rap out the rhythm on the wall. He did that several times and asked Winslow, "You got that now? It's important."

"I got it," Winslow said, and at Stark's insistence he rapped out the tune himself. Then he asked, "Now, what am I supposed to do about it?"

Stark led him to the hatch and pointed at it. Winslow's eyes got big with surprise.

"You're going to stand right here," Stark told him, "and if you hear somebody tap that tune on the other side of the hatch, you come and get me right away. And there's no need for you to go and tell anybody about this."

"Is this going to help us get out of here alive?"

"Maybe," Stark said. That was still a long shot, but it wouldn't hurt anything to spread a little hope around.

"Then I'll do exactly what you say, Mr. Stark. You can count on me."

Stark clapped a hand on his shoulder and said, "I hoped you'd feel that way, Simon."

He left Winslow guarding the hatch and went back out into the main part of the wing. Things had finally settled down somewhat as more of the prisoners went to sleep, although a few arguments were still going on between the regular inmates and the terrorists. The correctional officers who had holed up in here were taking turns sleeping, too.

Alexis Devereaux and Travis Jessup were stretched out on pallets made from blankets spread on the floor. With drool leaking from their open mouths, neither of them looked ready for prime time anymore. Alexis looked especially haggard, and Stark wondered if that was from not only fear and the physical toll of their ordeal but also because she'd been disillusioned in her admiration for the Islamic extremists.

Doubtful, Stark decided. People like Alexis who had made a religion out of their liberal politics couldn't allow anything to shake their faith, or else the whole underpinning of their existence would fall out from under them.

Riley Nichols came out of the restroom used by the correctional officers. She nodded to Stark in the dim light and said, "Everything's quiet, isn't it?"

"For now," Stark said. "It's a while yet until dawn, though."

"Hamil's deadline."

"Yep."

"I'm a little surprised the President hasn't issued an executive order telling you to release those terrorists. It seems like something he'd do. Democrats all love executive orders—when they're in the White House."

"And that's a permanent state of affairs now, most folks believe," Stark said.

"Probably. As long as things are the way they are now." Riley smiled. "Things have a way of changing when people who used to be free get beaten down long enough, though."

"Until the last ten or fifteen years, I'd have said you were right. Now . . ." Stark shook his head. "I just don't know anymore. It may be that the country's too broken to mend itself."

"You're not saying we should give up hope?"

"Never," Stark said. "As long as good folks are drawing breath, there's still hope."

"Even if they're outnumbered?"

"Even if they're outnumbered," Stark said.

He had a feeling the world might be seeing that for itself before too much longer . . . even if he wasn't around to witness it.

"Where's Lucas?" Riley asked.

Stark hesitated. Kincaid hadn't told her what he and Cambridge were going to do, even though Stark had hinted that maybe he should. Kincaid had said there was no real need for her to know. That was true from a strategic standpoint. Stark wasn't sure it was from an emotional one, though.

"He's around, I suppose," he said.

Riley's eyes narrowed with suspicion. She had good instincts, Stark thought.

"He's up to something, isn't he?" she said. "But what

in the world could he do? He's trapped in here like the rest of us."

The hell with it, Stark told himself. It couldn't hurt anything to tell her about it now. Kincaid would either make it back . . .

Or he wouldn't.

Compared to some of the places he had been in Iraq, Afghanistan, and Pakistan, these tunnels weren't too bad, Kincaid thought. The ceiling was high enough he didn't have to stoop, the concrete floor wasn't covered in sewage, and low-wattage bulbs mounted in wire cages every so often provided light.

And nobody down here was trying to kill him . . . yet.

"Where do you want to go first?" Cambridge asked.

"Where does the tunnel to Administration come out?"

"In Warden Baldwin's office."

"Good a place as any to start, I guess," Kincaid said. "There's a chance nobody will be in there. None of the security systems are run from there, so there's no real reason for the terrorists to leave somebody on guard."

"I agree. It's this way."

Cambridge seemed to know where he was going. After they had trotted through the tunnels for a few minutes, making several turns seemingly at random, Kincaid asked, "Have you actually been down here exploring before, Mitch?"

"Well . . . no," Cambridge admitted. "But I've studied the plans extensively."

"What if something got built a little different from the plans?"

"I can't think of any reason why it would." Cambridge shrugged. "But if we run into that, I guess we'll just have to figure it out."

That was no more of a risk than any of the others they were running, Kincaid thought.

A short time later they came to steel ladder rungs set into the wall. Kincaid looked up a short, circular shaft and saw a hatch similar to the one in the maximum security wing.

"What if it's locked on the other side?" he asked.

"It shouldn't be," Cambridge said. "All the hatches can be dogged down from the top side, but the plan was to leave them where they could be accessed from underneath. Otherwise they wouldn't serve the purpose they were intended for."

"Again with the plan."

Cambridge shrugged and said, "Let's go find out."

He started to grab hold of a rung, but Kincaid said, "I'll go first."

"Why?"

"Just in case there's trouble waiting for us up there."

"I can handle trouble. I've already fought with those terrorists."

"I've tangled with a lot more of their cousins," Kincaid said.

"Overseas, you mean."

Kincaid just grunted. He had already spilled his guts to Stark, and he still didn't know what had possessed him to do that. He wasn't going to tell his life story to Cambridge, too. For one thing, there wasn't time.

"I'll go first," he said, his tone not allowing for any argument.

Cambridge grunted and said, "Up you go, then, if you feel that strongly about it."

Kincaid went.

The hatch cover wasn't fastened down. He spun the wheel and raised it without any trouble. The two men emerged in a closet that opened onto a darkened office. A little light penetrated the room because the door into the outer office and the door beyond that into one of the main corridors were both open.

Kincaid's jaw tightened as he looked around in the dim glow and saw how thoroughly the place had been trashed. The terrorists had had fun breaking and ripping and even pissing and shitting on things, judging by the stench that filled the room. They were animals, Kincaid thought, then corrected himself because that comparison wasn't fair to the animals.

Voices from somewhere outside the office made him stiffen.

He motioned to Cambridge and then ghosted across the room toward the door. They eased through the outer office and then paused in that doorway.

Two of the terrorists were coming along the hall, talking to each other in Saudi. Kincaid understood enough of the language to know they were talking about the American girl who had been raped to death the day before. When they laughed, it was all Kincaid could do not to step out into the corridor and hose them both down with the semiautomatic rifle in his hands.

That would make a lot of racket, though, and he wanted to avoid that as long as possible. Instead, he and Cambridge hung back in the shadows until the two men passed the door.

Then Kincaid stepped out, caught one of the guys from behind with the rifle across his windpipe, planted a knee in the small of his back, and broke his neck with a sharp tug and push.

A few feet away, Cambridge used his rifle to cave in the other terrorist's skull.

They dragged the bodies into the office. It might be a while before anybody came looking for the dead men.

It was a start, Kincaid thought.

For the next hour and a half, he and Cambridge moved through the sprawling prison like phantoms. They waited for good chances to strike, killing terrorists one, two, or three at a time. Once they opened fire on a group of six men, cutting them down before they knew they were in danger. By the time any of the other terrorists responded to the sound of shots, Kincaid and Cambridge were back down in the tunnels.

Kincaid could just imagine how the rumors were starting to fly up there. Men were dying, and no one would know how the Americans were managing to kill them. Some of the terrorists were probably starting to get pretty spooked by now.

Kincaid wasn't sure if this would do any good in the long run, but it sure felt good to deliver swift, irrevocable justice to those scum. He had hoped they would find Phillip Hamil somewhere in the prison. If they were able to capture the Sword of Islam's leader, that would give them a bargaining chip they might be able to use. So far, though, they hadn't been that lucky.

"It's not long until six o'clock," Cambridge said. "We should probably start back."

"Yeah," Kincaid said. "Wouldn't want to miss Hamil's deadline at dawn."

They had only gone part of the way, though, when a massive explosion shook the entire prison, even down here in these secret tunnels.

CHAPTER 45

Men ran to meet Hamil as he brought his car to a screeching, skidding halt inside the prison compound. The guards outside the prison had let him through since they recognized his vehicle.

"Where is Raffir?" he snapped as he got out of the car.

"I've sent someone to get him," one of the men replied.

"Never mind. Take me to him."

Hamil stalked into the prison's main building, where Raffir met him in the lobby, hurrying and looking sleepy. It had been a long night.

"We saw an explosion in town," Raffir said. "What happened? Did the Americans—"

"Never mind," Hamil interrupted him. "I want us to break into the maximum security wing. Now."

"Doctor, you don't know what's been going on out here. Somehow—I, I don't understand it—but somehow the Americans have been able to kill some of our men—"

"Listen to me," Hamil said. "I. Don't. Care. Get into that wing and kill them all."

Hesitantly, Raffir said, "If we use explosives powerful enough to breach the sally port, we'll be risking injury to some of our imprisoned brethren."

"There is no gain in life without risk. If some of them are injured or even killed, the rest will be freed. Those who die will be holy martyrs."

"Of course, Doctor. I'll give the orders."

"See that you do," Hamil said.

Raffir rushed off. Hamil paused and rubbed his temples. He had thought that he slept restfully, but now weariness had settled in on him. This had gone on too long. The best, most effective strikes were those that were over quickly, leaving death and devastation in their wake.

He thought about what Raffir had said. It *was* troubling that the Americans had been able to fight back and kill some of his men. They should all have been bottled up in the maximum security wing. It was possible, Hamil supposed, that a few of them had managed to hide while his forces were making their sweep through the rest of the prison, but not likely.

Troubling or not, the problem was irrelevant. Soon *all* the Americans would be dead, those unjustly imprisoned would be freed, and he would be a hero from one end of the Muslim world to the other.

And this was just the beginning, Hamil vowed. Soon the Muslim world would have no end. It would encircle the globe, and rivers of blood would run in every country as he and his fellow warriors claimed the planet for Allah's greater glory.

"Doctor," Raffir said, breaking into Hamil's vision. "The device is ready."

"Then use it," Hamil said.

Stark still wore a watch. Many of his generation did, even though younger generations relied on their phones to tell them the time. Those phones did practically everything except tuck you in bed at night. Some of them probably had an app for that.

When Stark looked at his watch and saw that the hour was getting on toward six o'clock, he thought about Kincaid and Cambridge and wondered where they were. Kincaid had said they would be back by six. Dawn, the deadline that Hamil had set, was less than an hour after that.

It would be here before you knew it, he thought.

Riley came into the guard station. She had been pacing worriedly for a while, ever since Stark had told her what Kincaid and Cambridge were doing.

"They should have taken me with them," she said. "I used to be a Marine."

Stark smiled.

"Yeah, I know. You told me."

"Well, I could have helped," she insisted.

"I don't doubt it. It wasn't up to me, though."

"Evidently it wasn't up to me, either," Riley said. "I swear, if Kincaid went off and got himself killed—"

"Hold on a minute," Stark said. He had been watching the video monitors, and he had just spotted movement on one of them. He leaned forward for a better look. Riley came up to his shoulder to join him.

"What is that?" she asked as they watched an ungainly object rolling along the corridor toward the rubble that blocked it. "It looks sort of like . . . a hotel serving cart. Like they use with room service."

"Nobody's pushing it, though," Stark said. "That's some sort of remote-controlled robot."

He had a bad feeling about this.

Suddenly, he told Riley, "Get everybody back along the cell block as far as you can, away from the doors."

"Crap, crap, crap," she said under her breath as she started out. "That thing's some sort of bomb."

"That's what I'm thinking," Stark said as he hurried to the sally port's inner door. He started firing his rifle through the gap at the advancing robot.

His shots didn't do any good. The thing was heavily armored, he thought. But it couldn't reach the outer door because the corridor was blocked. In fact, it had bumped up against the rubble now and stopped. It couldn't come any closer.

The top of the box-like object slid back, and something started to rise out of it. Stark recognized it as a rocket launcher. He fired several shots at the rocket, hoping to detonate it. But again the bullets just bounced off harmlessly.

Stark leaped to the control panel and slapped the switches that closed the doors. As they started to grind shut, he offered up a silent prayer that the reinforced doors would be strong enough to withstand whatever was coming.

The doors hadn't quite closed all the way when the rocket launched, trailing smoke as it flew the fifty yards along the corridor. It wouldn't have mattered if they had.

The explosion blasted both doors to smithereens and threw John Howard Stark backward into blackness as if he were a rag doll.

While Stark was shooting at the robot, trying futilely to stop it, Riley ran into the wing and started shouting.

"Everybody wake up! Wake up! Get to the far end of the wing! Now! There's a bomb! Run, damn it!"

She paused and bent to grab Alexis Devereaux's arm. She hauled the older woman to her feet and gave her a shove.

"Move!"

"What—what are you doing?" Alexis demanded. "How dare you—"

"I'm trying to save your life, you stupid bitch," Riley snapped. "Your friends are about to unleash hell on us."

J.J. Lockhart ran up and asked, "What is it, missy? What's goin' on—"

She pushed him toward the far end of the wing, too, and told him, "Just go!"

Everyone—guards and inmates alike—stampeded away from the entrance, yelling about a bomb. The terrorist prisoners in the cells started clamoring. There was nothing Riley could do about them, but she herded everybody else away from the sally port.

Satisfied that panic was going to clear out this end of the wing, she turned around and started back. She didn't see Stark anywhere, and if he hadn't been able to stop what was bound to be a lethal robot, he needed to get out of there.

Before she could reach the guard station, an explosion rocked the floor under her feet. A giant ball of fire bloomed at the entrance to the wing, and a wave of concussive force slammed into her, lifting her off her feet and throwing her backward.

She slammed into the floor and blacked out, but when she began to regain her senses she could tell that only a few seconds had passed. Smoke billowed from the area where the guard station had been. It stung her eyes and nose and made her cough as she pushed herself up on an elbow.

Everything was oddly silent. She realized the explosion had deafened her, and she could only hope that her hearing would come back.

Of course, that might be a minor worry in the long run.

She looked around and saw a crumpled shape lying a few feet to her right. She recognized the man as Stark and scrambled onto hands and knees to crawl over to him.

As she did, she took stock of her own condition and realized that nothing seemed to be broken. Her body worked all right, even though it ached like it had been pummeled by giant fists.

The blast must have blown Stark clear of the guard station, she thought. He was lucky it hadn't incinerated him. He still might be dead, though. The bomb's concussion might have broken his neck and pulped every bone in his body.

Riley grabbed Stark's shoulders and rolled him toward her. His eyebrows and mustache were singed, and blood oozed from several small cuts on his face. She didn't see any major injuries, though, and when she searched for a pulse in his throat, she found one. He was alive, although she couldn't have said whether he had any internal injuries.

"Come on, Mr. Stark, we need to get out of here," she said. She heard the words only vaguely as an echo inside her skull.

Stark didn't respond. His eyes remained closed. Riley glanced toward the wreckage of the guard station and the doors.

Ruthless killers were going to be coming through that cloud of smoke any second now, she thought.

A massive form suddenly loomed over her. She looked up and saw Billy Gardner reaching down for Stark.

"Let me give you a hand with him, ma'am," the former gangland bodyguard and enforcer said.

Gardner's voice was tinny and distant, but Riley heard it. That was one small sign of encouragement in the violent chaos. She scrambled to her feet as Gardner lifted Stark—who was a big man and no lightweight himself—and draped him over a shoulder.

Angelo Carbona had followed Gardner. He urged, "Hurry up, Billy! Those terrorist guys gotta be on their way in."

Riley spotted a rifle and a pistol lying on the floor nearby. She grabbed the rifle and used her foot to send the pistol sliding toward the old mobster.

"Mr. Carbona!" she called to him. "Get the gun!"

She knew Kincaid had been opposed to the idea of arming the inmates, but he wasn't here right now and neither was Cambridge. Stark was unconscious.

So Riley was going to do what she thought best.

"Thanks, doll!" Carbona said as he reached down and picked up the pistol. He straightened, pointed it at Riley, and opened fire.

She realized—luckily in time not to kill him—that he was shooting *past* her, not at her. She turned and saw several figures emerging from the smoke. They had scarves wrapped around the lower halves of their faces and carried rifles and machine guns. Riley started shooting at them as she backed away.

She and Carbona dropped three of the attackers and made the others scatter. That gave Riley and Carbona the chance to run after Gardner, who loped along easily with Stark's senseless form over his shoulder.

Several correctional officers ran to meet them. They provided cover as Riley and the others retreated. As she hurried past an open door that led into a maintenance area, she saw Simon Winslow standing next to the hatch where Kincaid and Cambridge had left the wing a couple of hours earlier.

"Simon, come on," Riley called to him. "We've got to pull back. They've breached the doors!"

"Mr. Stark told me to stay here," Winslow objected. "I'm supposed to listen for a signal and unfasten the hatch when I hear it!"

More gunfire filled the air as the guards battled with the terrorists. Winslow probably wouldn't be able to hear anything, even if Kincaid and Cambridge returned and gave the signal.

Maybe they were safer down there in the tunnels, Riley thought. With the bloodthirsty terrorists now pouring into the cell block, lying low might give them their best chance for survival.

Riley found that she was surprisingly okay with that. She wanted Lucas Kincaid to come through this alive, even if she didn't.

"Come on, Simon," she said again.

He swallowed hard.

"Do . . . do you think I should unfasten the hatch?"

Riley shook her head and said, "Leave it dogged down."

She hoped Kincaid wouldn't wind up hating her for that decision.

Winslow joined her and Carbona. She hustled both of them along the cell block. At the far end, benches and tables had been piled up to form a makeshift barricade. It would give the defenders some cover for a little while, but it wouldn't hold back the terrorists for long. They swarmed like vicious, mindless insects, willing to die for their twisted, hate-filled beliefs.

With bullets whipping around and above their heads, Riley, Winslow, and Carbona made a run for that small measure of safety. Somebody on the other side of the barricade pulled a bench aside, and the three of them darted through that opening. Men shoved the bench back into place.

As the shooting continued, Riley paused to catch her breath and look around. She saw Alexis Devereaux huddled in a corner, disheveled and red-faced from sobbing in terror. Travis Jessup stood near her, pale with fear but holding a rifle, Riley noted with surprise. Evidently, desperation had forced the newsman to find a little courage deep inside himself.

John Howard Stark was conscious and on his feet, although he looked pretty shaky and Billy Gardner stood next to him with a hand on Stark's arm to steady him.

"Mr. Stark," Riley said, "are you all right?"

Stark tapped his left ear and said, "Can't hear you very well, Riley. I was too close to that blast. But I reckon you asked if I was all right. I am, especially considering that I could've been blown to bits."

"Can you take over? I don't know what to do now."

"Only one thing we *can* do," Stark said. "Fight as long as there's breath in our bodies."

CHAPTER 46

"They've blown the doors in the sally port!" Kincaid said as the ground still trembled under their feet. "We've got to get back there!"

Cambridge grabbed his arm to stop him.

"Wait a minute," the young guard said. "We can't waste this chance, Lucas."

"Chance?" Kincaid repeated. "What the hell are you talking about?"

"They'll be throwing everything they've got at the entrance to the maximum security wing. We can come out behind them and catch them in a cross fire."

"Two men can't catch five hundred guys in a cross fire!"

"I wouldn't be so sure about that. There'll be so much racket, so many bullets flying around, we might be able to kill a lot of them before they even realize we're there."

Even though Kincaid's instincts made him want to rush back to where he had left his friends, he realized that what Cambridge said made sense. Effectively using the things you had on your side was often at least half of winning a battle. He said, "You can put us in the corridor behind the main bunch of terrorists?"

"I can," Cambridge stated.

"Let's go do it, then," Kincaid said with a nod.

Raffir argued that his leader should stay back where it was safe. Dr. Hamil meant more to the Sword of Islam than just another fighter to be martyred in their holy cause.

Hamil appreciated that sentiment, but after everything that had happened, all the months of preparation, all the blood that had been spilled, there was no way he was going to miss out on the culmination of this glorious triumph.

He wasn't going to throw his life away recklessly, though. He wore a bulletproof vest and carried an AK-47. He thought he looked rather dashing—although Allah frowned on vanity and hubris, of course.

With satisfaction, he looked at the damage that had been done by the remote-controlled rocket launcher and bomb. Beyond the piles of rubble and the gaping holes where concrete walls had been, a crescendo of gunfire continued as members of the Sword of Islam fought their way along the cell block toward the last bastion of defenders at the far end.

"Another few minutes, Doctor," Raffir said. "Another few minutes and it will be over. Our brothers will be free."

"Have we lost many men?" Hamil asked.

Raffir shrugged and said, "Some. The Americans fight well . . . for infidels."

"A thousand Americans will die for every Muslim. This is only the beginning, Raffir. Only the beginning."

Raffir smiled and nodded. Then his head jerked a little and his eyes widened. A red-rimmed black hole had appeared in his temple. As his eyes glazed over in death, his knees folded up and dropped him to the debris-littered floor.

Hamil had no idea where the shot that had killed Raffir had come from, but he leaped behind a pile of rubble anyway, taking cover as he looked around frantically. With the air so full of gunfire, there was no way to isolate and identify a particular shooter.

But several men who stood nearby began to fall, blood welling from their wounds. Hamil remembered what Raffir had told him about someone killing some of their men earlier, before the final assault began.

American snipers were loose in the prison, Hamil thought. Even though he would never have admitted it, the thought struck fear in him for an instant.

Then he shoved it away. Allah would protect him.

But just in case, maybe it would be a good idea to stay here behind this rubble . . .

During a brief lull in the fighting, Riley Nichols said to Stark, "I don't want them to take me alive."

"That's probably a good idea," Stark said with a nod.

"I mean it. I'm saving one bullet for myself. Just like in the old Western movies. Unless I can count on you to . . ."

Stark grimaced and said, "I'm liable to be pretty busy. But I wouldn't go giving up just yet."

Riley looked around the makeshift fort. About half of the guards and some of the inmates were dead. Several of the defenders who were still alive had been wounded. A bullet had broken Simon Winslow's arm. The hacker cradled it against him with his other arm. J.J. Lockhart's corpse sprawled to one side, a couple of bullet holes in his chest. Carbona and Gardner were both sporting bloody creases.

"They're going to overrun us any minute now," Riley said.

"More than likely, but that doesn't mean we should stop fighting."

A faint smile curved Riley's mouth as she said, "Remember the Alamo, is that it?"

"Something like that."

"You Texans are a stubborn bunch."

"Yes, ma'am, we are," Stark said, "and here they come again!"

Colonel Atkinson left a few dozen men in Fuego to finish mopping up there. The rest of his force piled into whatever vehicles they could find and headed for Hell's Gate.

The sun was coming up behind them.

Lee and Gibby were in a van with Atkinson and Sgt. Porter. The colonel had another cigar clenched between his teeth, holding it at a jaunty angle. Lee knew it was a pose, but he had to admit it looked good on Atkinson. And the colonel was one hell of a fighting man, that was for sure.

The prison came into view. Smoke spiraled up from it in several places. Even from a distance, it looked like the battleground that it was.

"We'll hit 'em hard and fast, boys," Atkinson said. "I don't know where the folks still alive in there will have forted up, but we should be able to follow the gunfire."

"Are we gonna wind up in federal prison for this, Colonel?" Lee asked. "Assuming we live through it, that is."

"Well, I don't know, Officer Blaisdell. If the feds come in and try to arrest us when this is all over, we may wind up with another fight on our hands. Are you ready for that?"

Lee thought about Janey and the new life they were going to bring into the world, and he knew what a sorry state of affairs it would be if Bubba had to grow up in a country where up was down and right was wrong.

"I'm ready for whatever comes, Colonel," he said. "As long as we've got good men to lead the way."

Atkinson grinned back at him from the shotgun seat and said, "You're one of 'em, son. You're one of 'em."

"That's Hamil," Kincaid said to Cambridge as they knelt behind a fallen steel beam from a collapsed wall. "I recognize him from that TV broadcast we saw last night. This is our chance, Mitch."

"Chance to do what?" Cambridge asked.

"Grab the son of a bitch and use him to make the others give up."

Cambridge shook his head and said, "Do you really think they'll do that? They're fanatics. They come from a long line of people willing to blow up themselves and their loved ones to get back at their enemies. Even if you capture Hamil, the others won't stop now."

"Maybe not, but it's worth a try. Give me some cover."

Cambridge started to say something else, but it was too late. Kincaid had already darted out from behind the beam and was running in a looping pattern toward the pile of rubble where Hamil had taken shelter.

Hamil was watching the attack on the maximum security wing and didn't see Kincaid coming. Some instinct must have warned him, though, because at the last instant he twisted around and fired the AK-47. He hurried his shots and missed . . .

Except for one bullet.

That slug laced into Kincaid's side and knocked him

half around. He lost his balance and fell, skidding behind the rubble. Hamil pounced, kicking the rifle out of Kincaid's hands. Then he stood over Kincaid, pointing the Kalashnikov down at him.

"Infidel," Hamil sneered, "do you know who I am?"

Kincaid's jaw was tight against the pain that filled him. He ground out, "You're the head bastard."

"I am the Sword of Islam! The living personification of Allah's great and glorious cause! I am the man who will bring your satanic country down to its knees and then crush it!"

"What you are is batshit crazy."

Rage darkened Hamil's face. His finger started to tighten on the AK's trigger.

An explosion hammered the building. More gunfire rang out, and between the shots Kincaid heard voices shouting.

American voices.

Hamil had hesitated, and that was all the break Kincaid needed. He kicked the terrorist mastermind's knee and rolled aside at the same time. The burst of lead from the Kalashnikov chewed up the floor but narrowly missed Kincaid. He hooked a foot behind Hamil's ankle and tugged. Hamil was already off-balance from the kick. With a startled yell, he toppled over backward.

Kincaid went after him, ignoring the pain in his side as he scrambled up and landed on Hamil in a diving tackle. He grabbed the rifle with his left hand and wrenched it aside, while his right sought a hold on Hamil's throat.

Kincaid had changed his mind about capturing Hamil. He didn't know what was going on around him—all hell was breaking loose, from the sound of it—but it didn't matter. Hamil was too big a threat to the country.

He had to die, here and now.

Hamil twisted and rammed a knee into Kincaid's

wounded side. Agony flamed through Kincaid's body and mind, but he fought it back and locked his fingers around Hamil's throat.

Hamil heaved up from the floor and with a surge of maddened strength broke Kincaid's hold on him. Kincaid hit him on the inside of the elbow and knocked the rifle out of his hand. For all Hamil's arrogance, fear showed in his eyes as he tried to writhe away.

Kincaid caught him from behind, looped his right arm around Hamil's neck, and locked it into place with his left hand on his right wrist. As Kincaid started to tighten the choke hold, Hamil gasped, "Who—are you?"

"Just an American," Kincaid said. He leaned closer to Hamil's ear and whispered, "Just an American who knows what you and your kind are planning for this country . . . and I'm going to stop it."

Then he broke Dr. Phillip Hamil's neck with a sharp, clean snap.

Heavy footsteps made Kincaid look up as he let go of Hamil's sagging body. He saw a tall, lean man with graying fair hair and a close-cropped beard grinning down at him. The stranger wore camo and had a cigar clenched between his teeth.

"Good work, soldier," he said as he extended a hand to Kincaid.

Kincaid knew an officer when he saw one. He had been on the run for so long that he hesitated before reaching up and clasping the man's wrist.

But only for a second.

Somehow, he knew he could trust this man.

They came like the howling horde of barbarians they were. The last defenders of Hell's Gate, only two dozen of them now, stood at the makeshift barricade and fired until their weapons ran dry, and then they fought using rifles and pistols as clubs, along with anything else they could get their hands on.

In Billy Gardner's case, that was the body of a terrorist whose skull he had caved in. He picked up the corpse by the ankles and flailed around him with it, driving back the savages. Bodies piled up around him, but the only one that really mattered lay at his feet. Albert Carbona might be dead, but Billy would protect him to the last.

They had to shoot him at least thirty times before he went down, and when he fell he toppled across Carbona's body.

Somebody had had to show Travis Jessup how to fire a gun, but he had fought as long as he could before collapsing as blood flowed from his wounds.

When Jessup fell, Simon Winslow got in front of Alexis to shield her with his body. He had never been a fighter, never been physically adept at anything. That was one reason he had gotten so good with computers. But he gave it everything he had, even with a broken arm, and it was to his credit that it took six of the terrorists to haul him down and hack him to bits with knives.

Stark and Riley fought side by side and then back to back, and even in that desperate moment it occurred to Stark, who had two sons, that he would have been proud to have a daughter like Riley Nichols.

Then he grabbed one of the howling terrorists by the throat, took the man's pistol away from him, and used it to blow the bastard's brains out. Stark hung on to the corpse, using it to block some of the bullets aimed at him as he and Riley backed into a corner. As at least fifty more terrorists got ready to charge them, he thought about what she had said earlier about not wanting to be taken alive. That was pretty unlikely, but he could make sure of it.

Then he looked at her, saw the fierce snarl on her face, and knew he didn't have to worry, and neither did she.

There was no way in hell those grubby little varmints were going to take Riley alive.

She'd see to that—and she'd take as many of them with her as she could.

"Mr. Stark," she said, "if by some miracle you ever see Lucas again, could you tell him—"

"Tell him yourself," Stark said, "because here he comes now."

It was true. The terrorists started falling like bowling pins, chopped down by relentless fire from behind them, and leading the way were Kincaid and Cambridge, their faces streaked with gore and their clothes stained with blood and the guns in their hands spouting flame and righteous vengeance on the murderers who had invaded Hell's Gate.

When the last of the terrorists were down, kicking out their worthless lives, Kincaid rushed forward and swept Riley into his arms. She clutched him with equal desperation.

Stark didn't know how they were going to work things out, but as he limped out from behind the barricade, he thought there was a good chance they would find a way.

Then he frowned as he looked at one of the men with Kincaid, the one who seemed to be in charge, in fact. And in that man Stark saw something familiar, something that took him all the way back to Vietnam and a skinny soldier who always seemed determined to do things his own way, no matter what his orders said.

"Private Atkinson?" Stark said.

"Good Lord," Atkinson said. "John Howard Stark! You turn up in the oddest places, Lieutenant."

"Yeah," Stark said as he shook hands with his old acquaintance. "And I'm getting too old for it, too."

"Nah," Atkinson said. "Because that would mean *I'm* getting too old, and that's never gonna happen. Men like us, we just go on fighting as long as there are wrongs to be righted."

Stark was too tired to argue.

Besides, Atkinson was right.

This wasn't over.

"The death toll, including the alleged terrorists, now stands at 1,247 and is expected to rise. The details of exactly what happened in Fuego, Texas, and at the nearby Baldwin Correctional Facility yesterday and early this morning are still very unclear and open to speculation. In a statement from the White House, a spokesman said the preliminary investigation indicates that overreaction by local law enforcement personnel to a peaceful protest may have sparked a riot as the protesters attempted to protect themselves.

"This stance would seem to be at odds with the broadcast from Fuego last night by Dr. Phillip Hamil, who perished later on in the disturbance. Dr. Hamil, a well-known academic and advisor to the administration, claimed in the broadcast to be the leader of a fundamentalist group calling itself the Sword of Islam. It appeared that several hostages were executed at Dr. Hamil's order during the broadcast. The spokesman for the President says that he believes Dr. Hamil was being coerced, that the man he knows would never be responsible for such an atrocity. The President was quoted as saying, 'Islam is a religion of peace.'

"Also in relation to this ongoing story, representatives of the Department of Homeland Security had no comment when they *were asked about reports that some sort of paramilitary force entered Fuego early this morning to quell the disturbance. Governor Maria Delgado of Texas also had no comment.*

"In other news, members of the Muslim community in cities across the nation continue to protest the deaths of several of the inmates at the prison, who were killed during the violence there. They say that these were political executions and the prison staff should be held responsible for them, with appropriate criminal charges filed against them. However, only a few of the prison employees actually survived the incident, among them Warden George Baldwin, who is in serious but stable condition at a hospital in El Paso.

"The correctional facility, known locally as Hell's Gate, has now been placed under federal jurisdiction for the time being."

"You get that Mexican bitch on the phone," the President raged. "She can't get away with taking military action in defiance of my orders! I'll put the whole damned state under martial law! I'll remove her from office! I'll throw out all the Republicans down there and be done with it. Somebody should have cleaned out that rat's nest a long time ago. They've been holding up our progressive agenda for too long."

The advisors stood around in the Oval Office in uncomfortable silence and let the President pace back and forth and rant. When he finally ran out of steam, the chairman of the Joint Chiefs of Staff ventured to say, "If you do that, sir, you'll have a fight on your hands."

The director of the Department of Homeland Security sneered and said, "I don't think we have to worry about a bunch of redneck yokels kicking up too much of a fuss."

"I wouldn't be too sure about that," the Attorney General said. "But in this case, Mr. President, we don't have any real evidence against Governor Delgado. We don't have grounds for any federal charges—"

"Screw grounds!" the President screamed. "I'm the President of the United States! The people have spoken! I have a mandate! I can do anything I want! My word is law!"

"But sir, the Constitution—"

The President raised both fists over his head, shook them furiously, and roared, *"Fuck the Constitution!"*

Later—much later—after he had calmed down, he made a call on a special encrypted phone that not even the Secret Service knew about. When a familiar voice answered, he took a deep breath and asked, "What should I do? Is it time for the endgame?"

"Not yet," the man on the other end of the call said. "The day is not here." He paused. "But it's coming. Soon."

Lee Blaisdell was made acting police chief of Fuego. He didn't really want the job, but somebody had to do it. Putting the town back in order was going to take a long time.

There were mass funerals for two weeks. It took that long to lay all the innocent victims to rest.

Nobody knew what happened to the bodies of the terrorists who had been killed. They were loaded onto trucks and taken away, presumably by the federal government. Good riddance, most people thought.

Jerry and Lara Patel were both buried in Fuego, however. The authorities weren't quite sure what their connection to the whole thing had been, so they were given the benefit of the doubt.

Lois Frazier had lost both her husband and son to the

savages. Within a month, she sold her house and went to live with her sister in Houston.

Ernie Gibbs's parents hadn't been at church that fateful Sunday morning after all, because Mrs. Gibbs had turned her ankle in the garage when they were walking out to the car to leave for Sunday School. Together they mourned Chuck, the family's lost brother and son, and three weeks later, when Fuego High School reopened with a much diminished and much saddened student body, Ernie was among them. He knew Chuck would have wanted it that way.

Lt. David Flannery resigned from the Texas Rangers and dropped out of sight.

The last network Travis Jessup worked for aired a thirty-minute special about his life and career. It got even worse ratings than their usual programming.

Alexis Devereaux never shut up. She was on some cable news show or other every day for a solid month, telling anybody who would listen about how none of the tragic events in Fuego would have happened if not for the reckless policies George W. Bush had set in motion more than two decades earlier.

Hell's Gate was shut down, its remaining inmates transferred elsewhere. In the case of some of them, no one really seemed to know where they had gone.

Mitch Cambridge was hired as a correctional officer in another facility.

One of the other officers, Lucas Kincaid, was on the list of those killed in the incident.

"Cigar?" Atkinson asked Stark.

"Don't use 'em," Stark said.

"Suit yourself."

"I wouldn't say no to a cold beer, though, if you've got that."

"Of course I do. Sit down and I'll be right back."

Stark sat down in one of the rocking chairs on the front porch of Atkinson's rustic, isolated home. From here he could look out over the rugged, wooded slopes of the Palo Pinto Hills, and he thought it was a mighty pretty sight.

"Here you go," Atkinson said. He handed Stark an ice-cold longneck dripping with condensation, sat down in the other rocker, and took a long swallow from the bottle he had brought for himself. "What do you think of the place I've got here, John Howard?"

"Pretty nice . . . if you want to hide out from the world."

Atkinson snorted and said, "The way the world is today, wouldn't you want to hide out from it?"

"Some of the time," Stark admitted. "We still have to live in it, though."

"That's true." Atkinson took another drink. "You hear anything from Kincaid?"

Stark smiled and shook his head.

"That boy's so far back in the woods we may never see him again . . . especially since Riley went with him. He said he'd check in from time to time, just to see if we needed him for anything."

"We're going to need him," Atkinson said, his voice growing solemn. "When the showdown comes, we're going to need him to prove what's really been going on."

"You think people will believe it? Enough people?"

Atkinson sighed and said, "That's a damned good question. I wish I knew the answer. But one thing I *do* know—that showdown *is* coming."

Stark heard wheels rumbling on the narrow gravel road that led to Atkinson's house. He sat up straighter and asked, "Are you expecting company?"

"As a matter of fact, I am."

Stark and Atkinson stood up as a nondescript car

drove into view. It stopped in front of the porch, and a man and a woman got out. Stark knew the man.

"Lieutenant Flannery," he said with a nod of greeting.

"Just Dave now," Flannery said. "I'm not a Ranger anymore."

"Yeah, I knew that."

Stark looked at the woman and recognized her as well, even though they had never met. As she came up the steps, she held her hand out to him and said, "Mr. Stark, it's good to finally meet you."

"You, too, Governor," Stark told Maria Delgado. He glanced at Atkinson, who was grinning. "I reckon Tom asked me to come out here today so we could have this little get-together?"

"That's right. We have something to discuss. Something important."

"What would that be?"

Maria Delgado took a deep breath and said, "The future of Texas. The future of our country."

"Got more chairs here," Atkinson said as he waved a hand at them. "We might as well sit down and enjoy this pretty day while we talk."

So that was what they did. They sat there on a beautiful autumn afternoon in Texas and talked about the days that were coming.

The bad days that were coming.

Visit our website at
KensingtonBooks.com
to sign up for our newsletters, read
more from your favorite authors, see
books by series, view reading group
guides, and more!

Become a Part of Our
Between the Chapters Book Club
Community and Join the Conversation

Betweenthechapters.net